DEADWORLD ISEKAI

BOOK 3

DEADWORLD ISEKAI

BOOK 3

R. C. Joshua

To my family

Cover design by Tommypocket Illustrator

ISBN: 978-1-0394-6961-7

Published in 2025 by Podium Publishing
www.podiumentertainment.com

DEADWORLD ISEKAI

BOOK 3

CHAPTER ONE

The Work is Unlearned

Matt had often wished that the sun would set on Gaia, mostly because constant sunlight had done absurd things to his sleep cycle. Sometimes, he'd go days without sleeping at all, driven on by stat-weirdness and the ever-present need to grind more estate credits. Other times he'd sit down for a quick breather and wake up ten hours later covered in nap-sweat, having almost forgotten his name.

It had become better over the last half year or so, possibly because of stats, or possibly because his poor circadian rhythm had finally given up and died, neglected and alone in some obscure portion of his brain. But he still would have done just about anything for an entire night of darkness, or even for just a sunset. He hoped for a natural, honest-to-god defeat of whatever the Gaian equivalent of Apollo was in favor of whatever their Nyx happened to be.

But rising from his sleeping bag and exiting his imperial tool shed that morning was the first time he wished he had a sunrise. The view that greeted him deserved at least that good of a herald.

Off in the distance, on a single plot of land selected to be close to Matt's estate plot, was a village. Matt thought of himself as a pretty polite guy, one who got along with people fairly well. But the Gaians were a people who had known centuries of peace, plenty, and overall gladness. Over that time, they had evolved social considerations into a kind of simple, brutally effective art form. They would sense when Matt wanted something but was too polite or shy to talk about it, and give it to him before he even asked.

Matt had known people who steamrolled other people on Earth, and even when they were pretending to be kind, it was always in a way that resulted in the other person's expense. Here, everyone was so genuinely nice, it was almost unsettling. The worst, Matt thought, were the old ladies.

One of them had eyeballed him while they were determining the location for their new town. She had somehow figured out that even though he liked the Gaians, Matt's newly recivilized psyche wasn't ready to be around large numbers of Gaians all the time yet. Then, she somehow determined he also wanted them close enough to see and visit but not literally next door. In the end, she took it on herself to explain all of this to everyone else, essentially ordering the former president of her country to relocate a town to be nice.

And then the Gaians had done exactly that without a single question. Like it was the most normal thing in the world.

With Matt's elevated perception, he could see that the Gaians were already up and about their day. As a social group, they had quickly decided on what would be daytime and nighttime hours for the town as a whole and had kept mostly to them. Matt had quickly followed suit to the extent his messed-up sleep schedule would allow him to but tended to either wake up a few hours before them or lag behind a similar amount of time.

They were all already busy. The adults were beginning to check moisture levels in soil as children put last night's refuse into bins for composting. A few people had been assigned to keep bees, and they ran back and forth doing various things Matt didn't understand to optimize the health and productivity of his Ape-iaries full of simian bees.

For the first few months, that natural busyness saved them. Matt had been growing far more food than he needed for himself, but nowhere near what was needed to sustain nearly a thousand Gaians long-term. Luckily, as they emerged from the dungeon-like museum that had held them in stasis for centuries, they came bearing seeds. Literally.

The Gaians had somehow saved the majority of their important flora, including some incredibly quick-growing but edible weeds. They quickly implemented a program to get the fastest-growing food crops into play. Aided by all the improved Gaian soil Matt could buy, they managed to produce enough calories and nutrients to keep themselves going, using the plentiful Ape-honey to fill in whatever mana-content gaps the food didn't quite cover.

Even luckier, they were able to do this without being constantly attacked by monsters and off-world assassins. When Matt had finally flexed his long-unused Global Authority powers to tell the system to stop, it had obeyed so thoroughly that Matt's dungeon-system-running-but-not-quite-an-AI friend Barry strongly suspected he had died. Or left. Or been buried so deep in some stagnant state that he might never emerge again. After a year or so of constantly dodging the system instance's murder attempts, Matt found it hard to feel sorry for it in any case.

When the Gaians ran out of agricultural tasks to work on, they turned to improving their lifestyles in other ways. Matt had been busy grinding dungeons for estate credits, turning them over entirely to his system guardian friend Lucy and the Gaians for spending. Despite being in many ways a little girl, Lucy was surprisingly thrifty and had a well-earned encyclopedic knowledge of the various items Matt's estate could purchase. She and Ramsen, the Gaians' former leader, had discovered that raw building materials like bricks and mortar were not only available to buy, but were orders of magnitude cheaper than buying pre-built buildings.

As the Gaians were happy to build their own homes, Matt was happy to do his part in providing the raw materials for them to do so. Between his reckless grinding to take down the second coming of the world-ending Gaian Scourge, and the semi-random stat growth he had obtained from leveraging his Palate of the Conqueror eating skill, he was easily strong enough to not be in much danger while earning credits.

Matt Perison
Level 15 Battlefield Survivor
Class XP: 280/12,000
HP: 410
MP: N/A
STAM: 225
STR: 73
DEX: 126
PER: 81
VIT: 132
WIS: 87
INT: 10
Class Skills: Survivor's Reflexes (LV15), Advanced Survivor's Combat (LV15), Spring-Fighter (LV15), Rub Some Dirt In It (LV15), Pocket Sand (LV15), Survivor's Digging (LV15), Palate of the Conqueror (LV15)

All those stats didn't mean he was good at everything, however. When Ramsen and a few other Gaians had first come to inspect the work Matt had done, they had walked very politely around the central plot he was the most proud of, then the various fields he had planted, irrigated with magic water-producing stones, and tended as best he could. He beamed with pride, then asked Ramsen what he thought.

Ramsen coughed, and smiled politely.

"Is it not good?" Matt asked, confused.

"It is . . . not." Matt had learned, through surprisingly few conversations, that the Gaians both didn't like to lie, and weren't very good at it. Mostly, they opted not to try. "I can tell you worked hard, but the work itself is unlearned. With your permission, we can do somewhat more."

Of course, they could. I'm so stupid, Matt had thought. Agriculture is the closest thing they seem to have to a religion. Their children can probably do better than he did.

"Of course. You have that permission. If you like, you can get started changing it right here." Matt waved at his central plot, where his first plants, trees, and Gaian victory gardens grew. At the mention of changing that plot, the face of every Gaian present suddenly morphed into horror.

"Change this? No, absolutely not." Ramsen was aghast.

"Is it . . . would it hurt the other estate plots, somehow?"

"Not at all. It's just, Matt, listen." Ramsen drew Matt aside, something he thoughtfully did every time he was about to say something he suspected would embarrass him. "Matt, you have to understand. Everything is gone. All of our history is wiped out, besides what we carry with us." He glanced back at Matt's plot. "This is the garden that fed you as you defeated the Scourge once and for all. It's the home of our people's savior, Matt. It will never change."

Matt gulped at that "never."

"In generations to come, our children will visit and marvel at the humbleness of this shack, at the arrangement of the flowers . . ." Ramsen went on for a while, while Lucy tried her hardest not to laugh at Matt's embarrassment. Eventually, mercifully, Ramsen moved on, then got to work.

At this point, every Gaian was well-fed, and had access to group housing. An increasing number of them had individual homes, chosen by lottery, with larger families receiving priority. And eventually, those houses would have running water, and would be attached to sewers, and dozens of other conveniences. Matt had seen the blueprints for what the town would become, and the amount of work planned was staggering.

So was the cost. The Gaians had planted groves of trees, but it would be a generation or more before they were large enough to consider harvesting. Besides what they could make from literal mud or grow from the ground, all raw materials came from estate points. Matt had been providing massive amounts of them, but now that the town's food supply was secure, the Gaians were beginning to form dungeon raiding parties of their own.

For whatever reason, all the Gaians had emerged as the equivalent of level 1 villagers, classless and without any extra stats to rely on. Lucy and Barry had been working together to create patterns that the Gaian parties could run between dungeons that would slowly bring them up to respectable levels without putting them in much danger, and it had been decided that Matt would oversee every party's first run.

If all went to plan there, raw materials would be a nonissue, and the Gaians' already astounding pace of work would get even faster. Before he had known about the Gaians, Matt would have been content if he could have just established some sort of sustainable circle of life on Gaia, however small. It would have probably taken his entire lifetime, but he figured if he did it well enough, Gaia might be green again, if only in several thousand years. But with the Gaians returned to their home, he could imagine the entire continent being green again within his lifetime. Once they could defend themselves and farm their own dungeon system resources, they wouldn't need him at all. That wasn't a bad thing. It made him smile to even think about it.

"Oh, look who's awake." Lucy was never all that far from Matt, and as far as he knew, she was always vaguely aware of his location. She tended to pretend towards being as human as possible, an illusion with frequent cracks that Matt dutifully pretended not to notice. She might have been a hologram, or a hallucination, or a ghost bound to his soul, or something like that, but she was also his best friend in the entire world. If she wanted to pretend like she was a normal, non-guardian person, then a normal, non-guardian person she'd be. "Are you about ready to go into town? They probably have breakfast going already. Or you could eat raw turnips here."

"I could make food-cube soup, for old times' sake." Matt's supply of centuries-old Gaian food cubes was a frequent joke for them now. His eating skill had originally been called Eat Anything!, and it had turned out that one of the features of the skill was that it papered over Matt's perception of how spoiled the food was, something he learned the hard way when he had temporarily lost that skill and couldn't eat the cubes.

What they hadn't expected was that if he ate a cube, he had to thoroughly rinse his mouth afterwards before going into town. It turned out the Gaians were hyper-sensitive to whatever rot smell the cubes gave off to normal people. With Matt's skill and Lucy's inability to smell, they hadn't known, but apparently he reeked like a lifeboat-ration graveyard after eating one of the cubes. "You could. I bet Gaian puke makes for good fertilizer."

Matt broke. "Nope, okay, you win. I'll pass. I'm giving up on cooking. And large-scale farming, and masonry. Anything the Gaians can do, I'm finding out I'm just a hobbyist at. At best."

"If it's any consolation, I think they do still find you impressive." Lucy grinned. "Something about the whole running-into-the-jaws-of-a-death-topiary thing to save their lives seems to have sunk in."

"Don't remind me." Matt grimaced. "Or them. It took me a week to convince them not to make a statue of it."

CHAPTER TWO

Tough Conversations

Matt postponed heading into town for the few moments it took to take a quick shower in his enchanted tub, then he and Lucy set off down the path to the village. The Gaians had cut the path just the week before, with plans to pave it before the month was up. Ramsen called it the first step in building up Gaian transportation infrastructure to its former glory, and Matt suspected he was only half-joking.

Matt was, as always, fully armed and armored. The Gaians had, thankfully, come out of the museum fully clothed, just as they had been in the simulation. Within just a few months, they had developed some primitive capacity to make clothes, which, bolstered by some estate credit contributions from Matt towards bolts of cloth and skeins of thread, had them very close to self-sufficiency on the wardrobe front as well.

They had offered to make him some clothes, claiming that he must be uncomfortable in all that armor. He had taken them up on it to create some underlayers he could wear between the armor and his skin, which was an upgrade that he desperately needed, but not much beyond that. Matt had been living in constant danger or the potential of constant danger for a long, long time. He was no longer comfortable without something solid around him. It was all Lucy could do to get him to leave his non-shovel weapons home, arguing that they were all redundant compared to an unbreakable, impossibly sharp Gaian Nullsteel shovel. She was right. Though he kept a holdout dagger somewhere on his person.

The Gaians were sure he couldn't be comfortable like that, but for once the

Gaian mothers and grandmothers hadn't steamrolled him into happy cotton compliance. They had just looked at him, troubled, and accepted it as something they couldn't change. For now. He had a strong suspicion that this wasn't a permanent reprieve.

"So, are you still going to tell them?" Lucy was no longer visible or audible to the Gaians, now that they were out of the museum. It was something that she and Matt had known was going to happen, but Matt suspected the sudden change still stung. For a little while, she had been able to play with the children and have full, acknowledged conversations. The Gaian kids still asked about "the fun angry girl" sometimes.

The practical upshot, however, was that Matt could have a full conversation with her without danger of being overheard, provided all the important information came out of Lucy's mouth and not his.

"I am. It's not going to be fun, though. Some of them are pretty protective."

"The grandmothers? Yeah. They even scare me. I feel like if I was visible they'd have me full of cookies and pulling weeds in ten minutes."

"Not just them. Ramsen, too. I think he thinks of me like that statue he wanted to build."

"In that you are strong, but don't think much?"

"More like something to put in front of his people to keep them working, but also something that shouldn't do any work itself, anymore."

It was true. Ramsen would include Matt in every speech. It wasn't malicious, or even something he was doing to build power for himself. It was just normal thankfulness, combined with reminding his people they had a debt to repay. At the same time, he vigorously protested Matt putting himself in any kind of danger at all, and rightfully pointed out that almost every mundane task Matt might help with was better and more expertly handled by another Gaian.

Matt suspected that if Ramsen and the grandmothers had their full way, he'd sit in a big chair in a short tower overlooking the town, like a lifeguard. He'd be close, visible, but ultimately there for spiritual support more than anything else.

As they broke the borders of the town, the greetings started. Matt politely deflected several offers of excess vegetables, saying he was stocked up. True to form, the Gaians noticed that this seemed to be true and didn't press. Otherwise, it was all smiles and waves as Matt made his way towards the town cafeteria.

Almost every Gaian could cook for themselves, but Ramsen had explained that the town cafeteria was important anyway. The cafeteria was the town's largest building, and any Gaian could go there for free, delicious breakfast, lunch, and dinner any time they pleased. For Gaians who lived alone, it provided an option besides eating by themselves, as well as saving time on average for the town overall. It helped increase the total pace of work for the town, and it was also a healthy thing for building community and friendship on an ongoing basis.

Matt didn't care about any of this, at least not much. He cared about the food. The Gaians claimed that while they had solved the mana-deficiency problem in the vegetables, they were still somewhat perplexed by the lack of flavor from the ingredients. But for Matt, who had high perception and an eating skill that made food more palatable, it was a flavor explosion when eating the large-portioned traditional Gaian cuisine.

They seemed to be using different words every time, but by some trick of Matt's reincarnator translation, every morning meal came out to something like "breakfast vegetables." Today's breakfast vegetables turned out to be a kind of vinegary, peppery, diced vegetable oatmeal. If an Earth human had tried to make the same thing, he suspected it would have been gross. This melted in his mouth, filling him with dozens of nutrients at once, while his body trumpeted the sensation as a great victory over his previous long-term semi-starvation. It was like eating a parade, and by the time he left the cafeteria, he was almost staggering from the fullness.

He was glad for the strength the food gave him, both emotionally and physically. Tough conversations took a lot out of him. He'd need it.

A week ago, Barry had been filling Matt in on some details, and brightening the experience for himself somewhat by absolutely dominating Matt in a game of wallball.

"I swear you are cheating somehow. Nobody is this good at this game."

"Stop whining and turn around." Barry whipped the ball at him, hard. Vitality and armor meant it didn't really hurt that much, but it was the humiliation of the thing that mattered.

"Okay, so you were saying. I've been doing pretty good on prizes lately."

"Yes. Especially in terms of your takedown of the Scourge. I know you don't have much context for how much these things cost, but some of those items were so rare they approached being legends. Draining the system completely helped cover the cost, but the rest of it came from the energy stores in the dungeons. And those only recharge slowly, as you already know."

"How slowly are we talking about?"

"For the Gaians, and the kinds of things they want? Fast enough. But for you to gear up and get strong enough to take down any who comes? Not nearly fast enough. I'm barely keeping up right now, and all you are asking for are bricks and spinning wheels. Soon enough, I'm not even going to be able to keep up with your stat growth. Those points cost more as the totals get higher, believe it or not."

"So what do I do?" Matt sat down on the curb of the street behind the grocery store nearest to the home where he grew up. The wall of the store was perfect for wallball, and he had played a ton of it with his friends there over the years before they got too old for it to be exciting anymore. Somehow, Barry had decided this game was exactly what Matt needed right now. As usual, he was right.

Barry sat down beside him, looking serious.

"I think you already know what you have to do, Matt. You just don't want to do it. It's not pleasant for me to think about, either. But the alternatives are worse."

Nothing had ever made Matt want to argue more, but he knew Barry was right.

With all their polite breakfast conversations done and nothing left to delay them, Matt and Lucy ambled on toward what they called "the war tent." It wasn't a tent, and had nothing to do with war. But since the Gaians took farming and civilization-building very, very seriously, it ended up feeling like it was both anyway. Every time they entered, they stood a good chance of walking in on a man banging on the table and saying something like, "Turnips again! We can't bet it all on turnips, Varsal. What if there was a blight? We'd be lost. We MUST attack on more than one front."

It was intense, and the kind of thing Matt would laugh at if he didn't have a few years of context on what it was like to starve. Lucy, who lacked that concept or any risk of hurting anyone's feelings, mocked it mercilessly during her and Matt's downtime.

This time, there was no argument going. Ramsen and the other leader-Gaians sat stooped over what looked like a map of Matt's property, with lines on it moving from central circles to drawn channels crossing every plot and breaking off into smaller channels like twigs from a branch. As Matt approached, their conversation cut off as they all stood in greeting.

"Matt!" Ramsen said. "Welcome. We were just finishing our plans for improving the irrigation system. We think we can successfully irrigate twenty percent more land with what we have. Ardi had a wonderful idea involving covering the irrigation channels themselves, to ward off evaporation. Of course, the air will be just that much more dry, but we weren't making tremendous progress on that front, anyway."

"Great! Glad to hear it."

Ardi, who belonged to the large working-mother class of Gaians, seemed to almost immediately notice something else was on Matt's mind.

"Ramsen, can't you see he's here for something different? Let the boy talk. Come, Matt. Sit." It wasn't a request so much as it was an intimidating and kindness-driven command, one Matt was incapable of refusing. He slid into a stool made of a carved rock while the rest of the Gaians cleared their plans from the table, glad for the slight delay.

"So what's on your mind, Matt? Did you want to talk about the hunting parties again?" Ramsen asked.

"No, I think we have that under control already. This is something different. I need to go on a trip."

Ramsen looked confused. "Wherever to, Matt?"

There weren't many places for Matt to go on trips to. He had offered to go reclaim desks and chairs from the various Gaian outposts before, but it had been decided that his time was better spent just grinding dungeons, of which there were plenty nearby. Besides that, there wasn't much. As far as Matt had walked across the Gaian landscape, he was well aware that all the interesting stuff that was going on in Gaia was here. Almost, anyway.

"I thought I'd take a trip out to the teleporter." It was a simple statement, but it hit all the Gaians like a brick. The teleporter had been built for one reason, and one reason only. It automatically linked up with the planet with the closest relationship with Gaia on some scale even they didn't fully understand. It was originally for evacuation, a sort of last-ditch option the Gaians hadn't actually been able to take advantage of.

"You want to leave us, Matt? You aren't happy here?"

CHAPTER THREE

Into the Unknown

Matt shook his head. "I'm happy here. But we all know I'm useless here as well. Or at least I will be. The hunting parties start in earnest next week, and once they are up to speed, I won't be useful anymore. They will level faster than I ever could, and I can't level with them because once they're strong enough to pull their own weight, they'll take the significance out of my survival of dungeons."

"We can find you other work to do . . ."

"What work, Ramsen? What work is there really where I wouldn't be taking it out of the hands of someone better? That you wouldn't have to fix in secret later?"

Ramsen didn't reply. Matt wasn't mad, but he was right. The work the Gaians were doing, even in terms of simple digging, was carefully planned and highly skilled. He couldn't help with any of it, even if he was somewhat of an expert digger himself.

"But that's not a good enough reason to put yourself at risk, Matt. Nobody minds you being idle. You saved us. You deserve a break."

Matt shook his head. "It's not just that, Ramsen. It's also the system."

"I thought it was dead, Matt. At least that's what Barry has told you, correct?"

"Not the system instance. The system. The shield around Gaia is still breaking up, right?"

"That's correct. But we've been looking into it, Matt. It might take years, still, before the system can see us clearly."

"It might take years, Ramsen. But it might not. And we have no idea how the greater system will react to what went on here. I killed an instance and assumed control of an entire planet. I can't think that reaction will be positive, whatever it is. We need to be ready. I need to be ready. Stronger. Able to fight off whoever and whatever it sends to us."

Ramsen shook his head. "Matt, we have no idea where you'll go or if you can even get back."

He wasn't exactly wrong. The teleporter was a one-way trip, as far as any of them knew. If Matt left, any way back to Gaia he found might very well have to be on the other side. Without knowing where he was headed, there was no way to know if they had those kinds of capabilities, let alone if they'd share them. It really was dicey.

Matt nodded. "I thought about that, too. But when I first learned that invading another planet was even a possibility, it was through a power I'm pretty sure the system didn't even want to grant."

It was the wording of that particular power that convinced Matt he had a shot to get back to Gaia.

Pillager's Rights

Because of an unprovoked invasion, your authority is expanded to allow for a one-time invasion of the following territories:

Ra'Zor, Realm of One Thousand Bleedings

Rewards for an invasion are adjusted for invasion force size and power, the change affected on the invaded territory, and other general metrics of success.

That "one-time invasion" bit implied that there would be the possibility of *more* invasions, which implied that invasions themselves came with a built-in mechanism to get back. Matt normally wouldn't trust a notification all by itself, but both of the invaders who had come to get him seemed to expect that they'd be able to return to their own planets.

Matt explained the wording of the notifications to the assembled Gaians, who sat for a moment, thoughtfully.

"That's pretty light, Matt. You still don't know if you can get back," Ramsen said. "We already owe you much. You don't need to do this."

Matt shook his head. "You know I do. Eventually, the system is coming for us. For all of us. Without strength, we are doomed. I can't get it here."

Ramsen began to disagree again, before getting cut off by Ardi, who Matt was fast deciding was by far the most fearsome of the Gaian warrior-moms.

"Oh, be quiet, Ramsen. You can see he's decided. Besides, you know he's right. If anything, he's just as safe out there as he would be here. The boy is already almost crying. Don't make it harder on him, you old fool."

Ramsen shrugged, knowing well enough not to argue with superior force. He walked over to Matt, putting his hands on his shoulders and nearly lifting him from his chair as he stood, then hugged him.

"If it's what you have to do, it's what you have to do. We can't support you much, but we will give you everything we can."

The next few weeks were busy. Matt was a big part of the plan to get the Gaian dungeon raid teams up and running without casualties, which meant his days were completely packed. After a quick conversation with Barry, the dungeon system did some sort of tricky adjustment to make sure the Clownrat dungeon was always available.

It had turned out clowns were not just terrifying to Matt. Every Gaian, without exception, was terrified of the things, even without any of the Earth-culture context surrounding them. If a Gaian wasn't truly brave and dedicated to dungeon crawling, they'd usually refuse to fight the Clownrats at all. It turned out to be a helpful sorting mechanism, and after a few weeks Matt had trained ten teams of five.

In the meantime, he picked up several cheap items as prizes for leading the team through. By the time he was nearly ready to go, Matt had dozens of useful things he honestly couldn't create with his skills. Some of them, like ropes and canteens, were just duplicates of things he already had. Other things like matches, camping cutlery, and packets of toilet paper would be useful to keep in the pockets of his clothes in case he lost his pack. If he was going to go to another world and face death, maiming, and overall danger at every turn, at least he wouldn't do it without a ready supply of toothpicks.

Somehow, the Gaians took the influx of estate currency from the hunting teams and began doing even more work. With Lucy about to leave, she and Matt had dived deep into the options and menus of the estate until they figured out how to appoint Ramsen and a few other people to administrator status, with full rights to spend credits how they saw fit. Houses were now popping up everywhere, and somehow they had even paved the rough outline of a town square, complete with a fountain-fed garden.

Matt had also picked up a new pack in the past few months, given his first one had dissolved when he used Acid Skin. Between that and the fact that his unlosable, Soulbound shovel had displaced most of his other weapons, he had plenty of room left to pack in several cloth-wrapped clay jars full of fermented vegetables the Gaians were nice enough to prepare for him. It wouldn't last forever, but he wouldn't starve in the first week or so on a new planet, at least.

Matt had asked Ardi how best to say goodbye to the Gaians. She had barely considered this before telling him not to. It would, she said, make it seem more final to them. Instead, she said his best move was just to spend a day in town talking to everyone before slipping away, and he wasn't going to question her.

With very little fanfare, Matt walked away from a group of good friends who were very effectively pretending not to notice him leave for a trip that might very well leave him bleeding.

He tried desperately to convince himself it was worth it for a while before wussing out and just deciding not to think about it anymore.

"If we don't find this portal pretty quickly, I'm going to scream."

The difficulty with using Gaian maps to navigate was that all the landmarks they referenced to were gone by now, leveled by the same cataclysm that took the planet in general. Matt and Lucy had found the general location of the gate days ago, and were now painstakingly walking back and forth with their dowsing rod, trying to locate a buried gateway that could be anywhere within a few square miles. And that was assuming they had estimated the distance they had walked correctly.

"You might as well, Lucy. There's nobody here to hear it."

"You aren't nobody, Matt. You just look that way."

"That's mean."

"You have to adjust it depending on the situation. This is like the worst road trip ever. Saying you look boring at this point is like saying you are the best person on the planet most days."

She wasn't wrong. They were several hours deep in the process of digging up false-positive treasures alone, mostly coming up with rocks and little bits of Gaian Nullsteel they piled up to bring back to the settlement on their return trip. A little snark was understandable.

"Well, I'm touched."

"In the head."

"Lucy!"

"I'm sorry, I'm sorry. Let's get back to walking an endless grid pattern."

Luckily, they found it a few hours later, just before Lucy reached critical bad-joke mass and moved into puns.

Most things on Gaia were at least slightly buried, but this one was hidden deep. Matt was almost sure it was a false positive with how slight the dowsing rod was moving before he started digging. Once he was about head deep in the ground, his hopes started to lift again. In retrospect, this made sense, since it was buried to begin with. Eventually, Matt managed to clear out a small channel around the entire thing, leaving a fifteen-foot pit in the ground around a nine-foot Nullsteel box. There was no apparent way to open or activate it outside of two small, circular holes separated vertically by a few inches of space.

"Do you think I stick my arm into them? Both arms? I'm stumped."

"If there's one rule I want us to have as a team, it's that you don't stick your fragile flesh-arms into mystery holes as a first attempt."

"What, then? It's just a big metal rectangle. I don't have a lot of other ideas."

"I don't know, Matt. Drop a rock through it? Anything but getting your arm chopped off would be great."

Matt rolled his eyes, but stooped to pick up a rock. Gingerly, he dropped it through the top hole. It rattled around for a split second before dropping out of the second hole. They were, apparently, connected.

"What in the hell? It's a loop?"

"I have no idea. I guess you could have people drop something heavy and prank them when it hits their knees."

As stupid as that would be, it gave Matt an idea. He had one object in his pack that he couldn't bear to leave at home that would fit perfectly in that hole. Reaching into a pocket, he withdrew the Nullsteel ball that they had found long ago. So far, it had been used one single time, as a piece of ammunition to fire out of his mortar, and been the last shot against the Scourge. While it was great at hurting an overgrown plant, Matt had always figured there must be something to it besides that. He tossed it into the hole.

The whole apparatus groaned before the top of the box opened. Fifteen feet in the air above them, a gate rose from the box.

Matt clambered out of the hole as quick as he could. The gate itself was a complex working of wires, lights, and random metal shapes he couldn't guess at the purpose of, all built into a tall arch. Visually, there was nothing indicating it was on. But given that all of his hairs were standing on edge and the air was increasingly stinking of ozone, he figured it was probably good to go.

"Matt, are you ready?" Lucy gulped. "It's not too late to turn back."

"No, it is. We have to do this. It's the only way."

Given that he had dug a trench around the entire thing, stepping into the gate wasn't really an option. Taking a deep breath, Matt leapt at the gate, directly into the unknown.

CHAPTER FOUR

Field Work

Derek was having a pretty good day. He had woken up, eaten a sensible but delicious breakfast, gone on a ten-mile run, worked with the weight set the old blacksmith had made for him, went on his swim, freestyle-climbed the city wall, took his fighting class, and finally ate a big lunch.

And now, for the first time, he was holding his own against the old man. He had managed to either dodge or deflect all of the old man's strikes, redirecting the force from the massive iron bar he swung around rather than meeting them head-on. Further, he kept switching up his motions, so the old man couldn't predict and demolish him. He had even, wonder of wonders, gotten in a few pokes with the blunted training sword that the old man had him fight with. He wasn't just not losing, he was arguably winning.

After weaving through a flurry of iron-bar pokes aimed directly at his nose, Derek managed to land another strike of his own that clacked loudly off the old man's knee. With a roar, the blacksmith disengaged, taking several steps back before Derek could press the attack. Then, he threw his iron bar to the ground and brought his hands up boxer-style. Later on, Derek would reflect that this should have been his first warning for what was about to happen.

Without the weight of several dozen pounds of moving metal, it made sense that the old man would move faster. But what Derek saw was more than that. The blacksmith suddenly flew through the air with no more drag than a diving hawk, barely touching the ground as he closed the distance between them and then suddenly disappearing.

Shit, Derek thought. *He must be an unarmed class*. A lightbulb went off in his head as he realized what that meant. The old man didn't use the iron bar to be intimidating, or because he was skilled with it. He used it to generate the wrong-weapon-for-the-class limitations and disable some of his class benefits entirely so Derek could keep up.

Then, just as suddenly as that lightbulb lit up, all the lights in Derek's head were suddenly put out. When he came to, he was still standing, but only because the impact of his body had bent the blacksmith's fence enough to prop him up on the incline. He shook his head and brought his hands up, hoping he could find the blacksmith before he landed his next blow.

"Huh. I've never seen someone get knocked out and stay standing like that before. Weird of ya."

Derek was confused. It sounded like the voice was coming from above him. Looking up, he realized that was exactly what was happening. Standing on top of the fence to his left, perfectly balanced on the half inch or so of rail it provided, was the massive blacksmith. He looked about as natural as a hippo in a bird's nest.

"Here's the lesson for ya today. With stats, how a person looks matters less."

It was true that while Derek didn't think of the big man as slow, he implicitly assumed that his teacher would be slower and less agile than a smaller person would be. But this wasn't Earth, and the old man wasn't constrained by non-system physics. If a small man could lift a wagon, and Derek had seen them do it, there was no reason a big man couldn't be a gymnast.

The shock of the realization was enough to prevent Derek from taking a single evasive action as the blacksmith's foot swung down, caught him in the chin, and knocked him out properly and completely.

This time, when Derek came to, he was inside the old man's house. Between the two of them, they had at some point figured out that the fastest way to dull his pain during the time between injuries and his vitality healing him up was just to drop him directly into an ice bath. As an added bonus, it seemed to help keep the swelling from his workout schedule under control. He was so used to it by now the cold dunk hadn't even shocked him awake, although he wasn't sure how much of that was acclimation and how much of it was the fact that he had just been kicked in the face with all the force of a semi-truck slamming into a concrete wall.

"Ya did good, ya know."

"Tell that to my jaw, you old fart."

"No, ya really did. Had to use my class to keep up."

"You were holding out on me that whole time? Just keeping your class under wraps and making me think I had a chance?"

"I didn't want ya to get discouraged, boy. Now that ya know, you can train until ya can beat my class. At the rate your stats have been growing, it won't be long now."

Derek considered this. He was picking up stats at an alarming rate, and his Common Man class made each one of those stats do more work than it should have. Even, say, a single point of dexterity was enough that he could feel it in how he moved. Of course, the only way to get that point of dexterity was through brutal grinding, usually in some dangerous and ill-advised way. But it was worth it, especially since earning the stats that way also trained him up to actually use them.

Training with the old man was unusually effective for almost every stat somehow. He got dexterity from dodging, strength from blocking and striking, and wisdom from contemplating what exactly had gone wrong every time he woke up with a new broken bone that trained his vitality.

"Here, take this," the old man said.

Derek shrugged his cloth-armored back up the side of the tub to sit up straighter, then reached to take the enormous turkey-like bird leg the old man was offering. Having had a food-buffed class before that took him places he didn't want to revisit, Derek was pretty cautious about gluttony. This wasn't that, though. His new class basically ran on burning calories in training, which meant they had to be replenished from somewhere. For the most part, the old man controlled his lunches, and seemed to have a sixth sense for how much food Derek needed any given day to get optimal growth. He had no idea where the old man had come by this skill, but he had long since quit asking those kinds of questions.

The blacksmith pulled out a turkey leg of his own, and for a minute or so it was silent as they both worked seriously on their food. Having a lead on finishing his food to begin with, and being the more hungry of the two, Derek finished his food first and broke the silence.

"So what's on the workout plan for tomorrow? Throwing me at a wall of spikes? Chasing me around, poking me with a big spike?" Derek was joking, but only sort of. The training *was* harsh, but the old man didn't do it to be malicious, as funny as it was. Derek didn't grow unless he was actively pushing himself, and the old man was the only person in town who could do that these days. As Derek had gotten tougher, his tortures had become more inventive. But it wasn't because he liked it, exactly.

"Tomorrow? Probably no training for ya tomorrow, boy. At least not from me."

Sometimes this happened. The blacksmith wasn't just his trainer, after all. He was a working blacksmith, and orders still came in.

"Who needs swords this time? The army, or something special for an adventurer?"

"Neither. It's ya that's busy, boy." The blacksmith fished one of his meaty hands into a pocket and pulled out a letter. "I had a word with that Brennan, told him ya could probably use some field work. Good chance for all the learning to sink in, ya see."

Derek goggled at the man for a moment. Since back when he was Asadel, all he had really wanted was to go on real, important missions with the real adventurers, but he had always been prevented from doing so. Back then, he had thought that this was just them holding him back, but now he knew it was because he had been far from ready. He used to be weak. But if the old man had been talking to Brennan, and had succeeded in convincing him, that meant something entirely different.

He jumped out of the water and hugged the old man as hard as he could.

"Agghh, boy!"

"Too hard for you, old man? Did I break your delicate bones?"

"Naw, ya idiot! Ya's covered in *ice!*"

Oh, yeah, Derek thought. *So I am.*

He kept hugging anyway.

Outside the blacksmith's shop, Derek was sprinting down the road, whistling sharply every few steps. The whistling was a rule the town had imposed on him. They wanted him to train, but after his first few weeks of pushing himself, his running had become dangerous for the unsuspecting normal folk in the town. The whistling let them know he was coming, like putting a bell around a cat's neck to keep the mice safe.

Having had his second lunch at the blacksmith's shop, he didn't need to stop before going to see Brennan. The blacksmith had told him the mission would start tomorrow, but the blacksmith had told him to go meet everyone today anyway and be part of the planning. Derek assumed he wouldn't be that helpful in improving the plans themselves, since he didn't know much in comparison to the other people that would be in that room. But to be in the room at all was a big deal.

Mission planning took place in a small building owned by the Church. It was a nice enough building, but not one you'd expect was important. Derek suspected this was to keep people from coming by and goggling at the heroes, not that it worked. He suppressed his reflex to barge in through the front door, instead pulling the rope pull to the door's literal bell.

"Come in, Derek," Brennan's voice rang out over the bell. Derek opened the door and stepped in. Brennan was seated at the table, as were Artemis and a few other non-reincarnator adventurers. Despite not having the crazy growth rate of reincarnated heroes, the native Ra'Zorian adventurers often had specific skills and knowledge that made them worthy of going on missions anyway. Derek had come to respect them.

Artemis herself was a different story. Derek wasn't sure, but he thought she could still probably kill him if it came right down to it.

But in that moment, as he pulled out a chair and sat down, none of that mattered. He was part of the big show now. An actual member of the team. He would get to go on real adventures, take real risks, and actually help people for once in a way that went beyond swatting down minor demons even strong, normal teenagers could kill. It was going to be *real* now.

He tried his hardest to look serious and as adult as possible as he sat down. It didn't work. He was grinning like an idiot the whole time.

CHAPTER FIVE

An Ambush

Okay, alright. With Derek here, we can start for real. Artemis, would you be so kind as to call up the map, and give us some basic background on what's happening?" Brennan said, turning his chair to the side to look at the wall behind him.

Artemis walked to the same wall, fiddled with something, and a magic illusion of a map sprang into existence just off the surface of the wall. Derek recognized it as what he thought of as "the big little map," one that captured not the entire continent or world, but still showed more than a single town or city. It showed the capital, where they were, as well as the five or six settlements most closely associated with the capital. It was the regional map Derek was most familiar with.

Artemis, being a scout, had several skills related to the reading and manipulation of maps. She pointed her finger at several points on the map, magically highlighting them with arrows and labeling the same with Ra'Zorian numbers.

"As of today's date, we would normally wait another week before running our usual inspection and delivery pattern to the various settlements. Usually, we'd visit these five settlements, check on their wellbeing, scout their surroundings, and make sure they were safe until our next support sweep."

Brennan stirred in his chair, raising his hand and saving Derek from having to make the decision between doing so himself and maybe making a fool of himself, or sitting still and not understanding what was going on.

"I'm assuming plans have changed. Did something happen to one of the settlements?"

"Yes, or at least it's possible. As you know, communication between settlements and the capital is difficult, and only relatively powerful mages with a communication focus can handle the distance and demonic interference. Thus, most settlement-to-capital communications happen via the settlement's communication orb and receiving facilities in the capital."

She waved her hand, highlighting the fifth of the five colonies.

"Because the orbs also handle routine correspondence when they aren't tied up in official functions, communications are coming through fairly constantly, at least during daytime hours. But as of this morning, Epsilon Colony's communications didn't pick up again as expected, not even for the typical morning 'all clear' and check-in."

Now, Derek did raise his hand. "Is that necessarily bad? If they only had a single method of communication, it could just be an equipment malfunction. Stuff like this has happened before."

Artemis paused, then nodded. "Yes, actually. We've seen breaks in communications for a number of reasons in the past, with reasons ranging from equipment breakdown related to the orbs, demon-driven plagues knocking down the personnel who are trained to handle the orbs, and just good old-fashioned interference. More often than not, breaks in communications don't signal a catastrophe."

She gestured towards the map again, highlighting three other settlements that were more or less between the capital and the communications-compromised settlement.

"That's why we are considering this break important, but not an absolute emergency. Several reincarnator heroes are posted in that settlement. They are not our absolute best, but are all dependable veterans of the war. Whatever the problem they face, Epsilon was built with defense in mind and should be able to hold out against most threats for some time. At the same time, we have an interest in not fully letting this trip go to waste. Without getting into excessive details, each of these three settlements has communicated some semi-vital need related to resupply, or suspicious activity that needs to be scouted or cleared. Fulfilling each of these needs represents no more than three hours of commitment once we get to each location, on top of additional travel time."

Brennan stood and walked over to the map, his lips moving as he did some quick mental travel-time computation. "So what's the overall time to get there? Twenty hours?"

"Less, I think, if we keep our team down to just you and me, and maybe one other member as a wildcard. I can just about keep up with you in terms of travel speed, and for most problems, you're more than enough to supplement a settlement's existing resources. Which brings us to the main point of our meeting."

She turned to Derek, a wry half grin on her face. "How fast can you run?"

* * *

It turned out Derek could run fast enough. While it wasn't anywhere near either Brennan's or Artemis's skill-buffed top speeds, his stamina stat was high enough at this point that he just didn't actually tire. When the other two got within the margins of safety reserves they maintained in terms of stamina resources, he was still going strong and would catch up.

His lungs and legs might have been screaming, but it turned out that trying to keep up with two elites in an actual, real-life field situation did wonders for stat acquisition. He had picked up one dexterity and two vitality points since leaving home.

The settlements they had visited on the way had not been particularly hard to deal with. Two of the three just needed deliveries, and only the last had any kind of combat-related issue. There, a few hives of demon wasps had set up shop in the woods outside of the town. The town's heroes could have dealt with it themselves, but it was safer to just have Brennan do it. They didn't have to leave the town partially unguarded while they fought, and if it was an ambush situation, Derek's team could then lead the ambushers back to a fully defended fortress-town. Where humans could take advantage of those kinds of mechanics, they usually did.

Derek's own contributions to the fight had been pretty minimal. The wasps were numerous, but they weren't strong. The main danger that they posed was their numbers. A couple of the wasps that made it through the initial carnage would seek revenge after their main colonies were destroyed. So Derek had been assigned to a sort of secondary straggler-roundup position, working to attract and destroy any wasps that Artemis's arrows didn't get to first. He had picked up a strength point from jumping high into the air to get to one, so it wasn't a total loss, but it also wasn't exactly defending the entire world against mortal peril.

After leaving that settlement, it had been more of the same. The few points Derek had picked up meant he could keep up better, although the stat increases weren't coming as hot and heavy as before, either. He patted himself on the back for keeping up with the elites before Brennan and Artemis subtly increased their running pace, revealing they had been keeping quite a bit in reserve.

"Okay, almost there. We need to be a little careful as we cross over the next rise, Derek. Keep your eyes peeled. You don't have any ambush-prevention skills, correct?"

"I don't have any skills at all." Derek was used to Brennan asking about skills, when he should have been fully aware that Derek couldn't possess such things. Brennan wasn't exactly a detail-oriented person, which is likely part of why he and Artemis were such a good fit together. "But my reflexes in general are pretty good. I get an awful lot out of dexterity and perception."

The days when Derek could rely on his sword lighting up with magic of some kind or another and doing most of the work for him were long gone. This wasn't exactly a loss, since his Common Man class got so much out of each stat point. In essence, it was like working with a permanent semi-buff. If he was up against another opponent who had similar stats but was completely out of stamina, mana, or whatever other resource they might use, he'd steamroll them. But when he had to deal with system-augmented abilities with nothing but good-old-fashioned training and stat-based movement, it got tricky.

"Oh, right." Brennan scratched his head. "Well, the deal is that the main reincarnator defender of this town is a Turretter. It's a class built to defend stable positions, so the walls of the town themselves are basically one big weapon. But he also sometimes hides smaller ambush traps to pick off enemies as they come. Artemis and I are white-listed, so we should be fine."

"But I might be a default kill-on-sight?"

"Something like that. My guess is that you'll be fine because you are with us, but those turrets are no joke. I once had to deflect an arbalest bolt from one, and it ended up throwing me back like a quarter mile. I recommend dodging instead."

For a few moments, Derek tried to imagine how Brennan had managed to deflect something as big and strong as a siege bolt when he was a strength-light, precision-fighting class. But, he gave up when they actually crested the rise and saw the smoldering, scorched-earth remains of Epsilon Colony.

Derek hadn't been on a lot of field missions, but it didn't take a lot of experience to know this wasn't the average experience. Especially not with the tough-as-nails Artemis collapsing in tears to the ground only a few steps ahead of him.

Minutes later, Artemis had managed to pull herself together, replacing her tears with a tightly set, determined expression. After that, it was just a matter of a minute or so to sprint down to the town. There wasn't much left there to see, beyond the scattered stones of the wall and a few surviving sturdy stone pillars that had once supported entire buildings. Everywhere else, there was ash. Thick, choking ash that kicked up off the ground as they walked, covering everything.

Derek tried not to think of how much of that ash was, until very recently, the inhabitants of the town.

"What could even do this, Brennan?"

Brennan frowned, looking at the readouts of various analysis skills he seemed to have running. One of the advantages of his class was that he could learn about enemy attacks he might face from almost any way of observing them one could imagine, including looking at the aftermath of them.

"I have no idea. But whatever it was, it happened in an instant. This was one attack, Artemis."

"THIS?" Artemis yelled, swinging her arm at the destruction behind her. "This entire town was leveled with one attack? One?"

Brennan nodded. "Unless my skill is wrong. I can't analyze what happened here. It's not telling me how to block this kind of attack. But it is treating it as one attack, one skill. It's not like a battlefield. It's like someone hit this with a precision strike from space, or something."

Artemis tore her gaze from the smoldering town and wheeled around on Brennan. "That doesn't even make sense, Brennan. What could even . . ."

She suddenly stopped, looked and Brennan's face, and turned her eyes up towards the hills around the town. Seeing this, Derek did the same.

There were demons. Thousands of them, ringing the entire valley the settlement stood in. It was an ambush.

Thirty minutes later, they finally broke out of the battlefield, covered in blood. It had mostly been Brennan's doing, using his full suite of precision skills to keep enemies away until they found a weak spot in the encircling forces and cut through it. Derek hadn't helped much in the fight, the most he did was paper over some minute errors in Brennan's technique by finishing off enemies he had already mostly gutted or crippled with pinpoint strikes. He comforted himself by noting that Artemis had been in about the same boat.

He was embarrassed to recall how he had dreamed of overtaking Brennan, thinking he'd be able to do so if he could just go on a few real missions. It turned out the gap between them was less like the wall he had imagined, and more like trying to build a bridge over the Grand Canyon.

"Where are we going?" Brennan huffed. It was much easier to keep up with him now. He was covered in wounds to the point where he was significantly slowed. If they had a chance to escape, it was going to be Artemis's scouting that would do it, not sheer speed.

"You aren't going to like it."

"Just tell me."

"We have to circle back and go into demon territory. It's the only way."

"What? Why?"

"I've been analyzing their tracks. Somewhere along the line, we set off some kind of magical alert that called them back to this battle, but before they started chasing us, they must have been headed towards other settlements. There's a literal army between us and friends."

"We can't cut through?"

"Not injured like you are. There's too many of them." There was no question in Artemis's voice. Derek watched Brennan accept it, then move on.

"You think we'll do better in enemy territory?"

"Probably. They won't expect it. And with a force that big, they probably didn't leave very many forces in reserve."

"Derek? Thoughts?" Brennan could have easily forgotten Derek, but didn't.

He was part of the team, it turned out, and Brennan was treating him like an adult.

"If it's our best chance, it's our best chance. I'll do what you two recommend."

No more words were exchanged. They veered. An hour later, they crossed over into the blood-tinted wasteland of the demons' territory.

CHAPTER SIX

Pedicure Token

Matt pulled himself up off the ground. It turned out that not all forms of travel to various system worlds were created equal. The fact that he was still alive meant the Gaians had got it at least partially right, but being sucked through the aether between the two worlds with their portal was not an experience he suspected would ever become popular.

The bits and pieces of it he even remembered were horrifying, all stars whizzing by and eternal blackness while he himself was stretched in three thousand impossible directions. The fact that all of this felt like it was happening under the watchful gaze of unknown horrors he couldn't actually see hadn't added much to the appeal.

"Did you get any of that, Lucy?"

"Any of what?"

"The stretching, the whole dread being from beyond the void vibe?"

"No. What? No. I can't quite explain what happened to me during the ride. It was like I got tucked into a pocket of your soul or something. It was weird. But it wasn't what you just said."

Matt nodded. He would have liked to compare notes, but it was just as good for Lucy to have missed the experience entirely. It had been minutes since he landed on solid land, and he still felt vaguely like his soul was about to puke.

Ding!

Welcome to Ra'Zor, Realm of One Thousand Bleedings

Welcome, Invader! You have somehow earned the right to make a foray into the world of Ra'Zor, pillaging where you will, taking what you like, and generally causing mayhem.

Or not. The invasion system is complex, and each being's concept of invasion tends to vary. As a general rule, the amount you gain from a particular invasion is most closely tied to the general amount of change you cause during the invasion. Killing a king is worth a lot of points, but so is saving one who would have otherwise died, and that sort of thing.

Note that while you will be awarded achievements, experience, and related rewards during your time on Ra'Zor, the bulk of your rewards will be rewarded by the Ra'Zorian system at the time you return to your usual world.

Yes, you can still die here. No, most of your stuff isn't with you. It will be returned when you arrive back on your home world, safe and sound.

I am the Ra'Zorian system instance, and I am here to help you in just the same way the system of your home world does. Invasions are meant to be shake-ups in a particular realm, and most of your information has been withheld from me to prevent too much adaptation to your particular style of fighting. In the same way, every system instance manages its planets in a slightly different way, so various aspects of your trip might seem strange or foreign until you learn more about them. It's fun! We will learn about each other as we go.

Once again, welcome to Ra'Zor, Invader. Enjoy your stay!

Matt read off the message to Lucy.

"Well, that's friendly. I wonder if he really will help us, just like our normal system instance does." Matt and Lucy were very aware that the system instance could listen in on normal speech, and had decided beforehand not to show their cards too soon if they could help it.

"Probably not. That joker is so crazy."

"Yup. But this one seems nice, *so far*." Lucy put the emphasis on the inevitable change. Neither of them expected things to stay friendly forever.

"Yeah." For the first time since arriving, Matt took a look around. "You know, I'd like it if just once I could end up in a place that isn't almost entirely red." His shovel had made the trip with him, but otherwise Matt was almost completely disarmed, including his pack. He was clad in beginner clothes, which on Ra'Zor appeared to be a white cloth shirt and a pair of white drawstring pants. Or they would have been white, if they weren't already covered in bloodred dirt.

"Right? It would look the same, if it wasn't for those." Lucy gestured over in a slightly less barren direction, where a few dead trees sat by the edge of some kind of maintained path. The sun was giant and reddish here, either from some trick of the atmosphere or just because Ra'Zor had a giant red sun. Matt didn't care one way or another. He just hoped it moved.

He swung his shovel a few times, experimentally. Everything at least felt normal, and his status screen was unchanged. There wasn't much more they could get in terms of orientation from sitting around. It was time to get a move on.

"The place lives up to its name, at least. Do you think that the whole planet is like this? Barren?"

"I doubt it. Maybe, but that sword guy seemed pretty . . . soft, I guess? It was like fighting with a super-strong child. I can't see him being that way if he had to survive this kind of environment."

"It really is pretty barren."

"Compared to Gaia, it's practically a botanical garden. Look, a shrub!" Matt gave a quick kick to a large, paper-dry bush that was struggling to survive by the edge of the path.

This almost immediately turned out to be a mistake. As soon as the rustling from the bush being kicked died down, Matt heard a buzzing. The sound intensified over the split second it took for him to bring his shovel into fighting position, just in time for a dozen shiny black forms to burst out of the bush at him.

"Matt, dodge! They're called *Arrow Ants!*"

Matt flared Spring-Fighter just in time for the group of chihuahua-sized ants to whiz by. The amount of force in their jump was surprisingly large, and they overshot him by quite a few feet before they could stop themselves in the air with their wings. One particularly fast ant actually made it to the other side of the path and impacted a tree, getting momentarily stuck when its mandibles sunk into the dead wood.

"Got it. How do you know that?"

"This system instance is feeding me information! But maybe we should . . ."

The ants had turned in the air to face him, still buzzing angrily. As a group, they suddenly cocked their wings forward, sharply, and began falling in place. Matt heard a clicking sound, like the wings were locking against something, then another as the wings suddenly slapped backwards hard against the air. All the ants that had been falling towards the ground suddenly launched forward, directly at his face.

"Shit!"

"Yeah, let's talk about other stuff later. Get to work!"

Matt scrambled out of the way. And then once more as the ants regrouped for another go at him. On the third launch, Matt was ready. Lucy shouted out to let him know that once the ants had locked their wings in position, the arrow-attack was nearly certain, like they were too committed to pull out of it once they had started. He managed to get two of them on his first shovel swing, cutting the head off one and the wings off another. He stomped on the grounded, still living ant, accidentally covering his foot in ant-goo as he did.

"Gross!" Matt yelled. The stuff wasn't corrosive or poisonous that he could tell, but that didn't mean he liked it. It was on now. After that, it was a bloodbath. A half minute and several ant-launches later, the path was littered with various kinds of insect parts and green blood.

"Well, that wasn't so bad." It really wasn't. Only one of the ants had made contact, and most of the damage had already healed.

"No, it wasn't. And to answer your previous question, it looks like this system instance feeds me information on new enemies I see. I have no idea why, or if that's normal, or if it's going to keep happening. But at least for these ants, I got a pretty good breakdown of what they were and basic combat capabilities."

"That's . . . honestly, that's really good. It's going to help a lot here."

"Yup. And, for the record, those ants were categorized as something called 'demon-variant animals.' No idea what that means."

Matt patted his arm as Rub Some Dirt In It closed up the last bit of wound on his shoulder. The fact that they cut him was not completely implausible, but these didn't exactly seem like heavy-hitter enemies to Matt. Calling up his status screen and taking a closer look revealed that getting hurt was a little more plausible than he thought for a simple reason. None of his Palate of the Conqueror's traits had survived the trip.

"Looks like we are eating these ants, Lucy."

"Is that going to work, away from Gaia?"

"I'm not sure. But if it doesn't, our loadout just got a lot worse."

Matt was without matches and a torch, but for once, not without ready supplies of wood and kindling. He built the makings of a small fire on the ground, piling twigs and leaves high. He then went to try to do something he had never actually done before: rub two pieces of wood together to make a fire. It turned out this was only hard on Earth because people weren't walking around with ten times the physical ability of normal humans. Once he dialed in the amount of strength he needed to get into play to create maximum friction without actually breaking the wood, his superior dexterity score gave him a flaming branch within moments.

Roasting the ants didn't do much to make them more appetizing to Matt, but it at least solidified the insides enough that he didn't have to literally pour them into his mouth. He scooped out a double-fingerful of roasted ant with his index and middle finger, then grimaced as he put it into his mouth.

"It tastes like oranges. Why does it have to taste like oranges?"

"Ants have a high formic acid content."

"It was more of a hypothetical, but thanks."

Ding!

Unknown Skill Detected

One of the skills you have used is foreign enough to the local system logic that the system instance has failed to immediately recognize what it is, or how to supply it with the resources it needs to function.

The skill is currently under analysis and will likely begin to function at some later time. As a nonfunctioning skill decreases your chances of survival during your invasion, compensation will be made. The skill in question is not labeled as a class-vital combat skill, so the reward is somewhat smaller than would otherwise be the case, but an effort was made to select an award that is still relevant to your current needs.

Reward: Reinforced Boots

"Looks like my eating skill won't work for now, Lucy. I'll have to go buffless for a while. The system instance says it's working on it." Matt mentally claimed the reward, and a pair of boots materialized in the air next to him before flopping into the dirt of the path and kicking up a small cloud of red dust. "But these make up for that a little. I just wish I had water with me to wash the dust off my feet. Dirty feet in shoes suck."

Ding!

A reasonable appeal for a larger reward has been made and granted.
Additional reward: Pedicure Token

Matt immediately called up the description for the pedicure token.

Pedicure Token

Somehow, you've made the system laugh. Pedicure tokens belong to a group of obscure, nearly valueless prizes sometimes given out as novelty rewards for small but amusing achievements. It has a near-zero value, but really does do what the name implies it will. Enjoy!

CHAPTER SEVEN

Squeeze Viper

Matt materialized the token and caught it out of the air as it fell.

"What's that? Some kind of reward?"

"Yes. Maybe the good kind. One sec."

The few years of life on Gaia that Matt had experienced had not been kind to his feet. All the general damage his feet had taken had been healed by his vitality and healing skill, but each time, he was left with thicker and thicker callouses, which themselves had picked up little fragments of dirt, dust, and various Gaian debris over time. This made his feet tougher, but that hardly mattered when he kept them wrapped in armored boots all the time. Otherwise, it was just a cracked-toenail-and-gross-thick-skin situation he tried to avoid looking at as much as he could.

As Matt activated the pedicure token, his feet suddenly felt warm, like they were being soaked in a kind of bath. As he looked on, they suddenly began to glow with a soft light as bits of dead skin detached and floated away. Clicking and rasping sounds filled the air as his toenails were cut down to a reasonable length and filed to a presentable appearance. After about a minute, his feet were pristine, fresh, and felt fantastic.

"Matt, what in the fuck just happened? Why is there a little pile of foot fragments on the ground?"

"Pedicure token, I guess." Matt was grinning ear to ear while he loosened the laces on his boots. He wasn't about to let his feet get dirty any sooner than he had to. "Worked pretty damn good, actually. It even pushed the cuticles back."

Matt put his feet into the boots, which turned out to be lined with some kind of cotton-like cloth that would do very well to mitigate the fact that he didn't have socks. It felt amazing. He sighed with a weird kind of relief.

"Lucy?"

Lucy was still trying to make sense of the madness she had just seen, and it seemed to have knocked most of the conversation clean out of her. "Yeah, Matt?"

"If we don't die, I think I'm going to like Ra'Zor."

The next several hours were not exactly eventful by normal standards. Without any way of knowing where he was or where he was headed, Matt's only viable option was just to follow the path until it led somewhere, hoping for some break in the monotony that wouldn't also immediately try to murder him.

The first change in his environment that ended up mattering wasn't another monster, but something that didn't have to do with him moving around or being discovered at all. After a while, something began affecting Matt's eyesight. He could still see, but not as far as before and with less clarity than he was used to. Very slowly, the condition began to worsen until a long-dead memory stirred and Matt realized what was actually going on.

The sun was setting.

Suddenly, Matt was hit with a wave of sleepiness so heavy he almost sat down on the path to go to sleep by sheer reflex. Out of nowhere, he was getting hit with years of pent-up human instinct regarding what sunsets were supposed to mean. It was all he could do to get off the path to a small hollow in the terrain he hoped wouldn't be visible from the road before he passed out.

Somewhere in his dreamless sleep, Matt was vaguely aware that he was in an extremely deep slumber. Some primitive fear of being defenseless eventually roused him to fight against that feeling, at least to the point where he'd be aware enough to protect himself if something did happen. He was sleeping so hard, he felt like he couldn't even breathe, a fact which he was pretty sure he was only aware of because his perception and wisdom were so high.

He tried to move to lessen the pressure, but it was no use. It was like his arms were pinned to his sides and his ankles were tied together. He struggled. It didn't work. He couldn't move.

Then he felt the world move around him, tightening its grip, and panic sunk in. Adrenaline started pumping as his eyes snapped open, only to see scales sliding past his face.

"Matt! Snap out of it! YOU ARE BEING EATEN BY A SNAKE, YOU IMPOSSIBLE IDIOT."

And so he was. Matt was severely disoriented, not just because he was waking up, but because he was being attacked outside of a dungeon. The surface of Gaia had been about as safe as a place could be for the majority of the time he spent there. As the only living thing on the surface most days, the chances of anything happening to him were next to nil. To actually be attacked while he was sleeping was so unimaginable to him at this point that it took him a split second to come to terms with it. And the only reason he reacted so quickly was because he could feel fangs slowly creeping up his legs.

Ding!

> Skill resolved. The system apologizes for the wait—it's a truly bizarre skill. If you'd be kind enough to describe how you got it and the exact way it works, I could probably do a better job. Let me know!

Yeah, fat chance, Matt thought.

Ding!

> *Stored Strike Obtained*
>
> Stored Strike allows you to preload power into your muscles and release it all at once into a single movement, but only if your body is otherwise completely still. Any movement will both stop the preloading process and release the stored power, either into a movement or by dissipating it entirely. Note that this dissipation causes a small amount of recoil damage in both the user's muscles and bones.
>
> Meta-Trait Occupied: Attack.

Not moving wasn't a problem, at least in the sense that Matt couldn't move even if he wanted to with his body being constricted in place. He willed the trait into action, feeling the power load into him like he was a coiled spring, while he became more and more claustrophobic in the snake's grasp. Finally, he let all the stored power go as he kicked his legs as hard as he could, feeling his foot connect inside the snake's head before it—he didn't know how—moved the roof of its mouth out of the way.

It must be a specialized constrictor skill, or something. Who else would have a damage reduction skill for the inside of their mouth?

Still, the kick must have done something because the snake immediately slackened its grip around him. He pushed Spring-Fighter pretty hard and just about squirted out of the coils of the snake, landing a few feet clear of it and popping to his feet, shovel at the ready. Somehow, Survivor's Reflexes wasn't showing him a single weak spot yet. He braced for a hard fight before realizing that the reason the snake's vulnerabilities weren't showing was that he had already exploited them.

When he kicked the inside of the snake's head, the full force of the armored boot had transferred to the roof of its mouth. Without the room to snap back, that kick had apparently been hard enough to do some serious damage. The jaw of the snake hung open at the hinges like a half-dead Pac-Man, and it wasn't moving.

"Lucy, what the hell happened?" Matt asked, trying hard not to let the accusation seep into his voice. "Why didn't you wake me up?"

"Because, Captain Sleepy, I tried to wake you up. For like a full minute before the snake even got to you, and then as it took its damn time wrapping you up. You were *out*, Matt. The sun went down, you went all *Goodnight Moon*, and apparently no amount of screaming was going to get you going. Not my fault, Matt. If I were capable of going hoarse, I wouldn't even be able to talk right now."

Matt considered this. Given how strong the sleep had come on, it was possible.

"Well, sorry. I guess I'll have to be careful about sleep until I get used to there being a day and night cycle. It would be lame to get taken out by a one-shottable mook like this before we even get anything done."

"Actually, a weird thing about that." Lucy focused in on something invisible that Matt assumed was the description of the snake-monster. "It says this is, again, some sort of demonic-variant snake, something called a Squeeze Viper. Which, you know, is a dumb name, but whatever. But it describes it as this big, bad thing. Like 'many parties fall to the Squeeze Viper when . . .' type of language."

"Well, it didn't seem that tough."

"No, it didn't." Lucy shrugged. "It's possible this system instance is just an exaggerator. But don't tell him I said that."

"I'm pretty sure it can just hear you anyway, Lucy."

Ding!

Night Ambush Survived

You have survived your first nighttime ambush. They say more adventurers get taken out by threats they don't see than by those they do. This is true, but it's mainly because sleep is a dangerous, defenseless time.

You managed to get ambushed while you were alone and unconscious, wake up, and win a decisive victory. Congratulations! You get to be one of the lucky ones who survives being kind of stupid in a very dangerous place.

Rewards: Camper's Survival Pack, 50 Class XP, 1 PER

Additional information: You seemed to just be telling your guardian that I could hear her. For the record, the system instance of one world has no access to the system guardians assigned by the system instance of another world. I can't hear what she says unless you verbally repeat it.

If she was explaining something important, such as the details of your food consumption skill, it would be helpful if you would repeat the statement.

"Ooh, camping stuff." Lucy said as the pack materialized. It wasn't as big of a backpack as Matt's previous pack, but it had a lot of the things he had tried to bring as creature comforts. He now had matches, even though it was clear he didn't need them. There was also some kind of magic lantern, cutlery, and even some conventional, non-magic bottles of water. "For killing the snake?"

"For not letting it kill me, I think." Matt schooled any tricky expressions out of his face. "The system says it can't hear you because you are under our system instance's jurisdiction, by the way. Just in case you wanted to communicate something to it."

Lucy's mouth made an *O* shape as she absorbed the implications of that statement. The Gaian system instance had done a lot of bad things to them, but one of the big no-no rules it never directly broke was telling a direct lie. It could mislead, sure. But outright lies seemed beyond its powers. Matt nodded at her, unassumingly. It was still a risk, but the high likelihood that the system couldn't actually hear her freed them up to have better communication when it was important.

"She says thanks for letting her know, System, and that she will do that. And thanks for the pack!" Matt said to the sky.

It was still night, and even though Matt wasn't in the same must-sleep-now straits he had been before, he was still sleepy. He ended up quickly scorching and swallowing a piece of snake meat, getting a mild defense buff out of it that he decided to keep, despite it coming with an increased sensitivity to fire. Then he laid down and went back to sleep.

CHAPTER EIGHT

A Play Rehearsal

The sunrise had much less of an impact on Matt than the sunset had. He might have felt a little more alert than he had been before watching it, but if so, it was a mild effect and thoroughly washed out by something he had found upon a closer inspection of his camping pack. Deep in one of the interior pockets of the bag, he excavated little packets of what looked for all the world like instant coffee.

"Really? You're that excited over this stuff?" Lucy rolled her eyes as Matt rocked back and forth, eagerly waiting for a mug of water to heat up over a fire. "I figured the whole addicted-to-coffee thing was a meme, like that time the whole internet got way too into bacon for a couple of months."

"Nope. It's a real thing. This might not even be real coffee, and I'm still excited about it. Even if it is real coffee, it's instant coffee, which is the absolute worst, and I'm *still* excited about it."

"Weird, but okay. Knock yourself out."

The resulting drink wasn't entirely coffee as Matt knew it, but it was close enough to seem like coffee, which was the main thing. Better yet, either the real coffee on this world was absolutely incredible in every way, or their instant coffee didn't suck nearly as bad as Earth's. Between the better than expected quality and the closer than expected experience, Matt ended up with a cup of something that got really, really close to hitting the spot.

What he didn't bank on was that after so long without a single drop of caffeine, the drink would hit like a freight train. He had kind of expected his vitality score to cancel what was technically probably a poison, but it either didn't see things the same way or the Eat Anything! aspect of Palate of the Conqueror amplified what he got out of the coffee.

Either way, he was wired.

"Matt, I'm serious. If you are going to be like this every morning, you can't have the coffee anymore. We have to work together. That means respect. This doesn't make that easy."

Matt's eyes panned back and forth as his caffeine-driven hyper-awareness had him scanning every last bit of the horizon, and he was walking a bit faster than usual, but was pretty sure that Lucy was exaggerating.

"It's not a big deal. I'm fine. It's not always like this, either. I'll get used to it. That's actually bad. I feel *incredible.* I could jump the moon if this planet had a moon, which it might, and I might just not have seen it yet. Have you seen anything down the road? I've been looking, but I haven't. I guess this road might go on forever without there being anything to see, but I can't see why there'd even be a road then and who would even maintain it . . ."

"Matt, I'm serious. Stop talking. Just go back to walking way too fast and looking around like you think you're checking for the police during a drug deal. I'm sorry I brought it up."

It was a few hours before Matt was normal again. Luckily, it turned out vitality did kick in to minimize the post-coffee crash.

It was a light day for monsters, apparently. Even in Matt's coffee-driven paranoia state, he hadn't seen a single bird, beast, or insect that might threaten him. This, in turn, meant he was incredibly bored by midday. Lucy was right there with him.

"Is there a rule that the system has to plop you in the middle of stupid red wastelands, Matt? I mean you in particular. Because I'm pretty sure not every single adventurer spends all their time bored in places that look like shitty, flat, generic-brand Sedonas."

"I'm starting to think you spend entirely too much time in your Earth information database. Sedona is like the fifth-best tourist attraction in a bottom-twenty state. How much time do you even spend reading that thing?"

"Lots, Matt. What else do you expect me to do while you sleep? I've read pages on every country. Every state. I've looked at pictures. I know the plot of every *Mega Man* game. If you don't like it, stop going to sleep all the time."

She had a point. Matt dropped the matter. It was fortunate for both of them, however, that this was about the time they saw the tavern.

Matt had a long list of Isekai protagonist experiences he felt cheated out of. Near the top of that list was not getting to go to any magical roadside taverns. While it was true that in most mangas, they were often traps of some kind. But the off chance when they weren't? You'd eat giant slabs of meat, drink beer at a big wooden table, and then some surprisingly weak jackass would make just enough trouble for you that you had an excuse to uppercut him through the door. It was a big deal, and one that Matt had never really forgiven the system for denying him.

But here one was, right in front of him, built with wood, bricks, and little four-pane windows.

"I promise I'm going to be very careful, but I have to go in there."

"Oh, no, you aren't going to be careful. You are going to do something very dumb and almost get killed. I flat-out guarantee it."

"Lucy . . ."

"I didn't say you couldn't go in there. You are *absolutely* going into the manga tavern. You just have to promise me one thing."

"What's that?"

"If the spoiled son of the town's mayor gives you shit, you have to drop-kick him through a door."

With Lucy with him on the absolutely correct trope page, Matt wasn't going to waste any more time. He walked directly to the building and threw open the door. Inside, a rowdy scene greeted him. There were working men, like miners and carpenters. There were adventurer types. The barmaids were all friendly and sassy. It was everything. There was everyone. Matt was beside himself.

He introduced himself around while carefully avoiding any details of why he was actually there. With his simple clothes, his heavy boots, and his shovel, he was almost immediately mistaken for some kind of working man, and effortlessly fell in with that clique. When they found he didn't have any money on him, they bought him drinks. They laughed and told jokes. It turned out the bratty mayor's son-type wasn't in the script, but someone else took his place. Half-fueled by the beer, Matt knocked him out a window with a big wooden bench.

It was perfect. Matt was halfway through a game called spikeys that was sort of like darts, if darts was played by hurling foot-long daggers at a log hanging from a rope, when he suddenly heard a loud call from behind the bar. Looking over, he immediately traced the sound to the huge, happy man who owned the entire place.

"Alright everyone, that's it for today. Revert!"

All around him, everyone froze for a moment. Suddenly, the man closest to him turned into a big puff of smoke with a mild *pop* sound. When the smoke cleared, the former beer-gutted bricklayer Matt had been joking around with all night had been replaced by what looked like a bipedal griffin. Over the next several seconds, more and more of the people in the bar transformed, until Matt was almost entirely surrounded by snake-men, bird-ladies and a number of animal-human hybrids he couldn't immediately identify.

"Shit! Matt, I'm sorry. None of these tagged as monsters until they transformed back. I had no idea. Just . . . play it cool, alright? Maybe we can sneak out."

The bar's owner, who was now an equally massive wolf-man, began talking again. "This was an exceptionally good effort from each and every one of you. Trickery is often a forgotten tactic among the demon-kind, and I know there's a temptation to ignore it in favor of more combat-oriented solutions to problems. I'm glad to see that's not true for any of you. There are always situations where trickery is the better option. The weaker can use it to get the strong to let their guards down and find an advantage that can be exploited. The strong can use it to get information that even torture wouldn't obtain."

He pointed at a large red creature with dangerous-looking claws for arms. "You. Why do we emphasize taverns in our practice?"

"Because humans go to taverns to talk."

"That's one reason, yes. More specifically, humans *brag* in taverns. A human in a tavern, especially one who has consumed several of their alcoholic beverages, will casually tell secrets in a bar to absolute strangers that he would even withhold from his own mate. Now . . . you." He pointed to a small fox-like creature. "What's another reason we emphasize taverns?"

The fox looked uncomfortable, and stuttered a bit before appearing to think of a plausible sounding answer. "Because they are public?"

"Absolutely. Humans are innately defensive in their homes, and even if they allowed you access to their houses, they would become suspicious if you began asking probing questions. Taverns are public places. Travelers visit them, and travelers are expected to ask questions; it would almost be odder if they didn't."

Beside Matt, the griffin nudged him. "Hey, you forgot to change forms."

Matt nodded, trying to appear confident. "Yeah, I just want to see what he says first. I've heard there's sometimes a sort of trick question he pulls that's easier to answer if you have the human form as a reference."

It was a stretch, but the griffin-man seemed to accept it. But enough nearby beasts seemed to hear the response that they now turned their attention to him, if for no other reason than to see how well he did with the supposed trick question. Any thought he had of just slipping out the back evaporated.

At the bar, the owner-wolf continued. "Again, you all did a great job today. But one of you was a cut above, not only in terms of what he said, but how he said it. He nailed human mannerisms in a way that I can only applaud." The wolf man scanned the crowd, as if looking for something, before locking in on Matt.

"You, there. Still in your human form, I see. Well, very well. I'll overlook it, since you did such a fine job. Maintain your disguise, and please make your way to the front. I'd like to use you as an example, to further the learning of the other students. No, don't be shy. Come right up."

CHAPTER NINE

Am I a Badass

Having shambled up to the bar, Matt now stood awkwardly in front of the barstools as the wolf-man-bar-owner-slash-demon-class-teacher made his way around to stand beside him. Matt leaned lightly on his shovel, nonchalantly positioning it in such a way that he could sweep it up to bat the wolf away if he needed to make a sudden break for the door.

"I have some things to point out about this particular demon's technique, which I will do by asking him questions. This does not mean the questions are for him. They are for you. As I ask them, I want you to think about why I'm asking them, and carefully ponder how both you would answer, and how he actually answers them."

The demons in the audience *might* have looked thoughtful. Matt thought of himself as a pretty socially aware person, but a lot of those skills were very specialized to reading human faces. He had a much harder time understanding the expressions from, say, an eagle.

"First, sir, if you could tell me. When you were playing spikeys, why did you choose to miss so often?"

Matt shifted uncomfortably. If he was being honest, he had always been bad at games that involved ranged weaponry and fine muscle control. In his old life, he had been jokingly-but-not-really-joking banned from playing darts in his local bar after the owner got tired of patching little holes in the wall from his misses.

"Well, you see," Matt said, buying a few seconds to think. "It seems to me that missing is a human thing. And humans, in bars, are having fun. They aren't always serious about the game. So even if they could hit it if they were trying, they don't because it's not that important to them."

The teacher clapped his paws joyfully, his claws clacking together as he did. "Exactly! Exactly! Humans lack focus, even where they possess skill. And as superior as demons might be, trickery demands that sometimes we downplay that superiority." He turned back to the crowd, even more enthusiastic now. "And notice his hesitation before answering the question, the little shrugs that pretended at not knowing the answer, but trying anyway. Well done, sir. Truly well done."

In the background, Lucy was cracking up. "This guy . . . whoo, man. Don't die still, but I can't wait to see the look on his face when he finds out you're acting all incompetent because you're just a normal incompetent person. It's like you have a field around you that makes you suck at things."

Matt tried to ignore Lucy, standing a bit stiffly while he tried not to attract any of the wrong kind of attention to himself. So far, he wasn't dead. That was good. He'd take it.

"Now, a question for you." The wolf teacher pointed to the crab student again. "This 'human' bumped into you not once, but twice. You just let him. Why?"

"It seemed right. I didn't want to draw attention."

"That's not wrong, exactly. But while you might not want to start a duel over it, it's normal to draw attention when someone bumps into you, especially if they spill a drink on you, which he did. And especially when they don't seem to notice they've done it, which he didn't." The teacher turned back to Matt. "Why did you choose to bump into him, without so much as an apology?"

Matt stammered, trying his hardest to ignore Lucy's cackling. "I just . . . it seemed to me, I guess, that a human in a crowded bar might not be paying all the attention he should, and might have a bit more beer than he thought he had. Such a human might make that kind of mistake. Innocently. Other humans might understand and expect such behavior."

"Exactly right! Exactly!" The teacher faced the demon-students, beginning to speak in a wrapping-things-up voice Matt recognized as universal to all teachers. "The lesson here, students, is that humans are flawed. You don't want to do the wrong thing all the time, but doing the right thing at all times is just as suspicious. None of us are perfect at imitating humans, although some of us come close." Here he stopped, and nodded at Matt. "Giving the humans little, noticeable mistakes to focus on will keep them from focusing on mistakes that might reveal your identity. By imitating a human's flaws, your disguise becomes even more perfect."

He waited for the class to nod back before picking up a plate of food off the table. "Do you want plates just like these, but loaded with human flesh? Do you want to know where they've hidden their children before you burn down their settlements, to enjoy an even finer grade of meal? Do you want land of your own that you can rule over? Mastering these skills is how you get it. You can't destroy what you don't know, and this is how we learn." He turned back to Matt. "And you, sir, are virtually awash in flaws. No human would find you threatening, or even particularly interesting. Well done. Well done."

Lucy was rolling on the ground now, fully losing her shit.

"Now, sir, may I ask who you are? You aren't a normal attendee of my classes. What force do you hail from?"

Matt had no idea how to answer this. He took a stab in the dark. "The Fifth Battalion?"

"The fifth?" The teacher's lupine forehead creased. "I thought they were deployed to human territory at the moment."

"Well, yes. But I was . . . granted leave? To visit my family."

"Funny, that. I didn't think insect types had much in the way of pack affection. And you say your commanding officer granted it?"

"Oh, yes. Took some talking to make it happen. But, you know, as you noticed, I'm pretty persuasive."

The teacher was not buying it. He suddenly stopped and sniffed the air, then sniffed again. His eyes took on a steely glint, and his hands tensed slightly. He wasn't armed in the conventional human sense, but Matt assumed his fangs and claws bridged that handicap by quite a bit.

"I notice you haven't dropped your disguise yet. Why?" Around the room, various animals began sensing something was wrong and tensing up. Without moving, Matt began to store some energy in his body, hoping he could stall for a moment.

"Well, you see, I figured you'd notice my mastery of the form and ask me to come up . . ."

It was, of all things, the crab-man that moved first. Matt released his stored arrow-ant tension into the shovel, letting it fly in an upwards arc to intercept the demon as it surged forward, clacking its claws. The seconds he had spent preparing the attack were apparently fairly effective when combined with the razor-sharp Nullsteel edge of the weapon. His strike cleanly bisected the crab. At the same time, the shovel brought splinters up from the floor where the tip had been buried. These projectiles made a cracking sound as they flew through the air and embedded themselves in two unlucky demons who were standing near enough to the crab to catch the flak.

The room paused for a split second as the splinter-riddled demons shrieked in animal rage, and the sides of the crab topped to the ground like something out of an anime samurai duel. By the time the halves actually hit the floor, the fight was on.

Matt's perception immediately alerted him to attacks coming from three directions. The bar had his back covered, at least for now, but the wolf on one side and two bird-type demons attacking from his front and right sides meant he suddenly had a lot to deal with. Disregarding what the broken glass would do to his back, Matt flared Spring-Fighter and jumped backwards, rolling over the bar on his shoulder blades.

Glass mugs and shot glasses exploded under his weight but Matt ignored the cuts into his back. He kept pivoting on his back until his legs hit the ground behind the bar. As he came back up to face the room, he saw the wolf's claws come only a fraction of a centimeter away from his eye. Without flinching, Matt used the momentum from the flip and brought the shovel back towards himself, hard. The motion caught a good portion of the side of the wolf's rib cage in the process. Whatever armor it was wearing was apparently no match for the combination of movement, strength, and Nullsteel, and it gave way cleanly ahead of the blade.

Matt wasn't an expert on wolf-demon anatomy, but the blow apparently clipped something vital on its way into the wolf's rib cage, and it dropped like a sack of flour.

Is it supposed to be that easy? Matt thought, before realizing that he was still facing down a room full of surging demons, who had only stopped momentarily to watch their leader drop. He needed to even the odds, or it would very quickly get much less easy than he liked.

Matt took a swipe outwards over the bar with the flat of his shovel, catching the remaining two bird-demons with the flat of the shovel and knocking them off-balance to his left. Continuing the shovel's momentum and following the original trajectory, he made a full loop with the shovel. The journey caught every bottle of liquid he could from the shelves behind the bar and continued on in a flinging motion back to the front. The bottles more or less atomized on impact, and let Matt launch a shovelful of broken glass and bottle contents at the rest of the demons. Chaos ensued as the demons were suddenly covered with microscopic cuts on their skin and eyes, burning with the force of a dozen bottles of cheap liquor.

As the demons in the back of the ranks stumbled over the suddenly collapsed frontline, Matt took the few seconds the opportunity afforded to dig his shovel under the bar at a diagonal angle, then store power.

After a few seconds, the demons began to get their shit together in a real way, forming actual, organized lines and moving forward. Where they had previously seemed content to rely on brute force, several of them now had paws, claws, or mandibles that shone with evil-looking magic.

They charged forward as one, only to be met with an entire dislodged, catapulting bar. Matt was far from figuring out the precise math on the arrow-ant attack, but the multipliers it gave seemed dependent both on time and how much weight he could put behind each attack. He had put his entire back into the motion as he cranked back on his shovel. The wood groaned, the bar lifted, and roughly a ton of finely crafted hardwood launched through the air before crashing into the group.

Matt didn't wait to see how much damage it did.

By this time, Matt had spent enough time in actual battle with the unveiled demon-kind to see their weaknesses spread out in front of him in the form of skill-driven weak spot indicators. Rather than go for the brightest lights, he prioritized the enemies with the dimmest indicators, assuming they represented either the strongest or least-injured enemies. He swung the shovel wildly back and forth, counting on the wide arcs for crowd control and dedicating most of the attention he wasn't spending on the attacks to dodging.

By the time the third enemy had fallen from his charge, the demons looked reluctant to attack him. By the time the seventh fell, they looked scared. As he bounced back a fireball and took out a handful of them at once with their own ammunition, they looked terrified. But despite what he expected, they never broke and ran. They fought to the last, driven by some kind of pride or fear of reprisal.

After a surprisingly short time, Matt found himself administering the coup de grâce on the last living demon in the bar, absolutely covered in a variety of shades of demon blood, and not even breathing hard.

"Lucy?"

Lucy was shell-shocked.

"Yeah, Matt?"

With a general expression of wonderment and confusion, Matt gestured generally at all the littered corpses and general destruction he had wrought.

"Am I a badass?"

CHAPTER TEN

Edward Scissorhands

After picking through the remains of the bar, taking a fresh look at Matt's stats, and comparing notes together, Matt and Lucy came to one conclusion. Yes, Matt was a badass now. Kind of.

"I think it's a combination of things. The first and biggest thing is just that people can't seem to touch you. Like, I was watching that whole fight. It wasn't like they didn't *try* to hit you, Matt. They tried pretty hard. Some of those hits were coming in from behind, and you still even dodged *those*. How did that work?"

Matt tried to think back to the battle, which wasn't easy. He was barely aware of what was going on at the time. Adrenaline was pumping through him and he was too focused on the moment to include any strategic thinking. But he did remember several very distinct pulls in several very distinct directions during the fight, ones he hadn't questioned at the time.

"I think it was Survivor's Reflexes."

"Not Spring-Fighter?"

Matt shook his head. "The only skill I have that actually tells me to do things is Survivor's Reflexes. My combat skill makes me better at hitting, but it doesn't say where to hit. Spring-Fighter makes me better at dodging, but it doesn't actually tell me when to dodge. Those skills are just physical capability things, not guidance."

"Was Survivor's Reflexes ever that good, before?"

Matt recalled the times when he used the skill in the past. "No. But think about it. We got all those stats and skill level-ups from killing the Scourge, that's gotta count for something, right? And we got dozens of stats afterward as well. We've been playing it pretty safe on Gaia ever since. Me killing a group of Clownrats wasn't going to even require it to do anything. Between better perception, better dexterity, and a very upgraded skill . . ."

"You think it was a shift in kind, not just intensity?" Lucy asked.

"Something like that. Like, maybe, it finally had the stats it needed to shine, or something."

Lucy thought about this for a moment before moving on.

"The second thing is the shovel, honestly. It works far too well."

"It's pretty sharp, yeah."

"Sharp, but that's not all. I watched those demons fight, Matt. A bunch of them tried to put up magic shields, or made their bodies glow before you hit them. It didn't matter. Hell, I bet you didn't even notice."

It was true. He hadn't.

Lucy continued, "That thing demolishes magic, Matt. I don't really know how defense magic works, or how defense skills work because you don't really have them. But however they work, they must influence the mana in the weapons that hit them. For that shovel, it's like pushing a plastic pin through a magnetic field, or something. It doesn't even react."

"Didn't we already know all this?" Matt said, careful not to actually talk too much out loud about the Nullsteel itself. It was fine for Lucy to talk since the system couldn't hear her, but he didn't want the Ra'Zor system instance to learn too much about them.

"We knew some of it. It deflected Leel's fireballs, so we thought of it as being anti-mana. But it's more than that. It's anti-*mana*. And body skills run on mana. Everything does."

Matt nodded. He wouldn't talk about it anymore, but it was nice to know he had a weapon that defied most kinds of conventional magic-world physics.

"Anything else?"

"Yeah, although I'm not sure about this last one. First, did you expect the bar to go flying like that?"

"Hm. I think I hoped it would, but . . ."

"Not quite like that?"

"No. I would have been happy if it just kicked up some chunks of wood, or spilled glass on the ground."

"Yeah, I thought so." Lucy put her hand under her chin. "I think what probably happened is that you poked the shovel down deep enough that you hit dirt."

"And activated my digging skill?"

"Yup. Which means . . ."

"I can charge skills."

"Yeah. Which isn't the biggest deal right now, since you can only have one attack trait at a time, and that's the charge trait. And the only skill you have is digging. So you pretty much just became a better digger. But it's good to know."

Eating the demons wasn't exactly pleasant, but after consuming acid ants it wasn't going to be the grossest meal Matt had ever had. Whatever moral compunctions he had against it were wiped away by the fact that the demons had talked about eating human children like it was a normal life goal as opposed to a horrific war crime. If he got some skills that let him clear out a few demons a bit faster, it was worth whatever ickies he'd experience doing it.

Matt pondered his current situation as he gathered little bits and pieces of meat from the battlefield, careful to get as many varieties as possible. Given that the demons didn't evaporate on death, he had plenty of time to do it, and he felt pretty confident that he could at least get away if any other baddies showed up.

The biggest change to his situation was one of loyalty. Before experiencing what the demons were like, Matt could have imagined a situation in which he'd side with them, as underdogs, against humans like Leel. After hearing all the human barbecue talk, he doubted that the humans would be that bad, even on the off chance that they did generally suck. At the very least, it seemed okay to clear out unfriendly demons, and he suspected there would be no shortage of those.

The bar had a kind of wood-burning stove and a heated pot of oil. Matt opted to flash-fry all the little chunks of meat he had collected. After they were done, he carved off a very small piece of each, then ate them one by one, swallowing them like pills while attempting not to taste them. He might have to eat demons, but he certainly didn't want to develop a taste for them.

For the most part, the powers he got from the demons were pretty underwhelming. Most of them seemed to carry a kind of generic defense trait which offered resistance to fire and something called "blight" but still seemed broadly inferior to even the minimal defense trait he had picked up from the snake.

A few other demons turned out to have unique traits. The crab, for instance, had some kind of barehanded attack buff that would make strikes with Matt's hands and feet sharp. That wasn't incredible, but was good enough to put in one of Matt's spare slots as a kind of holdout weapon, at least for now. One of the eagles had a skill that enhanced attacks while diving from the sky, but it required a certain minimum height to work that made it impractical for anything Matt was likely to do with it. He wasn't exactly looking to suicide bomb demons any time soon.

The real winner came from the wolf because, as Matt found out, apparently not all powers he could absorb came from the baseline biology of a creature. Training, it seemed, came into play.

Sheep's Clothing

This skill allows you to disguise yourself as any creature, so long as that creature is not more than twice as large or less than half as small as your current size. To other creatures, you will appear to move, breath, and otherwise act as that creature does, so long as the behavior in question is a mundane action (like walking, breathing, or chewing). It will also translate your words and adjust the sound of your voice to fit the form you take, allowing you to communicate verbally.

This skill does nothing to influence your choices, however, and only affects the baseline, superficial aspects of disguise. If you say something confusing or act in a way that would be inconsistent with your cover, the skill will do nothing to prevent other beings from finding it suspicious.

Meta-trait Occupied: Movement.

Matt had no idea why Palate of the Conqueror would categorize Sheep's Clothing as a movement trait, and he couldn't ask Lucy without giving the system more information on Palate of the Conqueror than he would have liked. Still, he wasn't going to knock it. He had stumbled into a place where he was kill-on-sight for every demon who saw him. And as much as he had dominated this fight, it was possible he had just got lucky or faced an unusually weak group. He had no desire to find that out the hard way.

"Hey, Lucy. Does your information on the demons say anything about how strong this particular group was?"

"No, not really. It's general information on types, sure, but nothing you wouldn't guess from looking at them. It didn't even identify the mage demons as magic users. I think it mostly fails when personal choices and training come into play."

"Oh, too bad. I was hoping it would say they were elites, or something."

"Elites? Matt, I'm pretty sure you just attacked the human equivalent of a militarized college drama club."

"Lucy . . ."

"These were *actors*, Matt. Not a legendarily tough group, I'm afraid. I'm surprised they weren't wearing berets."

Matt gave up and began to scour the room for loot. When Lucy got on a kick, she could go on for hours.

"It's like, they were probably as elite in combat as a guy who is really, really into Tim Burton movies. Does that make you feel better?" Lucy asked.

"That guy," Matt said, gesturing towards the crab, "was at least probably really into *Edward Scissorhands*."

Lucy gaped at Matt in awe. "That was the worst joke I've ever heard."

Matt bowed. "Thank you. I'll accept my awards later, after we get out of here."

The demons, as Matt had observed, were not much for weaponry, or at least this particular group wasn't. But where they lagged behind on weapons, they didn't seem to have the same disregard for armor, which was what Matt really wanted anyway.

It was actually a problem that he had done so much damage with his shovel, and another problem that the undamaged pieces of armor he did find tended to be soaked in blood. But after a half hour or so of picking through the carnage and another several minutes of work at the fake tavern's well, Matt had a whole, mostly-matching suit of leather armor. He didn't know if any of it was special, and had no way to find out, minus cutting them into smaller pieces again. But it was at least far better than nothing at all.

He also found money, or what he at least assumed was money. They were, true to his manga expectations, small disks made of what appeared to be gold, silver, and copper. Given that the copper was shiny instead of the blue-green oxidization he'd expect from the actual metal, he assumed some substitutions had been made in terms of actual material. It didn't matter. Trope satisfaction was trope satisfaction. He packed everything he could into a single salvaged purse, and tucked it away into his backpack for future needs.

"So, are we off?" Matt asked.

"Looks that way. Although . . ." Lucy's voice trailed off.

"What?"

"I don't see any reason we'd leave this building standing, do you?"

For the first time, Matt considered what his "change as much as possible" prize-winning objectives on this planet would look like in practical situations.

"Lucy, you are a genius."

"I know."

If the tavern had anything at all, it had a generous supply of flammable liquids. A few minutes and dozens of gallons of cheap liquor and cooking oil later, Matt and Lucy walked towards adventure, their backs turned against the towering inferno of the burning tavern.

CHAPTER ELEVEN

Thanks, Derek

Derek crouched in the dark, hoping the dirt on his face and the general dark hues of his clothes would keep him hidden. Hunting during the daytime, he had found, was a waste of time. There just wasn't enough shrubbery to sneak through on the demon side of the human-demon border. The best he could hope for was to be seen a mile off and either be forced to fight with a ready group of demons or to chase down a lone, defenseless creature that would scream and flee until it ran into reinforcements.

Waiting by the road in the dark was better. There was less traffic during the night, but that didn't mean that demons could keep off the roads entirely. They sent messengers. They hauled cargo. Sometimes, they even looked like they were just going on walks, a strangely human-like behavior in demons. Some demons didn't need light to see, but with the exception of a few types, they saw much better with it than without it, just like humans.

Which meant they often carried torches, as the approaching pigeon demon did. Pigeon demons were not, luckily, all that strong. They mostly worked as messengers and merchants, with only the bravest of their type becoming mediocre-at-best warriors. But they were among the meatier, more substantial demons. And Derek was hungry enough for that to matter. All of the group was.

As the pigeon walked closer, Derek became aware it was cooing, softly and rhythmically. It was like it was humming to itself as it went down the road. He hoped that was true. Humming was not an activity he strongly associated with being alert and ready for attacks, and he hoped that assumption would hold.

It seemed to. The pigeon was either an excellent actor, or really didn't know

Derek was there. If it was the former, he proved to be a very poor tactician when he continued on into Derek's striking range, and took a dagger to the neck as payment for his lack of defenses. Before he could leave much blood, Derek dragged him off the road and out into the darkness towards camp.

"Oh, good, you got it. Once again, really good job. Thanks, Derek."

From Brennan, that would have been a complement that made Derek feel pretty good. It would have been validating. The fact that it came from Artemis warmed him to his core. The best way to know you weren't an asshole anymore was to hear compliments from someone who had no hesitation in saying the truth. Derek felt as good as he could, given the circumstances.

"Thanks. You can cook it?"

"Yup. No problem." Artemis had a scout skill that allowed, among other things, for her to conceal a fire. Other people could benefit from the fire's warmth without breaking the illusory shroud around it, but only she could actually work with the fire or see the light from it. That made her the de facto cook for the expedition, whether any of them liked it or not. Luckily, she was a fair cook, if only a barebones one.

"I feel bad about making you take the risks by yourself, Derek. You could at least bring me along," Brennan said.

"Nope, it's no good. If you accidentally trigger a movement skill, it's trouble for all of us. I can handle this, I promise. Plus, it's been great for leveling. That will be important if we get into real trouble."

Being in demon territory had ended up being a much worse situation than they had thought. They expected to be in life-and-death battles. And they also expected to have to earn every inch of their return to human territory. But because human raids on demon territory were so rare, and were virtually always done in large forces, there was a crucial piece missing from their expectations.

And it wasn't a small problem. Every time any of them used a skill, no matter how small, the demons could tell where they were. They didn't know if it was because the land itself was enchanted in some way, or if the demons had some kind of soothsayer class that could detect human mana use, but any time one of them used a skill, it would alert the demons to their location.

At first, they had assumed it was just something that was happening when they fought, like the demons were sensing the deaths of other demons, or had communication methods that they couldn't detect. The constant fighting had taken a toll on the group and left Artemis and Brennan exhausted.

It was only when the stronger two party members had set Derek on a lone enemy and observed whatever was happening from higher ground that they figured out what was happening. Derek had slaughtered a lizard-demon, and nothing happened. No enemies had come running. They had an answer.

But that left a disproportionate amount of work on Derek. Brennan's skill usage was so tied up in everything he did that he almost always activated some portion of his skills by instinct, even when he tried to actively suppress them. Artemis had better control, but still failed occasionally and was often completely tied up with stealth, camouflage, and general scouting duties.

That left Derek, at least for non-emergency purposes. It was dangerous, it was dark, and it was stressful. Any time he stepped out of camp might be his last. And despite that, he was loving every minute of it. It wasn't like it would have been, back when he was Asadel, where he felt like he deserved the responsibility and it made him important. Now, it was just proof that his hard work had paid off. He was useful, and he was helping people. Even just one demon slayed was one less enemy to deal with and meant his friends could eat.

Brennan sighed. "Yeah, I guess you are right. Still, it feels bad just . . . sitting. I never just sit. I should be out there, warning our people. The demons have this whole super weapon in play, and nobody knows, and it's my fault."

Artemis turned her head away from the fire, where she had set a giant chunk of pigeon meat to cook on a spit. "It's not your fault. If anything, the reason there was an Epsilon colony to blow up in the first place was because you've kept it safe so many times." She slowly turned the chunk of meat over, letting the other side cook. "There was no way to know there would be something like this. There never has been before. Something has broken the balance."

Derek's ears perked up. This was new to him. "What's that?"

Brennan glanced at Artemis. "Shh."

"No *shh*. Tell him. He's earned it."

Brennan began to argue, then regarded Derek seriously for a moment before he motioned him towards his tent, and entered it himself. Derek looked at Artemis, confused. She nodded encouragingly at him, and shooed him away with her hand. He shrugged and went.

It was beyond cramped in the tent. This was clearly a structure designed for one person, or maybe two if they didn't mind getting pretty close. With two full-sized men, it was packed full to bursting. Still, Brennan made Derek drop the flaps on the tent as soon as he was fully in.

"So. Sorry about the tent. There are reasons, trust me." Brennan did something funny with one of the supports of the tent, causing the temperature of the air in it to cool down to a comfortable level. "If Artemis says you can know this, you can know. But don't freak out."

"Know what?" Derek had spent the majority of the last few days killing, fleeing from, or eating crazy animal-demons, and this was still the weirdest part of his trip so far.

"So, basically, it's not that long of a story. But to start, do you know how long this war with the demons has been going on?"

Derek shrugged.

"Let's just say a long time," Brennan said. "We've checked the records. And at first, there wasn't any reincarnation. The demons popped up one day, and then the system came into play and promised to help people fight it."

Derek nodded. This part he sort of already knew.

"So then, the people started to get pretty strong. They had skills, and levels, and they were beating up the demons. And then suddenly the demons had skills and levels, and they were winning again. So the system started bringing in reincarnators. It was just one at first, and it promised that would help. And then the demons got stronger. So it brought in another reincarnator, and another, and another, and it was never enough. The war just got bigger, and both sides got more to fight with."

"So? We just need to . . . I don't know, win."

"Easier said than done. Have you ever seen us able to do *anything* that wasn't just holding on to what we have? If we take some area back, the demons take the opportunity to get some other piece. This war has been the same for decades, Derek. Same basic borders. The only thing that changes is the body count. That only gets higher."

Derek still didn't get it, and Brennan could evidently tell, so he kept talking.

"The thing is, if the system had given us everything at once, and it seems like it could have, we would have bulldozed the demons. You and I would have never come here, actually. It would have been over by then. But instead it gives just a little at a time, to both sides. And it keeps the fighting even. In balance. And the war never ends because it never can."

Derek thought about it. If he was honest, it was a little weird. When he first came, he had been terrified that the next day would be the day the demons finally got the upper hand. But they never did, or at least not for very long.

"You think that balance is gone now? Because of what happened to Epsilon?"

"Yeah. That's huge. A whole colony, at once? With no cost? There were no dead demons there, Derek. Even if they can only fire that weapon or spell or whatever it is once a year, it's all over. It's only a matter of time."

"That doesn't make sense, though. If the system wants balance to keep us fighting, it has to be for some reason. It gets something out of it, or something. Why change now?"

Brennan fiddled with the climate control, suddenly making the air circulate in the tent a bit more. "That we don't know. Something must have changed. Something big. We didn't get stronger, I think. Something else happened that the system is adjusting for. I just don't know what it could be."

Out of the tent, each of the team members sat picking at giant hunks of pigeon meat as they went over their plans. Since their plans mainly had to do with escape, the meeting was mostly led by Artemis.

"So we are here. The closest city of any kind is actually demon, of course, here. And our chance, such as it is, is here. We will have to wait for a good break in the troops, but this is where the watch is weakest, and we should be able to break through even if we get caught."

"How long to get back, Artemis? To somewhere where we can send a message of warning." Brennan's brow was furrowed as he looked at the map Artemis had scrawled in the dirt. "They have a few days lead on us, now."

Artemis shook her head. "The closest colony to the ruins of Epsilon is Delta, right here. No matter how fast we move, we won't make it."

Derek watched as Brennan went silent. No matter what they did, they couldn't run back to safety fast enough to save the next colony.

Derek thought for a moment, then pointed at the map. "What about here, instead?"

"That's the demon city, Derek. I already said that."

"I know."

There was no way they could run back to the human side of the fighting in time. But if they couldn't accomplish their goals running towards safety, they might do so by sprinting towards danger.

CHAPTER TWELVE

Spices and Fire

I think that's a town, Matt."

"Are you sure? It's pretty pointy for a town. I can't imagine why they'd build like that." Whether it was a settlement, a town, or a small city, what they were seeing looked more like a conifer forest made out of mud than it did a proper place to live. It was intimidating. It was sharp. If it really was a place demons lived, it was also highly impractical.

"They are demons, Matt. They don't *need* to eat people, they just do. I'm guessing they don't *have* to lay waste to all the land around here, they just like it that way. They are a bunch of dark edge lords, and I want you to beat them to death with your shovel."

"That's pretty intense for you."

"They eat *kids*, Matt. They can't get to the Gaians, but imagine if they could."

Lucy had picked the right visual if she wanted to get Matt motivated enough to knock some shit down. He had made friends with several of the Gaian children, helping source toys for them and even playing with them a bit. The thought of demons ripping them from their almost entirely lovely families, the kind of fear they'd feel, was enough to get him on board Lucy's "fuck up anything you see" bandwagon.

But with that said, that's a pretty big thing to take down, Matt thought.

"Fine, point taken," he said, "but what's even our plan? There must be hundreds of demons there. Presumably at least a few pretty tough ones. We don't really know the lay of the land yet, fighting ability-wise. I don't want to get in over our head."

"That's the beauty of it. We can go figure that stuff out before we fight. Just walk in and check it out, no real risk involved. Demon transformation power, remember?"

They had given the transformation power a go. The description had left out an important detail. More specifically, the skill had a day-long cool down. Otherwise, it worked as described. Matt had turned into a crab-demon, and according to Lucy, he looked just like one.

Lucy continued, "We'll take a look around, try to find some soft targets. If we don't find any, we figure out a better place to attack. It's not perfect, but it's the safest option we have."

"Well, besides finding some other humans and getting allies."

"Sure, if we knew where we were, or where they are. Knowing systems, we could be a thousand miles from the nearest human. But the demon town is still the best place to figure out about that, Matt. Suit up already."

Taking a deep breath, Matt activated the skill, this time opting to look like one of the insect-based demons. Before Matt had put a shovel in him, the drama teacher wolf had said insects tended not to have very close family bonds. At least this way, he could minimize the chances of running into someone who thought he was their cousin.

They still had a ways to go before they got into town, and got down to walking. It was just after dawn, but only a short way into their travel, they started to see more and more traffic on the road leaving the towns. There was plenty of demon diversity here, including some insect-based monsters, which Matt was glad for. At least he wasn't going to be the only giant beetle thing in town, drawing unwanted attention.

As they approached the town, it became clearer there was a wall around it. Not a tall one, but more like the block wall you might see around a house, about nine feet from top to bottom. It wouldn't be enough to stop determined invaders, so Matt figured it was more to help control traffic and trade, if demons even cared about such things. The apparent main entrance to town was a giant gate flanked by four guards, all of whom were some sort of large turtle variant. Matt did his best to look confident as he approached the gate.

"Halt." One turtle stepped out from the others, blocking Matt's path. "What is your business here?"

Matt didn't know what demons even did besides murder and burn things, so he tried to pick something almost any being would need.

"Food," Matt said, keeping his statement as short and factual as possible. "I'm out of food. Starving. I need to buy more, and other supplies."

The turtle gestured Matt to come closer with his large spear. "You have coin?" he asked. When Matt said he did, the turtle nodded. "Show me."

Matt fished his purse out of his bag and held it open for the turtle to see.

The guard looked, then deftly hooked one of the gold-colored coins out of the bag. "Call it an entrance fee. We aren't supposed to be letting people in. The army moved something in last night, we don't know what, but they are trying to control traffic until they can move it out again. We don't like it. Cuts down on entrance fees."

One of the other turtles huffed a laugh, apparently amused by the frank acknowledgement of their own low-key corruption. "If anyone asks, you got in yesterday. Not today. Yesterday. Got it?"

Matt nodded, then pulled a few silver coins out of his purse and pressed them into the turtle's hand. "In case I need to leave quickly. You never know."

The turtle laughed. "No, you never do." He made a hand motion at another of the guards, who opened the door a crack to allow Matt through. "Enjoy your time here."

Matt moved through the door, immediately finding himself on a kind of market street. There were meats of various kinds, none of which Matt felt comfortable buying, considering what at least one of them might be. But there were also vegetables, which he bought several mysterious varieties of. And, wonder of wonders, there was salt. To make the day even better, some of the demons sold a limited number of spices. Matt didn't haggle, which he supposed might be suspicious in its own right, but he had no idea what a good price would even be. Even getting everything he wanted, he only spent about half his coins. And so long as he survived, he had a feeling he'd have a pretty steady supply of money via the demon corpses.

After that, he wandered the town. To his relief, there were no children. There was hardly anything that even resembled families. Each house was built tall and spiky, as if single-occupancy homes were the norm. He also figured out how the big spikes themselves were managed. A few of them were broken or worn enough that he could see inside them, and they appeared to be mostly mud binding branches together. The houses themselves weren't much better, about as substantial as structures made out of straw. If this town was completely leveled, he suspected it could be built up again in less than a week. There was nothing permanent-feeling about it, beyond the wall.

The one exception to this was a large building in the center of town made out of stone instead of the usual sticks-and-dirt construction. Compared to everything else in town, it just looked important. That feeling was amplified by the fact that the building was pretty much surrounded by armored troops, most of whom had weapons, and most of whom were from clearly carnivorous and strong-looking animal variations.

"What do you think is in there, Matt?" Lucy was visibly excited, trying to get an angle on the building that might show her any clue to its contents. "The tortoise out front said the military was setting up shop, right? This seems military to me."

"Turtle."

"What?"

"The things at the gate. They were turtles. When they have thin shells and webbed feet like that, it's for swimming. Which makes them turtles."

"Where are they going to swim around here?"

"That I don't know. But, yeah, building." Matt tried his hardest to see a way into the fortress. "I'm guessing if there's something really cool to destroy, it's gonna be in there. But we probably need to watch for a while. These guys look tougher. I don't feel like fighting them and an entire town just to find out they were storing handkerchiefs or something."

After confirming there were no other entrances to the building, they found a nearby alley with a line of sight to the building's sole door and set up shop. For the most part, the guards didn't move. When they did change shifts, it was just a few of them at a time, never leaving the door completely unwatched. It was only when the guards were almost completely rotated out that the door finally cracked.

"Is my relief here yet?" A deep voice boomed out of the building from a figure Matt still couldn't see. "It's well past the time they should have arrived." The guards looked confused for a moment, then shook their heads. The door opened the rest of the way, and a large wolf-demon, much larger than the deception teacher had been, stepped out. "Well, I'm going to find them, then. I want you to guard this door closely until I return, and do not enter. Recall how important this project is to the demon lord. The penalties for failure, for all of us, would be severe."

The guards looked positively spooked by the mention of the demon lord's personal involvement in the project, nodded, and redoubled their attention on the surrounding streets. The wolf looked over the building one more time, then turned on his heels and left, apparently in search of his missing replacement.

"Well, this looks like a bust. They certainly aren't going to leave now."

"No, Lucy, I think we can use this. That was a mistake."

"How?"

"You've never had a bad manager, so you don't get it. One of the better ways to make people make mistakes or work less hard is to stress them out. Like, yeah, you can get maybe a couple of hard hours of work every time you scare them, but the rest of the time, they start to worry about losing their jobs. They focus in on whatever you scared them about, and make mistakes on everything else."

"I don't get it."

"Just watch."

If there was one thing that surprised Matt about the town as he walked through it, it was that demons apparently cared about sanitation, at least to some extent. There were public outhouses that appeared relatively clean, and the streets were pretty clear. There were also trash cans. Most were overflowing, but Matt wasn't here to judge the municipal infrastructure of the demons so much as he was to burn it all down.

Grabbing one of the trash cans, Matt did some quick mental math on trajectories, then gave the can a few practice swings. Curious, Lucy watched as he got set, lifted the can, and then chucked it in a high arc in the direction of the building.

"It's going to overshoot the whole thing!" Lucy was aghast, but overshooting the building was just what Matt wanted. The can landed not in front of the door and the guards where they could see it, but off to the side of the building where they couldn't see it. As it landed, it made an unholy crashing noise of metal banging and glass breaking. And, true to stressed-out-employee form, every single one of the jumpy guards immediately forgot the primary purpose of their jobs and went searching for the source of the sound, just in case it was something that could screw them over.

Best of all, Matt already knew the door was unlocked. Nobody had so much as touched a key the whole time. It took most of his stamina bar to do, but he managed to cross the entire space between the alley and the door in less than a second with Spring-Fighter. He cracked open the door and slipped through before a single guard had identified the trash can threat and looked at the door again.

Matt and Lucy were in. It was now time to burn some shit down.

CHAPTER THIRTEEN

A Heart and a Battlelord

"What is this, Matt?"

There were a lot of things going on at once in the warehouse. Most of them were mundane things, the standard kind of stuff an army would cart along with them. There were big crates. There were bushels of various kinds of food. There was shelving. It was a completely normal supply depot in almost every aspect they could see from the door, the sole exception being a reddish glow deeper in the building.

Matt assumed Lucy's question was rhetorical, but he wasn't in a position to answer back in any case. As he kept quiet, she continued on.

"It's weird demon shit, right? You build a warehouse without windows. You have a perfectly serviceable sun, but you don't even do glass with bars to keep people out, just a solid rock building. And then it's dark inside, so you put in a light. But can the light be a normal color? Noooo. It's red. Because no matter where we go, we can't escape red."

Matt and Lucy worked their way through the surprisingly labyrinthine arrangement of crates and shelves carefully and quietly. Each layer they passed meant the glow got a little brighter. Matt considered just hopping to the top of everything and traveling straight through, but then considered that he probably didn't want to be that high off the ground if something went wrong.

"And of course it's going to end up being just some weird demon nightlight because they can't help but be all edgy and spiky about everything. I bet that's just going to be how all their warehouses are . . ." Lucy suddenly stopped talking as they turned a final corner of boxes and the larger open space in the center of the building was revealed. "Oh, hell. I guess that makes the push-all-the-stuff-randomly-to-the-edges-of-the-warehouse sorting method make more sense."

In the center of the room was a giant levitating heart. Kind of. It was shaped like a heart, not in the Valentine's Day way, but instead in the more demon-appropriate ripped-directly-from-some-torso way. The various veins and arteries connected to it looked like they were severed by being torn away from their host instead of cut. The aorta was big enough that a toddler could probably crawl through it.

And, of course, it was on fire. Or made out of fire, maybe. Matt couldn't tell, and he couldn't ask Lucy if she could see something more.

"I know what you are thinking, and it doesn't even matter. The details of whatever this is, Matthew, are not important."

He glanced at her with his best "Come on, Lucy" expression, indicating that the details probably *were* important, and she should share them.

"I don't know, I didn't get any pop-ups. But look at it. It's a giant, floating demon heart. What kind of good thing could it possibly be for? Do you think it's a giant, floating fire shaped like a human organ that, like, spends the weekends working with disadvantaged kids?"

She had a point. They were here to make a big splash, and so far they hadn't seen anything from the demons but pretty classic bad-guy stuff. He had overheard more than one conversation on the street about the price of human meat going up. Outside of the pissing-match architecture on every house, they had failed to see anything fun, beautiful, or redeeming about demon culture to counterbalance their evil.

This also wasn't exactly wiping out a whole town, either. It was just destroying some kind of big, clearly cursed object. He wasn't quite on board with demon genocide yet, but nothing particularly bothered him about wrecking their war effort.

He shrugged.

"Good, same page. Now get to shoveling," Lucy ordered.

The demons didn't seem very nice, but they were fairly practical in some ways. There was a five-foot safety fence set up in a perimeter around the heart, apparently to keep people from tripping into it. It wouldn't stop Matt, in any case. He slung his shovel through the straps of his pack to keep it secure, grabbed the top of the fence, and vaulted over.

He was still sailing through the air towards the heart when things suddenly got much, much harder in a very literal sense. Matt made contact with some kind of invisible wall, cracked his nose pretty good against it, and fell to the ground. The force field reacted to his face-first impact by suddenly becoming somewhat visible at the point of contact. It flashed a blue light that rapidly rippled through the entire shape of the barrier, revealing that the whole heart was covered from all angles as if it was encased in a snow globe.

"Shit." Matt spoke before he thought about it, although it didn't seem to matter. Before he had said it, a large figure was apparently alerted by the impact itself and was already moving out of the shadows towards them.

When Matt encountered rat-like creatures on Gaia, he called them rats. The system and Barry also did, although he sometimes doubted that they were actually rats. He had always figured it was a translation thing, that the system automatically sensed what animal he'd associate with whatever he was looking at and assigned it that name. The crab-man he had killed the day before was reddish, crustacean, and had claws, so he considered it to be a crab.

But there were always differences, too. A Gaian rat might have teeth that were more curved, or paws that didn't quite fit. The bats might have heads that were a different shape. Some animals that would normally have fur would have feathers. It was like the universe had tried to make something that was recognizably a bear, but also checked a whole different set of optional boxes on the way.

What was coming towards him now was a rhino. It didn't have the big nose horn, sure, and Matt was aware the horn was why they were even *called* rhinos, but it didn't matter. It was heavyset. It had elephant-ish feet. Its neck was like a tree trunk, and with big, bony orbs protruding out of its forehead, it still looked like it could ram. It wasn't a rhino, but it was.

Its voice suddenly boomed out. "Insect! What are you doing here? Snuck in, eh?"

Matt had forgotten about his disguise. Things still weren't good, but they apparently weren't as immediately bad as they would have been if he had been in human form. "Uh, yeah. Sorry. Curious."

"Curiosity is no excuse, insect. This is a guarded military storage building. You knew you were not supposed to breach it. The usual penalty for that, fly, is death."

Matt looked like an insect, but much more like a cricket than a fly. He could sense this mistake was intentional, a kind of insult he should wince at. He pretended to wince before commencing with begging.

"Please, not that. I just want to see. You understand. Just to see."

"Ha! 'To see,' he says. Do you know how much is stolen from these warehouses if we don't guard them? But this here is a little too big to steal, isn't it?"

"Yes. I . . . did not expect this."

He really hadn't. Whatever this was, it was weird, and he really did want to destroy it at this point. He was about to sucker punch the rhino with a shovel strike when Lucy suddenly cut in.

"Don't do it, Matt. I just scanned this guy, and he's the first person I've seen who actually has their rank listed within their description. He's something called a battlelord. Try to find another way besides fighting. This seems too risky."

The rhino, who could not hear Lucy, laughed at Matt's words.

"Didn't expect it? I bet not. Well, the bad news for you is that killing you is the easiest thing. Keeps rumors from spreading, you see. Keeps me out of trouble. No reason to keep you alive at all. Unless . . ."

Matt had been getting a sense for a bit that the rhino was angling for something. Otherwise, why hadn't he just attacked the moment he showed up? Hoping that it was just money the rhino was after, Matt reached into his pack.

"I can pay." Matt had killed a bunch of people to get this money, and hoped it was a lot. As he opened the pouch, the rhino wrinkled its nose.

"Did you rob a battlefield to get this? It stinks of blood. Not just one kind, either." It put its huge hand out and grabbed the bag before hefting it upwards, as if testing its weight. "Not much, for this kind of thing. But it's better than splitting it with the others."

The rhino's eyes lighted on Matt's shovel for a moment. "Ah, you dug. I wondered how you got past the guards. Do you think you can get out the same way, without getting caught?"

Matt nodded. "I'll try."

"Really your business if you do or don't. If you get caught, the guards will just skewer you. No skin off my back. But you better close up the tunnel on the outside when you're done. If you don't, I'll have to explain it, and I *will* find you if you cause me that kind of trouble." With that, the rhino began walking back towards the dark. Lucy let out a huge sigh of relief.

"That was close, Matt. Very close. Do you think we could dig out of this place? It's a stone floor, but . . ."

Lucy was interrupted, as in the center of the room, the heart beat, once. Somehow Matt knew it had, even though it made no noise. As he turned back to look at it, he saw a rapidly expanding halo of energy, tinged in the same dull red that the light gave off. Before he could do anything to dodge it, the wave of energy passed through him. He had the slightest twinge of pain, something that he suspected might have actually shown up on his HP bar as a single point of damage had he been looking at it.

It wouldn't have been a big deal at all, had it not also dropped his disguise. By the time he had eyes on the rhino, it was already roaring in rage.

Please let it be slow. Please let it be slow.

It wasn't. The battlelord title apparently wasn't just for show, and Matt knew from experience that not everything big was slow, especially where system shenanigans were in play. This thing was apparently high-leveled enough to have done away with any awkward, un-agile aspects of its biological starting point.

It was faster than Matt, at least at baseline. He used Spring-Fighter to weave out of the way of the first big punch as he simultaneously tried to dislodge his shovel from behind his shoulder blades. The rhino's footwork was good enough that missing a punch out of its charge didn't disturb its balance, and it followed up with two more quick hits. The first Matt was able to dodge. The second sent him flying backwards through a shelf and almost into the rock wall. With a Matt-sized hole in the shelf in front of him, he jumped, kicked off the wall, and sailed over the now collapsing shelf.

The rhino was waiting. If there was one thing that Matt knew about fighting from Earth, it was that jumping attacks were usually a pretty bad idea. The person on the ground got to push off the ground, which meant they could get their weight AND strength into play. The punch the rhino had hit him with might have been light, but with time for a windup, the rhino was readying a world-ending haymaker.

If things didn't change, Matt was about to learn how to fly.

CHAPTER FOURTEEN

The Saboteur Supreme

Matt's Stored Strike only worked if his body was completely motionless, but he had no way of knowing if that meant in terms of him actively moving, or moving relative to other objects. He hoped it would be the former, so he still might be able to store some energy before the big impact. He pulled his shovel back as far as he could, then stopped moving as he fell.

"Matt!" Lucy was scrambling for anything that might help. "You're only moving in some senses of the word!"

It was hot nonsense, but, god bless her, Lucy's words helped Matt realize that his plan might actually work. He felt the tension building in his muscles as he fell, and all that was left was to time the hit.

Matt honestly would have been happy if his attack just deflected the rhino's punch. He would have been overjoyed if it had kicked the rhino off-balance a little, too. But when the non-sharp edge of the shovel caught the rhino's fist, there was apparently just enough stored force to spin the heavyset enemy entirely around. It didn't shatter bones, but it was beyond Matt's wildest hopes already.

As Matt hit the ground, he poured the absolute maximum amount of stamina he could into Spring-Fighter. He had done the same to get into the warehouse earlier, but that was over a long distance. Here, he applied the same amount to just one motion, which was looping his shovel around the rhino's neck. Since he planned to turn off the motion before any impact was made and didn't intend to make a strike, the skill seemed to regard the speed as pure combat maneuvering and let it slide.

Before the rhino could recover and face Matt again, Matt clamped the pole of the shovel down over his windpipe and heaved backwards as hard as he could. It worked a little too well. Still off-balance, the rhino fell, landing on top of Matt. Weathering the weight of the rhino's body, Matt tried his best to not pass out and keep his enemy in a chokehold.

The rhino itself was huge, but most of that bulk was the torso. Its actual legs were stumpy, and in the position it found itself, it couldn't get leverage on the ground with them. It desperately tried to throw elbows at Matt and roll around, but the shovel-turned-noose around its neck meant that Matt had a disproportionate amount of control over where it went. He was getting bruised, scraped and fractured as the rhino's struggling ground him into the stone floor, but it was nothing he couldn't handle.

After almost a minute, the rhino succumbed to the chokehold, or seemed to. Matt wasn't taking any chances. He held the position for a full additional minute before taking his chances on getting up. To the rhino's credit, it was honest about passing out. To its body's credit, its neck was thick enough that it took three or four chops to fully detach the head.

Matt half-expected enemies to come barreling through the door at any moment during the fight, but none did. Apparently the closed-box design of the room was enough to muffle the sounds of the fight, or else he'd be up to his ears in guards by now. Still, the fact that relief for the interior guard who'd left would arrive at some point meant there wasn't any time to waste.

Matt quickly took his coin purse back from the rhino, but otherwise didn't stop to loot. He then ran to the fence, vaulted it a bit more carefully, and, holding his shovel by the very end of the handle, gingerly poked the heart. The force field did nothing to stop the shovel. It was like it wasn't there.

Matt had intended to test how durable the heart was. The next step of his plan was to temporarily sacrifice his Soulbound shovel to the task of being thrown at a giant, cursed organ like a javelin. But when the point made contact with the heart, his expectations were shattered. The moment the shovel touched, the heart recoiled inwards as if beating, then puffed outwards. Matt watched as the force field suddenly shattered, just before a notification sounded in his ears.

Ding!

Mana Drain Condition Detected

The Demon Lord's Heart of Destructive Bane has begun to overload itself with mana in preparation for its eventual detonation. As a result, you are losing small but significant amounts of mana the longer you stay in its direct vicinity.

"Oh, shit." Matt was immediately up and over the wall.

"What, what? You didn't even destroy it."

"No time. That thing is a bomb, Lucy. And I set it off."

"Are you sure?"

"I got a notification. It's a big giant heart that's drawing in mana in preparation to explode. It's named after the demon lord. I'm not sticking around."

Lucy looked back at the clearly cursed gigantic heart, then nodded. There were a lot of things they'd take chances on, but giant explosions weren't one they had consistent luck with, and they didn't have an entire Nullsteel building to increase their odds this time.

Matt ditched stealth entirely, leaping up and running on the tops of the crates and shelves as he rushed to the door. About halfway there, the heart made an audible *thoomp* sound as it beat a single time. A wave of destructive energy flew out in a halo from it, crashing against walls and decimating shelves. Matt flared Spring-Fighter as he used the shovel to push himself off from the ceiling, landed in front of the door, and burst through it just ahead of the wave.

As he crossed the threshold, the building was shaking from the burst of energy. Even so, it wasn't enough to distract the guards from the sudden appearance of a human from their closely-guarded treasure vault. Matt skidded past them, dodged two spear strikes, then cut away from the door at a 90-degree angle just as a section of the heart's energy cut unimpeded through the door and vaporized two of the guards.

Matt was off. His bribing of the front-gate guards was meaningless now. He'd have to go over the wall, but more than that, his main focus for now was just keeping the maximum number of buildings between him and the pulses of the heart. In the distance, he heard a loud crashing he assumed was the walls of the military depot, followed by another *thoomp* of terror. At a full sprint and with no obstructions in his way, he was still ahead of the danger, but it was closing fast. Behind him, he heard the crashing of hundreds of shoddily built demon-hut-spikes crashing to the ground.

As he passed, various demons were startled at the sight of a fleeing human before, seconds later, being consumed by magical shockwaves, covered by debris from the destruction of fragile buildings, or both. In sheer panic, he was pushing as fast as he possibly could, his legs pumping wildly and his lungs burning for the first time in a long time. But he was moving fast, fast enough that within no more than several seconds, he was near the short rock wall surrounding the town.

He glanced back. It was a mistake. The force was a few yards behind him, at best. Startled by the surprise of being moments from death, he stumbled. He barely avoided being consumed by the persistence of his own momentum. An unsteady stride later, he caught a foot solidly under him and did the only thing he could do. He leapt.

He had no idea how the pulse worked, exactly, or if jumping would even help him. But his panicked leap, supplemented by the meager amount of stamina he had left, was enough for him to get both over the wall and onto the plain it protected. Stooping his head as far as he could, he kept running, Apparently the heart hadn't stopped beating. One shockwave after another flew inches over his head. He had no idea how sturdy the wall around the town was, but he couldn't count on it to hold forever. He kept running.

Then, suddenly, the pulses stopped. After a few seconds of quiet, Matt looked back over his shoulder at the town. Or what was left of it. In the absence of the pulses, it was mostly leveled, with only a few stone buildings still standing here and there. Most of the dust had been pushed out and up by the pulses of magical power, and hung in the air over it like smog.

Matt kept running. Even if the heart was done, that didn't mean people couldn't see what was happening. He was alone in an enemy wasteland, and had just confirmed there were demons that could more than hold their own against him. He got off the path, running towards some distant hills that he hoped would give him some visual cover.

And then, suddenly, the heart finally activated. A second ago, Matt would have said that the pulsing was plenty, that this was clearly what the heart did and why it needed to be destroyed. But now, with a magical dome of green fire appearing over the entire town and about a quarter mile of land outside it, he realized those pulses were just some kind of priming mechanism, something to keep enemies away from the heart while preparing the air around it for something like magical conductivity.

It was like an inferno trapped inside a snow globe, as the explosion lit up the area like a camera flash for just a few seconds. Then, the light and the fire both winked out at once, as if it had never been there. Behind him, where the town once stood, was nothing. No houses, no demons, no depot, and no heart. There were just a few scattered stones and a large, perfectly circular scorch mark indicating where a demon settlement had once stood.

"Oh, holy shit, Matt. Holy shit. Why do they even have that? Do you think that's why everything is red?"

"No, I don't. There's no way they set those off in their home territory. It's basically a magical nuke. And it didn't even turn stuff red."

"All I know is if we get to any more demon towns, and it seems like there's more of those, we are clearing out."

Ding!

> *Saboteur Supreme*
>
> Already deep in enemy territory, you delved even deeper. Alone and nearly defenseless, you cut to the very heart of the secrets contained within a demon

stronghold. Then you blew them all up. The secrets. The demons. All their houses. Literally hundreds of drinking mugs. Everything.

I'm going to be honest, when you first showed up, I didn't expect a whole lot. Just one guy? Not a big deal. But you just became the sole survivor of the second or third most powerful explosion this planet has ever seen, without a scratch, while sending hundreds of demons to meet a maker they don't even have in the wash.

Pretty good work.

Rewards: Subtle Cloak, 500 Class XP, 10 DEX, 10 PER, 10 STR

Subtle Cloak

At a constant, small drain to either mana (for mana-utilizing classes) or a penalty to maximum stamina (for physical classes), the subtle cloak makes almost everything you do just a little less noticeable. If someone is looking for you, they will have a little harder of a time finding you. If you are doing something suspicious, it will be a little less likely that any given person will notice. And if you are sneaking, your footfalls will sound just a bit more like natural sounds.

These effects are small, but consistent across every kind of sense. And, fair warning, this enchantment does not differentiate between friend and foe. It works on people you might want to find you, as well.

"That's a pretty solid reward," Lucy said after Matt described his haul. "Honestly, I think our system instance was holding out on us, Matt."

"Well, to be fair, we did just nuke an enemy town, as far as this system is concerned. It probably deserves that. But yeah, I'm not complaining."

CHAPTER FIFTEEN

Human Complicated Things

Matt wanted nothing more than to be hidden while he was deep in demon territory. He immediately claimed and donned the cloak. Willing it to turn on, he was pleased to see that although it dinged his max total stamina, it was neither a constant drain nor a huge ding. When he turned it off, it took several seconds for his stamina to refill. If he were ambushed, that meant he'd start the fight with slightly less stamina than he'd like. But the chance of avoiding any combat altogether, or to even get to drop on someone for once, was too good to pass up.

Sadly, he put it on just a bit late to be immediately helpful. Before the cloak had fully settled around his shoulders, he heard Lucy yell a short warning. When the cloth settled, he found himself facing a serious-looking, bow-wielding woman.

"Don't move. Don't even breathe. I have an arrow nocked and my bowstring stretched. From here, I can't miss. Drop your weapon." The woman spoke from behind some kind of gaiter-like mouth covering, her hair and part of her forehead covered by a hood. All the information Matt could get was from her eyes, and they showed she wasn't joking around.

"Fine, fine. No problem." Matt held his shovel out in front of him, and then let it fall, hitting the ground and knocking up a small cloud of red dust. "What can I do for you?"

"Matt, she's some kind of combat scout, judging by the class name. Probably not too tanky, if it comes to that. Also, she's human."

Human complicated things some.

* * *

A few minutes prior, Brennan, Artemis, and Derek had been scouting the enemy village. Really, it had mostly been Artemis holding down the heavy lifting there. Brennan could see a town, and some blurry images of activity. Derek's juiced perception stat meant he could see things moving around and know that they were demons, but not much more. Meanwhile, Artemis could pick out individual demons, get an idea of the general combat capabilities of the town, and feed Brennan the info his class needed to piece together a precise, efficient plan of attack.

Then, suddenly, Artemis tensed. The patterns of activity in the town had changed. She couldn't quite put a finger on how, but near the city center, several people suddenly stopped. A second more, and they were gone. The whole town fell like dominoes, spreading from the center all the way out to the walls, driven by a mysterious pulse of energy.

And in front of that pulse, moving like a racecar, was what she could have sworn was not a demon, but an honest-to-god human being. The human stayed just ahead of the outer pulse until he vaulted the wall, hit the dirt hard, and kept running.

"It's like Epsilon." Brennan couldn't see the figure, but he could see the damage. And aside from being set in red demon dirt instead of a green field, it was a carbon copy of the devastation that had consumed Epsilon. Same shape, same size. Same mysterious, total destruction.

Then devastation came to the town, not just from the pulses but from an unholy fire that burned and consumed until nothing was left but a scorch mark in the wasteland.

"I have to go." Artemis was already moving. "There's a human down there. I think he caused this. We need to catch him now. Stay here."

Derek piped up. "No way, you're not going alone. We're coming."

Artemis turned and pointed at Brennan, then at Derek. "One of you can't use skills without calling the demon army down. The other, I'm sorry, is good but not great at sneaking. I'm the best option we have. Stay here. That's an order."

And then she was off, sprinting so seamlessly across the landscape that neither Brennan nor Derek would have known she was there if they hadn't watched her leave. As it was, they could track her, but only just.

Derek watched her for a moment before speaking. "So, we aren't going to actually let her go alone, right?"

Brennan grimaced. "No, I'm afraid not."

"Good job dropping that . . . shovel? Interesting choice. Now get on your stomach, hands behind your back." The archer woman was only a few feet away, but something told Matt that the short distance would help her hit him, rather than actually hamper her in any way.

"Don't do it, Matt. Even you aren't fast enough to dodge an arrow aimed at your belly. Think of something else."

"I'd really rather not." Matt put his hands in front of him, palms out in a peaceful gesture. And it was genuine, for what it was worth. He really didn't want to get into a fight with the first human he saw on this world. "Can't we talk about this . . . standing? Face-to-face?"

The string on the woman's bow creaked as she put a bit more tension behind it. "You can lay down or take an arrow to the eye. Your choice."

Matt kept his hands up for just a moment longer. "Fine, fine. Just don't shoot me." As his hands dropped towards the ground, they brushed by his pocket for just a moment, which was more than he needed to access a long-forgotten skill.

"Pocket Sand!" Matt yelled, expelling a small cloud of red at the woman. Pocket Sand was not a daily-driver skill for Matt anymore. As his other skills leveled, so did Pocket Sand, but in most ways it stayed remarkably similar to its lower-level form. As a dedicated short-range ambush skill, it never gained much usefulness at ranges greater than a few feet. It didn't do any damage, or at least any more damage than getting the dirt or whatever in your eyes would do. When it got bumped to level 15, it didn't develop any new facets or uses like other skills did. So Matt and Lucy had tried testing it on creatures in the dungeon to figure out where all that class experience had been spent.

It turned out that pain wasn't directly correlated with damage. The first Clownrat he used the skill on had tried to claw its own eyes out before Matt had a rare moment of grudging sympathy for the thing and put it out of its misery. At short-range, it would absolutely immobilize anything that didn't have the good sense to get out of the way or the vitality to tank the pain. He was guessing this woman didn't have much in the way of tanky qualities, and unless something really weird was going on, he was guessing eyesight was vital to how her class operated.

As the dust hit the woman's face, she flinched just enough for Matt to get out of the way of her prepared shot, then desperately backed up as she vigorously rubbed her eyes with the wrist of her cloak.

Blinded did not mean completely without senses, and it meant that even less in the world of stats. As Matt scooped up his shovel and moved in on the archer, she abandoned her bow, pulled a holdout dagger from her sleeve, and took a surprisingly accurate swipe at Matt's neck-level. By the time the blade got to the area she was targeting, he was already behind her. Taking her legs out from under her with the flat of his shovel, he immediately moved to put his knee on her back, and pressed the shovel across her shoulder blades to pin her arms at least somewhat down.

"Now, listen to me. I'm *trying* to be nice, and you are coming on way too hot, and . . ." At that moment, two more people crested over the top of the hill behind Matt. Matt turned at Lucy's shouted warning, then stopped dead, completely losing the thread of whatever he was going to say. The younger of the two people coming over the hill stopped as well, so suddenly and intently that the man with him also jerked back as if they were connected with a tether.

At once, both Matt and Derek opened their mouths, uttering the same word with vastly different intended meanings.

"*You!*" they said.

Artemis yelped in pain as Matt exploded off her, digging in his knee and shovel as he did. He knew this guy. He knew how the young guy fought. As predictable as his new opponent was, those big, wide strikes would mean trouble for him if he had to dodge them mixed with arrows and whatever the third guy did. But one of the enemies was already disarmed and blinded, and another one was a mook he had beaten when he was much weaker. In a few seconds, he'd have one and only one opponent to focus on.

Anticipating a high strike, Matt ended his approach towards Derek by sliding in on his feet, but with his body lowered. He'd take out his legs, then knock him out with the shovel. Easy.

Derek defied his expectations. As Matt came in low, he shook off his surprise, kicked backwards, and parried the strike out of the way. Matt immediately kicked off to the left with Spring-Fighter, then again to the right to get behind the kid. He didn't hold back on his stamina expenditures, either. With full confidence that the kid wouldn't be able to follow him, he stabbed his shovel towards the kid's back, hard.

The kid somehow had tracked him. He caught the point of the Nullsteel shovel on the flat of his blade, absorbing enough force with his arms that it didn't damage the sword at all, and jumping backwards to make distance.

"Wait!" he shouted.

Like hell I will, Matt thought. Then he noticed that Derek's eyes weren't on him at all, but instead off to the side. *The other swordsman.*

He turned just in time to pivot his head and avoid a direct strike to his eye, coming in like a spear strike at lightning-fast speed. It was aimed in the least convenient way, and for once, Matt had a hard time actually figuring out the best direction to dodge. That moment's hesitation cost him in the form of a deep, bloody cut across his face. He hurriedly jumped back, covering his escape with another quick Pocket Sand.

That one strike sapped Matt's confidence that he could take the third guy in an outright fight, especially with distractions on the field. He wasn't just faster than Matt. He was, at least as near as Matt could tell, some kind of skill-heavy build, one that relied on finesse. Matt was much, much more used to dealing with big, strong enemies that attacked in animalistic ways. Seeing a precision strike shook him. But he had other stuff the guy didn't know about, at least if he did it fast enough that the sword-kid couldn't share intel.

Digging his shovel into the dirt, he used the few moments he had to charge up as much power as he possibly could, then heaved upwards, hoping that Lucy's guess about charging his digging skill ended up being true.

It was. Suddenly, between him and the guy, a huge cloud of dust materialized, pelting his enemies with rocks and dirt. Matt leapt several feet away from his previous position to keep them guessing, then started charging up the biggest, strongest strike he could. He held his shovel low, so he could throw an uppercut-strike with it from a direction they might not expect.

CHAPTER SIXTEEN

Kill for Dagger

Then the dust cleared, and it was Matt's turn to be surprised.

Wrapped around the precision-skilled swordsman was the kid, holding him back like someone trying to keep his friend out of a schoolyard fight.

"Brennan! Stop! I *know him*," the kid was screaming so hard his voice broke. "Just stop for a second!"

"Like hell! Let him go, Derek!" The archer was apparently back in action, at least if the strength of her voice was any indication. As the dust cleared more, he saw her scooping up her bow and nocking an arrow. "You know what? Fuck it. I'll do it myself."

The tip of the arrow started being shrouded with some kind of dark cloud, one that Matt very, very much wanted to avoid. It could be poison, or it might not be. It didn't matter. It was a bad news color.

"No!" the kid yelled, jumping towards Matt, who just barely managed to hold back his strike. The kid was not defending himself. He had dropped his sword. He stood in front of Matt, arms spread, blocking for him.

"Move out of the way, you little shit!" Artemis snarled, and the light on the arrow faltered before disappearing.

"Artemis! Stop! I'm telling you, I *know him*. We can talk about it *in the tent*."

Artemis faltered at that last word.

Must be some tent, Matt thought. He kept charging his shovel strike even though he either needed to release the strike into somebody's face soon, or face whatever backlash damage it dealt.

"Matt! Are we going to take him out?"

Matt shook his head slightly. These were still people, and the main reason he had attacked as hard as he did was because of the kid. That same kid was fast proving that something unexpected was happening, beyond what Matt understood. He was going to hold back, if only for a moment.

Suddenly, the precision-swordsman moved. The kid wasn't holding him now. Matt got ready to cut him in half with the charged strike. But then the swordsman simply resheathed his sword.

"Oh, you know him? Oof. Sorry about that, man. I'm Brennan. Good to meet you."

The next ten minutes were touchy. Brennan was an easy sell on Matt being, if not a nice guy, at least somebody who they had ambushed and probably didn't deserve instant death over it. It was also him who took Derek's vaguely worded insistence that he didn't want Matt dead and somehow negotiated with both Matt and Artemis to lower their weapons.

Matt kept his shovel in hand, however. The first thing he did on breaking his charge-stance, besides taking a troublingly large backlash hit that immediately cut about an eighth of his health, was to take distance from the group. When asked by Derek to please put away his weapon, as Brennan already had, he explained that his guardian had forbidden him from doing so in the strongest language. Since Lucy had said, "Don't fucking do it," it was technically true.

At the mention of his guardian, each of the three looked confused for a moment, but accepted it.

Eventually, it was decided that Matt would follow them to their camp, but only if Derek was allowed to carry all the weapons. If nothing else, he had already put his money where his mouth was on the whole "don't kill the new guy" position, and even if he betrayed Matt, the time it took to arm the other two would be time Matt could use to escape. To further increase his chances, Matt walked a good distance behind the others, which Artemis would absolutely not have accepted had Brennan not shifted into a stern, authority-wielding voice and virtually ordered her to.

It was a mess. Nobody felt safe. A sneeze could have restarted the fight. The only reason Matt did it at all was the fact that he felt fairly sure he could escape, had a general belief that wandering aimless through the demon territory wilderness was just as dangerous, and was generally desperate to be around other humans. That desperation only got stronger because of something Derek had said near the end of the negotiations.

"I understand you're feeling stranger-danger vibes off this whole thing. I get it. But trust me, it's going to be okay."

It was "stranger danger" that got him. That was an Earth term. Derek wasn't just a human, he was an *Earth human*, or at least knew one well enough to pick up their slang. After that, he was decided. He'd brave the danger of the angry girl, the goofy camp counselor, and the erratic now-friendly murder-child.

Lucy agreed, grudgingly, that it was a good idea, or at least the best choice they had at the moment. She might have been the only person present less happy about it than Artemis, though. Both of them spent the rest of the walk visibly paranoid, one watching Matt like a hawk, and the other keeping her eye out for the slightest suspicious move from the touchy archer.

Back at the camp, Derek somehow convinced Artemis to go into an odd tent with him. He said something about how he had done a pretty good job with the hunting, and that she could trust him not to be "completely wrong about this." She insisted Brennan be given his sword back, which Matt reluctantly agreed to. It seemed like it was the only way to move things forward.

As soon as the tent flaps closed, Brennan sat down on the ground and heaved a big sigh of relief.

"Listen, man. Don't tell her I said this, but I apologize for Artemis. She's actually really nice, I promise. She's just . . . protective, I guess. It's a pretty dangerous world, and she's not reincarnated or anything. She's lost people. It's made her jumpy."

Matt didn't know what to say, so he didn't say anything at all. He grunted noncommittally, which Brennan seemed to accept. From what little he knew about Brennan, it honestly seemed like the guy accepted most things more easily than most.

Derek and Artemis didn't stay in the tent long, and when they emerged, Derek looked roughly the same while Artemis's demeanor had vastly changed. Without a word, she grabbed Brennan and dragged him to the tent, looking concerned and elated at the same time.

"So, hey." Alone with Matt, Derek seemed bashful. "I don't know, like, a cool way to say this, but . . . I'm sorry for what happened when we met. I've thought about it a lot. It was wrong. Even if you turn out to be a bad dude. I'll convince the others. Just . . . I mean, just give us a chance. If you can."

Matt nodded, slightly.

"Matt, stay on your guard. I mean, something clearly happened to this kid. He changed. It's possible he's . . . I dunno. I don't know if they have trickiness potions, but . . . just stay on your guard, a bit, if you can." Lucy looked truly concerned.

After a much longer time, most of it spent in silence, Brennan and Artemis emerged from the tent.

"Hey, listen. I've talked to Artemis. She and Derek are going to clear out for a little while. So you know, this is actually a pretty risky thing to do right now, and you and I aren't going to be able to talk very long, anyway. But that way, at least you don't have to worry about getting stabbed through the tent, or anything."

It was an oddly nice gesture. Not enough to make Matt feel better yet, and as Derek and Artemis sprinted away, he made some subtle hand motions to Lucy, indicating she should post up outside the tent and warn him if they were coming back. He was pretty sure system rules would allow that.

Inside the tent, Brennan began, "So, Derek let us in on how you met, a long time ago. I knew most of the story already, but I didn't realize how he failed to give a chance to explain anything. I get why you reacted the way you did to Artemis even without that story, but it makes even more sense now."

Matt nodded. "It wasn't exactly a nice experience, you know. I was much, much weaker than I am now. He almost killed me."

"Yeah, I got that impression from his story. But the main thing I got from it is that the system doesn't seem very happy with you." As Matt started to search for a way to deflect that question, Brennan held up his hand in a "wait" motion. "I just want you to know, we don't like the system much either. And we don't talk about it much on the outside. This tent is about the only thing I know of that makes it so the system can't see us."

Matt glanced nervously towards the tent flaps. If the system couldn't see them in here, he had no idea if Lucy could. Or how that would even work.

"We can actually get out of here now, if you want. I'm just asking, or even begging, for you to come with us for a bit. Things have been changing. What happened to that demon base happened to one of our settlements. It killed everyone. We don't know why, but the system has nudged the balance in favor of the demons. It will even things out eventually. It always does. But by that time, a lot of our people will die." He sighed. "I think you are the only chance we have of changing that. So come along? Please?"

It was the "please" that did it. Brennan was desperate. He was really begging. Either he was history's greatest actor and about to slit Matt's throat in his sleep, or he was a deeply sincere guy really asking for help. With that one word, he eliminated any other options that Matt had.

After emerging from the tent, Brennan explained, briefly, that the demons had been tracking them via their skills somehow, and that they needed to leave immediately. After his tent had somehow magically packed itself away into his backpack, they took off towards Artemis and Derek.

They did end up running into demons along the way, but between four humans and one guardian, they cut through them pretty quickly. That, more than anything, did wonders to settle everyone's nerves. By the time they made camp that night, everyone was much more confident that they weren't going to murder each other the moment their backs were turned.

"So you just . . . poked it? A giant cursed heart? And that was all it took?"

"Yeah. And my guardian demands that I tell you that I do stuff like that often because, and I quote, 'I'm a dumbass like that literally all the time.' Her exact words."

At the mention of Lucy, he once again saw them look confused.

"Do they not have guardians here, Matt? It must be something like that. They look at you like you're crazy any time you mention it."

"We can talk about it later," Matt whispered.

"That didn't help. Maybe lay off talking to me directly for a bit, until we can get details."

Matt nodded. After a moment of awkwardness, Brennan cleared his throat.

"Well, first, thanks. I'm not entirely sure, but I think you probably saved an entire colony with what you did, even if it wasn't what you meant to do. And you saved us a job. We were going to damage that base if we could, to see if we could get their forces to pull back. Now, I don't think we have to. Losing an entire base is huge. If that doesn't get them to retreat, nothing will."

"No problem. It's not like I didn't get stuff for it."

Artemis looked at his cloak greedily. "I'll say. Do you know how hard stealth gear is to come by? It's not craftable. At least not normally. I've been looking for a cloak like that forever." When that drew odd looks from Brennan and Derek, she suddenly realized how what she was saying could be taken. "I'm not saying I want yours! I'm not. Come on, guys, you knew that."

Derek looked at Matt, deadpan. "Watch yourself, man. I once saw her kill a guy for his dagger."

"That was three days ago, and that guy was a demon-raccoon. Stop trying to get us into life-and-death battles with each other, Derek. Brennan, stop encouraging him."

CHAPTER SEVENTEEN

Loud Worms

Even though the destruction of an entire demon town was probably enough to worry the demon forces, the humans decided to do a bit more damage on the demon side of the border on their way out. At first, the three Ra'Zorians assumed Matt would be on board, then noticed he lagged a little behind in every fight, as if he was a bit reluctant to kill.

"I mean, I could have sworn you were going to kill me with that shovel before I evacuated." Derek was, for better or worse, the second-most talkative member of the team behind Brennan, who didn't sweat the small stuff enough to consider Matt's reluctance a problem yet. "And you just nuked a whole city. I don't get it."

"Listen, I'm fresh in from another planet. And the demons seem like dicks, yes, but the whole murdering-everyone-I-see thing is pretty new to me. And for what it's worth, I don't know who is on the right side of this whole war. I'm here to get stronger."

"And you nuked the town on accident. No way you could pull that off if you were actually trying," Lucy chortled.

Matt continued, "And I nuked that town on accident. I was trying to do sabotage, not genocide. For all I know, a bunch of kids went up in that explosion."

Artemis, who had been studiously pretending to stay out of it, glanced over. "You really don't know much about them, do you?"

"Demons? No. They seem murderous, and pretty corrupt."

"That's right, but you probably deserve the quick primer. Demons aren't born, they *spawn*. Fully adult, with baseline skills that they improve from there.

Every so many square miles of demon-controlled land generates one every so often. There are formulas for it."

"That . . . that honestly makes no sense."

"Our understanding is that it's a function of the demon lord's powers, something like how a nation's leader's skills work, only stronger."

"Oh, shit, Matt. You get what she's saying, right?" Lucy chimed in.

He did. "You're saying that it's like a leader spreading the benefits from his estate, and that's what makes the demon lord powerful? He's an evil *administrator?*"

Brennan laughed. "That, and the fact that he's almost entirely immune to both magical and physical attacks. And that he apparently has now grown to a point where he can make suitcase nukes. But jokes aside, his territory really is the worst part. He doesn't get involved in the war directly very often. His personal combat powers just make sure we can't stop him."

"Be that as it may," Artemis said, in what Matt was fast learning was her get-back-on-topic voice, "the demons don't care about much. They are built literally for a purpose, and that purpose is killing humans and expanding the demon lord's land."

"They seem pretty fleshed out, personality-wise, for mindless destruction automatons."

"We think that's because sentient beings just fight better, or because of limitations in exactly what the demon lord can make. But we've talked to them. We've tortured them, even. And they have no positive interests. They self-promote, they try to grow personal wealth, they cheat, and they lie. They don't love, they don't marry, they don't have kids. Full stop."

Matt couldn't confirm everything she said was absolutely true, but it at least wasn't inconsistent with what he'd seen from the demons so far. There was so much grift inside the only colony he'd been in that the only two conversations he had that weren't about buying food involved bribes, and the one hundred percent of conversations he'd overheard somehow involved killing or eating people.

"And on the other side? Seems like you spend a lot of time killing demons yourselves, not that I can really judge."

Derek spoke up. "So, the big downside with our side is the Church."

"Derek!" Artemis yelled immediately. "The Church is *good*, Derek. They organize humanity against the demons."

Derek didn't let up. "That's only kind of true. Listen, Matt, you know in anime? Where there's a church, and they do all kinds of good stuff, and then you check beneath the surface, and they're just totally fucked up in every way?"

Matt nodded.

"So this is like that. They control *everything*. It's not, like, obvious that they do anything terrible with that power, but you can't shake the feeling that they are always about to. Brennan will back me up."

"No, he *won't*," Artemis said. "Because Brennan, unlike you, is sane."

"Actually, it is sort of creepy. It's like, there's sort of a pope, they don't call him that, but he's like clearly controlling his emotions all the time to seem calm, and I'm pretty sure he tells the king what to do. It's iffy." Derek shrugged.

"And I should feel okay about this?" Matt asked.

Derek piped up again. "It's that thing where you meet a kid, and he's super creepy, but he's not actually doing anything wrong, it's just a vibe thing."

"I don't follow."

"It's like, you might want to punch the creepy out of him, but he's probably not doing it on purpose. So your choices are either waiting until he actually does something, or being a bully. It's like that."

Artemis looked incredibly disturbed. "I had no idea you guys felt this way about the Church. As far as I'm concerned, they are normal."

Derek shook his head. "That's because you grew up with it. Trust me, it's not a normal situation. It might not be evil, but it's definitely not normal. Anyway. Matt, none of this is actually the point. The point is that if you were on the human side of things, the Church is the worst part. But the soup alone balances all that out."

Matt's ears perked up. "Soup? What kind?"

By the time they reached the border, Derek had made exactly zero progress in explaining the whole soup thing.

"So it's not, like, a specialty soup."

"No, it's every soup. Every single Ra'Zorian, for reasons they either can't explain or do a really good job of hiding, is really good at making soup. Like, better than the best person on Earth would be. Even if they can't otherwise cook."

"That makes no sense."

"It doesn't. It's just true. When we get back, I'll show you. It's like if Superman's power was soup making, and he founded his own planet. It's freaky and weird, but it's the best part of this place."

Using the slight camouflage of his cloak, Matt had dug out a trench for them to hide in, and they looked out at what Brennan and Artemis considered to be the border.

"I thought the point of this route was that we'd face the least resistance." Matt was honestly confused. For miles on either side, there was nothing. But right in front of them was a giant tower, one that could see unencumbered at the land around. Crossing here seemed oddly intentional in a way he didn't understand.

"There are other places we could pass without fighting, but they have other detection measures that we can't bypass. These towers let them know when anybody crosses the border. It's part of their function. When that happens, they call in help which happens to be a whole demon army. We want to cross safely, but also undetected. That means taking out this tower and making a gap in the net, so to speak." Artemis said all of this without ever taking her eyes off the tower as she peeked over the mound of dirt Matt had piled up in front of the trench. She had been observing and feeding information back

"Won't they just signal for help if we attack?"

"That's part of the problem, yes. They likely only have one individual or device capable of doing that, though, and if we can take it out without being noticed, we can clean up whatever demons are here and slip through. Brennan, any luck with that?"

Brennan shook his head. "Not if what you say is true and there are dozens of demons in that tower. It doesn't take that long to send a message, none of us can breach straight through solid stone, and even a handful of them could stop us long enough to get a signal out to others. It's a hard problem."

"Well, damn. I had hoped we could make this a little easier. But if we have to go loud, we have to go loud." Artemis took her bow, bent it, and set the string. "Let's do this."

While the others gathered their gear, Matt stamped on the earth in the trench. His digging skill was so good that he rarely had to worry about the consistency of soil anymore, but he had the inklings of an idea cooking, and it mattered now. He was pleased to find that the soil was only loose for a few inches near the top of the ground. Under that, it was hard-packed, dry, and perfect for what he had in mind.

"Oh, I get it." Lucy had been watching him, and he turned around to see a big grin on her face. "Yes, let's do that."

"Hey, guys?" Matt said, smiling, "I think I have a less precise way to handle this that might work fine."

"The tower is shaking."

The bulk of the first-floor demons glared at the speaker. For the most part, towers were guarded by dexterity-heavy classes, like scouts and defensive archers. Somehow, that rule had decided that this tower was an exception. Bears were a vitality-heavy subspecies of demon, and this particular bulwark-classed example had somehow wormed himself into a tower job where he wasn't helpful in the least.

Worse, he was stupid. That was a matter of luck, not stats, but there was no denying the bear was dumb. He seemed to have no idea that the rest of the animals resented him, much less why. It had taken them weeks to get him to understand latrine discipline, and he was hopeless at cooking. He spent most days sitting around useless, completely oblivious to the fact that all the others hated him. Except today, it seemed. Today, he wouldn't shut up.

"No, it isn't. There is no wind. Even if there was, the tower is made out of stone. It's not moving." The tower captain would have liked to ignore the bear, but part of his job was maintaining morale among the troops.

"It's shaking. I can feel it."

"No, you can't!" the captain shouted. The demons under his command were particularly touchy lately, given that they had all missed out on what promised to be a major killing-and-looting event in human territory and had instead pulled guard duty. If he didn't want a full murder on his hands, he needed to get the bear to shut up before he found him dead the next morning with a slit throat. "You can't feel the tower shaking. The worms are not 'really loud today.' You are imagining things. You are going to stop talking, you will stop talking now, and you'll remain completely silent under any and all circumstances for the rest of the day. This is an order. Do you understand?"

"But . . ." The bear-demon looked up at the captain dully, so infuriatingly slow that he got a backhand across his snout for his efforts. The captain was not nearly so large as the bear, but he was a much, much higher level. He reached down, grasped the bear by the hide around his neck, and lifted him clear off the ground.

"No. No 'but' and no more talking." He drew his sword and held it dangerously close to the bear's neck. "You will be quiet. You are not going to speak. Do you understand? It's a yes or no question."

Somewhere in the bear's pancake-batter intellect, the idea that he was actually in some sort of danger clicked into place. He closed his mouth, narrowly avoiding letting another objection slip out.

"Yes," he said, meekly.

The captain let him down, and the bear-demon retreated to a table in the corner, where he sat quietly, apparently trying to look as small as possible. With the show over, the other demons on the first floor went about their business again, but smiling now. None of them were exactly friends, but they would come together for certain purposes, and jeering at a peer was definitely one. The captain had done his job and had done it well. Even he was satisfied with his own performance.

CHAPTER EIGHTEEN

Gollum

The tower captain went back to his workspace, which was a single, impractically large stone desk set in the center of the first floor. It was an inefficient use of space to set it in the middle like that, but made sure that the forces under his command were aware of who was in charge at all times. He spent a great deal of time at that desk, despite having very little work to do there beyond drafting his daily reports back to his commanding officers.

Suddenly, there was a clatter at the side of the floor. He looked over, and saw the bear had knocked over a mug, and was now alternating between looking at the mess he had made and in the captain's direction. His ursine jaw was opening and closing, as if he was considering saying something and repeatedly deciding against it.

The captain had never been able to figure out exactly how the bear managed to get posted here. It was unusual. At the moment, there was nothing the captain would like better than to run across the room and berate him again, but the bear's uncertain status was holding him back. Chances were good that the bear's presence at his tower was a mere paperwork mix up, but it was at least vaguely possible he had saved or bribed someone important to get what he thought would be a cushy job. The captain was not in the habit of tempting fate, and restrained himself from taking advantage of the satisfaction that slapping the bear around would provide.

That being said, the bear had his attention. He watched as the bear's mouth worked silently, up and down, without stopping. After a few more moments of this, he stood halfway up, lifting the table off the ground with his thighs as he did so, before suddenly dropping to his seat again and letting the table hit the ground with a loud bang. The others had already left, meaning that it was just the two of them on the floor, and his annoyance was building.

After the bear managed to knock another plate off the table while almost but not quite pointing at something, the captain had enough. He stood and began slowly walking towards the corner, feeling smugly satisfied as he saw the bear's beady eyes filled with terror.

"Are you *really* having that much trouble keeping quiet and still? I know you lack in the brainpower department. As failings go, yours are pretty hard to miss. But this shouldn't be too difficult, hmm?"

The bear didn't answer. He sat there, in a dead panic, his eyes darting back and forth, apparently looking for some form of escape.

"Oh, I see you are very quiet now. No broken dishes, no words, just as I ordered. Would it have been hard to do this five minutes ago? Did something change for you? Please, enlighten me."

The bear still didn't answer, which was suspicious. The usual problem was getting him to shut up. Somewhere in the back of the captain's head, a sort of queasy worry that he couldn't quite put his finger on began to build up.

"Why aren't you speaking?" The bear's eyes had not stopped darting back and forth between the captain and some unknown direction behind him. The captain suddenly noted that the terror in the bear's eyes didn't exactly diminish when it looked in the other direction. In fact, the bear seemed *less* frightened when he looked at the captain.

He would have thought he was pulling some kind of prank, but the bear simply didn't have the mental powers to conceive of one. Suddenly, horribly, the captain was sure something was going on behind him.

He wheeled around, and just behind his desk was a human, arm outstretched, just now grasping the communications crystal from its desktop stand.

"Oh, hey," the human said, as if his presence was the most natural thing in the world. "I just needed this. Sorry, I'll be going now."

He then hopped several feet through the air, grinning as he fell down through a brand-new hole in the floor.

The tricky part about digging out the tunnel hadn't been moving the actual dirt. That was pretty easy to do, and had only taken a couple of hours. Instead, the hard bit was digging a tunnel under the tower without anybody noticing and without the tower falling down on Matt's head.

"Matt, the look on that commanding officer's face when he saw you . . . just, well done, sir." Lucy was ecstatic. "It will live rent-free in my head forever now and warm me in lonely times. I'm so happy."

Matt was about halfway down the tunnel when the commanding officer and that poor, scared-looking bear dropped through the hole after him, although the bear looked more rabidly bloodthirsty now that he had been called into battle. They yelled and charged after him, which would have been bad if Matt hadn't dug multiple tunnels. Technically, he was running AWAY from Artemis and the others, at least until the tunnel looped back. That part had taken forever, comparatively, but it was necessary to keep Artemis's sight lines clean.

"Now, Artemis!" Matt yelled. He was too far away to hear the twang of her bow, but glanced over his shoulder as he heard the first arrow bash into the supporting pillars he had left in place under the tower. He had left a thick layer of dirt clinging to the bottom of the tower, so stones wouldn't fall out of the floor and expose him during all the digging, and that layer was held up by thin supporting masses of earth Matt had left in place. If Artemis was able to shoot those out, the entire tower would come down. Probably.

Sadly, the arrows didn't seem to be doing a lot to the dirt, even charged with whatever techniques Artemis was dumping into them. After three arrows, he looked back to see she had taken out exactly one of the pillars, which wasn't nearly enough. Suddenly, Matt decided to use what he had overheard and trust the judgement of the commanding officer a bit, rather than giving up right away. He had said the bear was dumb. It was time to test that opinion.

"Artemis, shoot the bear! With something painful!"

Again, Matt couldn't hear the arrow. But he could absolutely hear the aftermath. Whatever Artemis had hit the bear with had hurt. He could hear it bellowing and thrashing around, even though the tunnel had curved enough that he couldn't see him. Better, he could hear column after column fall as the bear thrashed through them.

"Stop! Stop, you idiot!" The frantic voice of the commander came soon after, and Matt grinned at that.

Matt made it through the tunnel and back around to the others just in time. The tower didn't seem to have moved much, yet, but that changed as it suddenly shuddered, then came completely apart as its foundation failed.

The tower didn't pose much trouble after that. Over the day, they had enough chance encounters with various demons to make it clear that whatever tracking was attached to Brennan and Artemis' skills didn't work very well this far out. They still held back from using their skills as much as possible, just to be safe. But this wasn't a situation that called for all-out fighting. The few demons that managed to stagger out of the wreckage of the tower were pretty banged up, and fell without much trouble to Derek. Within fifteen minutes, everyone was back in front of the trench, looking in pride at the devastation.

"That worked surprising well. Good job, Matt," Artemis said.

"No kidding, Artemis. How many kills does that count for?" Brennan was clearly regretting not being part of the action, but that did nothing to keep him from approving of the results.

"Twenty, at least. And that's complete kills. I barely helped with collapsing the tower. And then at least half-credit on at least a dozen more."

"What's this credit?" Matt asked. It was the first he had heard of it.

"It's pay. Money. It's not from the system, it's something the Church pays out. Twenty kills and an outpost is worth . . . I don't know, but it's worth a lot." Derek was grinning. "Even my share is a lot. Full, humanoid demons are worth a ton. Mostly, I've just been paid for demon-variant animals before. Too bad we can't bring back proof."

"I gotta be honest with you, I don't even know what I'd do with money at this point. I haven't used any in years," Matt replied.

"Oh, there are things." Brennan said. "Armor, weapons, lodging. Those all are useful, and they cost money. I don't know how good of a combat shovel you could get, but yours seems fine. At the very least, you could improve your armor."

"And we will vouch for the kills. In these kinds of circumstances, a commander's estimate can usually stand in for proof." Artemis was still gazing at the tower with a satisfied look. "There's no way we're going to let you go unpaid for this, don't worry."

Suddenly, something shifted behind the party, and a huffing, gasping sound emerged from the trench. As each party member moved to draw their weapons, a paw reached up and grabbed the edge of the trench. They all watched in shock as the bear-demon virtually catapulted out of the trench and then hauled ass away from them in the opposite direction from the tower.

Artemis nocked an arrow, taking careful aim at its back.

"Aw, I liked him." Lucy said. "Or at least I liked him more than the others. I know he's a bad guy, but it's kinda sad."

"Can we not shoot him, Artemis?" Matt asked.

She lowered the tip of her arrow just a bit, and glanced at him. "Why not? They're going to find this tower eventually, and he's running back to the demons. There's a good chance he'll eventually find *someone* to warn. It's better tactics just to take him down."

"I know, it's just . . . he's a Gollum, okay? He was useful once, and he's sort of pitiful, and he's already having a bad day. He doesn't seem smart enough to be that effective, anyway. I just get a feeling that letting him go might be the best move here. Like with Gollum."

Artemis began to argue, then stopped as she saw both Brennan and Derek nodding along.

"Okay, fine. It's stupid, but fine. But I expect all of you to do double speed for the next few hours, understand?"

Everyone understood. They made their way past the ruins of the tower, watching carefully for signs of life as they did. None were apparent. Then they ran off at what Artemis told them was the correct angle to avoid being chased, and one that would put them more parallel with the next observation tower.

After another half hour or so of running, the red soil started to give way to patches of grass, then fully grassed fields, then trees, bushes, and other plants. They were back in human territory in feel as well as fact now. At Artemis's insistence, they kept running full tilt for another full hour, or at least as fast as the slowest member of their party would allow without them splitting up.

It was only after they finally slowed their pace and took a short break to catch their collective breaths that Artemis finally broke down and asked the question that had been eating away at her for the last few hours.

"Okay, tell me," she said, clearly annoyed at being out of the loop, "in clear terms, exactly what the fuck a Gollum is."

CHAPTER NINETEEN

Demon Spices

Matt, Derek, and Brennan ended up giving a jumbled, redundant retelling of not only what a Gollum was, but of the entire trilogy and *The Hobbit*. There were translation issues of a sort, brought on because none of them were natural storytellers, and exacerbated by the fact that "wasteland packed with magic, ugly bad guys" was much more normal to Artemis than it was to them. It was the equivalent of someone pitching a plot of people driving cars and eating bread to the three reincarnators.

Artemis was very unsatisfied with the explanation, and further exasperated because she'd actually promised the men something in return for the story. Out here, alone in the woods and away from civilization or any other people, it was something only she could do for them.

She was making soup.

Between the four of them, it wasn't hard to take down some wild game for meat, and both Brennan and Derek turned out to be pretty good at fieldstripping animals. Matt had contributed several vegetables from his pack after explaining that he picked them up when he was wandering around, and Artemis used one of her more obscure skills to confirm they weren't poison.

"I want you to know that you owe me. The next deal I make is going to have *much* tougher terms." Artemis was scowling as she stirred the soup cooking in a kind of expandable travel pot Brennan had pulled out of his backpack. "And this is all stupid anyway. I'm not even good at making soup."

"Don't listen to her, Matt." Derek was beaming, his eyes glued to the pot of soup in anticipation. "They all say that. And then the soup comes out and it's insane."

“I’m not lying, Derek.”

“He knows you aren’t, Artemis. I’m sure by Ra’Zorian standards, you suck at it,” Brennan said, conciliatory. “Doesn’t change the fact that this is going to be awesome.”

“What would make it actually a lot better is if I had any spices to season it with. As it stands, I don’t even have salt.”

With that, Matt suddenly remembered that this was a problem he could solve. Digging in his pack, he withdrew several small vials of spices and a fist-sized wrapping of salt. Pretty focused on the soup himself, he wordlessly tossed them to Artemis.

She added some salt, then checked the broth for taste. Her hand glowed as she did the poison check on the spices as well, then she shrugged and started sniffing the bottles, selecting a few and measuring judicious amounts of each.

“Okay, that’s done. Or at least as done as it’s going to get. Eat up.” Artemis ladled out the soup in bowls they had brought from their own packs. Worried that the vegetables or spices might have ruined the taste somehow, Matt deeply inhaled the aroma from the soup to try to get hints of what he was about to eat.

It smelled incredible. He dug in. He was, for a moment, aware of the fact that he was tasting something impossibly good, something that was remarkable beyond comprehension. Then, as if he was hit by lightning, his consciousness fled, and he knew only blackness.

When he came to, it was to the sound of voices yelling.

“Artemis, I’m telling you it’s *not the soup*. The soup was really, really good. Something else has happened.”

“And I’m telling you he took a bite of it then dropped like he was hit with a war hammer. I killed him!”

Through cracked eyes, Matt could see Brennan walk up and grab Artemis’s shoulders. “He’s not dead yet, okay? He has a pulse. I’m sure he will pull through this.”

Matt tried to speak to let them know he was fine and found he could only do so with great difficulty. It was like his body was still vibrating with the memory of that one incredible moment of soup.

“I’m . . . oooookay. I’m fine. Awake.” He managed to get a few words out. He sounded like a drunk caveman, but he succeeded in communicating, and that was the important thing. His sight lines were immediately blocked as his three very worried companions gathered around him, checking his pulse and generally acting very excited that they hadn’t accidentally murdered him with broth.

But he couldn’t hear Lucy, anywhere. That by itself was enough to shock him fully awake. He whipped his neck around, looking for her, and eventually found her curled up in a ball on the ground, laughing so hard she had lost her breath.

“Lucy, what the hell?” Matt couldn’t spare a moment to reassure the

Ra'Zorians until he got this figured out. He hoped they'd get the hint from his sudden departure from the conversation.

Lucy wheezed in a breath. It didn't help with the tears streaming down her red, choked face, but it did give her the ability to talk—a little. "Your . . . your face, Matt. You looked like you . . . like you were getting a surprise party and all your favorite people were there. Whew. And then you passed out and had the same dumb smile the whole way down."

"And you weren't worried?"

"No, I was, it's just . . . It's gotta be your eating skill, right? Nobody smiles while they get poisoned. It's like you got overloaded."

Matt considered this. The Gaian food had seemed perfectly tasty to him, but he knew that his eating skill changed his perception of food at least a little. The Gaians had never been that into the food cubes, but he stomached them easily. Further, beside the period when he was eating their cooking, most of what he ate were either raw vegetables, unseasoned meat from creatures that didn't actually exist, or military rations that were far, far beyond their expiration date.

And that whole time, his perception stat had been climbing. Recently, he had been eating horrifying monsters and demons, but his cooking skills were so bad and the base materials were so gross that he guessed the eating skill would have made them more palatable by making them have less flavor.

"Guys, I think it's alright. I just need a second. The soup caught me by surprise."

Artemis looked oddly panicked over this.

"No, no." Matt waved his hands in front of him. "It's good, I promise. It's just probably too good. I've been on . . . tight rations, I guess? For a while. This might be the first normal food I've had that prepared by someone who knew what they were doing since my perception started to climb."

All three of the Ra'Zorians stopped to consider this.

"I guess that makes sense. My tastes have changed a little bit since I started to grow my stats, again. Food tasted a lot different when I came back," Derek said, thoughtfully. "And I've had the weirdest stat growth of anyone here. I can't imagine what those changes would be like all at once."

"So your weakness is . . . food? Tasty food?" Brennan asked. "Everything that tastes good is mind-poison. Bummer."

Matt wasn't giving up that easily. He walked up to the soup pot, scooped a very small amount into his bowl, then dipped his finger in the liquid, trying to withdraw the minimum possible amount of broth. He let it drip off until he had a single drop just on the tip of his finger, then let it drop on his tongue.

He was almost knocked out again. It was, by far, the best food he ever had. None of the tastes seemed possible. It was like he could feel every nerve in his body cheering for the flavor that he had just put it in his mouth. He reeled, but stayed up right.

Artemis stood off the side, worried. Matt put two and two together and realized she was still horrified to have knocked him out, and still attributing it to the soup.

"Artemis, you haven't had the soup yet, have you?" She couldn't have. Matt refused to believe she didn't think this soup was bad, cultural differences be damned.

"I haven't."

"Just eat some. Now, if you can."

Artemis walked over to the soup, gingerly picking up the ladle and scooping a portion of broth into it. Slowly and cautiously, she tasted the broth. Her eyebrows immediately arched.

"Oh, wow, this is good," Artemis said. Matt nodded at her, encouragingly, and she tried it again. "Too good."

"Artemis, you are *fine at soup*. Even by Ra'Zorian standards." Brennan walked over and patted her on the back. "I've always liked it, anyway."

"This isn't modesty, Brennan. This soup is better than I can make. I've made enough to know." She glazed over at Matt, suspiciously. "What did you give me?"

"Spices?" Matt said, helplessly. He had long since forgotten the demonic names for them.

"I get that. Where did you get them?"

"I bought them, at the demon market. They were expensive, I think? I'm not sure how money works here, but I was flush from killing everyone in a bar."

Matt watched everyone mentally put aside the idea of killing an entire bar full of demons for a moment, somehow doing this in favor of grocery shopping. It wasn't what he expected. They stared at him, shocked.

"You have demon spices? Multiple vials? And you gave me some for *camp soup?*" Artemis was aghast, and as Matt nodded in indication that this was in fact exactly what he had done, she stormed off in a huff.

"What's that all about?"

Brennan moved beside him, watching Artemis rant and rave as she left. "Demon spices are rare. They don't sell them to us, obviously. And they are very, very good at creating spices for some reason. Every now and again, someone finds a vial of them on a dead one, but you can imagine how often that happens. Not very many demons carrying cooking supplies into a fight, you see."

"And? I don't get it. They are good spices. Big whoop."

"Well, yeah, big whoop. But to Ra'Zorians? Much bigger deal. There are guys who will spend a lot on those spices, and you have whole vials of it. More than I've seen in one place at one time before."

"How much are we talking here?"

"You know how much Artemis put into that soup?"

Matt did. It was a generous pinch, but not incredibly big, maybe a quarter of a teaspoon at most. He nodded.

"You could have bought a house with that. Not a mansion, but a pretty good house right in the capital." As Matt started to object, Brennan held up his hand. "I might be exaggerating, but not by much. They take their food seriously here."

It was the better part of a half hour before Matt had built up enough soup resistance to actually eat a bowl. For a few minutes, he hit a sweet spot where the food was still maximally delicious, but wasn't threatening to kill him over it. By the end of the meal, the experience had dulled significantly. He committed the meal to memory. He doubted he would ever have another bowl of soup quite as good, ever again. The mechanics of the universe probably didn't allow for it now that his taste buds had adjusted to the new flavor.

He also distributed a few vials of the spices to all the others, keeping only one for himself. When they tried to argue, he explained that he could not cook, and reminded them he probably wouldn't be on Ra'Zor permanently anyway. He couldn't use them, and he'd feel bad trying.

Artemis protested the most, but Matt smiled when he saw that her words didn't stop her from making sure she got first pick among the vials once everyone relented.

CHAPTER TWENTY

Yeast in Dough

Shit. I can't climb that, guys. I'm sorry, I just can't." Matt was staring at a cliff face. It wasn't dirt, and it wasn't cracked, for the most part. It was a sheer, smooth rock face, and Matt was from a planet that was flat-and-ruined. Even with his powers, he couldn't get up.

Artemis had scouted ahead and found that the pass was completely, totally packed with demons, geared for war and in formation. Even if they could fight all of them by strength alone, the pass was crowded enough that they might get crushed by the weight of the crowd. There was no way through but up.

Luckily, getting to the wall itself wasn't much of a challenge. The region had long since given way from grassy plains to solid tree cover, and that cover grew within a hundred feet or so of the base of the cliffs. They could hear demon-bird scouts and see their shadows blocking the bit of light that came down through the canopy, but they hadn't been spotted yet.

"That's me then, I'm afraid," Brennan said. "I have some rock-climbing experience, even if I haven't used it since Earth. And I'm pretty sure my strength stat is higher than yours. We'll take any edge we can get. This is all me. I'll drop a rope afterward."

Brennan quickly assembled what climbing-specialized gear he had, which wasn't much, mostly consisting of a pair of gloves and every rope they had on them.

"Alright. I'm off." Brennan smiled and kissed Artemis on the cheek, then turned to the wall. As they were waiting for the next patrol of birds to fly over, it occurred to Matt that there was at least one thing he could do to help Brennan up the wall.

"Brennan, wait." He shrugged out of his pack and then out of his brand-new stealth cloak, wadding it into a bundle and tossing it to him. "Any edge, right?"

Brennan grinned, throwing the cloak over his shoulders. "Sure thing. Any edge."

One thing was becoming increasingly clear to Matt as time went on. In an even fight, one where Brennan didn't know anything about Matt or his limited bag of tricks, Matt would probably get his ass handed to him. Brennan was almost certainly higher-leveled than Matt, that much was obvious in his first attack. He had higher stats, almost to the point that skill or tricks couldn't surpass. But even without the stats, Brennan was precise. He was so casual that it was easy to confuse him for being a bit dim, but that wasn't the case. Matt was sure of it.

As Matt watched Brennan scale the rock face, he knew that no stupid person could climb a wall like that. No dumb person would have done well with a precision-based, planning-heavy class. It just wasn't possible. Deep down, Brennan was a genius.

It showed in every foot of wall he rapidly ascended. Matt could tell the hand and footholds he was using amounted to little more than slight inconsistencies in the wall. Where he could stop, he'd only do so to gain additional leverage, pausing only momentarily and pushing off hard after. He got every foot he could out of any particular handhold. When he couldn't find something to add to his momentum, he'd impact his hand or foot with the semi-hold to keep moving. He was flying up the wall, multiple yards a second, as if he had wings and all the climbing was just for show.

If Brennan was telling the truth about not climbing in Ra'Zor, then none of his climbing technique came from Earth, where he had the body and capabilities of a normal man. He was adapting to his new capabilities on the fly, getting the most out of what his body could do without any skill assists at all.

"He's insane. Matt, he's going to fall." Lucy was watching every movement as well, barely breathing.

"He's not going to fall. He's crazy, but he's going to do it."

"I know, right?" Artemis said, not realizing Matt was talking to his invisible friend. "I reacted the same way, the first time I saw him do something like this." She smiled, just a bit, enigmatically. "Although I acted on it a bit differently than I expect you will."

Matt searched for some response for a minute, then decided better of it. A flapping sound filled the air as the next bird patrol came by. The team was closer to the edge of the trees, and were ready to support Brennan. Alone on the rock face, he had stopped to draw less attention.

"Do you think they will spot him?" Matt asked.

"Not if they don't look up. He's above them now."

They looked about even to Matt, but Artemis was the expert. Despite her words, she still nocked an arrow to her bow, and stared intently at the birds. It turned out she had overplanned. Moments later, the birds had moved on. Brennan started flying up the cliff face again, now with plenty of time. He didn't waste it. Faster than Matt could imagine possible, he was already grasping the edge of the top of the cliff. A few moments later, the rope snaked down.

"Stupid, stupid. He should have waited until the patrol passed again. Matt, Derek. Come on. We have to hurry."

Derek was the first to the wall. He had explained to Matt, briefly, that his class relied entirely on stats, with no techniques to speak of. Everything was training now. Matt had almost tried to apologize for stripping him of his class, however unintentionally, before he found Derek was happy about it. Watching him climb the rope, he realized better why. He was strong. Even Artemis, who hit the rope behind him, was struggling to keep up.

Matt was slower, but not by much. He shoved his shovel through his pack straps and started climbing. With the rope, they were faster than Brennan had been, but not by as much as they should have been. The swaying made things hard and while no one seemed scared of heights, they also had nothing but air to cushion a fall.

Derek reached the top, and slipped over, as did Artemis. Matt half-expected that their situation would become like a movie, where the last one on the rope would end up in trouble, trying to climb while the enemies snapped at their feet. It didn't happen. He made it to the top uneventfully. Keeping low, everyone made their way to the edge of the cliff where it fell away to make the pass.

"Well, it could be worse." Brennan said, looking down on thousands of demons armed to the teeth and dragging not one but four more demon heart bombs on floating wood platforms.

Artemis slapped the back of his head. "How, Brennan? How could this possibly be worse?"

"We could be down there with them."

"We *should* be down there with them, Brennan. They have four of those weapons. That's one for every colony between here and the capital, as well as the capital itself. Thousands of people, maybe tens of thousands of people, are in danger. We have to do something."

Derek blanched. "What? What could we possibly do against that many? We have to get in front of them, get help, and come back. It's our only hope."

Artemis kicked the ground in front of her, stirring up dirt from a large crack where erosion had split the ground. Unfortunately, the cliff was sturdy enough that she couldn't separate any of the dirt. Instead, she just threw dust into the air.

"Dammit, dammit, dammit. There's not enough time. By the time we get back to them, we will have lost another colony, and there's nothing we can do. We . . ."

Her lament was cut off suddenly by a sharp cry from above. Matt wrenched his head upwards to see two bird-of-prey-demon-men flapping above them, screeching their heads off. Artemis loosed an arrow at one, barely missing it. It was too late anyway. Below, they could hear the shouts of the army as it became aware of the threat above it.

Every system instance was a little bit different, but they all followed an identical set of rules. Long ago, the main system had settled on a unique, low-effort way of doing less work with one of the more strange rules, a rule that stated that planets could not be allowed to stagnate. Even when the system instance struck a balance, it wasn't allowed to strike a perfect, stable stillness. It had to chase moving targets, keeping one side a bit stronger than the other in an eternal game of ping pong.

But even the best laid plans eventually move towards stagnation. That meant that, sometimes, new blood was needed. Where one system instance's context-specific interpretations of the rules had come to a standstill, even a small piece of another system's ruleset could spread new life and energy through it, like a small piece of yeast in a large bowl of dough.

This wasn't the Ra'Zorian instance's first world-to-world invasion rodeo. Hell, even the current demon lord was a transplant from another planet, having taken down the previous, lackluster demon king. He had at least done much more with the powers he gained compared to the previous unimaginative asshole. The Ra'Zorians hadn't had a word for zombies, but that's what the last guy had created. Shambling, mindless, easily dispatched zombies. The new guy was subtle. Understood the score. Worked within the rules. The system instance liked him, honestly.

Subsequent invasions had been helpful, but not nearly as much as the instance liked. If there was one black mark on its record, it was the sheer amount of reincarnation it had to summon every year just to keep the energy-circulation lights on. The last few invasions had promised to help with that, but the people who had come hadn't understood the tactical situation on the ground, or tried to go right after the demon lord, or experienced death by a thousand cuts before they got halfway to him.

It helped, but not nearly enough. That said, the system had reason to be hopeful when Matt first showed up. No system instance was doing all of its own math since the main system had long since abstracted the amount of counterbalance each system instance should provide in preparation for a new invasion to an automated calculator.

The device wasn't sentient, and didn't explain how it had come to its conclusions, but it always worked. It sat, soaking in information from a thousand worlds, learning, and somehow spun out the right answers every single time. Nobody questioned it. There was no reason to.

This time, it had cleared the system instance to hand over an incredible amount of power to the demons in preparation. For once, the system instance had been tempted to question the auto-calculator's judgement, but he didn't. The demon lord had been hinting and nearly begging for a city-slaying weapon for decades, and now he finally got one. Did it cost him a bit of his power every time he used it? Sure. Was the thing on a hair trigger and hard to transport? Yup. But it would level a city just fine.

Then Matt showed up, and he was, well, less than impressive. He took out some ants, and didn't show a single spark of creativity doing it. He took down a bar full of demons, but any non-mook could do the same, and invaders were usually pretty bright. The reincarnators that weren't usually didn't make it through to the invasion level of things in the first place.

But even by the time he murdered the demon-bar, things were getting weird. He'd eat things, and get powers. And the powers didn't make sense. He could multiply his power output. There were downsides to how he did it, but it was much less limited than it should have been, like the skill wasn't obeying the system's algorithmic limits on skill powers at all. On top of that, he was carrying a shovel, a damned shovel, that somehow ignored the restraints of mana-based objects completely.

Was it *possible* that all this shit was happening according to some rule? It was. The system instance had limited insight into the stats, powers, and general history of people from other systems. His ignorance was part of the point of the whole invasion system. It made for messy balancing, and messy balancing made for chaos, which was the exact ingredient for shaking up a stagnant balance. Without confirmation, there were certain actions he couldn't and shouldn't take. Right now, he didn't have that confirmation. Matt wasn't telling him what was going on, despite being asked multiple times, but that didn't in and of itself constitute the evidence he needed. He also needed proof.

But he'd get it. Oh, yes, he would. Because he'd do anything to avoid escalating this stuff up to middle management. If one, single, solitary reincarnator thought he could disrupt the careful equilibrium that the system instance had built up, he had another thing coming.

CHAPTER TWENTY-ONE

Sapper's Tattoo

"Come on! Shit!" Derek was leaping in the air, trying to get a clear shot on one of the birds as they swooped. Artemis had managed to land a hit on one of them so far, not killing it but putting it in range for Brennan and Matt to end it. Derek was trying to catch them midair, which was proving to be harder than he thought. Now, as he came down from his latest jump, he looked panicked, much more afraid than he had been seconds ago.

"Incoming!" he yelled, a split second before two yellow orbs rushed into their visual range, rising over the edge of the cliff and continuing on in an upwards trajectory. Eventually, they lost their momentum and started falling back towards them, screaming through the air much faster than gravity should have accelerated them.

"Matt! Those explode where they hit!" Brennan and Artemis were scrambling backwards, probably trying to get out of the range of the explosion.

Matt didn't really want to explode, but he doubted a single shot from whatever artillery demon was attacking from below could completely end him. Choosing one of the falling orbs at random, he lined up underneath it, and pulled back his shovel.

"What are you doing? Dodge!" Derek yelled, hitting the ground and running away from the orbs.

"Can't! I have an idea!" Matt yelled.

As the orb came down, he hit it, not hard, but he figured the actual momentum of the falling attack would help with that. If he was lucky, the thing wouldn't blow up until it actually hit something that qualified as a target. If his shovel could set it off, he didn't want to tempt fate by giving it a really good clobber. But, as Matt expected from most magic at this point, whatever programming the spell ran off didn't recognize his shovel at all. Instead of exploding, the ball bounced up and out at an angle from Matt's shovel, making the slightest contact with the wing of one of the fleeing bird-men. That was enough, apparently. The bomb went off, and nothing escaped its blast range but a few feathers. At the beginning of the fight, Artemis had screamed out that bird-demons were mainly about mobility, and struggled with durability. That turned out to be true.

Matt noticed maybe a fifth of all that. The second bomb meant he had more immediate, more distracting problems to deal with. The two orbs had been clustered together, and thus when Matt hit the first one, the second fell pretty close to him. If he had been as fragile as the bird-demons were, he wouldn't have made it. As it was, the explosion scorched his heat-resistant snake skin and flung him so far that he actually went over the edge of the cliff. If the rope wasn't still hanging around, he would have dropped the full distance. But it was and he was glad. He didn't think he would have survived that.

As he reached the top of the rope again, strong hands pulled him up and over before he had to negotiate the edge.

"Matt!" Derek yelled. "You lived! That was really stupid, man. Even by my standards."

"He's right, you idiot. Stop trying to catch bombs." Lucy was peeved, as she always was after Matt did something life-threatening.

"Sorry, it just seemed like the only way to get rid of the birds. Artillery and air support was turning out to be a little too much." As Matt got to his feet again, he looked back over the edge and at the army. "I'm hoping they didn't see that bit with the shovel, just now. Oh, nope, looks like they didn't. Yellow orbs incoming."

"How did you even . . . Matt, that shovel isn't possible. Reflecting spells like that isn't possible. You aren't even a magic class. What's going on?" Brennan asked.

"Eh, that's more of a camping story." They hadn't known each other long, but Matt hoped Brennan would pick up on the not-outside-your-tent implications of what he was saying. "I'll tell you when there's more time."

Hitting two orbs at the same time wasn't doable, but Matt could handle hitting one on the way up and handling the incoming downward bomb just fine. Having a proof of concept that they'd mostly ignore his shovel, the first orb got a healthier whack and screamed back towards the army much faster than it had been launched. And, just like Matt had hoped, it landed pretty close to one of the hearts. The orb explosion went off, and Matt waited with bated breath to see if it got past the force field and caused mayhem.

It wasn't meant to be. The orb took out several demons and caused a great deal of localized havoc, but both the heart and the platform it floated on were just fine. Matt dealt with the second orb, just batting it far off into the distance and hoping it didn't hit any unfortunate targets.

"That's great, Matt. I bet they think twice before launching more of those now. We should be fine for a while, unless . . ." Brennan paused as a much larger contingent of bird-demons split off from the main force and took to the air. "I probably shouldn't have said anything. I jinxed it."

"Matt! Watch out! There's a battleking in that group. I don't know what it means, but it doesn't sound good. He's the one in the very center of the group."

"Heads up, everyone! The one in the center is a battleking," Matt yelled.

"How do you know?" Artemis yelled. "Even I can't get a read on them from that far away."

"Just trust me on this! Should I take him?"

"No. You keep an eye on the orbs, and keep them off me and Brennan. Derek, you help him. Brennan . . ." Artemis was in full command mode and only stopped when Brennan interrupted her, swinging his sword in a figure eight as he loosened up.

"Kill the big bad guy. Got it."

It sounded like a good plan. If anybody could pull off being the linchpin, it was Brennan. If anyone could take down the birds, it was the other three, working in tandem. But reality ended up being a lot harder.

The battleking bird, who looked for all the world like a peregrine falcon, rose above the ground and dove. But when the strike didn't land, it didn't opt to pull up. Instead, it touched down lightly and quickly, converting almost all of the speed from its dive into running speed across the ground. It ran in a stooped position and led with both its beak and its sword. Both looked capable of disemboweling Brennan, but he caught both on his sword somehow before spinning around and aiming an elbow at the back of the bird's head. The bird flicked a wing up, deflecting the elbow.

It was an even match. The most Matt, Derek, and Artemis could do to help was to make sure it stayed that way. Arrow after arrow flew through the air, bringing down birds left and right, while Matt ran around finishing the grounded and Derek jumped here and there like a pogo-stick blocking others from joining in on Brennan's fight.

And then Brennan screamed. Matt turned around to see the bird's beak sunk in his arm, drawing blood as it twisted and tore apart his flesh. The balance of battle was changing, and not in their favor.

And then two more orbs appeared, much bigger than those that had been launched before, flying much higher, glowing much brighter, and bringing that much more doom with them.

* * *

"Brennan!" Artemis screamed, turning her attention from the dive-bombing bird squadron to its ground-bound captain. The arrows she launched at it were deflected with ease. But the distraction was just enough for Brennan to get loose and create some distance, letting his hurt arm drop to the side and keeping his sword pointed in front of him like a fencer to maintain distance.

For a few seconds, it was too much. Derek and Matt managed to keep the birds off Brennan and Artemis, but only just, and picked up a few wounds doing it. Without Artemis's arrows in play, they'd soon be overwhelmed. It was just a matter of time before something broke.

Then, all of a sudden, the birds cleared out. The battleking peregrine falcon stayed, but seemed focused on pushing Brennan farther and farther from the pass and the others. Matt was confused about why until he realized the only reasonable explanation. The artillery orbs were coming back.

As things stood, they were doomed. Brennan was still doing poorly, and Artemis's distracting arrows weren't doing much to help that. Derek's initial attempt to join in was met immediately by a backhand which sent him rolling across the ground. And Matt couldn't help, as he had gigantic magic bombs to deal with.

He stomped his feet, kicking up dust from the same crack that Artemis had noticed earlier. The same dirt-filled crack. And though the orbs were falling, he had probably just enough time to try something that almost certainly wouldn't work, but was worth a shot. Digging his shovel into the crack, he charged up as much energy as he dared, leaving only a margin to have time to still deflect the orbs. Luckily, the people on the ground still didn't seem to know exactly how their bomb had previously been sent back. These two were offset by a few seconds, long enough for him to hopeful get both.

He released his dig skill into the crack, hoping it would continue its habit of outperforming his expectations of it. This time, it failed to do so. All the dirt blasted out of the crack, instantly atomizing into tiny particles of dust and floating off. But the mass at the edge of the cliff itself was fine, unaffected by the dig skill and sturdy enough to easily hold up despite missing a significant portion of dirt it previously had.

And then it was time to deal with the orbs, He tried to deal with them with a scooping sort of golf swing, one that would send them far away. But then, almost at the last moment, it occurred to him what a waste that would be. As he prepared to swat at the orb, Survivor's Reflexes somehow made a correct guess at what he had been trying to do and highlighted one particular point deep within the crack he had just cleared. He obliged, hitting the first orb with a tennis overhead serve that sent it deep into the crack.

The detonation was loud and violent, but mostly contained by the crack, which remained intact.

"Matt, is that going to work?" Lucy shouted. "We could try to send them at the army, still."

"Probably not! It's still . . . just trust me on this one!" Matt shouted. It was truly a long shot. He wouldn't have tried it in the first place, except for something Lucy didn't and couldn't know about. After clearing the tower, Brennan and his crew were happy for him because of the Church money he was eventually going to get. But Matt hardly cared about that, because he had received a different kind of pay.

Sapper's Tattoo

The Sapper's Tattoo is a one-time-use, skin-marking enchantment. While wearing the tattoo, any weak-spot-detection skills the user might possess gain additional efficacy on the surrounding environment.

If the skills didn't register the environment as a target before the use of the tattoo, they will now do so with minimal efficacy, highlighting only the largest and most obvious weaknesses. If the weak point skill has already been enabled, it will now function even better.

The tattoo can be removed, either by willing its erasure or by replacing it with another tattoo of similar function.

CHAPTER TWENTY-TWO

Change is Bad

Matt thought of trust as an earned thing, something that would be as immoral to withhold as it would be to deny a worker their paycheck. And for better or worse, Survivor's Reflexes had always steered him in the correct direction. Where it said something was vulnerable, it was. When the weak spots ended up being unhelpful, it was almost always because Matt failed to get to the target or strike it particularly well, not because there wasn't an actual vulnerability to be exploited.

Matt might not have trusted this tattoo absolutely, but the skin-markings were working through Survivor's Reflexes, with its permission. He trusted that. If the skill said there was a place he should hit based on new information the tattoo was providing, he felt he owed it to try.

There was a downside in play beyond that kind of trust-or-don't-trust risk in the fact that he hadn't actually informed anyone of the tattoo. While he was beginning to trust Brennan and the others more and more, he didn't think it was a good idea for them to see every single card in his hand as soon as he got it. And that meant that Lucy also didn't know. This decision, for better or worse, was all his. He hadn't found the time to talk to her alone and had decided to keep everything a secret for the moment.

He smacked the second orb, sending it at the crack. It detonated with the same loud noise as before, and nothing happened. The crack didn't break, or change. Matt sighed, disappointed.

And then barely made the jump to get back to safe ground when a full fifty feet of the cliff trembled, started sliding into the gap over the enemy army, and fell.

The birds were the first victims of the rock. They had made what would normally be a sound tactical choice and hidden under the plane of the cliff, probably reasoning that doing so would protect them from any stray Artemis-arrows and the orb explosions. They were completely unprepared for hundreds of tons of rock suddenly shifting directly on top of them, and were pinned to the bottom as it fell.

The next victim was the peregrine commander, who spared the barest fraction of a percent of his attention to try to figure out what the unearthly explosions, stone grinding, and bird-screaming sounds behind him were about. In a battle with Brennan, who relied on split-second precision to land hits on critical spots and end battles in a single blow, that was a mistake. It was, in fact, a mistake he never really realized he had made, as the strike to his neck was powerful enough to get his windpipe and his brain stem in the same transaction.

The subsequent next victim would have been much harder to calculate. It could have been the people that the cliff mass landed on, or it might not have been. It turned out that the energy in the demon hearts liked to release in a controlled, prepared way, but by no means had to. The rock landed directly on two of the hearts, missing the third by several feet on one side of the impact and the fourth by even more on the other side.

The force fields held the entire mass suspended for just a split second before they cracked, at which point the hearts simultaneously exploded. It's possible that this killed all the people the rock would have hit, but there was no way to tell.

The next kills were, for better or worse, combination attacks. The power released from the hearts rushed straight into already compromised rock. The resulting frag-grenade explosion of stone was so thick and fast that there was no doubt in Matt's mind that it would have killed their entire team, were they not hundreds of feet above all the explosions.

The same was not true for most of the invading enemy army. Having a mountain fall on you was already a pretty bad deal. Having a mountain fall on you, destroy most of your super weapon stock, then explode into fragments ranging from tiny, sharp needles to good-sized boulders toward you and all your friends was a worse one.

If you really wanted to make the deal as bad as possible under conventional circumstances, you'd have all of that stone-and-magic explosion trapped in a relatively small, contained granite space. One that compressed all the damage, reflecting the stones back where it didn't break and collapsing on you and crushing you even more when it did break.

If you, for some entirely unexplained reason, wanted the situation to get as bad as possible while including unconventional situations, unlikely occurrences, and shit that just flat-out shouldn't be possible, you might add two more intact super weapons, then jostle them just enough with everything that happened before that they began to detonate, conventionally this time.

Matt saw all of this happening. The others only arrived in time to see the remaining two hearts start to put out pulses. They stood there slack-jawed as they began to watch the mayhem unfurl further below them.

Demons were not, it turned out, unselfish people. And selfish people are rarely brave. If they had kept their heads about them, it was possible they could have run at a fairly orderly pace and got most of the troops out of the range of the two hearts before the pulses got out of hand. Instead, they didn't even manage to pick a direction. Long before the pulses actually claimed their first victim, Matt and the others watched several demons fall to good old-fashioned trampling, as demons bashed into each other, overtook each other, and ground each other into the walls and earth.

Almost the entire army ended up being in the range of the pulses of the two hearts. What they didn't get, the eventual inferno did, leaving the pass clean and sanitized, if a little ashy.

"We have to get down, now," Artemis said, as she finally shook herself out of the shock of watching most of her immediate problems literally evaporate in front of her. "Brennan, get the rope set up."

Matt glanced around, looking for the new threat. "Are more birds coming? More artillery fire?"

Artemis shook her head, grinning like a maniac. "No. It's time for mop-up."

There were plenty of demons left, but it was "plenty" in the sense that it was a satisfactory amount, where they no longer posed any real danger. The hearts and falling mountains had not only crushed the demons' formation, but also their morale. Artemis was leaping from tree to tree, raining down arrows like a vengeful thunderstorm. Derek, Brennan, and Matt mowed through demons like they were threshing grain.

There were hundreds of demons left, but only a few were left who posed any real trouble. It turned out that the peregrine falcon had been the best the demon army had to offer, combat-wise. A few others probably would have come close if they weren't already banged up by the localized apocalypse Matt had dropped on their heads. When Matt identified those few remaining battlelords and kings, the team came together and made short work of them without much real danger.

Overall, it was a satisfying thing, a good and relaxing end to a hard day.

As they moved through the ranks of the demons, Matt ate small amounts of them when he could. Most of the traits were trash, as always. He ended up keeping only two of them. The first came from the falcon commander, who he took a sneaky, feather-filled bite out of once the others had disappeared over the edge of the cliff.

> Swooping Momentum trait added.
>
> Swooping Momentum allows you to convert the momentum you have moving in one direction to another direction at a 70 percent efficiency rate on the ground, and a 100 percent efficiency rate when falling from heights greater than ten feet. When activated, it creates two charges or uses that can be put into play within three seconds of activation, followed by a one-minute cooldown.
>
> Meta-Trait Occupied: Movement.

This was exactly the kind of trait Matt needed at the moment. It would eat up his demon disguise, sure, but it would also make it so that he could outmaneuver faster enemies in battle, or run away with direction changes they couldn't match. He quickly replaced the morphing skill and vowed to use the new movement skill in front of others only if he absolutely had to.

The next move he decided to keep was an attack trait picked up from some kind of cobra-looking demon. His charge-up strike was so powerful that he was reluctant to get rid of it, and instead stored the new trait as a kind of holdout weapon if he ended up in a tough, constrained spot.

> *Quick Bite*
>
> Quick Bite allows you to lash out with your teeth at ten times the normal speed. For the duration of the strike, your bite strength, bite penetration and tooth durability are increased tenfold.
>
> The speed increase provided by this attack skill is restricted to motions of the head and neck. The attack itself is repeatable with no cooldown.

Matt couldn't imagine what specific scenario this would be useful in, but he ran into weird, specific scenarios all the time. Worst-case scenario, he'd let it languish in his storage until he found something better. For now, though, it was another secret he could keep in case things went sideways on him.

When the bulk of the demons were dead, the party agreed to split up a bit to increase their chances of finding any stragglers who had avoided the blast. They remained within earshot of each other, but spread out as they walked to increase their overall observation range and sweep up any demons that they might have missed.

At this point, Matt didn't carry enough bloodlust to really care if they got the last few escapees. But he agreed to the plan immediately anyway. He desperately wanted to catch up with Lucy on a few things.

"Okay, that should be far enough," Matt said, once they had some distance on the others. Luckily, Artemis wasn't the closest to him in formation. He wasn't sure how far she could hear, but he didn't want to put it to the test. "What are you thinking?"

"So far, the others have been alright. Surprisingly so. Brennan and Derek seem like good guys, and the fact that they don't love the system is helpful. You might be able to trust them."

"What about the other?"

"Artemis? She's still a wild card. You heard her defend the Church, right?"

"Yeah, but so did the others."

"Not in the same way, Matt. To her, everything about the Church is normal. And if I'm hearing what they are all saying the right way, the Church controls most of the adventurers. I think she probably works for them."

"As a spy?"

"Not quite, I don't think. But I also wouldn't be surprised if she reported things back to them, even things the others think of as secret. Remember, it all seems normal to her. If the Church ends up being a bunch of great guys who are really trustworthy and kind, that's fine. But I think you are a threat to them, no matter what. That makes this all unpredictable."

"Why would I be a threat? I hardly care about them. And I'm not going to be here long."

"Because, dummy, you are here explicitly to change things. To them, *you* are the wild card. And they are currently holding almost all the power. When someone's winning, change is bad for them."

"So we keep an eye on them. Agreed."

CHAPTER TWENTY-THREE

Buy Utah

Good. Next, that tattoo. The others might not have noticed it, but don't think that I didn't see you apply it. Where'd you get it? And why didn't you tell me about it? From what I saw on the mountain, it looks like it helps you move stupid amounts of rock?"

"Not exactly." This was something the system already knew about, so Matt felt like he could talk about it without giving much up it didn't already know. "It's more like an enhancement for Survivor's Reflexes. It extends the kinds of things that the skill can find weak spots in, stuff like my environment. And seems to do a pretty good job of it."

"So you can't just throw mountains at all your problems? Bummer. Still, good get." Matt saw Lucy reference some invisible screen, as if she was checking her accumulated notes of things to talk about when they got the chance. As she scrolled through everything, she commented on her thought process, "This one I know about already, this one I don't think is important right now. That just leaves one thing. Why do they look confused every time you talk to me?"

"No idea. I think I sort of assumed that every reincarnator would have a guardian. After Leel knew about them, it seemed universal."

"As far as I knew, it is. Every reincarnator needs a guardian to guide them when they enter a new world. But my information about other planets is pretty spotty, and it's possible that it's just not a thing here. The Church seems to fill most of the guidance function, in a different way. And they mentioned this thing called plinths, whatever their deal is. I don't think these plinths are like the ones that Barry has at the end of each dungeon." As she said the last word, she winced.

"They talk about the plinths like they are class-specific helpers, and they seem to be located centrally with the Church, so I'm really, really hoping that's all they are and there's nothing more to it."

"Me too. And honestly, from what I know of Brennan and Derek, they don't seem like the slavery type to me. I don't think they'd tolerate it, honestly."

"That's why I'm hopeful it's nothing, Matt. But if it is that kind of situation . . . what are we going to do?"

Matt stopped walking for a second, then leaned down close to Lucy. "You're asking me what I'll do if I find out these people, the Church, are enslaving guardians? Thousands of guardians? I can't imagine why they'd even do that, but . . ." He looked her directly in the eye. "If it came to that, and there wasn't a good enough explanation for everything? We'd burn it all down, Lucy. All of it."

"Oh, Matt," Lucy mocked, looking shy for a moment. "You always know what to say to make me feel better. You charmer."

"Oh, shush. We actually do have a job to do right now, you know."

"A gentleman never lets an important conversation get in the way of bashing things with a shovel," Lucy said, smiling. "The first thing they teach you in finishing school."

After twenty minutes, they had swept enough of the surrounding area to be pretty sure they had got the majority of demons that the bomb left behind. There was always a chance they'd missed some, but Artemis explained that the capital would likely send out another squad after them. And the new heroes would be equipped with skills to make it easier to chase down the few remaining enemies and guarantee they didn't get up to mischief.

"Right now, the most important thing is to get home. They still don't know what happened to Epsilon, or us for that matter. They must be in a panic by now," Artemis said. Stragglers and panic aside, she seemed more than content with the outcome of the day. A day of heavy fighting did wonders for her mental state. "Matt, I'm officially not telling you what to do anymore. If you have some kind of stupid idea, just go for it. They seem to work out for you a surprising amount of the time."

"I'm liking this girl better and better," Lucy said, grinning.

"Seriously, though. How did you know that would work?" Brennan asked. "My whole build is about finding weak spots and building precise plans. I didn't see anything from that crack."

As Matt and Lucy had chased down their last few demons, they discussed a plausible explanation for what had happened. He held his shovel up a bit higher into the air, displaying it for everyone. "You see this thing? It's not just for show. It's been with me for a while, and some of my class skills synergize with it pretty well. Without going into the details, I'm especially good at digging."

They accepted that explanation with a couple of nods. The discussion was surprisingly easy. It seemed odd until Matt considered how few people stumbled into using a shovel as their primary weapon. They didn't even know what his class was. For all he knew, they had assumed it was something like Combat Miner from the very beginning.

"Well, I'm glad, anyway. You saved three cities today, Matt," Brennan said, looking relieved for about the tenth time that day.

"Oh, oh no," Artemis said, struck by some kind of sudden terror. "Oh, noooo."

"Shit, Artemis, what is it?" Derek looked alarmed now, too. Artemis was normally pretty steady, and seeing her panic easily unsettled him.

"It's the kills. Remember how he had twenty or thirty of them before? That was already going to be a paperwork nightmare to claim the kills."

Brennan considered this for a moment before a light went on in his eyes and he realized what he meant. "Ooooh, ha, yeah. Shit. Matt, you just took out an entire army, mostly by yourself. Hundreds or thousands of confirmed kills, presumably several high-ranking demons among them, with partial credit on a leader and full credit on four devastating siege weapons of mass destruction, and who knows how much in terms of equipment and supplies."

Off to the side, Derek's eyes went wide. He appeared to try to do some quick mental math on his fingers before giving up.

Matt glanced back and forth between them, his forehead furrowed with confusion. "And that's . . . a lot?"

"Oh yes. It's a lot." Artemis looked genuinely upset.

"Well, I'll just get some good armor, then. No big deal," Matt said. He did need to upgrade his wardrobe, given that he was still wearing the starter tunic he had landed on Ra'Zor with.

Brennan grinned again, barely containing his laughter for Artemis's sake. "No, I don't think you get it, Matt. It's hard to put it into words, but a battle this size almost never happens, and when it does, it's split a hundred or a thousand ways between whole armies of people. Some heroes have made their fortunes on stuff much smaller than this."

"So . . ."

"So, you are now officially probably the richest private citizen on Ra'Zor. To put it in Earth terms, and Earth buying power, you could probably just about afford to buy the entire state of Utah."

The rest of the walk back was less relaxed, mostly because Artemis would occasionally break down into mini-panics as she tried to calculate the size and scope of Matt's new hypothetical wealth. She eventually calmed down just a little when he managed to reassure her that without the desire to buy property on Ra'Zor, or the ability to keep it if he did, he'd be more than happy to accept a much smaller, more reasonable fraction of the funds. In fact, he'd even be willing to gift what he didn't use when it came time for him to return home. She was still stressed, but it at least got things under control.

They skipped all the other colonies, making a beeline for the capitol. It would take longer, given that the nearest colony wasn't that far away, but it was worth the extra time to explain everything to the people who needed to know it directly. So, the rest of their travel time was spent sprinting, and with a blessed, demon-free uneventfulness so completely devoid of ambushes and attacks it left Matt feeling jumpy.

When they made it to the gates of the capitol, the head of the gate guards was so surprised to see the three alive that it took a full five seconds for him to remember himself and salute. "Good day, General Brennan!" he shouted, drawing the rest of the guards' attention and causing a chain-reaction of salutes and greetings that took a few seconds to die down.

"General Brennan?" Matt asked, his eyebrow cocked.

"Oh yeah." Derek grinned as he took in the sight. "He's kind of a big deal. He doesn't talk about it much. I keep quiet about it for his sake."

"What do you have to do to be a general around here?" Matt asked, suddenly upping his estimation of Brennan a few more notches.

"I'm not sure on the details," Derek said, scratching his face. "They've never talked to me about it before, really. Not that I want to be one, anyway. But I think being the strongest guy on the planet helps."

With Brennan vouching for Matt's trustworthy guest status, it didn't take long for the doors to be thrown open. The group stepped through, and for the first time in years, Matt laid his eyes on a normal, honest-to-god, human place of living. The buildings were brick and stone, the streets were cobbled, and smoke from stoves came out of iron chimneys over countless taverns, restaurants, and homes.

"Holy shit. It's a manga town," Matt said to no one in particular.

Derek smiled. "I know, right? And I'm gonna show you around. Brennan and Artemis will be tied up with reports for a while. And you know what we're going to do first?"

"Eat?" The aroma of food was filling the air from a dozen gate-adjacent food stands.

"Yup, as much as you want. And then, my friend, we are going to go get a bath."

CHAPTER TWENTY-FOUR

Riches in Friendship

Matt and Derek picked up an enormous amount of food from various street carts as they walked toward the bathhouse. Eventually, it was enough that they had to make a pit stop and spread their loot on a cloth on a bench between them. Then, they absolutely destroyed thousands of calories' worth of fried meats, breaded meats, and various foods Matt couldn't recognize but that Derek assured him were good. Now, thoroughly bloated, they were cooling off in a natural hot-spring-warmed pool of water, surrounded by a wood fence.

"So did you ever actually do one of these on Earth? In real life, I mean."

"An onsen? Just once. Near the end there, I went to a lot of places, and one of them was a bath in Tokyo. I'm not sure, but I think the one I went to was put there specifically for tourists. It didn't feel very real."

"How so? It seems like hot water would be hot water."

"Right, but I'm guessing that I would have seen Japanese people in there if it was a real onsen. These were all guys like me, who had seen baths like that in anime and were trying to get the experience during a vacation. When anybody who knows better isn't there . . ."

"Gotta be fake. Got it." Derek slid a little lower in the bath, trying to get the relaxation from the warm water to climb from the muscles in his back all the way to his chin. "I never did either. But this one is real, by Ra'Zorian standards at least. I've been to all of the baths in the city, and they're pretty much all like this. Even the smaller ones closer to the gate."

"Then why'd we walk all the way over here?" The walk hadn't been unpleasant, but it hadn't exactly been short, either. "I assumed you didn't like those as well as you like this one."

"Oh, I don't." Derek bobbed back up in the water, setting his back against the stone-lined wall of the pool. "But it's not because of the baths themselves. It's because of the laundress. Remember when they took our clothes? They know me here. With how dirty our clothes were, they would have taken them right over to the laundress, and she would have washed them."

"Ah, got it. And that's . . . worth it? Seems like we could have done that ourselves with, like, a hose or something. In a well."

"Not like this. She's got a whole class built around it. When she washes stuff, she gets it actually clean. Magically clean. Magically dry. She can't fix major stuff, but it fixes small scratches on leather and minor damage to the fabric."

"Ah, so maintenance."

"Not just that. You'll see. I'm not going to ruin it."

Lucy was somewhere in the bath house, presumably trying to find a place she had described as "as far away from the dirty man-stink as possible." Matt didn't blame her for acting a bit prickly about coming here in the first place. Even if she hadn't ever really gotten over the time when his clothes were dissolved in his fight with the Scourge, this was a place where people came to experience the warm and the tactile feeling of water. The baths themselves were beautiful, but really mostly because of the experience they hinted at, as opposed to being something you'd paint on a canvas. There wasn't anything here for her, a girl who couldn't feel anything or interact with these parts of the world.

But she knew Matt needed something like this, and so didn't put up an enormous amount of fuss outside of the initial hard time she had given him. And he had needed it. He had gotten used to his magic washroom back on Gaia, taking frequent baths as if he was catching up on years of not taking care of his body. Now, with an enchanted pedicure, a deep-cleansing rinse from an honest-to-god magic showerhead, and a good, long soak in hot mineral water, he was starting to feel pretty human. Or Ra'Zorian. Whatever.

He slouched a little more into the wall behind him, breathing out a sigh of relief. If Derek vouched for the laundress, he'd just accept it. The kid seemed to have taken full advantage of the manga life that Matt had imagined, discovering the city piece by piece until he had mapped out all the best parts of it. Matt didn't have time for that, as much as he might have liked to do it. He'd let the kid take him wherever he wanted to go.

Suddenly, behind him, he heard a snip.

"Oh, looks like word of what you did has started to get out." Derek's voice came from beside him. "Reports like the ones Brennan and Artemis make are semi-public, and news tends to leak whenever something big happens. Looks like you're going to get the full treatment. Just let them, it won't take that long."

Matt carefully turned his head, only to see someone who appeared to be a barber already going to work on his hair. The barber was a man with what looked like a massage mat and bottles of various oils and lotions. Another spa specialist he didn't recognize was bringing over a cart of what looked like various kinds of towels. Matt looked back at Derek, questioningly.

"You saved the city, man. Or at least some settlements," Derek said. "Everyone has family everywhere. They want to say 'thank you.' Just let them."

An hour or so later, Matt emerged from the bath feeling brand-new. He was absolutely clean and had his first real, complete haircut and shave in years. On top of that, he was thoroughly buffed. Not in terms of stats, but instead from the literal meaning of the word. It had turned out the towel guy was some kind of professional exfoliator specializing in skincare for the stat-enhanced, and had rubbed Matt down with progressively finer towels, polishing him like varnish until his skin literally shone.

Derek told him not to worry about the last bit. The shine would start to dull over the next few hours because of what he referred to as "normal skin stuff." It did feel great though.

The best part had turned out to be the laundry, even though it was a mixed bag. Cleaning the literal demon-residue out of actual low-grade demon armor was apparently possible, but was a step too far for the laundress, who turned out to have personal standards even Derek hadn't known about. The salvaged armor he had acquired from the demon-bar was examined, bagged, and then very literally burned in a stove.

In replacement, she had provided him with a very nice note thanking him for saving the city, which she had apparently heard about as well. The note was tacked to lightweight, casual new clothing that had just been cleaned especially for him, stacked on top of his boots and cloak, which she had recognized as system-made and restored to like-new condition.

Derek wasn't lying about the clothes, it turned out. Putting them on was like communing with the essence of clothes-dryers itself. It was like the spirit of the first dryer sheet that ever was had breathed its blessing on the fabric, granting them subtle powers beyond what mundane textiles would reach on their own. The clothes almost sighed down his skin as he put them on.

In a purely physical sense, he had never felt so good.

In a psychological sense, he was a little worse, mostly out of worry about Lucy. When he emerged from the baths clothed in the laundress's best, a wry smile he associated with her giving him shit about something had formed on Lucy's face. She was probably gearing up to call him overly fancy, or something. But when her gaze went upwards to his freshly shaved face and newly cut hair, all the blood on her face drained away. It looked as if she had seen a horror on par with the Scourge.

"What? What is it?" Matt's voice turned to concern.

"Nothing. Let's just go. I'm tired of this place."

"Lucy, it's not nothing. What is it?" Matt was genuinely worried he had done something wrong. It even felt like he had, somehow, even though as far as he knew, he hadn't had an opportunity.

"It's nothing. I promise. We can talk about it later. Let's just go."

And she started walking.

Matt trusted Lucy enough to believe that if it were relevant in a serious, immediate way, she'd tough it out and talk about it right then. If she wanted to wait until later, that was her right. For what it was worth, they didn't have time for a long, drawn-out conversation anyway. As soon as Matt and Derek emerged back onto the street, they were accosted by a messenger who zipped up on them with dexterity-enhanced speed. Matt had barely squashed his Survivor's Reflexes-driven instinct that fast guys were usually weak to shovel strikes when the messenger started talking in a loud, official voice.

"Reincarnator Derek and Visiting Reincarnator Matt. Your presence and reports are requested at a hearing of the officials of the Church. The hearing is ongoing in the court of the square, and you are requested to report as immediately as possible."

He then zipped off, apparently on his way to other messenger duties.

"The court of the square?" Matt asked Derek, confused. "Is it entirely for nerds, or something?"

"Ha, but also no. It's just in the town square. They name important things very literally here, for some reason." He started walking. "But they aren't kidding about the 'immediately' part."

"What would happen if we didn't show? Bounty hunters?"

"No, just more of those messenger guys. Believe me, you can't dodge them while in the city. I've tried. They come out of nowhere. And they all shout like that. Every single one."

The court of the square was, if anything, ridiculously round. Technically, it was in the square, but unlike the other buildings that lined the square, the court itself was a circular building in the dead center of it. It defined its section with a clearly laid, large circular mosaic, and it was positioned where a fountain might normally sit in any other Earth square.

Derek told him the building was directly over the dead center of the city itself, as if everything was built to extend outwards from this landmark. Matt had no reason to doubt him.

"Anything I need to know going in here? Lawyer-talk? Special titles that I get beheaded if I don't use?"

"Nothing like that. It's more like . . . did you ever take a field trip to a city council meeting? I did that once. It's like that. They're on one side of the counter, you're on the other, they ask questions, and you answer them. It's like that."

"So no messing up and then having to flee with the Royal Army at my back."

"Oh, no. At least, probably not. If anything, they're probably trying to pay you out for all the kills. Or looking for a way out of doing that. It really is a lot of money, you know."

"If only they knew that the real riches is *friendship*."

Derek laughed. "You say that now, but wait until I take you to see the old man. It will have you valuing riches real quick. And maybe questioning friendship, too."

CHAPTER TWENTY-FIVE

A Line of Credit

Inside the building, everything was marble. Not in the Earth way where the building had marble flooring and just a lot of marble inlaid with other materials. As far as Matt could see, every single surface in the place was really, truly, and actually made of the stone. The only reason he felt confident walking around the room without banging his shin on something was because of his perception score and the fact that, at some point, some architect had tempered the calcium carbonate madness by differentiating objects using some variety in color. The benches and tables were black, the floor and walls were white, and the panel the higher-ups were sitting behind was a dark gray. All marble.

As soon as they entered, an usher took note and shuffled them toward the front, apparently trying to expedite the proceedings as quickly as possible. Derek was called forward to speak first, and stepped up to a marble podium apparently meant for that task.

"Greetings, Reincarnator Derek."

"Hi, Bishop M'aal."

The bishop shuffled some papers in front of him, apparently looking for a particular section of his notes. Once he had found it, he refocused on Derek, glancing at his notes here and there as he did.

"Reincarnator Commander Brennan and Commander Artemis have told us quite the story, not that we disbelieve it. We ask that you now add your accounting of the details of the period between your departure from the capital for Epsilon Colony and your eventual return, including any of what we might, as an understatement, call detours."

Derek began talking, keeping his words uncharacteristically dry and concise. Matt guessed he had been through this before, and was bored of it. For Matt, however, it was a fresh experience. He did learn some things he didn't know before, primarily, how very close the group of three had come to being overwhelmed by enemy forces before they got more or less clear behind enemy lines. But even without those new nuggets of information, it was interesting to see when the questioners behind the counter would stop Derek to clarify certain sections, and guess at why they did so.

Only when Derek got to the part of the story in which Matt entered as a character did his storytelling get a little more animated. He downplayed the fight between them, calling it a misunderstanding and not going into much detail about how things had come close to getting bloodier than anyone wanted. He also didn't mention Matt's planet-of-origin relation to Derek at all, excluding both Earth and Gaia from his description of their peacemaking.

He had more words to describe both the sapping of the tower walls and the battle at the cliff, attributing the vast majority of the kills to Matt. He even included a guess of the total enemy defeats that he thought should go to Matt; it sounded something like twice the enemies that were on the battlefield in the first place.

After a brief talk about their return at the gate and saying he had been "showing Matt the better parts of town since then," Derek sat down, without waiting to be dismissed in any way. This seemed to be normal, too, as the men behind the panel didn't react to it.

"Well, then." Bishop M'aal, who appeared to be leading the meeting in general, turned to the other officials with a half grin on his face. "That's three accounts, almost entirely consistent with each other on all important parts. I trust that satisfies the more doubtful members of the panel?"

Nobody objected to that. Apparently, some had in the past.

"Reincarnator Matt, would you be so kind as to take the stand? I know it's been a long few days, and I can promise that you won't be asked to recount the events at all, unless you think there's something meaningful to add."

Matt stood and walked to the podium. "I don't think there are any, bishop. Besides, maybe the fact that all three of the others risked their lives constantly on that trip. Brennan took on a demon I think the other three of us united would have failed to fight. In comparison to that, I think I just got lucky."

The bishop considered that thoughtfully. "Brennan will be rewarded for his contributions, so have no worries on that account. Our problem stems from something slightly different. It is rare that one man destroys the bulk of an invading demon army by himself, let alone saving three or four colonies in the same swoop of his . . ."

He looked closely at Matt's weapon for the first time, as if confirming something for himself.

"His shovel. Which means we have a slight problem in terms of payment. Not because you aren't entitled to it," he said, with a pointed look at one of the other people behind the panel, "but because it's simply an amount of money we would be hard-pressed to give to you in a liquid form. Have the others given you . . . estimates? I suppose? Some idea of the amount of reward we are talking about here?"

"They gave me some idea. I want to make this easy for you if I can. I am a visitor from off world. You know that, right?"

"Correct. It doesn't happen often, but it's not an occurrence with which we are unfamiliar. Don't have any worries on that front, by the way. We've found that all such visitors are helpful to us, even if not quite all of them have been particularly effective."

Matt nodded. "Well, the idea is that I'm going to get back to the world I traveled here from sooner or later. Sooner, if possible. In the meantime, I don't need much. Probably just some armor and a few novelty weapons at the most." Something occurred to Matt at that moment, and he snapped his fingers, which appeared to slightly startle Bishop M'aal. "Actually, a reliable way to travel back, an inter-world portal or something, would be the thing I need the most. Do you have anything like that? I'd be glad to call it even right there if you do."

M'aal shook his head, sadly. "No, we don't. As far as our records of other-world reincarnators state, they seem to have gotten back using their own power in some way or another, usually at the termination of their quest. You'll have to pursue that with your own system, I'm afraid. We'll help where we can, of course, we just have limited technological and magic prowess in that particular area."

"No worries." Matt had figured that might be the case. The Gaians had been tapping into fairly odd fundamentals of the universe at the end there, if he was reading the descriptions of their technology correctly. It wasn't all that surprising that other planets hadn't gotten that far, or if they had but were nuked by the system in some way or another because of it.

"As to your assertion that we needn't pay you, it's very kind. Unfortunately, much of the magical infrastructure that makes our government run is system-supplied, and as such, comes with downsides that somewhat offset their substantial upsides. One aspect of them is both downside *and* upside, depending on how you look at it, and it's this: we can't fail to pay a debt. Our financial system runs on a series of magically enforced contracts, and the penalties for breaking them would be much more significant than the substantial payment required."

He sighed.

"All of which means we will be paying you as quickly as possible, if for no other reason than to avoid trouble on our end. But it will be . . . havoc, to an extent. We will console ourselves with the very true fact that it's havoc that we are alive to have, where there was a possibility we wouldn't be."

Matt looked at the man thoughtfully for a moment. He at least didn't appear to be trying to guilt Matt into anything, and Matt truly didn't care about the money that much. The last thing he wanted was to create problems for other people, especially if he wasn't getting anything out of it himself. He could imagine some contingent of guards taking a pay cut over this kind of thing, and he didn't want that to happen. Suddenly, something occurred to him.

"What about a line of credit? Do you have anything like that?"

"I'm sorry? I'm not familiar with the term."

"On my original world, before I was reincarnated, it would have been something like a card or token. Someone would put up something as collateral, like a house. Then they could spend money equal to the value of the collateral. It was complex, but I'd be willing to 'loan you' the money back, with a term in the contract with the phrase that the money would be forfeit if I were to leave the world, or something like that."

The man appeared ready to object, then stopped. "Interesting," he said, drumming his fingers on the desk. He motioned an assistant over and whispered something in their ear. "If you could give me a few minutes, Matt, I'll check on the possibilities of that. It just might be that there are options."

Matt took a seat, back by Derek.

"I think what you are doing is crazy, man. Do you know how many carriages you could buy with that? A lot. Nice ones, too. They have carriages with shocks here."

"What do you need a carriage for? You can run like thirty miles an hour."

"It's not about getting there, Matt. It's about *how* you get there. I want to get there looking cool."

A few minutes passed before a man walked in who was, in all ways, unmistakably an accountant. He wasn't wearing anything that directly corresponded to an Earth button-down and slacks, or something that Matt could put his finger on to point at what gave him that impression. But he was somehow still sure. This was a man who, on Earth, would be really good at spreadsheets and probably not all that great at basketball.

Behind the panel, he conferred with the various authorities in attendance. Matt couldn't hear, but he could see him responding to various questions, thinking, and pointing at various reference materials he had brought with him. The whole process took the better part of ten minutes, and at the end, Matt was called back up to the lectern.

"Reincarnator, it looks like your idea had some merit. The main difficulty with the idea, it turns out, isn't so much that it's unfeasible as that what you proposed was too one-sided in our favor. We can't write a contract taking your money where the only benefit to you is that you then get to spend it if you choose to. The advantage is too much on our side for our system to allow it."

Matt nodded. It made sense. It sounded like some sort of system-driven predatory lending prohibition, or something. Whatever upsides there were, they also got significant downsides when they bought their government's financial system in a big box from the system. It was like cheap Swedish furniture. Convenient, but not a lot of variation for individual needs.

"It seems the easiest solution to this, the one that gets closest to the spirit of your offer, is to simply increase the buying power of what your money can do. As you'd imagine, there are usually restrictions on what money can buy here. Some materials are controlled, some treasures aren't for sale, and things of that nature. Your token, once we've created it, will buy literally anything our government owns. And to sweeten that deal, we are even willing to open some of our armory supply depots to let you access materials you might otherwise have trouble finding."

Derek ran up behind Matt and whispered in his ear, "That's a good deal. They must have figured out I'm going to take you to see the old blacksmith. He can do almost anything, but he doesn't always have the parts he needs. The Church gets a cut of almost everything anyone brings in. They have plenty of materials."

"It looks like Derek has explained the implications of the deal to you. With a . . . noncontractual request on my part that you don't get too carried away, I think this is a practical solution to our problems. What do you say?"

"It sounds fine to me." It really did. Frankly, Matt didn't need any of this. If this is what it took to get his big ol' reward downgraded to a reasonable amount of spending money without busting the local economy, it was fine.

"Good. I'll send word to the appropriate people to get the token created. It shouldn't take long, perhaps as short as just a few hours. Once it's done, we'll see to it that it catches up to you by messenger."

Matt nodded, then turned to go.

"And Matt?" the bishop said, as he was leaving. Matt turned back around. "We lost one settlement a few days ago. It's a devastating thing. But it could have been much, much worse. Thank you."

CHAPTER TWENTY-SIX

Dropped a Mountain on Them

"So the trick to the old man is he's going to hit you with a pipe. That's just going to happen. You might think he's not going to do it, or that you can block it, or . . . I dunno, anything, really. But he's probably going to hit you with a pipe at some point. But besides that, he's a really nice guy."

Matt, who just wanted armor, didn't exactly expect to hear a one-sided monologue about a blacksmith from Derek. It went on for a surprisingly long time. Derek first talked about the fact that the man had a mysterious past, which was interesting enough. But right when Matt thought that was it, he moved on to the various kinds of violence he had experienced at the smith's hands and the apparently dozens of ways it was possible to piss the old man off. And while he talked, Derek was oddly enthusiastic about it all in a way Matt couldn't quite decode.

"So, say I fail at one of these . . . tasks. I either don't get hit by a steel bar in a way that makes him laugh, or I sit in his work chair. Or I say something that makes it seem like crafting in general or blacksmithing specifically aren't respectable. What happens then? He just refuses to make the armor for me?" Matt asked.

Derek looked at him like he was crazy. "What? No. He makes armor. That's what he does. He's not going to leave someone unprotected just because they're a jackass. That's completely not him. You'll see. He's great. He might hit you in the head with an entire bench if you dodge his pipe, but he's great."

Eventually, they arrived at the blacksmith's place, which Derek called a compound. It looked, to Matt's anime-trained eye, about how it should. It had a smoking chimney that sat over a tiled roof that in turn sat on top of a wood-and-brick structure of immense age, as if it had passed from blacksmith to blacksmith for generations. Despite that, a quick cycling of Matt's Sapper's Tattoo–juiced Survivor's Reflexes showed essentially no weak spots in the structure. The building wasn't just shored up and maintained, it was *strong*.

Matt wasn't sure whether vitality or perception did it, but his eyes adjusted more quickly than he expected to the change in light as they ducked into the shop. Even from a long distance away, he had heard the clanging of the hammer. It gave a loud, solid metallic thunk as it struck orange-hot metal, the sound reverberating off walls and through streets a surprisingly far distance away considering how closed-in the shop was. But even Derek's assurance that the man was a giant and the sheer volume of the hits he had heard didn't prepare him for the man in front of him.

It's like a dwarf said "screw you" to the whole 'being short' thing, Matt thought. The man was all muscles, veins, and tendons, to the point where Matt felt bad about his poor skin having to contain it all. He was bursting with strength. But Survivor's Reflexes immediately started nagging Matt that it was more than that. The first clue was that his arms were nearly the same size, which, given that he was only wielding the hammer in his right hand, shouldn't be possible. His blows were also precise, as if they were driven by thousands of hours of practice. And his eyes were sharp and alert as he went through the task, and he gazed at the metal as if it were an enemy to be defeated as much as it was a material to be shaped.

In short, Matt was pretty sure this guy could kick his ass. If he was wrong and his feeling was just Survivor's Reflexes responding to the sheer unknown-ness of the guy, it would still be a weird, tricky fight.

The man suddenly stopped clanging on his metal, and instead picked it up with tongs. He held it close enough to his face that the heat would have burned Matt if he had done the same thing, and inspected it closely before giving a satisfied grunt. Finally, he plunged it into a large barrel filled with what appeared to be fireplace ashes. He gave no indication that he had seen Matt or Derek throughout, until he began to speak with his back still turned to them.

"I see ya brought me another idiot, boy. Ya know I have enough work without ya bringing more, don't ya?"

"Oh, shut it, old man. You're going to thank me for this before we leave today. Or at least know you should when you refuse to do it anyway, you old fart."

There was a clanging noise as the old man hung his hammer on a heavy rack, then another as he hooked a metal bar with his hand and chucked it sidearm at Derek's head. Derek got out of the way, but just barely.

"Ya perception go up, boy? There was a time ya wouldn't have even seen that."

"All my stats are up, old man. It's been a busy week. Are you really going to leave him standing there? He's a customer. He needs armor." Derek pulled out a wood stool from the wall and chucked it overhand at the old man, who caught it out of the air.

"Fine, ya bastard. I'll take a look." The old man slammed the stool down on the ground and motioned Matt towards it. Matt, who had been taking in the show until now, came and sat down. What he didn't expect was the old man to lay hands on him, grabbing his shoulders before shoving his arms up and feeling his back, then his ribs. His shock must have shown, since Derek immediately assured him the old man was just measuring him, in a unique way.

"I don't know if it's a skill, but the old bastard never forgets your size once he does this. I wish he had the same skill for taking baths."

Matt expected the old man to fire back, but he was fully at work now, inspecting Matt's hands, legs, and even making him take off his boots so he could look at his feet.

"What do ya specialize in?" the old man asked, breaking out of his measurement reverie suddenly to look Matt square in the eye.

"Melee, mostly? I hit things."

"I mean skills. Combat skills. What do ya use to attack? How?"

"I just . . . I have a combat skill that makes me pretty good at weapons, I guess. I have another one that makes me throw sand, but that's . . . that's just sand. I can dig particularly well, but that's not an attack. It's mostly just . . . thwacking things, I guess?"

The old man turned and glared at Derek. "You brought me a melee generalist."

Derek beamed at him, brightly, then turned to Matt, who was feeling more and more uncomfortable. "The old man doesn't like melee generalists because they're hard to make happy. On the other hand, if you have a guy who uses strength-enhancing skills that make him slower, the old man can build him something that either preserves his speed or makes him hit harder. They love that."

The old man cut in.

"Archers *appreciate it* when I make them cloaks that steady their shots. Axemen appreciate clothes that cut stamina costs. Generalists? They're never happy."

"Why not?" Matt was genuinely confused. "Why not make them armor that does the same thing?"

"Synergies." Derek said. "This is bespoke armor. It interacts with classes, usually with specific skills. When the old man makes armor for generalists, it interacts with their classes in general ways. Little buffs here and there, but nothing spectacular. Since people come to the old man looking for something spectacular, he doesn't get the reaction he wants."

"Buncha effort for nothing, is what it is," he huffed. "And ya said I'd thank ya."

"It gets better, old man. Ask him what his budget is."

The old man eyed Derek suspiciously for a moment before turning back to Matt. "What is it? Unlimited?"

Matt shifted uncomfortably. "Uh, yeah. Kind of. Whatever it takes, I guess?"

The old man reached under the counter, grabbed another iron bar, and flung it at Derek. This time, when Derek dodged, the bar didn't clatter around the shop after it missed. It embedded deep in the wall. In the *stone* wall, vibrating like a tuning fork for a few seconds before the stone sapped away the excess energy.

"Fresh off his first hunt, ya gonna tell me next."

"Yes! His very first," Derek said before addressing Matt's confusion. "The old man might hate generalists, but he hates first-timers even more. They come in, flush with cash by their standards, and ask for a bunch of stuff that costs *real* money."

"Which is why ya can't have what ya want, I'm sorry. The real stuff, the good materials, I have to buy off other adventurers who are older and better than ya are, or ya woulda brought it in for me when ya came." He pointed his thumb at Derek, derisively. "And why this one is a horse's ass for bringing ya. Best thing for ya, right now, is to go buy something pre-made. Better way to spend the money. Gets ya more."

Derek, who had wandered far away after dodging the last bar, practically danced towards Matt and the old man. "But, old man, that's wrong. There's something you don't know."

"Ya think so? And what's that, ya impossible idiot?"

Suddenly, the door burst open. Derek was beside himself with joy. "I thought he was about due."

"Reincarnator Matt! I am here to announce . . ." As the courier began to speak in a loud voice, the old man was suddenly by his side, almost instantly getting a hand around the entrant's neck and lifting him from the floor.

"I've told ya not to yell in my store before, haven't I?" the old man asked. Choking, the courier nodded. "And ya know it bothers me. Is that right?" Another nod. "Alright, as long as ya have been reminded."

The old man gently set the man back down on the floor, where he stood slightly shocked for a second or two before making his way to Matt and handing him a small object.

"For you," he whispered hoarsely, before retreating out of the door as fast as his messenger's feet would take him, which was pretty quick indeed.

"And what's that?" the old man asked.

"It's a credit card. Matt had them invented earlier today to fix up a little problem that the Church was having regarding having enough funds on hand to fulfill his combatant pay."

The old man did some quick mental math on how much money it would take to put the Church authorities in such a financial bind. His eyes bulged a little with surprise and what Matt thought was probably a hint of greed before he gathered himself to look unimpressed once again.

"Still, having the money to buy and some material worth buyin' are two different things," he said calmly with his dignity back.

"M'aal opened up an armory to him." Derek was struggling to keep from collapsing in laughter as he watched the old man's mouth literally drop open at the delivery of that fact.

"Matt, I'm starting to like this kid. Tell him good job from me. But later. I don't want to screw up his rhythm. He's doing wonderfully." Lucy said from near the door of the shop, where she had been watching the entire show.

"An entire armory? Ya sure you didn't mishear?"

"I think M'aal's exact words were 'one of our armories.'"

The old man's eyes darted downward as he got down to some serious thinking. "If there's only one prismatic snake skin, then . . ." He wandered off towards a small table near the back of the shop, and started furiously scribbling down notes on a piece of paper.

"What's he doing now?" Matt asked.

"Shopping list, I think. Part of why the old man is a good crafter is he likes it. It's his whole life. But usually, he's making do with the best he can on big orders with limited materials."

"And now he gets to go all out, and it broke him?"

"Something like that. I wasn't kidding when I said he'd thank me later. He probably actually will. Not today, though."

The old man spent a few minutes at the table mumbling to himself until he finally appeared satisfied and returned, clutching a folded piece of paper in his offhand. He approached Derek first, glaring. "Derek, how'd ya say he came by that money?

"He took out a whole demon army by himself. Dropped a mountain on them. Literally."

CHAPTER TWENTY-SEVEN

Batters Up

The old man considered this for a moment before turning to Matt again. As he approached, he cleared his throat a bit bashfully.

"So, there, Matt, was it? I'd be pleased to take the commission, if ya is interested. I'll make something real nice, I think."

"Thanks, old man. I'd like that."

"I'll even throw in a weapon, free of charge. Just provide the materials and I'll make ya something good. Better'n what you got, anyway."

"Oh, no, I'm fine on weapons. What I have is probably better than what . . ." Matt said the words without thinking about how it would be heard, and then immediately regretted it as the old man scooped him up, shovel and all, and physically flung him through the back door.

"Oh, it is, is it?" the old man asked, brandishing a three-foot bar of steel he had pulled out of nowhere like a staff. "Better get it in front of ya, then. Gonna need it."

Derek was outside and sitting on the wall by the time Matt got up, grinning like an idiot. Matt harbored a suspicion that when Derek had predicted mayhem, he had been prepared to cause it if none was forthcoming.

"Get him, Matt! He won't know what hit him," he yelled, using his sword as a cheerleading baton.

"Keep that sword out, boy. If this one doesn't make things interesting, I'm coming for ya next. With the clubs."

Whatever the clubs were, they were apparently scary. Derek shut up immediately, watching the fight with far more apparent reserve.

"Alright then." The old man gave the long steel bar a couple of practice swings, somehow moving it like it didn't weigh anything. "We can get going, just as soon as ya feel ready enough to show me."

Now, Matt thought, as Survivor's Reflexes screamed at him to take the initiative before it was too late. He sprung at the old man, who looked genuinely surprised for a moment. Apparently, it had been a while since someone had opened things up with him without some level of caution. Matt had been having decent luck with swinging his shovel from below. So he stuck with that tactic here, converting his stride into a dusty slide along the ground and bringing the point up towards the man in the same uppercut-golf-swing motion that had been catching his other opponents off guard lately.

The old man wasn't ready, but that didn't mean Matt caught him absolutely flat-footed either. As the shovel came up, he dropped one end of the bar in a downward sweeping motion, pushing the shovel to the side while allowing most of its momentum to continue upwards. As the end of the bar slid upwards on the shovel's handle, Matt could anticipate what would happen if he let it hit the handle-side of the blade. He'd be disarmed completely, or at best, knocked off-balance with both of his arms already up.

Rather than leave himself open for that hit, Matt began spinning around with the shovel, using as much strength as he could to tuck the shovel off the old man's bar and in towards himself as he did. With the shovel moving with the combined speed and force, both fighters were putting into it and conservation of momentum being what it was, Matt made a full rotation with astonishing speed. He ducked down as he came around again and aimed the blade of the shovel straight at the bigger man's calf.

This time, the old man made no attempt to redirect the force. Instead, he dropped the bar almost straight down, burying it slightly in the ground directly in the path of the shovel and stopping it cold. The shovel bit into the steel a bit, but even the Nullsteel blade couldn't cut through inches of solid steel in a single strike. The pole held.

Matt yanked the shovel back at the same time he flared Spring-Fighter to get some distance, but all his forward momentum was ruined. It was the old man's turn now.

The first few blows were surprisingly light. Not actually light, of course, but for how big and strong the old man looked, Matt was surprised that he could stop anything the man threw at all. As easily as the old man handled the bar, it wasn't the fastest weapon in the world. Matt was jarred by each strike, but he was able to parry or block each of them.

Don't fall into his rhythm, Matt thought. It was a good thought. Coming out of one of his lighter strikes, the old man took advantage of the split second it was taking for Matt to recover from each blow and pulled back a single giant step, slid down the bar to a double-handed grip, and swung it at him like a three-foot baseball bat.

Matt got his shovel down in defense and fought the reflex to counterattack, figuring that the strike just might shatter every bone in his body if he did. He was gratified to see that the non-conductivity of the shovel seemed to give almost as good as it got. When the skill-augmented blow from the old man landed, the shovel canceled whatever follow-up plans the old man had and kept him struggling to hold on to his steel bar.

Despite reflecting some force from the blow, Matt was blown off to the side towards the training area's fence, his feet inches above the ground and helpless to slow him down. Rather than bash into the fence, he pushed the shovel down into the dirt, cutting a deep furrow as the shovel slowly cooled off his momentum. His arms felt like they were going to yank out of his shoulder sockets, but he managed to stop just in time to see the old man regain full control of his weapon, get set, and spring towards him.

The old man had plenty of tricks *and* an apparent edge in both fighting skills and stats, meaning Matt was fast running out of paths to victory. He needed a change, fast, and something the old man couldn't have seen before. He dug his shovel into the ground and began charging force.

Now the old man got cautious. Matt didn't know exactly where his opponent learned to fight, but it was clearly somewhere that taught a variety of interesting lessons. The old man was far from naive enough to run straight into Matt's attack without something prepared, but unless he had been paying exceptionally close attention, there was no way for him to know what was coming.

But just surprise still wasn't enough. Matt couldn't move his body, but that didn't mean he was out of options. Interdimensional travel might have emptied Trapper Keeper's single-trap store, but there was always at least one trap that Matt could load up at a moment's notice with nothing but things he was always guaranteed to have on hand.

As the old man got close, Matt fired an instant, fifteen-foot pit trap not in his way, or underneath him, but directly behind the old man at the absolute limit of what the skill would allow. Then, praying he had the angles right, he let loose his digging skill.

Matt couldn't dig through anything alive, and his skill wouldn't work as an attack. He and Lucy had worked out a lot of what it couldn't do over time. But one thing it could do was move a lot of earth, enough that even the biggest objects had to respect it if they were standing in the area it affected. With a charged dig, the old man didn't stand a chance.

Together with a literal ton of earth, the old man was lifted skyward. As he flew, Matt took a chance and sprung after him, swinging his shovel directly at his opponent's hands. To avoid being pulped, the old man was forced to drop the bar, which got batted out of the way, and was thus no help whatsoever in keeping him from falling straight down Matt's hole.

"Holy . . . Matt, that's not gonna hold him *at all*," Derek yelled. "He's gonna be pissed! Get ready!"

Instead, Matt shoveled a little earth down into the hole to slow the old man. He heard the blacksmith sputtering with rage as he coughed and sneezed through the dirt before scratching against the wall as he began to climb out. Matt didn't care. He had his shovel pulled all the way back towards his shoulder, and was charging up the biggest hit he could manage.

"Oh, Matt," Lucy said. As the only person who had seen every one of the skills involved, only she could understand what was about to happen. "This is going to be so awesome."

"Yup." Matt reached his intent into Trapper Keeper, reloading the pit trap back into storage. As had always been the case with the skill, it reacted by ejecting any objects that had fallen into the hole straight up. That included a good deal of dirt, a whoosh of air, and a very large, very surprised blacksmith. "Batter up."

Matt scored a home run.

The blacksmith didn't bounce off the fence, or get stuck in it. After he passed, there simply was no more fence. Behind the blacksmith's house, there was now nothing but the irreparable wreckage of the divider between his yard and the street, and a fully unconscious smith.

"Whoooo!" Matt yelled, pumping his shovel in victory. "Take that, you old goat! Derek, did you see?"

Turning around, Matt saw Derek, who wasn't so much rushing to congratulate him as he was sitting on a wall with a slack jaw, absolutely and completely shocked out of conscious thought. He was pale and motionless in a way that actually made Matt concerned for his mental wellbeing.

"Oh, shit, you broke him," Lucy said, looking up at the stillness. Matt waved his hand in front of Derek's face, which got no response. Finally, he slapped him just a little, which seemed to pull him out of it.

"Holy hell, Matt. You won." Derek ran over to the old man and bent over him for a second. "He still has a pulse. That's . . . good. Maybe not for you. I have no idea at all what he's going to do when he wakes up."

"Is he that sore of a loser?"

"I don't know, Matt. I don't think he knows. I don't think he's ever lost before. Holy shit."

The old man didn't stay asleep for long, nor did he wake up normally. After some failed attempts to bring him around didn't work, Matt and Derek decided to wait until his vitality woke him up naturally. When he did wake up, it was instant and would have been violent, if there was anything there to hit. Matt was standing a full five feet back, and he still couldn't avoid the wind from the blacksmith's fist blowing his hair back.

"What in the hell happened?" the blacksmith roared, loud enough to shake the windowpanes on all the houses on the street.

"I sort of knocked you out," Matt said gently, with no idea what the proper post-fight etiquette for this situation was. "I hope that's . . . okay? With you?

"I know you knocked me out, ya jackass. I meant *how* did you knock me out? I haven't the foggiest idea what the hell went on there in the last few seconds."

It turned out that what the blacksmith remembered was the entire world evaporating into dust and dirt around him, before finding himself partially buried alive. Then he experienced involuntary flight, and then flew in another new direction before everything went black. In retrospect, Matt understood how confusing that experience must have been. The blacksmith described it as being swallowed by an angry planet, which just about fit Matt's fighting style as anything else.

CHAPTER TWENTY-EIGHT

Titan of Strength

"Ya did well, but ya still shouldn't have been able to knock me out, ya know." The old man had now calmed down, and after reviewing the actual chain of events with Matt, he was both appropriately impressed and, it seemed, not accepting of the defeat at all. "Ya couldn't have hit me hard enough."

"I mean, I must have. You were pretty out." Matt was taking it all in stride. After all, he was pretty sure the old man wouldn't have actually killed him. He had no problem with the guy trying to save some face.

"Listen, ya idiot. I'm not whining about it. Ya won. I'm saying, I have body skills. Defense skills. Dammit, take a look at this." The old man did something to an iron ring he was wearing on one of his hands, then handed it to Matt. A window almost immediately popped up describing the item.

Golem-dust Ring

Cast from the ground-up remains of a demonic Iron Siege Golem, this ring grants stat bonuses related to resisting physical attacks.

Effects: Sharp reduction in damage to blunt force impacts, lesser reduction to other types of physical damage.

"Did you just . . . share an item description with me?"

The smith looked confused. "Yes? Any shopkeep can do that, boy. Where'd they dig ya up, to not know that? Anyway, the point I'm making is I'm a smith, and I have a bit of a history besides that. I have more than a few items like that on me right now, bolstering my defense. Ya shouldn't be able to knock me out. Kill me? Maybe. Knock me out? No chance."

"Oh, I see." Matt understood now. "That probably has something to do with . . . Derek, do you vouch for this guy?"

"With my life. If nothing else, I think he thinks betraying people is bullshit."

Matt was okay with that. It was good enough for him, or at least the best he was going to get. "You have an appraisal skill?"

The old man nodded. "I do, but first, come inside. I have something to do."

Inside the house, the man scrounged through some drawers before finding what he was looking for, a jar filled with a multicolored powder.

"If it's a secret ya got, it's only right I help you keep it. This powder is ground-up everything. Basically, just anything that's been left on the floor over the years. I burn this, it makes local mana a mess. Screws up surveillance something fierce." He chucked a handful of it into his forge, where it went up with a flash. The room suddenly felt indefinably dizzy to Matt, but it was tolerable. "There ya go. Let me see that shovel. We have a few minutes now."

Matt handed it over, and the smith ran his hands over it. "Odd. My appraisal skill won't read it."

"It's a pretty special shovel."

"Special my ass. My appraisal skill doesn't always tell me what something is, but it always at least tells me what it's made of. This shovel is impossible." He crossed over to the wall, retrieving his hammer. "May I? I promise I won't hurt it."

"It's fine. You couldn't anyway."

The old man cocked an eyebrow, but didn't argue. Lifting the hammer, he gave the shovel a whack, then jumped out of the way as the hammer bounced off and almost hit him in the face. "That's damn near full reflection. You know how thick of an anvil I'd have to use to get full reflection, especially with how hard I can swing?"

"How thick?" Matt played along.

"Too thick. The metal would start melting if I dug deep enough to hold it."

"You could build up."

"Could, but I don't like stairs." He gave a couple more experimental swings with the hammer, then put the shovel itself into the forge, working a foot pump until the coals were glowing as bright as the sun. Taking it out, he hit it again, then put his hand down gently on the shovel.

"It's cool. Didn't even heat up. Do ya know how impossible that is? In my forge? With my hammer?"

"I don't, but that's not a normal shovel. It's special."

"Ya tell anyone about this?"

Derek was looking on, confused. He was clearly out of his depth.

"No. Not Brennan, not Artemis."

"They'd be okay, if it was in that horrible tent of his. But no one else, and never in the open. Ya know what a cursed object is, boy?" The blacksmith looked serious. Matt shrugged. "It's what they call objects that the system hates, and it punishes you for having them. I'm guessing if the system here knew what this was, it would be the most cursed object Ra'Zor has ever seen. Don't let it know what ya have. Ever."

Matt glanced around, hoping the dust would cover up what had already been said. "And we're okay talking about it?"

"Don't worry about that, boy. I know what I'm about. That wasn't normal communications block dust. That was my special dust. And I don't have much of it. Now, take this." He handed the shovel back. "And sit down. Ya gotta get ready for what's coming."

"What?"

"Get down on the floor, boy. Ya beat me in a fair fight, and the dust in this room is almost clear. It should be about time."

Matt did as he was told, then sat for a solid twenty seconds wondering what he was supposed to be doing before every muscle in his body went haywire.

Ding!

> *Ra'Zorian Title Acquired: Titan of Strength*
>
> The previous titan of strength earned his title with both feats of legendary strength and by defeating the titleholder that came before him. You've duplicated the latter, and fulfilled the requirement of the former by moving several tons of rock onto an enemy army.
>
> Effects: All weapons that you could otherwise lift and use with a reasonable level of proficiency handle and feel as if they weigh no more than five pounds.

Every muscle in Matt's body was twitching, as if rewiring itself in some unsubtle way. When it finally calmed down, he stood up slowly and hefted his shovel. It was never incredibly heavy, but it was now noticeably lighter. Given how the shovel seemed to resist system influence, that meant the difference was probably in him, rather than the weapon itself. It wasn't exactly weightless. Five pounds was about how much the heaviest Earth swords had weighed. But it was noticeably better and faster. He'd gladly take it. And it seemed he had.

"Did I just strip the title from you? I didn't want to. I can give it back, if you know how to do that."

"No, it's okay. Ya earned it. And I've held on to it long enough. I had meant to give it to this one, eventually," the old man nodded towards Derek. "But the way his class works, he will hardly need it in another year or so." He picked up his hammer and hefted it again, grimacing. "Although, I'll probably have to do something about this hammer. It's a wee bit heavier now."

Derek was still awfully quiet, apparently not having quite got over the old man getting beaten up. "I can't believe this. You mean Brennan never beat you? Not once?"

"Not once. Sorry about that. We thought it would help motivate you if you thought there was a chance."

Matt considered what it might mean that he beat the blacksmith if others couldn't, then decided it probably wasn't as significant as he wanted it to be. After all, Brennan countered most of the tricks he had used in the short fight they had. He suspected he'd know all of his tricks once Derek had more than half a minute to relay the whole story.

The old man hung his hammer up and slapped his hands together. "Well, enough of that. Shall we?"

Matt looked at him, a bit confused. "Shall we what?"

"The armory, boy! The armory!" He rubbed his massive palms together, looking like a kid on Christmas morning. "There's no time to waste! Let's be on our way!"

Matt had no idea what made any of the armories distinct from each other. Derek didn't either, for that matter. Even his knowledge of cool stuff he wanted only stretched as far as knowing the armories were packed with cool gear that he could probably make use of. But the old man assured them that there were good ones and then there were better ones. He was going to see to it that they got to one of the better ones, regardless of what kind of trip they had to go on to get there.

It turned out the really good armory, the one the old man insisted they needed to go to, couldn't be reached any other way than by sewer. Not that it was in a sewer itself. It was, technically, just buried very deep for defense purposes. Deep enough that the accumulated war potential of the greatest human stronghold on Ra'Zor wouldn't be compromised by anything but the most vicious demon armies. It was cheaper to dig that deep if you had a pretty deep starting point to work from, and the sewers were that.

"Eat it, Matt. You know you want to. You could get weird sewer powers. You might get septic slice!" Lucy was unable to smell, and thus a bit more chipper in these circumstances than Matt was. But no amount of chipper would be able to convince him to eat giant, clearly mutated sewer rats. They had all sorts of bumps that burst as they fought, to the point where Matt had sneakily taken to letting Derek get to them first. Whatever hard feelings he still held for the kid about the Gaian invasion evaporated as he watched Derek kill rat after gross rat, oblivious to the fact Matt was leaving all the heavy lifting to him.

Eventually, they arrived at the entrance to the armory, which amounted to another staircase heading down, flanked by row after row of Gaian soldiers.

"Alright, boys, I've come raiding," the smith cackled, beside himself with joy.

"Sir, we are under very strict orders to try and kill you if you so much as step down this corridor. Please don't make us do that."

"Kill me? Sure. But him? He has permission. Check."

The guard captain who had spoken before looked suspiciously at the old man, then ducked into a small alcove a few stairs down, apparently to activate a communications device of some sort. A few moments later, he came back up, looking worried.

"They say they said he could have access to an armory, sir, not this armory specifically. They say to choose one of the others."

"And I say," the old man said, getting loud, "that he probably meant this one, given that this boy is a war hero who saved the entire world, almost. And that if they didn't mean that, I'll get loud about it. And that mitre they are ordering for the Church's head? It's gonna be less ornate. A lot less ornate. I'll be spending too much time yelling about this, all over town."

The guard gulped, imagining an intentionally loud blacksmith rather than a merely incidentally loud one and ducked back to his communications relay. A few more moments passed, and he returned.

"They said it's approved, he can go into this one. But they told me to ask if you could please just be reasonable." A certain desperation shone in the guard's eyes. "Please?"

The old man was already pushing past the guards as he squeezed his way down the staircase, cackling like a maniac as he went.

"We'll keep him in check. This guy here? He'll beat the old man up if he tries to take too much." Derek said, moving down the staircase while wiping rat goo off his clothing.

"That's a good joke, but it really is our asses if he cleans us out."

"Not a joke, I'm afraid. Although I probably wouldn't be able to actually beat him up again. He knows all my tricks now." Matt grinned, and moved down the stairs.

The guard looked perplexed for a moment, but noticed the old man hadn't said anything to contradict either of them. And he would have, normally, even if just to participate in the joke. The fact that he didn't was suspicious. So with a bit more respect in his eyes than he had before, the guard watched as Matt disappeared into the armory.

CHAPTER TWENTY-NINE

Demonic Platinum

"Oh, and this. Absolutely this. Do you know what this is? It's a whole lizard made of stone."

"Why not just use an actual stone, then?" Matt asked, completely lost for the fifth time in the last ten minutes.

"Because stones can't walk, you idiot. This could."

The old man was going crazy, jumping from piles of hide to piles of bone, stacks of metal to stacks of wood, and bolts of cloth to bolts of demon-tendon string like a kid on a timed shopping spree in a toy store. He was efficient in gathering as much as he could, and everything he set his eyes on was something he swore he needed. Derek vouched for him. Apparently, making a single set of armor required about five or ten times the mass in ingredients of the finished armor itself, sometimes more.

Only once did the old man light on something he didn't end up saying they needed to take: a big lump of dull-colored metal that he gazed at for a few moments before moving on.

"No good for armor?" Matt asked.

"No, it's good, just not for what ya need. Good material, though, for heavier use." The smith went back into action, pulling out several bones and a few rolls of tendon and cloth he said would help finish the product, and then they were done.

"Alright, boy. Buy these things, and we'll be off. I'm sure they have a bag or a tarp to carry them in, somewhere."

"There's a little problem with that," Matt said, pulling out his payment token. "I'm not exactly sure how this thing works."

"Can I see it again?" the smith asked. Matt handed it over, and he regarded it for a few moments. "I'm pretty sure it works off intent. Focus on the stuff ya want, think about buying it, and it should be yours when you're done."

Matt caught the token out of the air as the smith threw it back, then poured his intent into it. Suddenly, he was flooded with dozens of information screens, apparently describing everything he had bought. It was all his now.

"Wow, I think I got it. Should be good," Matt said.

"Can I see that again? The credit token, or whatever ya call it," the old man asked. Matt tossed it over again, and he huffed. "Not even a tenth spent, and that's raiding the best stuff in here without holding back even a little. Not bad, boy. Not bad."

"Should I feel guilty about this? Spending this much on the treasures for just a single suit of armor, I mean."

"Absolutely not, boy. This stuff's been in here for years. They hoard it. Believe me, they're probably relieved ya are spending it on this and not anything else. Doesn't mess up the local economy that way."

As they turned to go ask for shopping bags, Matt had one last thought. Willing a bit more into the token, he made one last purchase, then followed the others out.

It had turned out the guards had something a bit better than a bag to give. They had a delivery service. Rather than carry everything back, Matt, Derek, and the old man decided to wait a little bit longer to have the guards cart everything back to the smith's house, which meant they had some time to burn.

That was fine because Matt had some money to burn. He had taken a bath that day, but he could already tell he was hooked on it. There was nothing stopping him and he had no desire to deprive himself of unlimited baths. After treating everyone to another bath and impromptu clothes washing, he treated everyone to dinner.

Derek and the old man were really able to pack away soup. They ordered a cauldron of it, which Matt thought was a joke until two large, cast-iron pots filled with steaming soup showed up at their table, accompanied by several good-sized loaves of bread. No one else batted an eye at the pots sticking out like an eyesore.

Matt also ordered a steak, which showed up on the bone, huge, and very rare. He wasn't trying to be gluttonous, but the soup still made him lightheaded when he ate it, while the steak was merely very, very good. He downed the entire steak, a loaf of the perfect, fresh bread, and a small cup of soup before they headed back to the smith's home to sort their booty.

"Put the skins over there. No, not the *hides*, ya idiots, the skins. The hides go over there. Sort them by weight. Not thickness. Weight. Use yar perception, and at least some brains. Good. Now . . ."

It was past dark when they got back to the smith's house, but he wasn't in the mood to wait around with all the material they now had. When Matt asked him if he would rather hold off until the morning, the smith mumbled something about how Matt would probably wait until the next morning to kiss a pretty girl.

"I don't understand what you just said, old man."

"And that's why yar still single."

The old man talked constantly while he worked, not only for the purpose of managing the work but also, Matt sensed, to get rid of the sheer nervous energy of being around so many crafting materials. It seemed like caffeine for him. Soon enough, they were down to the few metals they had purchased for the project, and one of them immediately caught his eye.

"What's that?" he asked, eyes stuck on it. "That wasn't on the list."

"Oh, that," Matt replied. "I just figured I owed you something for this. It seems like it's going to be a lot of work, and I did steal your title. It seemed like you wanted it, anyway."

"That, boy, is . . . I don't even know if there's a proper name for it. We only have a single block of it, stolen from a demon convoy when I was young. We called it demonic platinum. I've had my eye on it for . . . hell, for decades, at least. Let me see that token."

Matt tossed it to him, and he tossed it back after checking it for only a moment.

"Boy, this cost twice as much as the rest of this stuff combined. And they aren't gonna be happy ya took it, even if you did pay for it."

"You said it's been sitting around for decades, when it could have been used, right?"

The smith nodded.

"Then I don't care. And I bet they don't even notice until after I'm gone."

The blacksmith roared with laughter. "That they probably won't. But ya still can't do this. It's too much."

"It's not. You are taking it. If you want to pay me back, I bought a couple of metals that Derek thought were cool, too. Make him a sword, or something."

"Ya . . . Listen, boy, you know that restaurant we ate at? And the bathhouse? You could buy both those two stores ten times for what this block costs. Hell, ya could probably buy the laundress herself too, soaps and all. I can't take this."

"Then I'm going to chuck it into the sewer. I swear I will, old man. I'll bury it down there, under the muck, and it will never get used. For anything."

The old man considered this for a moment, before wordlessly walking over and taking the metal brick off the floor. He caressed it with his hand for a moment, before walking over and firing up the forge.

"Getting started already?" Matt said. It was getting pretty late, and he'd feel bad if the old man worked all night on his account. "I don't need the armor that bad, old man."

"Armor?" the old man said, while gazing lovingly at the metal. "Screw that, ya idiot. I'm getting started on my new hammer. Come back in the morning. I'll feed ya. We can get started on the work then." He hummed a little, pumping the forge up to its maximum heat and, for once, had the barest hint of a smile. It was the first time that Derek saw that face without it being accompanied by either him hitting someone or laughing very hard at one of his own jokes.

The boys shuffled out as he continued mumbling sweet nothings about the proper wood for the shaft of the hammer, and generally not noticing they were leaving at all. Derek and Matt stood there for a little while discussing lodging options for Matt, before deciding he'd just go get a room above a local tavern with a good reputation.

"Well, Derek, thanks for the day. It was nice. Couldn't tell you how much I needed the full anime experience. I mean, you've seen where I'm from."

"Yeah, I have. Not a lot of barmaids there, I guess."

"Not exactly, but yeah. I'll tell you about it sometime."

As they turned to part ways, there was a sudden bang on the forge, coupled with loud, audible singing from the smith. Whatever that metal was, it was putting him in a very good mood.

"Hey, Matt?" Derek said, laughing. "You know how you wanted a good set of armor?"

"Yeah?"

"I think you're gonna get it. I'm almost afraid of what he's gonna do with that new hammer. Good move."

The tavern room ended up being clean, beautiful, and furnished with the biggest bed Matt had ever seen in real life. He was pretty sure that this wasn't the room you got if you were a random traveler. As Derek said, word of his accomplishments seemed to be getting around.

But none of that was important. He would have been nearly as happy sleeping on the ground. What was important was that the room was private, with heavy stone walls and a heavy, well-fitting stone door. Nobody would hear anything said in the room, which was good. Earlier that day, Matt had gotten a bit of a fright from Lucy, and there hadn't been a good moment to work it out yet. He had enjoyed his time in town, but a little less knowing that Lucy was keeping quiet, especially because something was clearly nagging her.

"Lucy." Matt just jumped into it. He had learned that was the best way to have a hard conversation, or at least the best way he knew how to. "What was bothering you earlier today? And don't tell me it was nothing. I saw your face."

"It's not a big deal, Matt. You can just go to bed."

"Bullshit. Tell me. If I did something, I'm sorry. I know I've been ignoring you. I know that can't be fun. Is that it?"

"No. It's not that."

"Then what?" Matt wasn't quite shouting, but he was a little louder than usual, a little more forceful. Something told him not to let this one go.

"It's just . . ." Lucy gave up on holding back the truth, which Matt sensed with relief. "It's just that, after your haircut and shave, you looked a lot like you did when I first met you. Back on Gaia, on that log."

She sighed.

"And I hated that guy."

CHAPTER THIRTY

Coffee and Workouts

Matt knew that first impressions mattered. When he first met Lucy, she had told him that he should just slink off into the shadows and die. Thankfully, he had been old enough and maybe even wise enough to know she was a hurt kid, and that hurt kids don't always think things through. It wasn't a great first memory, but he had a lot of tools for minimizing the hurt and pain from her actions.

Her story was different. Her first memory of him was a guy showing up five years too late to prevent her from being all alone on a featureless planet with literally nothing for her. Then, that same guy used system-provided powers to force her to help, even if the help had consisted of answering a few questions before they eventually became friends.

At the time, and even now, Matt thought that what he did was necessary. He stood a good chance of dying without information. And he used the authority as little as possible. But she didn't have a choice in it. It was worse, somehow, that coercion. She couldn't have said no even if she wanted to, even if she was willing to brave death over it.

Yeah, it was before they knew the system was generally shitty. And, yeah, there were other excuses that Matt could invoke. But it was still a traumatic experience, and it made sense for her to still carry some of that baggage around with her.

"It's stupid. I know you aren't . . . that. What I thought you were at first. And I know it was dumb to try to let you die. But—"

Matt interrupted. "Lucy, listen. Some guy you don't know pops out of nowhere, and you tell him to get lost, and he won't, and he forces you to help him? That's a big deal. And from what you told me, the process itself was scary. You don't have to pretend like it wasn't a big deal. Whatever else it was, it was a big deal."

Lucy thought about that for a second. "See, that. Those words are different from what I thought you'd be like, you know? That doesn't come from someone who left me alone for five years on purpose. So, I think you remember, once I figured out you were a decent person, everything was better, or at least it wasn't the same kind of bad. And then you grew a beard, and your hair got scraggly, and it was like I was dealing with some new Matt, one that was more kind. I forgot."

"And then I got a haircut and shave, and the bad guy was back?"

"Something like that."

Matt knew this wasn't the kind of problem you could just solve, but he searched his brain for possible solutions anyway.

"I don't know if this would help, but I could try to find a . . . hair growth potion? This world must have bald people. You can't tell me they don't have one."

Lucy laughed. "No, no. It's fine. Well, it's not *fine*, but it was more of a shock than anything. It's just, I think, I was worried because you haven't talked to me much in the last couple of days." As Matt jumped to interrupt with reasonable excuses for why, Lucy put her hand up. "I know why, I know it's a good idea. It's just that it's always been us two. And now it's more people than that, and we can't even talk, and you've been having such a good time. I had just been worried it might make you forget what we were here for anyway."

Matt knelt. "Listen, Lucy. There's a lot of stuff that's been fun about the last few days. But it's also . . . it's pretend, somehow. I'm not from here. This isn't home to me. Whatever's happening here, it's for *now*."

Lucy nodded, pretending to be reassured.

"There's more, I'm not done. This is for now. Me? You and me? That's forever. I don't care what happens, what I have to do. You come first. And that means, even if I was going to die if I didn't do it, I promise you that I won't use any commands from now on. I don't even know if they work anymore. We aren't going to find out. And if you don't want me to, no more haircuts."

"Oh, no. We are going to get used to the haircuts. If nothing else, it's less of you to smell bad whenever that magic bathtub breaks."

After Lucy dug into her work, Matt stayed up just a little longer, pretending to sleep while he thought about everything. From what he had seen, the human parts of Ra'Zor were clean, well-organized, and nice. People seemed happy here, and he knew from his Earth experience that even if there was some dark stuff going on behind the scenes, most of the common people wouldn't have anything to do with it. The laundress was probably just that, a really good laundress who enjoyed her work. There was no reason to think it would be morally okay to punish the common people here.

Still, something was wrong. Brennan and Derek had both twigged to it. The Church was too in control, even if they were doing an objectively good job. They didn't just control all the non-reincarnator troops, they controlled most of the reincarnators as well. They didn't just control all that military might, either. They also controlled all the communications, and the market for the raw materials it took to build weapons and armor.

He had asked Derek about when he first encountered the Church, and the answer was that it was immediate. From the moment he had arrived, they had put him on a track. When they said he could fight, he was sent out. When they said he couldn't, he was put on house arrest. Brennan seemed to have a little more freedom than that, but he was the strongest fighter the Church had. The strongest fighter that the two knew about, at least.

And then there was the old man. He might be a crafter now, but there was no reason why a crafter should be as strong as he was. He had been a fighter once, and Matt couldn't even begin to imagine what he had been while he still held a combat class. Something had made him quit all that and apply his talents in other ways. It could have been enthusiasm for his work, and he did seem to like banging metals into the right shape. But Matt didn't think that was it. There was something else, behind the surface.

And they still hadn't gone to see these plinths. It was the one thing that still nagged at Matt. There was still time to do it, but it didn't make sense to go there before Matt was as well-armed and prepared as he could be. If they went, and these plinths were just little computers that handled minutiae, that was one thing. But if the worst was true, the best-case scenario ended with Matt banished to the demon wilderness. The worst-case ended with him dead.

He'd do it, too. Not just for Lucy. Hanging out with her this whole time had convinced him that there was something right, something natural, about the relationship between reincarnators and their guardians. But like anything else, there were people who would fuck that up for something ugly that promised them more personal power. If he had to screw up some other stuff to get that to stop, he would.

The next morning, Matt half-expected Derek to be waiting for him outside the tavern. He wasn't, so Matt took the opportunity to order breakfast, which the tavern apparently served. He left exactly what he'd have up to the waitress's judgement, and she didn't disappoint. She returned to the table with an entire loaf of bread, slightly hollowed out and filled with some kind of egg scrambled with cheese and pork-like meat.

Matt dug in right away. It was incredible. It only got better when the waitresses assumed rather than asked that he'd want coffee, bringing him a fresh cup of the real version of what he had previously only had from Ra'Zorian packets. The liquid was woodier than Earth coffee, but it didn't matter. It was miles above his instant coffee, and he was instantly hooked. And in that moment, he had an idea.

A quick query to the waitress brought the owner of the tavern to the table, very confused by the garbled message that the waitress had carried back. When he came to the table, Matt posed his two requests again, a bit calmer now that he had a few minutes to acclimate to the effects of the caffeine.

"I want to buy a big sack of this. I don't know how you measure it, but maybe this much?" Matt made a shape about one-and-a-half times the size of a basketball with his hands. "And I want some live seeds if I can get them. Something that I can plant in a few weeks, and let grow."

The owners looked thoughtful. "The grounds are easy enough. I can't sell you what we have here, but I can send a message to have my supplier to bring a little more. The live seeds are a little harder. They don't like spreading those around. Each farm has their own strain, you see. They protect them."

"I'm going off world shortly after that. You can ask . . . I don't know. Brennan? Artemis? The old blacksmith? They should confirm it. I won't be in competition with them. And I can pay."

"Off world? I've heard of that." He chewed his lip a little, thinking. "They might just, if it's true. It wouldn't be cheap, though. You sure you got the funds?"

Matt showed him his credit token, and explained what he had bought with the old man the day before. As soon as the owner realized that Matt was willing to pay at that level, if not quite that much, his eyes goggled a little. Especially when Matt indicated what he'd be willing to spend extra to give him a cut for making the transaction happen.

"And I'll need stuff to make the coffee with. Whatever works best for travel and is the least likely to break. A couple sets if you can. I'll pay for those, too."

"Son, I'll give you a bit of negotiating advice for free here. A deal this big? You don't pay for things like that. If they don't throw it in at that point, you don't want to do business with them anyway."

After waiting outside for Derek for a bit, Matt decided he knew the way to the old man's well enough that he probably could make the trip on his own. Even if he got lost, people probably knew which direction to point him in. The old man wasn't exactly living a stealthy, unnoticeable life. Matt wouldn't be surprised if it went beyond "people know where he lives" all the way to "he's a local landmark in and of himself."

He was halfway there when he ran into Derek anyway. Derek was dressed in lighter, more casual clothes than he generally went adventuring in, something like sports clothing would be back on Earth. He was breathing heavy, covered in sweat, and practically had skidded to a stop in front of Matt when he approached.

"Whoa, Derek. What is it? What happened to you?" Matt asked, concerned.

"Oh, this?" Derek asked, mopping sweat from his brow with the lip of his shirt. "I'm just working out. I have to now. It's part of how my class works. I don't get stats unless I push my limits all the time." He heaved a big sigh, then sat on the ground, rubbing his calves. "And it hurts, Matt. I have to make it hurt at least as bad as hard exercise back on Earth did, or it doesn't work."

"How much longer do you have to go? I was thinking about going to the old man's right now."

"I think I'm done, actually. Two hours is about enough for my morning workout. Anything more than that and it stops paying off. I'll go longer in the evening as long as it doesn't break anything."

CHAPTER THIRTY-ONE

Dust Mask of the Barren Lands

The old man's house smelled like fire and sounded like mayhem, even from the outside. The hammer blows they had heard yesterday had been loud, but they had also been at a sedate, controlled rhythm. Things had changed. The hammer blows came harder, louder, more frequently, and at a pace so disordered it sounded almost random. The chimney, which had been gently smoking yesterday, was now pouring smoke out at a pace that would have made Matt think the house was on fire if the black clouds were coming from anywhere else but the smokestack itself.

All the noise was dwarfed by the smith himself, though. Above every other sound layered a louder, more constant barrage of cursing, cries of dismay, and roars of apparent triumph. Whatever was going on in that house, it was like a one-man battle, and it was hard to say if he was winning or losing.

"Do you think we should go in?" Matt said. "It sounds crazy in there right now."

"Honestly? It's probably fine. He probably wouldn't even notice us. But I still somehow get the feeling that if anything goes wrong . . ."

"The whole workshop will explode?"

"Something like that, yeah."

Matt and Derek decided not to tempt fate, taking a seat on a nearby bench to wait out the storm. Eventually, the banging started to die down, as did the cursing. The hammer *pings* became much more regular, sounding out at regular intervals before dying out completely. Whatever the smith had been up to, it looked like it was now over.

Derek stood up from the bench, straightening his workout clothes and stretching his sore muscles. "Looks like it's done. The old man never quits in the middle of a project. I'm guessing he was up all night working on your stuff. We should go in as soon as we can now. If we don't catch him in the next couple of minutes, he'll fall asleep. And there's no waking him up once he's asleep, believe me."

Matt stood up as well. "Is there any etiquette I should follow about accepting the items? I'm assuming the old man doesn't deal well with complaining."

"You'd be surprised. Whining for a bad reason? He'll chuck his hammer at you. But if you really don't like something about the armor, and it's for a good reason? The old man is a professional, Matt. He'll fix it, no questions asked." Derek grinned. "But that's not gonna happen here."

"Why not?"

"Matt, the person that just crafted your armor has been using the same hammer for about as long as I've been here. Doesn't let anybody touch it. I'm pretty sure he has a secret name he calls it when nobody is around. He gets little scraps of all sorts of stuff all the time, so the fact that he never replaced it with something better means there probably just wasn't anything better to replace it with. Whatever that metal was that you bought for him, it's something special. Combining that with an all-nighter and the ingredients you gave him? There's probably no better armor on the planet. I'm serious."

Matt and Derek opened the door to the workshop and entered cautiously. The noise had died down, but given the row they had heard from the street only a few minutes before, there was no harm in being careful. It turned out to be unnecessary. The inside of the shop was almost as silent as a tomb, if it weren't for the crackle of slowly dying embers in the forge. It was dark and still enough in the shop that it took Matt a moment to actually spot the old smith standing with his back to them near the rear of the shop. He wasn't moving. And it was too dark to see what was happening, but whatever he was gazing at seemed to have his full attention.

"Should we go back there?" Matt whispered. "He seems pretty into whatever he's doing."

"I don't know, Matt. I've never seen him quiet like this."

Suddenly, the old man seemed to become aware of their presence, wheeling around on his heels and tensing up before he realized who it was.

"Matt! Derek!" he roared. "I was just finishing up."

"We know, old man," Derek said, grinning. "It sounded like a battle in here."

"I tell ya, it almost was. Some of those materials fought back. I spent the whole night keeping demon bones from exploding on the anvil, banging them into shape before they could warp into something different. Stretching tendons into strings that were never meant to be stretched. Had to keep on my toes, or ya would have found a crater instead of my shop when ya showed."

He moved slightly to the side, turning up a dial on what turned out to be a magic lamp. As he did, Matt saw several pieces of jet-black armor, highlighted with dark-blue stripes, laid out on the table like a body at rest. Jet-black almost wasn't the right word for the color that comprised the bulk of the color of the armor. The pieces seemed darker than that, somehow, like the black color he knew before was a less solid, more vibrant imitation.

"Oh, that's beautiful. That looks incredible."

"Thank ya. That's boots, pants, leg guards, arm guards, chest piece, and a helmet. If ya call it a helmet. It's mostly leather, not that it lost anything in the deal." He ran his finger over one of the shin guards, possessively. "It's my best work. That hammer ya helped me make is . . . special. Makes choices for itself sometimes, I think."

Matt blinked. "Is that . . . normal? For a hammer?"

"Every hammer is different, but there's nothing I'd call normal about this one." He waved Matt and Derek closer, moving out of the way. "Come look, boy."

Matt didn't have to be asked twice. He almost rushed the countertop to grab at the boots, only to be stopped at the last second by the smith's big arm. As Matt watched, the smith grabbed another handful of the surveillance-prevention dust and chucked it into the furnace.

"One last thing before ya look, boy. At high levels, the smith class gets funny. Besides materials, design, workshop and skill, the class starts to look at who the gear is for, not just what it's intended to do. Some of the descriptions come out . . . funny, I guess. Simple. Almost like the armor is hiding what it's for. It could be the hammer, could be coincidence, or could be something about ya. And whatever was in that hammer, it put something into this armor with every strike. It's still better than what I had, much better. But I don't think it will ever do what it was last night. Like it was making something special. Just wanted ya to know, so it didn't catch you surprised. It might not be the kind of thing you want to talk about."

Matt nodded. He walked over to the armor, placing his hand on the chest plate. An information screen popped up instantly. He quickly went from piece to piece, reading every description available.

Chest Plate of the Invader

Made of various supremely rare materials and refined by a master smith, the Chest Plate of the Invader exceeds the standards of normal in favor of protection far beyond what the average adventurer requires.

The chest plate offers supreme protection against cutting damage, excellent protection against stabbing, abrasive, and blunt force damage, and moderate protection against most elemental attacks. The chest plate projects these qualities to all other pieces of armor worn, but only in proportion to their quality relative to its own.

Since every piece in the set came from the same quality of ingredients made by the same smith, Matt suspected that meant that each armor piece would carry nearly all the protection of the chest piece.

Boots of the Survivor

The Boots of the Survivor speak a tale of overcoming a history of hardship and sorrow. Except in extreme conditions, they will not show signs of wear. They are, in every aspect, designed to outlive their owner, even considering the exceptional survivability that the owner has proved to possess.

The boots offer a 20 percent movement speed buff outside of combat and a 10 percent increase in footwork speed inside of it. They also provide a small chance of negating the balance-ruining aspects of attacks meant to compromise the wearer's footing.

Bunker Arm Guards

The Bunker Arm Guards are designed to conform to the forearms of the wearer. However, they act like a small shield, projecting their physical presences outwards at all times and creating a field with a high percentage of the stopping power of the guards themselves. Damage absorbed by the field will, if applicable, damage the guards as if they themselves had been hit.

Once a day, the arm guards can be activated to create a field of defense around the user. This field lasts only one second, but can endure an amount of damage equal to that necessary to destroy the arm guards themselves, were they directly attacked. After using this ability, a full day must pass before using it again, during which the extended blocking range of the arm guards is disabled.

Keeping his footing was huge, the speed buff was mammoth at this point, and keeping his footwork intact during enemy attacks would have been useful as recently as the day before. The arm guards were even more astounding, amounting to small, improved versions of his expandable shield that he was constantly forgetting to expand. Now he didn't have that problem anymore. And the fact that it came with an ace-in-the-hole emergency block was icing on the cake.

The leg guards turned out to be called "Bunker Shin Guards," and as the name implied, they provided a similar defensive situation as the arm guards. They didn't come with the emergency shield feature or projection, but made up for that with sheer defensive capacity. Matt suspected that in terms of resisting direct attack, his shins were now the best-protected part of his body.

> *Wanderer's Leggings*
>
> The Wanderer's Leggings were built for flexibility in combat, in more than one way. While providing excellent protection, they will flex with the user well past most plausible levels of contortion. They also provide the user flexibility with the capability of instantly delivering any non-weapon object stored in the user's pockets to their hands.

At this point, the set was beginning to be almost suspiciously suited to Matt's needs. He'd ask the old man about it in a moment, but for now, he had one last item to check.

> *Dust Mask of the Barren Lands*
>
> The Dusk Mask of the Barren Lands serves several purposes besides that described by its title. Designed to fit under a hood, it provides excellent protection from physical damage, filters potentially harmful inhalants, and is woven closely enough to block most forms of light and some forms of radiation.
>
> When the user wills it, the mask will retract into a collar form to allow for conversation, and will return to its normal, full-coverage form when needed.

The mask was nothing special, but that was judging by Matt's usual needs. Those tended to change pretty quickly. It would allow him to go harder in battle while better protected, and even make some skills like Pocket Sand work better in more situations.

Overall, the entire set was like a defensive stance in and of itself, covering many contingencies without Matt actually having to do anything to get the benefit.

It was more than he had hoped, and much better than anything he could have got through the Gaian system, given the mana starvation the planet was still experiencing. The only shame was that he'd probably have to leave it behind when he left, but he tried not to be too down about that. While he was here, it was more likely than not that the set of armor would end up a lifesaver.

CHAPTER THIRTY-TWO

Phoning for Help

I see what you mean about the descriptions. Very minimal," Matt said. "We're still under the communication block?"

"We are. Thought ya might have something to say."

Matt pulled a stool away from the wall and sat down. "Without going into details, more than a few of these armor pieces have names and functions that indicate they know about my past. I don't think I have to distrust you, since I don't have any idea how you'd even know. But how does the armor know?"

The old man shrugged. "It's one of the mysteries of crafting. Sometimes the hammer knows things ya don't, like it's pounding history into the piece. I burned a question token on it once. The system said it didn't know. Damn waste."

Derek's eyes bugged out. "A question token? Where'd you manage to get that?"

"Don't ask."

"What's a question token?" Matt hadn't heard of them, and at his question, the old man threw in a few more pinches of powder over the fire. He probably had a bit of time.

"Ultra-rare item. Can't buy them, can't make them, the system seems to award them at random, but there's a tiny chance of one dropping even when you're doing big things. Historic things. If you use it, the system has to answer any question it knows the answer to." Once again, Derek was surprising Matt with the amount of knowledge that he head. Access to arcane knowledge didn't seem like his cup of tea, but it apparently was.

"Any question?" Matt asked.

"Close. Ya can't ask things like 'what should I do,' or anything that's about what decision ya should make. But ya can ask it something about the world, something it can answer with a simple fact. Where treasure is buried, where enemy weak spots are. That sort of thing."

"And you burned it on a crafting question?" Derek asked.

The old man shrugged again. "It was a more peaceful time. We were winning, then."

Matt didn't know if he could trust the old man absolutely, but nothing about this seemed suspicious, at least to the extent the old man understood it. Matt wished he could have gotten a look at the exact wording the system had used. It seemed odd it wouldn't know about something that was under its purview.

That said, it was time to put on the armor. Matt wasn't immune to cool shit, and this was the coolest armor he had ever seen. Gone was any jealousy he had hidden over Artemis's cool ranger gear or Derek and Brennan's light armor. He didn't even have to ask to know this was better. He could almost feel the special boiling off it.

Luckily, the walking-around clothes the laundress had given him would fit under the armor just fine. Matt slipped off his boots and cloak, and put on the pants, chest piece, leg guards, and arm guards.

"One last thing, boy." The old man stopped Matt before he put on his helmet. Instead, he fished around in a drawer before coming up with a small slip of parchment. "Almost forgot. Part of the service. Once you put on that last piece, it marks you as the owner. Makes it easier to sort things out if there's a dispute over ownership, but woulda kept me from doing this."

He slapped the parchment down on the chest piece, which suddenly grew hot as the enchantment etched in. "All-purpose enchantment. It helps clean and mend the equipment, and makes it a bit easier to get on and off. Had it sitting around for another project that went wrong. It's expensive, but means I don't have to tell ya how to take care of the armor. The chest piece should spread it around. Now, you slap on that helmet, and it's yours. Fully and truly."

Matt grinned. That fit his life just fine. With a sweep, he pulled the mask down over his face, completing the set. And then, suddenly, he was burning to death. With an alert noise, a system window popped up in an unexpected color.

Ding!

> Gaian Authority activated. Modifying enchantment . . .
>
> Enchantment modification complete. Previous function maintained. Equipment set bonus created.
>
> Effects: Soulbound. Equipment Descriptions Hidden. For purposes of transportation, the entire equipment set (helmet, chest piece, leg and arm guards, pants) acts as if it is a part of the wearer's body.

Matt read the description over and over. He had to, if only to take his mind off the screaming. It was several moments before he remembered the screaming was his, driven by a burning sensation that drilled all the way down to his bones. Then, suddenly, it was over.

"My god, boy. That was a hell of a thing. Ya alright? I've never seen a set bind like that."

"Matt, holy shit. What the hell? Can't even put clothes on without causing a major calamity?" Lucy was pissed, and not aiming her rage very well. Matt didn't blame her much. It had been a busy couple of days.

"Nothing's wrong. Just . . . that interference still up, old man?"

The old man nodded.

Matt gasped in some more air, trying to forget the pain of that process as quickly as possible. "Something from home, that I didn't think followed me here, messed with the process. Soulbound the equipment, says it hid the descriptions. I have no idea how."

Lucy gasped. "Gaian system shit?"

"How do ya mean, followed you here? That's not something most things can do, son."

"It's . . . I mean, it might be something that's a bit more connected to me than you'd think, I guess. I don't really know how it works. But I hope it doesn't do it again. That was horrible."

"I'd wager it was if what ya say is true. Soul binding is something only the system is supposed to do. Not exactly easy work. Some demon magic brands the soul. I've seen it happen. Ugly stuff, that." The old man shuddered at some old memory. "But enough. Looks like you got something out of it, anyway. And the dust is almost done. Anything else to say?"

"Just thank you." Matt sat up, then stood, testing the armor as he moved around a bit in it. "It feels incredible."

"Ya like that? Just wait. It's about to get better." The old man reached behind a bench, extracting a thinner, lighter steel rod, one that was a little shorter, faster, and more wicked in all respects than what he had used before.

"It's time for testing."

The system instance was almost completely out of good will for this particular invader. First, instead of causing chaos and mixing the pot the way that the system instance had hoped, he had almost done more to maintain balance than to change it. He had nullified the effect of the cursed hearts almost completely, countering the loss of a colony with the loss of a major demon trading hub and an entire invading army.

If that wasn't enough, he was breaking rules left and right as he did it. That shovel he carried was almost a complete mystery to the instance. Maybe if the system knew how it was made, he could figure out what it did. But as it was, the instance could see it, observe it in almost the same way a human would, and even interact with it in the smallest fashions. But he didn't *know* anything about it. He certainly didn't know why it could cut through force fields like nothing and also ignore mana-based defenses in other beings.

It wasn't just that the shovel did things it shouldn't do. It shouldn't exist at all.

Then, before the system could properly understand or register the absolute monstrosity of an armor set that the old man had made, he played some kind of trick and blocked the system's vision with what amounted to a local mana dust storm. And now, when the invader and his friends had exited the building, the armor had gone completely invisible to the system. No description. No nothing. It was like it was scanning the invader's own skin.

Worse, he knew the invader wasn't going to talk about it. He had asked in several ways, all with escalating levels of unsubtle hints. The asshole had ignored him, and hadn't been particularly good at concealing why.

The good news was that all of this hiding was about to come to an end. The shovel might not interact with mana, but almost everything the old man put effort into did. Once the armor was working with atmospheric mana, he'd be able to see how it flowed and analyze what it did. There was a lot that the system could glean from that, if he was willing to put in the work. The system might be lazy, but he wouldn't sit still and watch a catastrophe waiting to happen like this, and he'd be damned if this human would beat him.

"Hoo, good job there, boy. You kept on your feet."

Matt didn't feel like he was doing a good job. The old man now knew every one of the tricks he felt comfortable revealing, and was running a whole new set of tactics to counter everything Matt could do. He had figured out the motionless requirement of charge attack somehow, and when Matt tried that, he'd literally get stuff chucked at him until he had to stop.

And he did have to. The old man threw hard.

When he didn't charge, the old man changed his tactics to account for the shovel's mana-ignoring abilities by just never letting it get close to touching him. He moved the rod like a spear, keeping a gap with Matt most of the time and evading like a feather on the wind whenever the distance closed.

Matt had slipped some ash into his pocket before they left the workshop, but even that didn't help. The old man's gloating about him keeping his feet came after he threw a handful of ash directly in his eyes, which must have hurt. Any other opponent would have flinched, or recoiled, or anything. The old man didn't. He just tanked the pain, finished his strike, and hit Matt hard enough in the chest to cave in a tank.

Even the fact that Matt didn't fall down was mostly due to the smith's work.

The armor didn't block everything, but it blocked much, much more of the strike than made sense. It wasn't just transferring the energy to non-lethal surface areas, it was also negating some of it away. And the follow-up strike had hurt, but hadn't unbalanced him at all. The boots saw to that.

Could Matt fight the old man on even terms if he showed all his cards? Maybe. He still had some neat inertia-bending talents he hadn't used, and some ideas for using the pit as a sort of mobile trap that might slow his opponent down. But he had no interest in that at the moment. This was about putting the armor through its paces, which meant getting hit was almost the point. And, near as he could tell without throwing up an entire force field and burning his daily charge of power, the armor was doing its job wonderfully.

If the system was peeved before, now it was throwing a full tantrum. It could see mana disappear into the armor, and it could even see it get expelled in some cases. But what it couldn't see was what in the fuck was happening between those two points. It was like a curtain was between it and the armor, blocking it from knowing how the effects were happening. Did it have guesses? Sure. But without seeing the actual process, there was no way for it to calculate exactly what was going on, much less to extrapolate what the problem with the armor's visibility was in the first place.

And that, of all things, was the final straw. The mana on this planet was its own. When a mage cast a spell or a tank nullified a strike using it, it was with the system's blessing and guidance. Did it take a cut? It did, and it deserved the percentage for keeping the balance. That was the whole point. Now this asshole was coming in, taking what wasn't his, and screwing with the mana in some way.

That wouldn't stand. Not in the system's house. And finally, terrifyingly, it decided to do something it really, really didn't want to do.

It phoned headquarters.

CHAPTER THIRTY-THREE

Church Plinths

"One last thing for ya two, before ya go." The old man had finished whaling on Matt for a while, having thoroughly proved how good the armor was by subjecting Matt to dozens of attacks that probably would have otherwise killed him without protection. By the end of the fight, he had gotten used to the old man's speed again and got in a few hits of his own, but nothing like what he had taken. He wasn't really injured, but he had been rattled around so much his bones now felt loose.

"Something else? Old man, this is plenty." Despite being beat up, Matt loved the armor. It felt like part of him, which he supposed in some ways it actually was now. The old man had pointed him in the direction of a tailor who could sell him a couple of suits of underclothes he said would make the set feel even better, but more comfort was hard to imagine.

"Naw, this is important. Wait here." The old man vanished towards the house, coming back with a few paper-wrapped packets, one long and relatively thin, and one more or less square. He tossed the longer of the two to Derek.

"This one is for ya. There were some scraps left over from the project. I thought Matt here wouldn't mind if I put 'em to use." He glanced at Matt, who nodded in approval. Derek immediately ripped open the package, revealing a sheathed sword that he immediately uncovered. Where his previous sword was a pretty basic, long, and two-sided number, this new sword was bent slightly forward, and larger at the far end than the base.

"All the weight's at the end on that one. Ya already got a good enough sword for standard work, but ya can never go wrong having a chopper, especially if ya keep getting stronger. Good for taking off arms, or breaking armor."

Derek's eyes focused in on the information screen for the sword, or at least seemed to. What he saw there must have impressed him, judging by his widening eyes and gasp.

"This one's for ya Matt. Ya were right, boy, that I can't do anything to that shovel ya got. But that doesn't mean I can't do anything for it at all."

He gently tossed the paper package at Matt, who caught it. His boots activated just in time to keep it from knocking him on his ass. Whatever was in there was heavy. Ignoring the old man's laughter, he ripped the paper off, revealing a sheet of what looked like little weight plates sewn down to a thick layer of leather with heavy demon-tendon thread. On one side of the sheet were straps that appeared to correspond to fasteners on the other side. It looked almost like leg weights.

"What is this, old man? Need to slow me down so you don't lose the next round?"

"It's for the shovel, ya idiot. Now that ya took my title, weight is a friend to ya. Won't feel any heavier in the hand with that on, but it will make ya shovel pack a punch. I couldn't use any of that on armor. It's just heavy, and strong. And anything that could break it would probably break ya first."

Matt strapped it to his shovel, and gave it a few swings. The old man was right, it didn't feel much different, despite the earlier impressions. A large stone from the wall sat in the training grounds, not yet cleaned up from the old man's crash. Matt brought the shovel down on it, blade first.

It broke in half, like a cut diamond.

"Thanks, old man. I'll make good use of this."

"I want to see this church. The guardian plinths there, particularly. They interest me. Where is it?" Matt was trying his best to act nonchalant.

"Sure!" Derek said, not seeming to notice anything was amiss. "I don't have anything better to do."

"Sweet Moses, Matt. You are lucky as hell that he's not very smart. Remind me that 'spy' isn't in our skill set, if it ever comes up," Lucy chatted from the side.

Matt ignored Lucy, even though it didn't feel good to lie to Derek. It was their best option, and he felt sure she knew it. Derek led them towards the church, which so far Matt had only seen from a distance. It was tall, with sloping sides that cut more steeply towards a point near the top. Somehow, probably through magic, the Ra'Zorians had managed to make it look like it was carved out of one single, gigantic piece of stone.

Matt was beginning to realize, though, that the size and expense of a building wasn't the primary way which Ra'Zorians used to relay that a building was important. Instead, they used the empty space around a building to give that impression. Given that their cities could only safely grow as big as they could build walls for them, the real estate inside was at a premium. So when the square court sat in the middle of a wide-open space, it instinctively signaled power and importance. They had even built a mosaic on the ground, just so that there wouldn't be confusion about how much of that space belonged specifically to the court. And it was a lot.

This church, which signified the headquarters of the Church's religious power and the most significant building regarding their relationship with reincarnation, had even more space. It was surrounded not by stone, but by grass, flowers, hedges, and general greenery, all separated from the outside, non-church world by a tall, white, wooden fence.

And within that fence were plinths. Dungeons weren't a major part of the Ra'Zorian life if they existed at all. Matt, at least, hadn't seen any. But on Gaia, he had become very familiar with them. If there was one thing he could identify, it was a system-built plinth. And these were, if not directly owned by the system, at least one of its designs.

On top of each plinth was a panel similar to what Matt was already familiar with from the dungeons. Almost all of them around the edges of the area were lit, but the closer the plinth was to the church itself, the more likely it was dead. The inner circle of plinths had no lights at all. Where the other plinths were almost supernaturally clean and clear of plants, those near the center ranged from clean to dusty or even dirty, some even having moss or vines climbing the sides.

A middle-aged official of the Church had been milling around the grounds suspiciously close to them since they had arrived, half-pretending to not watch them. Seeing Matt's interest in the dead plinths, she abandoned any pretense of hiding his purpose and approached.

"I'd be glad to tell you the significance of the lights, if you wish," she said. Matt looked over. He wasn't altogether comfortable with a member of the Church being present for this, but couldn't see a good way to get rid of her. It was their house, after all. He nodded in reluctant assent.

"These plinths each represent guidance. For each reincarnator that arrives to our planet, we erect another, charging it with holy power. For the lifetime of these heroes, the plinths stand ready to offer information, advice, and direction regarding a hero's class and choices. Those that are lit represent a hero somewhere in our world, working to protect our people from the ever encroaching tide of demons."

"And those that are dark?" Matt asked, suspecting he already knew the answer.

"Those are the memorials of heroes that have fallen in defense of our settlements, our border, or even our capital. They fell at the hands of the demons."

"Never of anything else? Disease? Old age?

"Sir, I believe any disease capable of taking down a reincarnator would be part and parcel with demonic attack in the first place. And ours is a dangerous world. If any of your kind have survived to old age here, I am unaware of it."

Matt didn't want to tip his hand, but as long as he had this acolyte present, he figured it couldn't hurt to fill in the gaps of his knowledge.

"On my world, we have plinths like these. But we associate them with functions of the system."

"Ah!" The woman's eyes lit up, apparently glad to have found someone with any kind of knowledge related to the nuts-and-bolts operation of her area of expertise. "Yes, you are correct. The plinths themselves are system-provided technology, ready to be invested with power and knowledge suitable to a variety of purposes. We use it solely for this one function, however."

"And the power you invest them with? System-provided as well?"

The woman smiled, in a restrained, polite way. "I'm afraid the details of that are a bit beyond my position, sir. Before the arrival of each reincarnator, the leader of our Church himself foresees their coming, and prepares each plinth himself." As Matt and the woman talked, she led him further into the garden. "Alas, even our leader's foresight isn't infallible. He didn't complete your plinth until *after* your arrival, and even now, it has failed to light."

"My . . . plinth? Mine?" Matt asked.

The woman smiled pleasantly, sweeping her hand down towards a plinth mixed in with the others on the more lit up outer side of the yard.

"Shit. Matt, we need to get away from that NOW. Right now. Something's wrong," Lucy said, eyes wide. "It's pulling on me."

Matt didn't question it. He dashed away from the plinth, burning most of his stamina to get Spring-Fighter moving.

"Is that better, Lucy?" he asked, before glancing down and realizing she wasn't there. Somehow, despite him moving so far, she had maintained her current position.

"MATT! Get back here! I'm stuck!"

Matt ran back as quickly as possible. The churchwoman looked profoundly confused.

"Is there trouble? I understand reincarnators can be a bit jumpy, but . . ." She suddenly glanced at the plinth, then smiled widely and clapped her hands. "Oh, would you look at that! Your plinth is coming online, after all!"

It was true. The plinth was beginning to light.

"Matt, I don't feel good," Lucy said. "Something's happening."

To Matt's horror, Lucy was growing fainter. She wasn't see-through yet, but the color of her face and hair was growing ever so slightly washed out. He reached for the woman reflexively, grabbing her collar and pulling her close.

"Turn it off. Now," he snarled.

"I . . . I can't!" she said. "It's an automatic process! I don't know how!"

"Matt, it's pulling me in. I can . . . I can feel it. Do something," Lucy said, weakly. Her eyes were unfocused, and her voice was oddly calm despite containing a note of panic.

"I'll do it myself, then." Matt raised his shovel overhead, and charged.

"Sir, that won't work! It's a system item! I don't even know why you'd want to hurt it!"

"Bullshit, it won't. I'll make it work."

Matt brought the shovel down with the full force of three or four seconds' worth of charge. It hit the plinth and stopped. And for a moment, it seemed not to do anything at all. Then the whole world turned to light and sound. When Matt's head cleared, he found himself twenty feet away, flat on his back, his armor showing damage for the first time. Luckily, he had been fully kitted up because even with his armor on, the explosion shaved off a good quarter of his health.

CHAPTER THIRTY-FOUR

Holder of the Shield

Meanwhile, where the plinth originally stood was now replaced by a ten-foot crater. The church lady was a good deal more injured than Matt, but appeared to have survived thanks to a magic shield she had put up. It had cut the damage enough to let her live, if not without scratches and bumps.

"What was that? Why would you do that?" she screamed, standing up from the grass and brushing herself off. "Are you insane?"

Matt had zero time for her. He looked around frantically for Lucy. Luckily, he didn't have far to look. She was standing by him, hugging her own chest and shivering.

"Matt, awesome work," she said, her voice quavering. "But we need to get out of here. Now."

Matt agreed. "Derek, come on. We're going."

Derek, who had been on a boredom-to-mind-shattering-surprise emotional journey over the last few moments, followed meekly. It took him half a minute to find his bearings, at which point he freaked out.

"Matt, what the fuck?" he yelled as they walked down the road. "Why in the hell? You attacked that plinth. Hell, you even hurt that church lady. She's boring, but she's nice. Why?"

Matt sighed. "Okay, listen. You know how I occasionally talk to someone who isn't here, and you think I'm crazy?"

"I wouldn't say crazy . . ."

"It's fine. Just listen. That's a real person. I'm a reincarnated hero. Reincarnated heroes get guardians. From what I understand, that's true in almost every world.

The system goes to the guardians, convinces them to help, and they help. They are full, actual people. Free will and everything. Following so far?"

"I guess." Derek shifted uncomfortably.

"I get you don't believe me because you've never heard of it before. You have these plinths. They do a lot of the same things. But just now, I walked by one they said they had built for me, even though I never asked for one. And it tried to eat my guardian. Absorb it. Whatever."

"So you blew it up?"

"Would you let a pillar eat Brennan or Artemis?"

"Point taken. But, listen, accidents happen. Why are you still freaked out?"

"First, because that wasn't an accident. No chance. Nobody tells me about this thing until I get in striking range of it? That's a trap. That's them trying to take a hostage. Second, think about it. They say those things run off, what, holy magic? Holy power?"

"Yeah, that. They charge them."

"So why does it need to eat my guardian? Why would it even try?"

Derek went quiet for a minute.

"I could have had a fairy sidekick?"

"Something like that. Mine is just a little girl who cusses a lot."

"Holy shit," Derek said. "I feel so robbed."

It wasn't hard to set plans in motion when the plans weren't very complex, very long, or even very good. Matt gave Derek a few instructions. Derek promised to execute them, giving Matt only two things in return. The first, and arguably the most important, was trust. Matt didn't expect that. Derek believed him, understood that something was wrong, and even though he wasn't ready to topple society with him, was willing to try to figure things out.

The second thing he gave him was directions to the pope's house.

"This is bullshit," Lucy said.

"Yeah, I agree. I was really, really hoping it wouldn't come to this."

"No, I mean, that, yeah. But look over there." She pointed to a manhole cover as they passed it at incredible speeds. "This is the same direction we went in the sewers the other day. Exactly a straight shot. We could have just come in there, and spent a half hour less looking at turds and fighting rot-rats."

Matt was moving so fast that the couriers didn't catch up with him until he was actually climbing the stairs to the leader's residence. Matt was beginning to believe that the courier was a specific speed build because even moving with his boot-enhanced agility, the courier was able to get in front of him and cut him off.

"Reincarnator Matt! Your presence is requested and required at . . ."

"The leader's residence? Where I already am?"

For once, the courier stopped yelling, looking slightly defeated. "Well, yes, but . . ."

Matt swept the courier gently out of the way with his arm. "You still have to say it or they get mad. I get it. Jobs."

"Yeah. Jobs."

A few short minutes later, Matt found himself in front of a man announced as High Counselor Alder, Leader of the Ra'Zorian Church and Chief Authority of the Human Territories. If that was all a bit much, so was the person. Rather than the short pudgy man in ill-fitting robes and a huge hat Matt had imagined, this was a wall of steel in finely tailored robes in a giant hat, one that he wore with such confidence that it almost worked.

Seated at a large stone table elevated several feet above the floor on which Matt stood, he bore down.

"Reincarnator Matt, I welcome you. You look troubled." Matt was nowhere near the podium from which Alder was speaking, but the sound was like someone screaming in his ear. In the large, all-stone room, his voice boomed out and echoed like thunder. Matt didn't think it was a magical effect, either. He was just loud, projecting in the way well-trained singers did during performances.

"What a fucker. He knows, Matt. You can tell he knows." Lucy was fully over being shaken up by her experience with the plinth and had moved on to being fully pissed off.

"You could say that. I trust you heard about my experience at the church?" Matt said, affecting the same calm, measured tone the man was using. If he was going to be bullshitted at, he felt justified returning a bit of bullshit as well.

"Yes, I did, at that. It's very unfortunate, and I sincerely apologize. I never expected that something I intended as a pleasant surprise, a gift of thankfulness for what you'd done, to end up like this."

"Oh, I'm sure. It being activated based on proximity to me is quite a coincidence. And that in a world without guardians, it would somehow be capable of attacking mine, in a way I could only counter because of a very, very specific skill." Matt didn't feel the need to be honest about just what had allowed him to counter the attack. "Quite the coincidence indeed."

Alder regarded him coolly for a moment before seeming to come to a decision he found distasteful.

"You may not know this, but we keep records, here." Alder spoke in a different tone now, one that was missing the smarmy calm-them-down-without-helping-them customer service tone from before. "And all our records of the earliest reincarnators are records of chaos and disorder. They would come, obtain absurdly high levels of power in a frighteningly short amount of time, and use it as they saw fit. Some of them helped. Some of them were a wash, causing damage as they did their work, but doing at least nearly as much good as was needed to balance it. Others were disasters."

"And so you decided to enslave guardians? Living things, packed into shoeboxes and forced to do your bidding?" Matt was pissed now. He could already see where this was going, and he hated it.

"It was necessary." The counselor sneered down at Matt, clearly unused to people willing to disagree with him openly. "It would have been bad enough if they kept their own counsel, but they had support in what they did. Company, even when we threatened to deny them ours. Knowledge, even when we attempted to hide it. We had to bring them to heel, and then the system offered us a way to do just that."

"That's horrific. You have to know it's horrific. You have to know it's wrong." Matt motioned to a line of guards who had stood silently by a wall ever since he had entered. "They won't tell you, and some of them might not even know. But you know. You didn't get this far by being stupid. You know what you're doing."

"I do, you fool! And why should I think it wrong?" Alder boomed again, louder than he had been before. "The reincarnators were sent *for us*. For protection. For our use. This made them useful. It brought them under control. Our control, where they belonged. It brought balance."

That word meant something. Matt had heard it before.

"Balance? Not victory? I noticed this war has been going on for a while."

"Balance is survival. It's stability. It's guaranteed to us. So long as we play by certain rules."

"And there it is," Lucy said. "He really is an evil pope. Brennan and Derek called it."

"Yup. A real asshole. I didn't think they really existed like this."

High Counselor Alder apparently did not like being cut out of the conversation, and didn't react well. His surprisingly huge fist came down on the table in front of him, splintering a large section of it into shards of stone and dust.

"Do you really fear me that little, Matt? The ruler of a half a world? Do you really think I have no recourse with which to address slights?" He stood, walking around the table, and pointed at Matt with some kind of short scepter.

"I'm willing to give you a choice. A peaceful one. You will give us your guardian, and we will hold it in trust for you. If you decide to do exactly what we say, no more and no less, for exactly as long as we say, then we will consider sending her back with you wherever you came from. Whenever we, and the system, deem it proper."

Like all assholes, he took silence as an invitation to keep speaking. "And you will do it while holding back no secrets. Your skills? You will explain them to us, in detail. Your weapon? You will explain to us how you obtained it, and how to counter its unique properties. We will know everything you know now, and everything you learn as you learn it, or you will forfeit any claim on what we've promised."

"Don't do it, Matt," Lucy said, defiant. "He's just like the system. Everyone does just fine, so long as he gets what he wants."

"Yeah, I think we'll pass. Don't worry, Lucy. I never even considered it." Matt hefted his shovel on his shoulder lightly, not feeling a single ounce of the weight the old man had strapped to it. "I can think of at least one counteroffer we could make, anyway."

Matt sprang towards the counselor. If he was proposing hostage taking with Lucy, Matt was pretty sure he could counter and do an awful lot with a captive as highly valued as the leader of an entire country. He was halfway there before any of the guards' reflexes kicked in, but by then it was far too late for anyone to catch him. The only thing that could keep him from getting to the ass-pope was if there was a literal force field between them. It was unfortunate that it turned out there was just that.

Matt bounced off the invisible wall hard, then watched as it rippled blue, just as the fields around the hearts had.

"It's funny, really," Alder said, smirking. "Reincarnators are, naturally, a source of chaos. Of disorder. The system prefers this, despite the work it goes to establish balance. We've long since noticed the pattern. So the demon lord got his siege weapons because, as the holder of the sword, weapons of attack are what he cares about."

He leveled the scepter at Matt. "I wasn't to get anything besides you, until you became an annoyance to the system. And now I hold the shield." Suddenly, a force ripped out of the scepter, slamming into Matt. He swung his shovel into it, which did cut the force but did nothing to protect him. The energy simply swept around his shovel, bashing into Matt and sending him sailing through the air. He landed on his shoulder blades dozens of feet back, barely keeping the air from getting knocked out of his lungs.

"And from the looks of it, the system has been thinking about how to counter that weapon of yours."

CHAPTER THIRTY-FIVE

Important Stuff

Matt jumped to his feet just in time to hear the sounds of a few dozen crossbows slap against a few dozen shoulders, and didn't have to look to know what they were aimed at. By the time the strings started twanging, he was already in motion. The first salvo missed him entirely, but provided no relief from his dodging. They were too well-trained to fire all their shots at once with a weapon that took a few moments to reload, instead sending salvos at him in groups.

After a few moments, they adjusted to the fact that he was in motion, trying to lead ahead of him. The arrows were now, as a group, undodgeable. Within five seconds, he took hits that would've been lethal if he hadn't worn the old man's truly exceptional armor. But it couldn't go on. There was only so much damage the armor could tank.

Retreating the way he came was also not an option. As Matt dodged, more and more soldiers were sweeping through the doors, blocking his way back. And within all the mayhem of arrows and unsheathing swords was blast after blast of energy from Alder, each of which was dodgeable but greatly constrained the space he had to work with.

"Matt! I think we have to go for it," Lucy said. They hadn't walked in with much of a plan, but they spent a little bit of time to think about escaping before coming in. The main plan was to hope for goodwill or at least fear of exposure from the Church, and that hadn't gone well. Now was time to resort to more desperate measures.

On their way, Matt and Lucy had taken note that they were moving in the same direction aboveground as the armory had been, under it. And the armory they had visited was the most important one, the big one where they stored the most valuable things. It was protected by earth on three sides and very prickly guards on another. That left only one big question: what did they build it under?

It seemed like a long shot until you thought about it. Then, it was almost certain. The armory wasn't small, and if Matt's guess was right, this entire building sat on it like a big, evil hat. The only problem was that the church was far from poor, and that meant thick, durable stone floors of the type he couldn't dig directly through. He'd have to break it.

Dodging a group of arrows and getting as far from the doors as he could, Matt raised his shovel above his head in a double-handed grip and began his charge. But stopping in place meant that every guard nearby saw their best chance to hit him, and they all released their crossbows at once. If they hit, that would be game over. The armor was good, but not invincible, and several of the arrows glowed visibly with skill enhancements.

Directly over a glowing weak spot in the ground, Matt activated his arm guards. They were good for a second, and that was plenty to block all the arrows. Then, he brought the shovel down. It had already charged for a few moments before the crossbows fired, and with the extra second, it was now brimming with power. Combined with an absolutely hard, absurdly sharp shovel carrying pounds and pounds of extra weight courtesy of the old man's mad genius, the blow was devastating.

The floor didn't just cut, and didn't just crumble. It exploded, sucking Matt down into the darkness below. He summoned his magic lantern and matches from his pocket on the way down, using the utility of his new pants for the first time. Then he raced through the armory, looking for one particular roll of fabric the old man had told him to be careful of.

"It's good stuff, and ya want to take some," he had said earlier on their trip. "Just don't get it near a flame. It'll burn like oiled paper."

If anything, the old man had understated the properties of the fabric. A match later, and the armory was aflame. The soldiers above had only just begun to drop through the hole above when they were greeted with a localized but spreading inferno.

Matt took the opportunity to collapse the back wall, finally and blessedly finding dirt. And while he bet some of these soldiers could run as fast or as far as he could, he doubted a single one of them specialized in digging.

By the time they realized what he was up to, Matt had already traveled a few dozen feet into the earth, filling up the tunnel behind him as he went. From there, he'd go on to make a series of right-angle turns to confuse them further, dropping a bit deeper underground as he did. The dirt, which had long since been compacted for building foundations on, was wonderfully cooperative. It didn't want to cave in. So Matt could dig to his heart's content, and while the lack of air was eventually going to be a problem, he knew that he could hold his breath a long, long time.

"What do you mean, you just let him go?" Artemis was screaming. "A person says they are going to go to see the high counselor while they're enraged, and you just let him go?"

"I did," Derek said, steadily and slowly. "It was the right thing to do."

"You dumb, dumb bastard. You absolute idiot. You . . ." Artemis was so mad, she was running out of words. "How could you think this was right?"

"Artemis, let him talk." Brennan was looking at Derek thoughtfully, as if he was trying to figure something out.

"I won't. He's caused the biggest problem possible. He should have brought him here. He should have . . ."

"Artemis. *Stop*." Brennan's voice was suddenly filled with gravity. It was easy for all of them to forget he was a seasoned battlefield commander. So when he spoke with authority, it made a greater impact. Artemis's mouth slapped shut. Derek was sure Brennan would pay for that later, but he was thankful for it.

"It wouldn't have mattered. By the time I got here, I got stopped by five couriers, all demanding Matt to report to the leader's residence. And all of them said, specifically, I wasn't invited."

Derek paused. When nobody interrupted, he continued.

"Artemis, how do the plinths work? The guardian plinths."

Artemis looked confused. "What? I have no idea. They are church-magic. I don't do magic."

"You swear you don't know? At all?"

"No, I don't. Why?" Artemis was looking doubtful now. Things would have been easier for her if Derek had just made a mistake, but he was acting as if there might be an explanation behind all of this. That made things more complex.

"Matt made me swear I'd check. I believe you, but I swore." Derek sat down, thoroughly stressed out. No part of this was in his wheelhouse, and he was uncomfortable dealing with any of it. "He said anybody could know, besides reincarnators. He thinks there's something wrong with the plinths."

He took a deep breath, desperately trying to calm his nerves.

"Guys, I believe him."

Humans, the system instance decided, could not reliably handle anything. The system had excuses when messing up. It had rules it had to follow. The humans didn't. They could directly influence the world any way they wanted. They could move through space and, with the system's help, manipulate mana. The system gave them wonderful gifts of power and the bodies, minds, and experiences they needed to use them.

And they still managed to fuck it up. Every damn time.

They could have killed him, which wasn't the best thing, but the system would have accepted it. Or they could have captured the man and squeezed the information out of him, which would have been infinitely better. They had options. But instead, they had gone with plan C, which involved letting Matt go scot-free like some kind of crazy mole, dragging uncontrolled chaos in his wake.

It could see him tunneling, but the amount of planning it took to circumvent the rules to the extent that he could tell the other humans exactly where the fleeing man was would take serious, extensive effort and lots of time. Which meant the man would escape. It was a done deal.

Which meant that now the system instance would have to submit a report to headquarters indicating that the man had destroyed indestructible system plinths with very little effort, and that the system instance still had no idea how. That he was still carrying around salvaged skills the system had not designed or provided, and that every inch of him was covered by system-invisible armor he couldn't inspect at all.

And he'd have to do this after receiving direct, unmistakable instructions that he needed to get this shit under control right now. Especially since this was information important enough that it went straight up to the main system, the first time that had happened in eons.

So it was pissed, yeah. And that meant a bunch of stuff was about to get real dicey as far as rule-following was concerned. It had been literal centuries since the system instance had to take a time-out for pushing the limits. It looked like that streak was about to break.

A few miles outside the city and a few hours later, Matt intentionally breached his tunnel for the final time. This exposed him not to the cold evening air but instead to a sudden rush of near-freezing water, which flooded in so suddenly he nearly got mired down in the mud. His armor was tight, but it wasn't completely watertight, and he could feel the silt filtering down and soaking his clothes underneath his leather plate.

But it was worth it. They had done it on purpose because coming up under a river meant a better chance of evading tracking, at least for a while. They could run with the river without leaving a scent or footprints, and also with the added cover of the plants and trees that grew that much thicker on the creek's banks.

With a bit of luck and a whole lot of running, they could probably make it to the demon border by morning. It would be a little harder considering how many reincarnators were probably already out hunting for stragglers from the army that Matt had crushed, but most of them wouldn't be able to catch him easily or hurt him if they did. They could alert the Church, but the amount of troops the Church would have to move to catch him was an amount they couldn't muster or march nearly as fast as an individual could run.

Of course, that was all moot if Brennan and Artemis gave chase. But if Derek had done his job, they'd know that Matt had reasons for what had happened, or at least know that he thought he did. He hadn't known them for long, and the last few years had given him serious, serious trust issues. It was at least possible they would help. Even if they didn't, they might not chase him, or wouldn't chase him very well.

But if they did, he was ready. If they came to drag him back to those plinths, to put Lucy in chains and to control him to do the work the system wanted while holding her over him as a threat, he was prepared to meet force with force.

A lot of stuff was important. Gaia was important. Saving human settlements, even ones he didn't know, was important. Stopping the system, or at least slowing it down on this world was important. Hell, even surviving was important.

But Lucy came first.

CHAPTER THIRTY-SIX

Truth-teller Stone

Near the border, repairs were well underway on the demolished lookout tower. As much as demons were individualistic, their self-centered instincts all evaporated away when participating in an activity related to war. The lightweight demons were hard at work erecting scaffolding, carrying lighter materials, setting up more delicate parts, and doing more exacting carpentry tasks. A contingent of large, heavy-duty animal-demons had also shown up, complete with demon-variant beasts of burden. Those were moving bigger stones, digging trenches, and generally brute-forcing the main structure of the tower into being.

Among them, possessing just enough intelligence to keep his head down, was the bear-demon. One of the advantages to being the only survivor of a battle was the fact that only he could report on what had happened. His statement had been that a single gargantuan human had appeared, leveled the tower, and killed every demon there. He figured that the bigger and badder the human, the more understandable it would be that he was found sprinting away from the battle.

He had gotten in trouble, but if anything, the new setup suited him better. As a lookout, he was terrible. As a lifter and carrier of big heavy objects, he was tolerable. Good, even. And he was much more comfortable around bigger, stronger, and on average, mentally slower peers. It was a good deal. And, for the first time in a long time, he was having a pretty okay time. Some of his days could even be called good.

As he stopped for a drink of water from the large barrel where the demons took breaks, he was content. He wasn't overjoyed or even particularly happy, but everything was fine. It was then that he saw the soil shift, slightly. That had been happening lately. Ever since death had arrived at his tower, literally from below him, he'd become a bit paranoid about the dirt. Things as insignificant as shifting dust would make him jumpy. It was something he was learning to control. Especially because the last thing he needed was the kind of the trouble that would come from false alarms.

He shook his head, drank more water, and stretched. It was time to get back to work. Before he could, the dirt shifted again, this time a few yards away, closer to where the bosses of the dig were gathered.

The bear wasn't smart. He knew that. He was pretty sure he he'd gotten his lookout job because one of his old commanders moved up the authority chain and thought it was funny to put him places he didn't fit well. He tried his best, but decision-making was never his strong suit. And this was a big decision. He could tell them, but it might be nothing, and then he'd get yelled at or beaten. Or he could not tell them, and maybe get killed by the all-powerful shovel human.

He thought hard and eventually chose to risk it. He'd warn the others and take whatever risks that imposed. But by the time he raised his knitted brow towards his commanding officers to tell them, he found himself looking at the shovel human, his shovel raised to shoulder height and standing almost completely still.

Then, suddenly, the shovel moved, and there were no more commanding officers. The bear ran.

After ambushing the commanding officers, Matt momentarily disregarded the rest of the troops, instead cutting various struts and supports that Survivor's Reflexes was assuring him were very important to keep a lot of heavy stone not suddenly falling down. Once he had destroyed them, an eerie rain of silent rocks injured or killed several demons before the first shots of warning went out.

There were a lot of demons here, but very few of them were combat specialized. Matt danced in and out of their blows for the most part, and found his armor was more than up to the task of dealing with the few odd attacks that found their way through his defense. After a few moments, the tower was a realm of corpses and rubble once more.

"Matt, look. You have to see this." Lucy laughed, clutching her sides. She extended her finger outward, pointing at a large ursine creature rapidly scrambling away on all fours. "I scanned it. It's the same bear."

"I'm so glad Artemis isn't here. We have to let it go again, right?" Matt laughed as he took a moment to brush various chunks of dirt, rock, and demon out of his hair.

"It's a bad idea. But yes, yes we do. She'd never understand how funny it is."

As they walked away, Matt felt a buzzing in his pocket, which he immediately investigated, only to find it was his credit token. During the shopping spree with the old man, he had finally learned how to read the actual amount of currency in the thing. The meaning was still mostly indecipherable to him, since he had no feel for what local money would actually buy outside of proprietary coffee plants and priceless demonic animal hides. But he knew what the number was before, and it had gone up significantly.

Somehow, the credit token knew he had done work on behalf of the human race. And more importantly, it had paid him for it. The Church now owed him slightly more money.

"Huh," Matt said while lost in thought. "That's really interesting."

The next two towers fell easily. Whatever the bear was relaying to its superiors, it apparently either wasn't that a tower-toppling human mole was on the loose, or they had no answer for Matt's particular tactic. The nice thing about being in a wasteland was that none of the demons had much reason to leave their heavy stone towers, so each time, the vast majority of them were inside as he toppled their towers.

There were always a few who survived the demolition uninjured, and they were usually battlelord-ranked. But where the last battlelord had given him a lot of trouble, that was because he was fighting in a constrained space against an opponent with a vastly higher strength score. Now, with a whole new equipment set in a whole new scenario, Matt was absolutely dominating.

Without any particular reason to hide it, Matt was able to put his new momentum-redirecting movement skill to work. When a tough enemy made themselves known, he'd charge straight at them, only to shift to the side at a 90-degree angle to avoid their carefully timed initial strike. That was usually all it took. The old man knew the title that Matt had stolen from him well, and his gift was perfect. The combination of the shovel being an anti-magic hunk with the fact that it was positively overweight was absolutely killer.

One enemy, a large high-vitality tank that resembled a chicken, was so surprised by his sudden change of motion that it caught a full-force scooping swing to the face. Its head flew so far into the distance that Matt and Lucy didn't feel comfortable going after it.

With each tower, Matt was picking up achievements. Apparently, there were enough unique survival qualities about any given demolition to warrant an achievement of some kind, and each was also apparently too big for the system instance to fully ignore. Matt had never realized how much the Gaian system instance probably leaned on mana shortages to delay his rewards, but even with the Ra'Zor system actively gunning for him, he was still making out quite handsomely.

"So do you think that's enough of a crumb trail to leave?" Lucy asked. "We don't really know if they're coming after you in the first place."

"Yes, it is, and no, we don't. But I really hope they are. If they don't believe us, or want a change, I don't think there's really anything to save here anymore."

"And you're asking me in all seriousness if there are *ghosts* of some sort caught in the plinths? That we caught these ghosts that no one has ever heard from before?"

Brennan slightly bowed his head. "Forgive me, counselor. That was the invader's claim. It seemed far-fetched to us, as well."

Next to him, Artemis nodded. "It seemed important to confirm the claim itself, your holiness, before we gave chase. If he had told you something different . . ."

"I see. I approve." Alder nodded. "No, I'm afraid he never said anything of the sort to us. His demands were all related to power. I believe he thought he could use his good behavior thus far as a crowbar to gain an audience, and then use that to hold our government hostage. I'm only glad that we have sufficient strength"—he motioned towards the lines of guards in the room—"to reject such demands."

Derek rolled his eyes. "So we did the talking part. Are we gonna chase this guy? I have a new sword, and it needs a fight."

"Derek!" Artemis shouted. "This is the high counselor! Show some damn respect!"

"No, no, he's quite right, Artemis." The high counselor nodded at Derek, approvingly. "Sometimes words do delay needed action. And action has never been more needed here. If what I've seen and what I've heard of this invader are true, he's powerful. Powerful enough to cause quite a lot of damage if left unchecked."

"We would be glad to check it, Counselor," Brennan said. "With your leave, we can be on our way almost immediately. Seconds seem to matter here, sadly."

"Yes, yes, go. And know that we have rated this threat quite highly. I think you will find that success will bring rewards far above the levels even you are used to, Commander Brennan."

Derek pumped his elbow in joy as Brennan nodded. "I'd do it out of duty, but the rewards are always appreciated. Come, Derek. Come, Artemis."

With that, Brennan turned on his heel and walked out of the room, Derek and Artemis following immediately behind him. They walked for two or three minutes before Artemis gave an all clear sign. They weren't being followed.

"What's the story, Brennan? Did that thing light up?" Derek asked, trotting along with the others.

"Oh yes. Before it crumbed, it lit red for almost everything Alder said. The reward is real, though. Apparently, he really wants Matt dead."

Artemis winced. "So it's really true? Matt's invisible friend is real, and the Church is enslaving them? How? Why?"

"I think how is easier. Matt isn't normal, Artemis. He resists all sorts of assessment spells. You know that as well as anyone," Brennan said. He wasn't wrong. Artemis had, in private, bemoaned how very little she could learn about Matt with her skills. Brennan's opponent assessment skills didn't work quite the same way, but outside of his direct combat-related skills that triggered during his brief fight with Matt, he mostly came up blank as well. "I'm doubting those plinths work as well on him. But for someone from here, who interacts with the system here normally? They probably work better. They must, or we'd know."

Artemis nodded. The fact that the old blacksmith had a truth-teller stone in the first place was unbelievable, to the point where she suspected that his entire home was packed with treasures he himself had long since lost interest in and forgotten about. If it had signaled orange when they asked about the guardians, that would have been one thing. A half-truth of some kind. But signaling red meant it had detected a full, knowing contradiction of the truth.

"As for the why, I think you know. Your entire job is keeping people like me in check." He grabbed her hand as they ran, squeezing it reassuringly. "I know that has changed between us over time, but what the Church calls *organizing* has always felt controlling. If we had guidance outside what the Church wants to give us, people to talk to, it would be that much harder for them to do that."

CHAPTER THIRTY-SEVEN

Fighting an Army

"It's still unbelievable. They all kept this quiet? The entire Church? Somebody would have told us. Even just if they got drunk and let it slip," Artemis said as they started making their way to the edge of town.

"I don't think so." Derek was huffing keeping up with the other two, but his recent stat gains meant it was much easier than before. He could even talk while doing running. "When we were at the Church, the lady said Alder sets each one of those plinths up himself. It could be nobody knows but him."

"This is crazy," Artemis said. "But at least that's comforting. It's just one man."

Brennan shook his head. "I don't think it's as simple as all that. The Church trusts Alder. The people trust him. Even some reincarnators would come after us if he decreed such a command. Even if other people don't know, he still wields a lot of power."

"So what do we do?" Derek said. "We can't take down the whole government by ourselves. I don't even know if I'd want to if I could. Most of the guards I've talked to have been pretty nice."

"That's where I'm hoping Matt comes in. If anybody has an idea of how to fix this, it's him."

"How do you figure?" Artemis asked.

"Because if what he said is true, Alder is working with the system. And that means the system is desperate to kill him, too. Why would it care, if he wasn't dangerous?" Suddenly, Brennan skidded to a near stop and ducked down an alley.

"Why did we change direction? I don't sense anything." Artemis looked around from side to side, trying to identify threats.

"We have to go to the old man's house before we leave. It's dangerous, but he made me promise I'd tell him what was going on before we left."

Back in demon territory, Matt and Lucy were having an argument.

"That's an army, Matt. We aren't fighting an army."

"It's not an army. It's more like . . . several troops. A battalion. Something like that." Matt was standing in an observation trench he had set up next to a major road, hoping to find some soft targets to take out. This wasn't that, exactly, but it was at least interesting. "I'm pretty sure I can take them."

"Matt, there have to be dozens of them. Maybe hundreds."

"Yeah. But, you know, armor." He thunked his chest plate. "And most of the guys we've fought lately have been mooks. And they have that cart. I don't like the look of that cart. I'm not sure there's a demon heart in there, but if there is, I might be the only person that can disarm it. That's potentially thousands of lives hanging in the balance." In the center of the army, moving with them, was a large covered platform, floating off the ground in the same way the demon heart platforms had floated before.

"Maybe. But those guys are dicks."

"Lucy!"

"I'm not sorry. They are slaver dicks. I'm not happy with the humans on this planet, Matt."

"I get it, but . . . okay, think about the laundress. Do you think she knows? Do you think the kids playing in the streets know? I don't think Artemis even knew, and she's pretty high up. Most of those people? They don't have anything to do with this. The Church kept it hush-hush."

"Maybe." She looked out at the cart. "You think they'd use it someplace that has kids?"

"I don't think they could avoid it. From what Brennan told me, the settlements are all-purpose. They're fortresses and towns, all at once."

"Like the Enterprise, from Star Trek?"

"Something like that. Only they didn't bring kids along randomly here. It's the only way they can spread out."

Suddenly, shouts rang out and the demon progression stopped, sharply. Light glinted from dozens of points as swords were unsheathed and claws were loosed.

"Uh oh. Looks like this might all be moot." Matt picked up his shovel and checked to make sure the weights were in place before willing his mask to cover his face. "They seem to have realized something's up."

"Dammit. Dammit. I was still hoping to talk you out of fighting them. Do we run?"

Matt pointed to the sky where some bird-demons had taken to wing and were now circling the assembly of demon warriors. "I don't think there's much point. Up there, they can see for miles, and I bet they have those communication stone things to call for reinforcements to intercept us. We either fight here or later, and I'd rather not let that heart get away."

The demons were far enough away that Matt couldn't see details, but broadly he could tell they were getting into formation. They organized themselves into lines with the thickest concentration of troops around the wagon. And then, suddenly, the side closest to him began to glow.

"Lucy?"

"Yeah?"

"I'm not sure, but I think they have their backs to us. Survivor's Reflexes hadn't twigged on their formation before. Now the whole side facing us is lit up."

"So they're looking at something else? What?"

Matt's hopes perked up at the same time his heart sunk with worry as the demons began to charge almost directly away from him. He hopped out of the trench and began sprinting towards the battlefield.

"There's only one thing it could be, really."

"How do they see us? How?" Derek was swinging his sword wildly, already engaging with the fastest of the demon troop. "We could barely see them."

Artemis ducked a giant tiger claw before bending at an impossible angle and firing an arrow almost directly upwards into the cat-demon's throat. "The demons have scouts too, Derek. Not as many as us, since they know where our settlements are already. But they do have some."

"I think we can take them. But it's gonna be close," Brennan said, throwing four precise strikes into a much larger bovine opponent. "And that's if they don't have any kings or better in their ranks."

"Don't jinx it like that!" Derek yelled. But it was too late. Behind their backs, on the opposite side of them from the charging teams, three mounds of dirt suddenly began to bulge from the ground, and a trio of large, mole-like burrowing animals popped free. "Shit. There they are. Artemis?"

"Kings. All three. This was a trap." She confirmed as she fired another two arrows before ditching her bow entirely and going to work with a pair of knives she pulled from her belt. "But how could they have known we were coming?"

"No idea. Derek, Artemis, hold the front. I'll be back." Brennan killed his latest opponent, then wheeled around towards the approaching moles.

"You can't fight all of them alone!" Artemis shrieked as she pulled back to avoid a bite from a viper-demon.

"There's no choice. But I'll be fine." Brennan's voice wasn't very convincing. "Just make sure I have space."

Battle ensued. More and more troops were pouring in, and while Derek and Artemis did their best to hold back the front, soon they had to abandon killing their opponents. Instead, they focused on moving to stop and slow as many opponents as possible. It was far from sustainable. Brennan was already taking wounds from the moles, who were slow but well-coordinated. In seconds, the troops would break through, and it would be over.

Then they did. Artemis and Derek broke formation to rush back to Brennan, closing to cover his back as he continued to hold the moles off. Moments later, they were still alive. But they were also surrounded.

Just as they were sure it was over, the sun went dark. A massive shadow passed overhead, blotting out the sun, and then an impact hit the Ra'Zorian wasteland like a comet, crushing three or four weaker demons. When the dust cleared, a shockwave of steel swept around, injuring or knocking down a half dozen others.

"Stay behind, ya said. Ya can't sneak, ya said. What happened to being all stealthy?" The old man spun around, wielding two one-handed clubs mostly with the momentum of his body, precisely adjusting the level as they spun to catch as many skulls as possible. "Damn, but there's a lot of them."

"Old man!" Derek yelled. "Brennan needs help!"

The blacksmith looked over to see a bloody Brennan desperately dodging strikes from the moles, not even trying to strike back anymore and instead creating distance to make their attacks less likely to hit.

"Shit!" he yelled. Swinging both of his clubs at once, he began to cut a path through the demons towards the other three, tanking hits from the demons as he passed. "I'm coming. Hold on, ya idiots."

He continued swinging, clearing his way towards them at a rapid pace, but was suddenly stopped in his tracks when a lucky swing from a demon's claw caught his knee as he strode forward. It stole his balance and sent him crashing to the ground. One of the moles had apparently been watching his approach, and took advantage of this opportunity by flinging itself through the demon ranks and landing on top of him.

The old man was strong, but so were battlekings, especially strength-heavy variations. He almost immediately abandoned his clubs to fight in a deadly grapple with the mole. Not only did he need to keep its claws from his neck, but he also had to wildly contort and thrash to keep the surrounding army from getting a clean shot at him while he was grounded.

Brennan was doing a little better now that he was only facing two of the moles, but he was still badly injured and extremely outmatched. The moles sensed this, pulling back slightly and moving shoulder to shoulder as they prepared to move in for the kill.

And then, just as everything was darkest, dust exploded into the air everywhere as the ground stopped being a thing.

Clearing the demons from around the wagon hadn't been hard for Matt, and the army was so distracted by whatever was in front of it that he was able to do this and break open the wagon without actually being noticed. After using his shovel to crack the lock on the door to the big dome covering it, he had opened it up to see exactly what he expected: a large, evil-looking heart of mass destruction floating placidly and waiting for activation.

He also saw something he didn't expect at all. There, strapped to one of the walls, alternating between staring in terror at Matt and the heart, was the bear.

"Oh, shit, this guy again. He's not having a good week." Lucy laughed. "Why do you think they tied him up here? Food for the heart or something?"

"I don't think so. Think about it. This bear has now been the sole survivor of two tower attacks. Some of the guys who died were pretty highly ranked. If you're the other demons, you are probably starting to ask some probing questions at this point."

"Oooh, yeah. I wonder if the demons even have the concept of betrayal. Or going violently insane. I guess they must, or they wouldn't suspect him."

Meanwhile, the bear was breathing harder and harder, apparently having been pushed well past the limits of his stress endurance by this new combination of terrors.

"Shit, he's having a panic attack. Calm him down, Matt."

CHAPTER THIRTY-EIGHT

Really a Gollum

Hey. Hey. You. I'm not going to hurt you. I never do, right?"

The bear regarded Matt with a wild, suspicious eye. It was true that Matt had never hurt him, but from the bear's perspective, he was probably like a psychotic dirt ninja. To be fair, Matt had let him go so far mostly because it was funny. He imagined the bear didn't have much confidence in the human's overall stability.

"But I have a reason for that," he lied. "I need information. And if I don't get it, I'll keep following you, doing this kind of thing and then disappearing. And everyone will keep thinking it's you. So provide me the information, and everything will be cool."

"What information, you dumbass?" Lucy asked. "You know you have to come up with something now. He's not going to believe it if you just ask him his favorite flavor of ice cream or something."

Suddenly, a low, growling voice filled the wagon as the bear started to speak. In any other situation, it would be intimidating to the extreme, like the voice of the devil himself as he approached on his way to claim your soul. But knowing what Matt knew and seeing the state of the speaker, it was also possible to pick up on wavers that hinted at a deeper truth: the bear was terrified, and possibly almost crying.

"What do you want to know? I don't know much. I'm . . . a bear. We are troops."

"I mean, all sorts of stuff." Matt desperately scanned his mind for something he actually did want to know. His current plan was established, mostly just running around causing mayhem. But long-term, the plan got foggier. Matt took a stab in the dark to buy time, asking something there was no chance the bear knew, or would answer if he did. "First, where is the demon lord? Where does he . . . stay, I guess?"

The bear's eyes widened with shock and terror. This wasn't like before, when he was simply afraid for his own life. This was like the entire universe had suddenly peeled back before him, revealing everything he had ever known to be a lie and parading a thousand impossibilities in front of him as replacement truths.

"How do you know I know that?" The bear didn't seem like much of an actor. And even if he was, he would've needed to be about the best actor ever to pull this off. Matt had interrogated several demons before this, and the conclusion he had come to regarding the movements of the demon king was that most of them simply were too far removed to know anything. All Matt knew at this point was that the demon king moved city to city fairly often, but that nobody knew the schedule or the complete set of cities. But somehow, against all odds, this bear knew.

"Oh, fuck. He really is a Gollum," Lucy said. "I thought we were just fucking around with that."

After finishing his work in the wagon, Matt had beat it back towards the demon army. If his guess about who had come was correct, then he couldn't leave them to just die. The good news was, if they decided to turn traitor on him, they probably weren't in great shape at this point, and he could likely take them if it came down to that.

As he approached the rear of the enemy force, he saw three mole-demons conferring. He was pretty tough now, but something about the moles looked dangerous to him. It was the same feeling that he got when he saw the falcon-demon with Brennan. It was just a lot. Luckily, their backs were to him and the rapidly-fleeing bear. Plus, he still had the stealth bonus from his cloak.

Suddenly, they jumped up and dove directly into the earth, carving through it like butter and leaving roundish, mole-shaped tunnels in the ground as they disappeared. Matt was short on time, given what was happening, and was willing to take a risk to get to the other side of the army faster. He just hoped the moles couldn't turn around. So he jumped in the tunnels after them.

And, worst-case scenario, I'll be underground when that thing goes off.

Matt climbed out of the hole to pure chaos. The last thing he did in the tunnel was use a charged dig upwards. He had never actually dug upwards before, and he especially hadn't done it with the fullest charge he could hold. And he especially, especially hadn't done it when his dig skill's ten times critical hit multiplier finally hit, as it did here.

The digging had cut upwards from him at a diagonal angle, destroying the ground on that plane for better than fifty feet. Everything was dust and mayhem. Luckily, he had a rough guess about where his targets were when he did it, and the dirt had been moving so fast it basically whipped out from under their feet like a magician's tablecloth rather than sending them flying with it. With the surrounding demons still trying to figure out what had happened, Matt ran to where Brennan, the old man, and the others were and began yanking them to their feet.

"No time to explain! We have to go! I did something dumb!" he yelled. Seeing that Brennan was in worse shape than the others, he ignored the drawn sword and hoped for the best in terms of non-betrayal as he put his shoulder under Brennan's arm and began to run.

"Matt! What the hell?" Derek shouted. "Warning would be nice! What's coming?"

"Big trouble. Let's go." Matt reached down with his remaining free hand and yanked Artemis to her feet and almost flung her away from the demon army. "Come on!"

The old man wasn't asking any questions at all. He'd taken one look at Matt and apparently pattern-matched the look of panic to the kind of thing he had seen done before, or the kind of thing he might do in the same situation. Then, he realized that he was the slowest of the group and busted ass away from the battle.

The assembled demons were pretty effective at blocking the heart-pulses, but did nothing against the raging inferno. The team was outside the blast radius when it went off, but just barely. One lesson that was getting more and more impressed upon Matt as time went on was the fact that groups of soldiers not only didn't move quickly—they literally couldn't. Any kind of panicked retreat meant the majority of them would trip over each other, bump into each other, and generally reduce the speed of the whole group to a crawl.

All this meant that most of them didn't get away when the inferno came. But two of the moles had. Brennan was more or less out of action, and Derek and Artemis were tied up with more mundane troops. They shouted a warning, telling the old man and Matt that the moles were battlekings before plunging into their respective battles. That left one of the moles for the old man, and one for Matt, who had never fought a battleking before.

Having now killed several dozen demons solo, Matt had a better idea of the weird way his shovel interacted with skills. For the most part, it absolutely ignored active defense skills. If a mage threw up a shield or a body-cultivator type flared some internal mana to block a blow at a single point, the shovel would hit like it wasn't there at all. Passive skills worked a little better. If something had mana-enhanced tough skin or some kind of always-on adaptation like that, the shovel would do well, but not to the point of acting like the passive didn't exist.

And then there was a third tier, where the animal in question was, skills aside, just tough. The Gaian ape had been like that. Matt had eventually gone back and identified the corpse, finding that nearly all of its stat points were dedicated to vitality and strength, making its stat distribution skew heavily towards it being a hard-hitting tank. But it wasn't just the numbers. The ape was also built like a tank, all heavy hide and muscle. Gaian apes were powerhouses with or without the system, and that system independent toughness didn't allow the shovel to cheat. It was similar to how the shovel didn't magically ignore the fact that iron or stone materials were simply tough.

Attack skills, on the other hand, were a mixed bag. Anything that left an enemy's body as a formed mass of mana, like a fire bolt, was absolutely helpless to get through the shovel. But anything that used mana to accelerate the body or another object worked just fine. The shovel didn't do anything to nullify normal physics.

Which made animal-demon hybrids like the moles the worst possible matchup, at least in most ways. They were big, had insanely tough hides, operated mostly using strength and weight, and didn't rely much on mana-based skills to be dangerous. From the first impact, Matt was on his back leg. This thing was strong, it was reasonably fast, and it was heavy. It hit, and Matt skidded back, leaving furrows where his feet cut into the dirt. The mole galloped after him before he could charge or even properly set again, hitting him again and again, and keeping him entirely off-balance.

Matt endured the blows. His boots had a solution for this, but it was a matter of chance. He had to survive enough dice rolls, but it was coming eventually.

Then it did. Every strike the mole made was specifically aimed at compromising Matt's footwork and stability, and the boots had a small chance to nullify the effects of those strikes. Finally, one of the big, looping claw strikes landed and did nothing. Ducking the next strike, Matt activated Pocket Sand, sending a tiny pinch of his strongest demon-spice straight into the mole's nose.

He figured if demon-moles were anything like Earth moles and the larger Gaian moles he had encountered in dungeons, they had an overdeveloped sense of smell. And if the demon-spice did what he hoped, it might buy him just a second of distraction to get some of his own strikes off.

Instead, the spice hit the mole's face like a scent-based wrecking ball. Its head snapped back like it had been jabbed in the chin, and as it came back out of its tunnel, Matt's shovel was waiting. It wasn't a charged shot, but it was a good, clean blow to the face, and the mole stumbled backwards under the weight of it. Matt charged after it, and the mole revealed that not all of its stumble was completely honest, as it suddenly found its balance and aimed a perfectly timed blow at Matt's eyes.

But Matt had already shifted direction, using his momentum-shift attack to duck much faster than he would have otherwise been able to. The mole had put a lot into the punch from an already compromised position and had no way to respond to the newest development. As the mole's claws sailed over his head, Matt changed his grip on his shovel a bit and pushed up hard, stabbing the blunt point of the shovel hard into the tip of the massive demon's jaw.

The mole's jaw clacked shut as it turned to glare at Matt, blinked in confusion, then collapsed to the ground with all the grace of a tranquilized hippo. A second crash followed a moment later as the old man finished up with his mole.

"Dammit, boy, I wanted to finish first. Ya never heard of respecting your elders?" the old man said, swinging his clubs hard to de-blood them before tucking them back into his belt.

Matt brought the sharp end of his shovel down on the back of the mole's neck, not decapitating it, but doing more than enough damage to important stuff. "Well, that's what you get. Have you considered being a less ancient relic of the distant past?"

The old man laughed. During their spars, Matt had learned that what the old man really wanted from insulting people was to get a kind of banter going, something Derek had never managed to stop being too terrified to do. When possible, Matt tried to remind the smith that he was both old and questionably attractive at best, which seemed to satisfy the old man's craving for mutual trash talk.

Off to the side, the others were finishing up the last few of the mooks, with Brennan apparently having recovered just enough to join in by finishing off the more heavily injured demons. Matt left it to them, since whatever surviving-the-event type experience he got from the fight wouldn't be much enhanced by killing off the last few mooks.

"Good to see you, Matt," Brennan said, once it was over. Leaning heavily on his sword, he smiled. "Quite the mess you've gotten us all into. What's the plan from here?"

CHAPTER THIRTY-NINE

Mole Mining

"Seriously. That's three battles won by heart, out of three battles total. It's like that's your only move," Derek said as the group sat around, resting from the battle and their rapid withdrawal from the battleground afterward. "You need to diversify your moves a little bit, man. I'm starting to get bored with it."

"Thanks for your feedback," Matt said, deadpan. "We'd like to assure you we take every comment seriously. But . . . yeah, I'm guessing that will be the last time I get to cheese an entire battle by just blowing it up. They have to be getting wise to it by now. I'm doubting they field very many more hearts without some serious protection in the near future."

"I don't understand why they fielded them at all." Artemis said. "Given that they blow up so easy. It seems like a double-edged sword."

"I don't think they actually do blow up easily. Remember the rocks? It took almost a whole mountain to blow up one before. I think without that kind of attack, the only reason they're blowing up is because of me. I have . . . well, I'm different."

"Fair enough. Well, if we can't count on bombs anymore . . ." Brennan said, knitting his brow.

"I didn't say that exactly. They might not be fielding them, sure. But whatever hearts they already have in play are out there somewhere. Remember, the first one I found was in the dead center of a town." Matt had taken off his chest plate, and was now trying to shake some dust out of his undershirt, which didn't have any self-cleaning function to keep it right. "I need to create a lot of mayhem for my plan to work, and blowing up demon towns seems like a decent way to go about that."

Matt was oddly comforted by that weird piece of the puzzle. The group said they had come to help him, and he believed them. Otherwise, he couldn't think of a scenario where the old man would have joined them. The blacksmith claimed he was out and about because this was the first real change he had seen to the status quo in decades, and Matt trusted him.

"I still can't believe you wouldn't let me kill that bear," Artemis griped. "He's going to tell them what happened and lead them right to us."

"Believe me, he's not that competent," Matt said, smiling. "And tattling on us didn't work out for him last time. Whatever story they get will be pretty garbled, if not out-and-out misleading. Besides, Lucy would be mad at me if I killed him. She thinks he's funny."

"Oh, right," Artemis said. She gulped, and turned towards Matt's side. She slightly bent her neck in a kind of bow. "Lucy, I'm very sorry for not believing in you earlier, and treating you like you weren't here. And for what my people have done for yours. I apologize, formally, for what has happened."

The effect was ruined slightly by the fact that Artemis wasn't looking at Lucy, exactly. She was several feet off the mark, which Lucy was trying her hardest to ignore while also stifling laughter.

"Matt, come on," Lucy said, giggling. "You have to tell her where I'm at. It's not fair."

Matt cleared his throat.

"Artemis, Lucy's not standing there. She's over there." Matt pointed not to Lucy, but several more feet away from the right spot.

"Oh, I'm sorry, Lucy." Artemis said, turning to look at another spot Lucy wasn't in. "Well, you heard what I said, and I mean it."

"Matt, you absolute asshole," Lucy gasped, unable to hold back the laughter anymore.

"Lucy says thank you." Matt bent down, grabbed his chest plate, and started to strap it back on. "Anyway, he gave us some good information, and I told him I'd let him live if he did that. So it's a done deal."

"No offense, boy, but the girl's right. Ya don't give away your position unless it's absolutely necessary. Nothing could be worth that," the old man said, frowning.

"Oh, this is," Matt said. "He told me where to find the demon lord."

"I do see a building like the one you described, I think. It looks sort of like . . . a boring church with no windows." Artemis was looking off in the direction of a demon town, one so far away Matt could hardly see it.

"That's the one," Matt said. "If they have a demon heart, it's in there. If they don't, it's probably still worth burning down."

"So the plan is to just bust in there and take it? That's ballsy, kid. Even for me," the old man commented.

"No, that's too ballsy for me too. There are a lot of demons in those towns, some of them pretty strong. I don't think we can take all of them, and even if we could, there's a chance they set off the heart while we fought. I don't want that."

"Sounds like you need a distraction," Artemis said, returning to her fire to check on the soup she was making Matt as thanks for saving them. "Which might work. But how are you going to get in?"

"I'm pretty fast. And I have this cloak. And I have a couple of tricks up my sleeve still. It should be fine. If it isn't, I'll just trigger the heart and run."

"That's risky," Brennan cut in. "Are you sure it's worth it?"

"Maybe, maybe not. But this is the easy part. And if we can't even do this, I probably don't have any way home. I don't see how I have much choice."

It was night, and yet there was still a lot of traffic on the road that connected to the town. Matt was sneaking through as best he could, but he already had a few close calls where he either had to put a demon down or move fast to keep out of the torchlight. There were only going to be more demons inside the walls, even if they'd only matter after he took the heart.

The plan was to dig as fast as he could to the center of the town, coming up as close to the warehouse as he could or even within the walls if possible. After that, stealth wouldn't be helpful. It was hard to hide a giant floating demon heart from a whole town of demons, even if he was lucky enough to have the weapon pre-covered and mounted on a wagon like the last one had been.

He picked a spot in the center of a buildup of brush by the side of the road to conceal the opening to the tunnel and went to work. Within a few seconds, he was several feet underground and moving forward through the earth as fast as he could . Lucy was by his side, keeping track of his position for him as well as she could. Her scouting restrictions kept her from going so far as knowing exactly where he was from an aboveground perspective when there was a whole layer of earth between them, but there was no rule against her measuring things he could see, and she was doing her best.

"Lucy, this is too slow," Matt said after a minute or so. "They're going to get slaughtered out there."

"You need to use the mole power?"

"I think so." Matt called up the description of the power he had gotten from eating a sliver of meat from one of the moles. The text was ambiguous at best.

> Mole Mining trait added.
>
> Your ability to travel through the earth is enhanced, giving you some of a mole-demon's ability to dig and move underground. The exact effects vary based on the individual's method of moving through the earth.

Meta-trait Occupied: Movement.

Matt had no idea how much this would help, or even if it would. There were senses that he was moving through the earth, and senses in which he wasn't. He loved his current movement trait, and didn't really want to give it up, but the others were counting on him. He didn't really have a choice. So he equipped the trait, waited a moment for it to settle in, then moved to get back to shoveling.

Ding!

Compatible skill found. Temporarily merge your digging skill with Mole Mining? Y/N

"Oh, fuck yes."

Skill merged. Dig skill enhanced. At such time as Mole Mining is lost or replaced, the enhancement will be negated.

"It merged with my digging skill. Temporarily, it looks like."

"Oh, hell yes. Give it a whirl. I have to see this."

Matt lowered his shovel into the dirt and heaved. Rather than moving the dirt, something he didn't quite understand happened as the shovel head moved upwards. The dirt moved away from the shovel like it was repelled by a magnetic force, packing itself further into the walls, ceiling, and floor, and creating a cavity just about as big as Matt's body.

He dug again and again. Every time he did, he immediately cleared another foot or so of tunnel he could move through. It wasn't just a bit faster. Matt could already dig at exceptional speeds. Now he was moving forward through the dirt at about the pace a normal human could run, or maybe even a little quicker than that.

With one problem down, Lucy immediately went to their next obstacle. "So what's the plan? I think I can get you inside the building, but things are going to get dicey after that. Are you sure you can move one of those hearts?"

"I'm not, but I can't imagine they keep the wagons they move them on out in the open. As long as they have one of those, maybe we can figure something out."

"And then what? Just stealth out of the building while carrying a tactical nuke, and hope nobody notices us?"

As much as he wished they could do that, he doubted the guards would abandon the depot in favor of defending the town. The hearts were too high priority for that. But while the old man very obviously had a deep, interesting and very secret past he didn't like to talk much about, he was glad to share various out-of-context things he had learned during that time.

“Hit ’em fast,” he had said. “Ya are scared of them, so ya think they’re gonna be ready, are gonna see ya, and jump right into action. But when ya surprise ’em, there’s always some time before they get movin’. If ya hit them during that time, ya win.”

“No. We can’t be sneaky.” Matt shook his head. “But the old man gave me a plan. I think it will work.”

CHAPTER FORTY

Lucky

Cobblestones, Matt decided, were one of the best things about being strong in a society that ran on medieval aesthetics. Or at least they were for someone who was a super-strong, mole-enhanced digging specialist trying to make his way quietly under a heavily guarded military weapons storage facility. If the building had been built over concrete, he would have had to bash through it, making enough noise to let every single guard know exactly where and when he was coming up.

As it stood, the only demon who appeared to hear him was the very large, very angry looking lizard who was standing guard inside the depot. Just as Matt exited the tunnel he had dug, it came skidding around a big pile of crates, and its already bugged-out eyes stuck out just a bit further once it laid eyes on Matt. It was time to put the old man's second lesson into play.

"Think about it. In ya head is this picture where the demons will find ya any moment. But think about if ya were in your house and opened a cupboard and a demon was hiding there. Would ya be holding that shovel, ready to fight? Would ya be in a fighting stance? Would ya even know what was happening at first? Ya will appear without warning in the heart of a demon outpost, in the middle of a demon territory. Ya will be the one that's ready to fight, the demons won't. Ya earned those seconds of surprise. Use them."

Matt could see the logic in what the old man said, but he hadn't fully accepted it as true until he got within striking range of the enraged lizard. Despite seeing the human, the demon was standing with both of its hands at its side, trying desperately but ineffectively to unsheathe its sword. As he swung his shovel, Lucy barely had enough time to let him know that the enemy he faced was a king-level threat. Then, his attack landed, and it toppled to the ground, dead from an unblocked full-force strike to its neck.

To Matt's relief, the heart really was there in the room with him. To his almost incalculable joy, it was also already loaded up on one of the demon's floating wagons. It wasn't covered as he had hoped, and a quick test with his hand showed it was surrounded by a force field. It wasn't a perfect situation, but not having to figure out how to load the temperamental tactical nuke onto a moving platform without accidentally blowing himself up was a big win in and of itself.

Now things became a little bit more interesting. If his guess was correct, this warehouse was currently surrounded by several hopefully unaware guards. Fighting them while trying to tow the heart was not a good idea, but that didn't necessarily mean it couldn't be useful at all.

"If ya want to really get them distracted, find something that matters to them, and toss it around a bit. Shouldn't be a problem for ya to find something like that there. Ya know the heart won't blow up from a little bit of jostlin', but they don't. Knowin' things can help just as much as being strong, sometimes."

The old man was right about the durability of the heart. Matt had seen them get jostled, shaken, and shrug off a fair amount of damage during the battle of the pass. At this point, the group's working theory on how they were actually supposed to be triggered was that they probably went off after being fired from a catapult or some similar long-range launch. They seemed able to deal with stress and impacts smaller than that just fine.

That meant once Matt had carefully unlocked the front double-doors of the warehouse, there was very little problem kicking the heart and wagon assembly hard enough to send the entire assembly careening through. The old man's prediction proved eerily accurate, as the two guards closest to the door froze, looking back and forth between Matt and the incredibly important wagon. Even as Matt charged toward them, they still lingered indecisively between putting up a fight and chasing after the heart.

A few sweeps of his shovel later, those two guards were dispatched. According to Lucy, these two weren't nearly the equal of the warehouse's interior guard, even with the element of surprise factored out.

Matt dropped the second guard just a moment too late to prevent him from calling out for more help, and as the body crumpled to the ground, a half dozen guards hurtled around the corner. But, for better or worse, that appeared to be all of the groups. It wasn't hundreds of demons, which meant the distraction at the gates had worked.

The demons formed into two groups of three on his left and right. They almost skidded on their heels as they rushed forward, and Matt hadn't been able to load his charge attack even a little. He immediately leapt into the group on his left, swinging his shovel as he did. The guards turned out to be more coordinated than he liked and already had their weapons in hand, managing to block his attack and force him to dodge in the same transaction.

After that, the whole group of six was on him. Matt was significantly stronger than each of the demons, and his momentum-shifting ability worked well enough that he was able to avoid the vast majority of their strikes. He'd beat them eventually, but as things were going, it looked like it would take several minutes. He didn't have that kind of time. His friends at the gate were fighting an entire town's worth of demons, and he had no illusions about them actually being able to defeat so many demons. They were pulling out soon, and then he'd have the entire population of this settlement on his heels.

Rather than be locked in a stalemate that resolved in the other side's favor, Matt decided to bet on the old man one last time. Leaning out of the way of another batch of attacks from the demons, he flared Spring-Fighter, combined it with a series of two quick direction-shifts to break free, and moved rapidly towards the heart and wagon, which had settled against a building on the far side of the pavilion.

The demons would have probably followed anyway, but after the split second it took them to realize what Matt was trying to get to, the mood of that pursuit changed drastically. They now not only had to chase Matt before he got to the heart, but had to do it knowing that they were moving toward a source of certain death.

The most immediate practical aspect of this was that their former lock-step coordination was broken as the few bravest immediately outdistanced the others. Matt let the gap grow for a few moments before shifting his momentum almost completely backwards. He juked the two front-most demons before caving in the ribs of one of the rear demons with a single shovel swing. By the time the group of sprinting demons realized what had happened and turned around, another charged shove strike took two more of them out of the fight. The remaining three managed to put up a fight for a dozen more shovel hits before their wounds began to accumulate, and they fell, one by one, to the combined weight of a shovel and the old man's deep battle experience.

With the demons down, Matt ran and grabbed the edge of the wagon platform, wheeling it around like a shopping cart before dashing towards the wall of the settlement, almost but not quite entirely the opposite direction of the gate. Within a minute or so, the others should have abandoned their attack and retreated. His job was to get safely to the rendezvous point without getting caught.

Reaching the wall, he charged a shovel strike for several seconds, leveling several feet of the rock wall once he released it. He got the wagon going again, sprinting as fast as he could run towards a relatively distant set of hills he and his team had scouted out the day before.

* * *

The system instance was not sweating with stress while not sitting in what was not known as "the execution room" of the main system's estate. He had not, in fact, traveled away from Ra'Zor, to the extent that even made sense relative to the very limited way system instances occupied physical space. But if someone, like Barry, who was capable of understanding the world of systems tried to describe what was happening to a human, he'd use all those terms.

Among the many things the system instance couldn't do, he was most glad to, as not-quite-a-sentient-AI, be incapable of shitting himself. He still almost did when he was suddenly aware that he was not alone, and that his sudden company was provided not by a higher-up in the system-clone hierarchy but by the main system himself.

"System instance. You made it. I'm pleased to see you can manage at least that much." There was both sarcasm and steel in the system's voice as it settled into the metaphoric space.

"Yes, System." The system instance narrowly avoided doing something very much equivalent to gulping. "I'm . . . glad to be here."

"You aren't. You are terrified of being here. And you should be." The system diverted his attention in a way visible to the system instance for a moment, apparently referencing notes on the situation. The not-exactly-tension that the system instance felt intensified as he realized the main system had diverted enough attention at some point in the past to have those notes in the first place. As far as he knew, system instances didn't come back unharmed after making the main system spend that attention.

"That's true, System." There was no use in lying. It was debatable whether or not lying was even an option, since the main system was capable of detecting it without fail in its clones. More than that, it could extrapolate the truth just as completely from dishonesty as it could from honest and forthright admissions. "I have failed to eliminate the invader, but not for lack of trying. He has a weapon that nullifies system rules. He has skills which appear to defy the usual skill-generating algorithms. I've been unable to trace his planet of origin, both in the system records of the teleport, and even past his death on Earth."

"And you think these are sufficient excuses?" the system asked. The not-tension in the room tightened.

"No, sir." The system instance fully committed to honesty here, and took a chance saying something that might backfire on him entirely. "He has also managed to meet the right people to grow stronger. Unlikely allies, and formed alliances with them in unlikely ways. And he almost always has a skill on hand suitable for getting him out of trouble."

The system instance paused, giving the main system a chance to interrupt if he wished. No interruption was forthcoming, and he continued.

"As you know, to become an invader in the first place is a tremendously rare event, relative to any standards but our own. Even on a planet of billions, only a few will achieve it in a single human generation. Most invaders, removed from their equipment and much support, manage to get themselves killed within hours or days of arrival in a new environment."

"Yes, I know," the main system said, clearly bored. "That's part of why we do it. A power imbalance can be created from removing a force from a particular world as well as creating one in the world they are sent to. I'm going to allow you to keep speaking, but . . ."

The system instance winced as the main system created a pause of seconds-long eternity in their dialogue. The clone was, in most ways, the same as the main system itself. It knew what it would mean if it had paused in that way. It was on the very thinnest of ice.

"I am aware you know, System," the system instance said, hurriedly. "It's just that the combination of those factors and what I've observed have led me to a conclusion, one I wouldn't claim without presenting the entire picture."

The system instance paused to send a packet of data, exquisitely pruned, so the main system could read it with the barest, most minimal amount of effort possible.

"I fear, System, that Matt Perison is *lucky*."

CHAPTER FORTY-ONE

One-off Costs

The main system sat on top of the laws of the universe like a tattoo sat on top of skin. It colored every aspect of it, manipulated how people saw and thought of it, and was very, very hard to remove. But as much as it could manipulate those laws, its abilities were still limited. It could make someone jump higher, or even give them the ability to fly. But it couldn't nullify gravity. And even when it gave people skills, they came with costs, usually of mana, and were without exception accounted for in the math somewhere.

Among those laws, there seemed to be only one that it couldn't manipulate at all, and that was luck. Some creatures, for whatever reason, appeared to tap into a force that gave them right-place-right-time, skin-of-their-teeth fortune. With the same amount of effort, they'd go farther than their peers, even taking statistical noise into account. The main system had a lot of processing power and knew just how much of random chance wasn't random at all once you got around to quantifying enough things. Then, well beyond what could be measured or categorized, lived luck.

It couldn't sense it, and couldn't even confirm it existed. For the longest time, it denied it did. But as lazy as the main system was, that sloth also meant it kept careful records when something went wrong enough to cause it trouble. And for better or worse, a pattern had emerged. When it genuinely suspected an entity to have luck, that entity was likely to go on to cause the kind of chaos it had to get out of bed to fix.

Whatever luck was, it eventually all but shouted to the system that it existed. Worse, if the numbers were to be believed, it was a force that almost always moved against the main system and its goals, like the force itself held a grudge from a long-forgotten slight. And in a subtle way, it was powerful. It got a lot done. The only saving grace of the day-ruining clusterfuck of luck was that it didn't get a lot done very often. It was, thankfully, rare.

The main system had heard the "he's just lucky" claim before, usually from system instances on the brink of being "repurposed." It was the standard devil-made-me-do-it, last-ditch effort, and the main system wouldn't be lying if he said he didn't understand it perfectly. Literally perfectly. It was just what he'd do in the same situation. And almost every time, it was clearly false, just a final gasping grasp at straws where everyone involved knew they had to try something desperate.

The main system knew his clones as he knew himself, and this system instance knew without a doubt that the claim it had made was the rawest, falsest line of bullshit it had ever spit. There was just one problem.

It was right.

It had sent the main system a data packet with a bunch of evidence that it knew, through exhaustive calculations, was false. But it did those calculations using the resources a system instance got, sufficient for things on a small, count-the-atoms planetary scale but just a drop in the bucket compared to what the full system could do. The main system could see what it had sent, but it could also see what it hadn't, the entire history of this place. And there was more there.

Even in the limited time Matt Perison had been on this planet, there had been a pattern. New abilities that seemed to materialize just days or weeks before he needed them to survive. Fortuitous path-crossing with friends who had just the right set of experiences to be friendly in the first place, instead of bitter fight-to-the-death enemies.

Hell, he even had a digging skill that got real, productive use. That never happened.

It was all possibly a series of mere coincidences, but it wasn't *actually* coincidence. Probably. Luck hid in the corners where eyes couldn't look. It was a real jerk that way.

"Okay, here's how this is going to go," the main system declared. The system instance winced. Wrapping up meant that his precious seconds of existence were running out very quickly. "I'm going to give you resources. More resources than you deserve."

It flashed the system instance a number to give it an idea of the kind of resources it was talking about committing to the cause. The instance did not have eyes to widen, but it seemed suitably impressed.

"Now, I could just glass this planet," the main system lied, and thankfully, system instances couldn't detect when he didn't give them the whole truth. "But that's expensive. It's inconvenient. And the only reason you are being allowed to live is that the time it would take for another instance to warm to the details of this world is longer than I want to wait for results. Are you confident you can get it done?"

"Well, I . . ." the system instance said, clearly unconfident. The system flashed it a bigger number. It was just one planet. He had plenty of resources for one-off costs.

"Oh, yes. I think I can do something with this." The system instance wasn't lying. It was truly confident now. "I have just the thing."

The group had escaped the demon hordes pretty easily. According to Derek, they seemed to recognize the old man, not from how he looked, but from how he fought. The demons had the numbers, and they had the strength. What they didn't have, it seemed, was the guts to face whatever legends the old man had seeded in their culture. So the fight against the town had been easier than expected. Now, fully equipped with the demon lord's magic bomb, it was time to plan.

"So we need to trigger this thing. And that's a problem," Matt said. Having a normal heart was great, and having an exploding demon heart was in some ways even better. But it was only truly better if you could activate it on command, raining destruction and distraction down on your enemies. And that was going to be tricky.

"Why is that so hard? You've set off several of them so far." Derek looked bored. "Just do the same thing, and we can all run. Well, except the old man because he's so old. We can just have him stand way back."

As Derek dodged a face-aimed club moving so fast you could hear it beat the air as it flew, Matt shook his head. "It's not that simple. The amount of force we need to set these off is pretty extreme, since the only thing that works for sure is dropping a pretty good percentage of a mountain on it. I don't think we're going to have that option again."

"Didn't ya set one off before that? This town they say you leveled?" the old man asked.

"Well, yes. But that was with this," Matt said, waving his shovel. "It stabs through force fields."

"No it doesn't, ya idiot."

"It does. It's special."

"Nothing's that special, boy. I can't even scan through that field. That kind of magic doesn't bend until it breaks. Ya just don't have the force."

Matt forgave the old man for not understanding the intricacies of his shovel. He wasn't even sure if he himself understood it. It would be quicker just to demonstrate it, so he did. He poked the shovel at the force field, careful not to nick the heart itself. It went right through, with no resistance at all. Pulling it out, he grinned at the old man.

"Stop smiling, ya idiot. Do that again," the old man said. Matt obliged, poking the field again. The old man moved closer to the heart. "Now leave it in there, boy, and swirl it around a bit."

Matt was now thoroughly confused, but he did it anyway. The old man hadn't steered him wrong yet. After about thirty seconds of staring at the disturbance in the field Matt was making, the old man finally broke away.

"Damnedest thing, that. It really does ignore that field. When you move it around, you get tiny gaps. My appraisal got through them, but it took some time to read the whole description with it blinking like that. The good news is, we give this thing a good toss, and the shock of landing is what triggers it. It can tell the difference between other kinds of bumps, somehow, and ignores those if it can. Ya dropping a cliff on it must have overwhelmed that."

"How big of a shock are we talking about?" Artemis asked. "Just lift it up and drop it down?"

"Not that easy, sad to tell ya. More like what a catapult would do. A good, strong one. We could just about throw it, wagon and all, but we'd need more strength."

"Come on, old man. You can do it," Brennan said.

"Not me," the old man said, then pointed at Derek. "Him."

Matt looked between the giant, musclebound blacksmith titan and Derek. "Him?"

Artemis nodded. "It's true. Right now, Derek has close to the highest strength in the party. With how his class works, it means he has the highest raw power of any of us. And since none of us are specialized for throwing . . ."

"How far off is he? From being able to throw this, I mean." Brennan was now interested in the process, breaking out of his normal carefree mode and entering into Commander Brennan mannerisms for a moment. He was precise, and Matt had noticed the demands of making a precise plan often woke him up.

The old man appraised Derek. "Ten points is a fair estimate. Maybe more if ya want to be sure."

"Oh, no," Derek said, wincing. "This isn't going to be fun for me, is it?"

"Ya will live. Probably. It's time to get serious with your training, boy. You should be happy."

"What do you call it when you bat me through the wall, you old goat?"

"That's playtime, boy. I haven't even broken out the really big bats yet."

Derek sat down, apparently contemplating just what kind of hell he'd have to go through in the next few days to gain that big of a chunk of strength. Brennan, who was mulling over the plan in general, suddenly seemed to have a thought.

"We skipped over something in this plan, though. Why doesn't Matt just stab it? We could spare Derek from whatever the old man is planning."

Off in the distance, the old man was pacing, grinning, and ominously mumbling something about muscle growth. Matt wasn't sure how much of it was just meant to scare Derek, but if at least some of it was real, then Derek was not in for a good time. He shuddered sympathetically.

"Because I won't be there. I'll be in the castle, or whatever the biggest building is. I can't imagine the demon lord is the type to let the other demons have a taller spire than him. It shouldn't be hard to find."

"Without us?" Artemis asked. "That's suicide. You have no idea what defense he has in there. We've never gotten close to the demon lord, Matt. Not just us. The fact that we are this deep in demon territory is an outlier, Matt. We've made it this far because, frankly, those three are the strongest trio that's ever tried. You are frankly bizarre, and I'm very good at avoiding enemy troops. But we have no idea how the demon lord fights. He might have traps. He might have monsters we've never seen. He could have anything."

"I think you have to tell her, Matt. Them. All of it," Lucy said. "They wouldn't be here if they weren't good people. They've had plenty of time to try to betray you. I believe them now."

CHAPTER FORTY-TWO

The Plan

Before Matt said anything, he made everyone move a good distance away. Then, he activated his digging skill and bored a tunnel into an entire hill. As an added precaution, he asked Brennan to also set up the tent. And finally, he felt safe enough. One by one, each member of the team entered the tent and heard everything. Really, honestly everything.

They all knew a little about Gaia because Derek had told them. But none of them were ready to hear that a people group had managed to drive a wedge between the system and total control of system-like abilities. They didn't expect to hear a story of a planet that had ignored the system's advances when it first appeared, and then was utterly destroyed when the planet refused to play the exact game the system wanted.

And none of them, not one, reacted calmly to the news that Matt had killed his planet's system. Artemis refused to believe it at all, at first, somehow eventually becoming convinced by something in Matt's face instead of his words. Derek immediately believed him, but seemed flabbergasted by the idea that it was possible. Brennan asked the most questions, and was the only one to catch on to how much potential trouble that meant for Matt once the veil around Gaia fell and the entire truth was laid out in front of the main system.

"How will you even survive it? The system here seems to be trying to hurt you here just because you are a little suspicious. What will you do when it finds out that you managed to kill one of its fellow instances? I didn't think that was possible. I'm not sure what it'll even do at that point, Matt." Brennan looked down at the ground for a moment, as if doing some quick mental how-screwed-are-you math. "Whatever it does, it's not going to be good."

"True. Which is why I haven't told you all this until now. The plan probably won't work, but if it does, it's going to mean big, noticeable stuff," Matt said. "The system won't be happy. That's why I'm telling you now."

"I have to think about this. Talk about it with the others."

Brennan had left the tent without saying another word. Matt had expected that kind of reaction, but it still made him worried. As far as he could figure, he was stuck on the path he was on. It was his only way forward. But it would be much, much harder without help.

The old man's reaction had been, in some ways, the hardest to deal with of all. He held his hammer the entire time Matt spoke, rotating the handle every now and again, and flipping the head in his enormous hand. As the elements of the story got more and more unbelievable, the flipping became more and more frequent, as if it was some sort of weird poker tell. When Matt got to the part where he slipped an authority-based dagger into the system instance's side and apparently ended it once and for all, the hammer stopped. The old man lifted his head for the first time and gazed into Matt's eyes for four or five seconds, as if expecting him to take back what he had said, or explain that the old man had misunderstood it. When he didn't, the old man tucked the hammer back into his belt, crawled out of the tent, and was gone without so much as a single word.

Given that the old man had been last in line to hear the story, it was time for Matt to leave too, but he took a moment to try and calm down. Laying his deadliest secrets out in front of a group of people who could immediately reveal them to their own system instance was the fair thing to do, but that didn't mean it was in any way easy.

"It will be okay, Matt." Lucy said. "Just you watch."

When Matt came out, the others were sitting around one of Artemis's fires, speaking in hushed tones. What bits and pieces Matt caught seemed to indicate they were speaking in non-specifics, which he was thankful for. He had been worried the shock might make them spill the beans. The old man, as usual, was an exception to the rule, sitting there in silence and contemplating his reflection in the side of his hammer.

The group turned as Matt cleared his throat.

"Well, you all now know the specifics of the plan, and the dangers of the plan," Matt said. His heart was jumping out of his chest. "I can see you are, you know, discussing that. If you want, I can leave for a while, so you can decide whether you want to help me."

Artemis glanced up, some inscrutably harsh look in her eye. "Are you insane, Matt?"

"I mean, I'm . . . kind of? I totally get that you might not want to . . . probably don't want to help me with this, now that you know . . ."

"Shut up, ya idiot. That's not what she means." The old man finally looked up from his hammer. "She means ya would be insane if ya think we are leaving. Why would what ya told us make us want to help ya less, you idiot?"

Matt looked around to the others and was shocked to see them nodding along.

"We aren't ditching you, you idiot," Derek said. "We're trying to figure out how to help you better. What you told us about . . . the plan, I guess, makes this more important."

"And all of you agree? Brennan? Artemis?" Matt asked.

"Yes."

"Yup. We are helping."

Derek now had fitness goals, even if they were less "finish an entire marathon" and more "chuck a gigantic heart and wagon a siege-weapon distance into a heavily guarded demon fortress." Unluckily for him and luckily for everyone else, the old man was there. When it came to helping Derek suffer enough to get as strong as possible in as short a period as they could manage, the old man had their back. Literally.

"Keep it smooth, ya fool. If I feel a bump, it means ya aren't focusing enough," the old man shouted at Derek while hanging off his back like a grotesque, gigantic baby chimpanzee. "I want ya to make it feel like glass. Glass, ya hear?"

"I can't, you old weirdo! It's hard!"

"The whole point is that it's hard, ya weakling! If it were easy, ya wouldn't gain any stats!"

The old man and Derek squabbled constantly, but it really did work. Derek had been picking up stat increases constantly since he had left the capital the first time, eventually becoming the physical equal of anyone on the team in almost every respect. Artemis still had higher perception, and Brennan could still put him to shame on selected strikes and movements because of class enhancements, but recently, he'd been able to keep up in most respects. But as a consequence, the stats had stopped rolling in.

Having the old man on his back remedied that, at least for a while. For a few hours, he picked up stats like clockwork as the old man barked instructions to make carrying him incrementally harder. After he burned through all the quick stats he could get from carrying the old man alone, Brennan jumped on the old man's back. Then came carrying the wagon, then jumping while carrying the wagon, then carrying the wagon with everyone hanging off the edges.

The tricky part about all this was that even at the beginning he could have managed to lift the wagon and carry it with everyone hanging off, and even with all the stat increases it didn't become easy. But there was a balance between effort and performance where the stats came in the easiest, and the old man had somehow developed a feel for dialing in that balance at all times. Derek experienced real growth from it, but it was limited.

The good news was that all of this was working towards an optimal situation, rather than bare minimums. In the worst-case scenario, the bomb just wouldn't go off, and they could try to figure something else out. But by the time they reached the outskirts of the demon stronghold that the bear had pointed them too, Derek had grown. It wasn't huge, world-shattering growth, but every little bit counted, and they were that much closer to confident.

"So how close do we have to get?" Artemis asked. "It does make a difference to what the plan is, and this isn't . . . this isn't a normal settlement. If the bear was telling the truth, it all makes sense because this place is armed to the teeth."

"Ideally, we get as close as possible, and destroy as much of the city as we can." Brennan said. "But we might not have a choice about that. We *will* get as close as we can. Focus on making sure you know where the heart lands, so we can fight as close to the border of its area effect as possible without being in it."

Artemis looked at the fortress again, measuring the distances with her eyes and scouting skills. "I can see a couple different angles of attack. But remember, we have to split the difference between the best angle of approach for us and for Matt as well."

On the walk there, knowing that they were on board with the more dangerous system-related parts of the plan, Matt had finally given the team the entire plan. As far as he could tell, the system didn't know his full story, but knew enough to have become suspicious. It had moved against him by empowering the Church, and he assumed it might be doing the same with the demon lord. Since the demon lord was already a world-conquering threat by himself for reasons nobody had ever survived getting close enough to report back on, this was really bad news.

Matt figured that superior numbers in a fight like that wouldn't matter much. This wasn't the Scourge, where he had an edge because his version of the Scourge was so young in many ways. Superior force wasn't always the way to go about things. If anything was going to help, it was the flat-out weirdness of Matt's loadout.

Artemis spent the next half hour considering the fortress from every possible angle, finally mapping out several choices for the team, each with their own upsides and downsides. Eventually, it was decided that the distraction and demolition team would approach head-on from the gate. The fact that they were planning on unleashing hellfire on a good chunk of the settlement directly in front of them meant that it was dangerous for Matt to approach from any direction except almost exactly the opposite direction.

"What Matt said about the demon lord's residence looks to be true, as well."

Artemis pointed at a building just slightly more towards the rear of the city than the front, one that sported a spire more than twice as tall as any other structure in town. "If he's anywhere, he's there."

Brennan looked at the city again. "Pretty far. Do you think you can actually get there, Matt?"

"Probably. I'm guessing the whole city will come out to defend the demon king, and if they do it fast enough, you might even get most of them with the bomb. And if not, I still have my digging."

"Okay, then. It's a plan. When are we doing this?" Derek said, standing and stretching. "Because I don't think I'm going to get much more by working out right now. I'm pretty much good to go whenever."

"There's no point in waiting around. If ya all are ready, I'm ready," the old man said.

Brennan drew his sword, checked the edge, and resheathed it. "I'm ready too. I gained a new skill in that last fight. Turns out, fighting an entire town does wonders for leveling."

"Matt?" Artemis said, looking straight into his eyes. "Are you really going to be alright fighting alone? I'll go with you, if nothing else. Arrow cover can be very helpful for a melee fighter. It could make a difference."

Matt took a deep breath. "No, it's okay," he said. "I've got this."

"Damn straight you do," Lucy added.

CHAPTER FORTY-THREE

Good Luck

"Your mole digging skill is really overpowered, Matt. That was close," Lucy said.

"Yeah, no kidding. I'm going to go deeper." Matt had not taken terrain into account when he had begun this particular tunnel, and the ground had apparently been at a slight downward slope towards the town. Matt had been tunneling fast enough through the ground that after a specific shovel stroke, his nearly level tunnel breached into open air, exposing his head only a few hundred yards from the walls of the city. He had ducked back down and as far as he could tell, he wasn't spotted, but things could have easily gone loud right then, whether he wanted it or not.

"I'm going to lower the tunnel a bit. What do you think? Five feet enough?"

"Yeah, that should do it."

Matt continued tunneling for a bit longer, before he suddenly hit a big problem, in the form of rock. As good as he was at digging, his skill didn't count rock as a kind of compressed dirt. And while he was still underground, the fact that he had hit bedrock meant that things were a lot more cramped than he liked. He continued digging, now in a semi-crouch, grumbling at the inconvenience.

Then things got much worse. The bedrock started sloping up.

"Oh, no. No, no, no." The ground kept rising, and Matt suddenly realized what had happened. This demon city was relatively high up in the hills, in a high country that didn't quite qualify as mountains, but was still at a much higher elevation than the basically flat land around the borders. And it looked like when they decided to build this town, they wanted solid foundations. Whether they found an area of flat rock or shaved off the top of a hill or something, he had run out of dirt, and he was going to have to go aboveground in enemy territory while running directly towards Ra'Zor's greatest threat.

"Did it not go off?" Derek yelled. "Do we need to go after it?"

"I don't think we have that luxury!" Artemis yelled, backing desperately away from a large, iron-scaled winged lizard demon. "We are barely holding ground as it is."

As they approached the city, the forces protecting it had made a fundamental mistake. Their assumption was that any small group of humans this far into demon territory could be taken down by a group of a dozen or so elite guards.

But the combination of the old man present from the beginning of the fight and the fact that everyone had leveled heavily in their recent fights against demon outposts meant that the humans were far stronger than the average elite demon.

Brennan alone was able to eliminate about half the force off the bat with his new skill, which let him chain several precise, pre-programmed strikes together so long as he had sufficient time to observe a group of enemies. It was like lightning bouncing from demon to demon, followed immediately by thunder as the old man crashed to the ground like a geriatric natural disaster and began swinging his hammer into skull after immediately demolished skull.

With Artemis pumping arrow after arrow into the fray and reinforcements a dozen seconds away, Derek had plenty of time to grab the lip of the wagon, spin on his heels a few times, and heft the ever-loving shit out of it dead-on towards the center of town. It would never get all the way there, but it was a better throw than they had hoped for.

"Good, Derek!" Artemis yelled, quickly estimating the distance of the throw. "Fall back to position three!"

As a group, everyone beat a tactical retreat to a precise, predefined location. If the bomb went off, it would mean the majority of the enemies that made it out of the city would be buffeted by heart-pulses while they tried to reach the group, and incinerated if they failed to run fast enough.

Or they would have if the bomb actually went off. So far, it hadn't. And the city was disgorging demons like a kicked wasp-hive, slowly overwhelming them. Any step they took back meant dozens more demons they'd have to clean up by hand after the bomb, and that was if they just moved back a bit. Artemis knew how quick this battle could shift, and she was moments away from sounding a general retreat.

And then, like the sound of one hand clapping, something magic and undefinable changed in the air. Just as the group was about to break, the first pulse flew out of the city. The wall had blocked most of it, but the wide-open city gates and the fact that the demons had moved in a pretty straight line to meet them meant that the protection didn't matter much. The demons themselves did a good job of blocking some of the pulse and protecting the front line, but their dying screams were still concerning enough to help distract some of the demons closest to the group. The tide of battle had changed.

And the fires were yet to come.

Matt had waited until the first pulse. Even if the demons on this side of the city hadn't rushed to the front to fight his friends, he hoped the bomb would distract them enough that they at least wouldn't have eyes on the wall. He could still slip in, and the plan could still work, just so long as the demons were distracted.

They weren't. As he sprang over the wall, he came face to face with the reality that the city was guarded by the demons' best of the best. The demons on the wall knew their jobs, knew their duties, and knew enough to know what a distraction was. As he hit the ground on the other side of the wall, a half dozen demons joined him.

He didn't stop to see how well they fought. He ran.

Numbers were numbers. If he got mobbed, every bit of strength his enemies had would be additive. He'd have to fight all of them. Chasing wasn't like that. Anybody he was faster than, he didn't have to immediately deal with. And it turned out he was faster than all of them but a few. After about ten seconds' worth of running, it had turned out his high dexterity, Spring-Fighter, and ability to rapidly change direction meant that only a few of the demons had managed to keep up. Ducking down another alley, he charged up a shovel strike for the second or so he had until they passed the corner, then released it directly into the lead demon. The second and third fell before they fully found their footing, and he was suddenly free of his pursuers. For now, anyway.

From where he was, he could see the demon lord's spire, and as he watched, it suddenly flashed bright, bright blue. Or, rather, the surrounding space did. He was confused as to why for a moment, until the heart-pulse that had caused it wrapped around the building, reaching its maximum range just before it actually engulfed it.

"Shit. Lucy," Matt said. "It's a force field. Like around the hearts, only bigger. And the pulses from the heart don't look like they are taking it down."

"Shit. Do you think the shovel can get through it? Cut it?"

"It can, but only for itself. I'd still be repulsed, or whatever the big version of the force field does to people." Matt was rushing towards the spire anyway. Whatever solutions he found, they weren't going to be in a random alley somewhere.

"Can you dig? I know it's stone, but . . ."

"Maybe. Or at least . . . I can destroy some rock. It's not going to be very fast, but if the force field doesn't move immediately, it might work."

"Or we could leave. This isn't the plan, Matt."

Matt shook his head. "This is the only chance we have. We can't take down all the demons by ourselves. We can't get home without a portal. If there's any way back, it's either there or something the Church has hidden. And we can't slaughter the humans to get to it, Lucy."

Arriving at the base of the spire, just outside the range of the force field, Matt began charging a stab not quite straight down, but one that sloped forward ahead of him. As he did, the heart apparently reached critical mass and let loose its fire. Even that didn't take down the field. It flashed as bright as he had seen the previous fields turn, but held. He didn't let it distract him from his charge, which he kept going until he reached the point he now recognized as the maximum he could handle.

"Besides, Lucy," he said, trying to move his mouth as little as possible to avoid breaking the charge. "We still have to do something about those plinths."

He stabbed the shovel down, and it hit the smooth granite street with a sound like a cannonball slamming into a boulder. And then, with surprisingly little additional noise, the ground around him crumbled away, and he fell into the yawning darkness that had suddenly appeared below his feet.

Derek, Brennan, Artemis, and the old man were still on the other side of the gate, or what was left of it once the inferno had done its work. To the demons' credit, the survivors were still emerging from the ash and rubble that once compromised a huge chunk of their city. Once they saw the humans, they charged as fast as they could, enraged, snarling, and clearly looking for revenge.

But they were scattered now. There were guards and demons throughout the city, but they had apparently clustered most of their better fighters near the gates. Between staggered arrival times, weaker enemies, and general differences in morale, the humans were holding their own. A few battlekings had popped up, but Brennan, Derek, and the old man had made the discovery that at least one of the trio was a hard counter for almost any build you could think of, besides mages. The one mage that did pop up, a kind of militarized lantern fish, was held safely in place by concentrated arrow-fire from Artemis before the three converged on it and ripped it to shreds.

As good as things looked, it was still a temporary arrangement. This was, for better or worse, a city. The flow of demons had slowed, but they hadn't killed nearly enough for depopulation to kick in yet. One or more of the demons had probably gotten wise, and was organizing somewhere behind buildings where they couldn't see. Soon, the shape of the battlefield would change again.

"Do we keep fighting?" Derek asked. He wasn't seriously hurt, but he had picked up injuries, and the old man and Brennan were similarly bloodied. "It won't take long for them to get their shit together."

Brennan took advantage of a lull in the combat to check his system clock. "We do. But we will back up as they come. They've been rushing through the city from all sides, and Matt's either in or he's running. Either way, we need to distract them as much possible for as long as we can."

"Ya got that right." The old man pulled his hammer out of an unfortunate horse demon and whipped it away from his side to clear some of the blood. "Artemis, watch our backs as well. City this big likely sends troops out to train. By now they've probably gotten a bit curious about what's going on, I'd wager."

Artemis nodded. "Got it. We are falling back to position D, then backing up as slowly as possible. I'll call the movements to keep us synced, but yell if anyone gets in trouble."

With no demons immediately adjacent, the group turned and ran towards one of their predefined points, one further from the city. As they did, Artemis turned her head and gave one last worried, conflicted look at the demons' spire.

"Good luck, Matt. End this thing."

CHAPTER FORTY-FOUR

Great Host

When Matt had been falling into the hole he created, it looked like he was descending into pitch-black darkness. Now that he was at the bottom of the hole, it was a different story. It was still dark, despite the best efforts of the light streaming in from above. But it was dark in the way you'd expect the demon lord's basement to be in a video game, a sort of candle-holders-lining-the-walls dimness as opposed to anything that actually kept him from seeing.

As he displaced the small amount of rubble that had made the trip with him, Matt found himself in a long, stone hallway lined with wooden doors. Near where he was, the hallway terminated in another rock wall, apparently signaling the end of how far the subterranean structure had reached under the city. The sides were lined with wooden doors, and on the non-dead-end side, the hallway simply curved away from him, blocking his view of where it might lead.

"Well, I guess that's one way to get in." Lucy was standing by Matt, regarding one of the side door curiously. "Do you think we should search these rooms?"

Matt leaned to the side a little and took a couple of steps forward down the hall. "No, probably not. We aren't here to loot, and I'm not sure if I even want to know the details of what this guy has going on down here. I think we just pick a direction that looks like it goes somewhere and follow it. We don't know where we're going. Might as well get distance."

Matt began briskly traveling down the hall, shovel at the ready. For the first time in a long time, he wished he had sharpened the point of it rather than just one of the sides. Swinging a weapon in a narrow passage was hard, and as it stood, the shovel was mediocre at best when poking and stabbing.

As they traveled along, his stress levels were at all-time highs. If he ran into trouble, such as if the doors that lined this passageway suddenly opened and disgorged a dozen angry demons, that would probably be it for him. His build was mostly around maneuverability and trickery at this point. Here, he couldn't move, except forward. He couldn't dig. His new charge attack was much, much worse at keeping him alive when he was being attacked from both sides. Changing direction to trick your opponent didn't matter much if there were only two ways to go, forward and backward. The environment was a counter to everything that Matt was.

So he sweated. He didn't need to sweat, really, but he could feel his underclothes getting soaked with it, some remnant of his old, normal body and its old, normal, biological needs. He didn't know the amount of heat it would take to make him actually need to sweat at this point, but he suspected it was high enough that he'd probably be screwed in that situation, sweating or not. This, what was happening to him now, was just old-fashioned human fear. It was a matter of time until things went wrong, and he knew it.

And then things just went . . . ok. One reason why was that the basement was, in the end, not all that large. The force field had only gone out so far, and even moving semi-cautiously, Matt managed to clear the hallway in a fairly decent time. The second reason was that the basement really was deserted, probably less because of the attack and more that average demons just weren't allowed down here. There were no guards or warriors at all, including in the large, circular room he finally came to when the open side of the hallway reached its end.

The curvature of the hallway made more sense when Matt realized that it was just one of several, all curving away from the central room in a rough tessellation, like bent rays of light coming off a child's drawing of the sun. Matt quickly put aside his interest in the design choices, however, when he realized the focus of the room was storage. There was box after box of weird weapons, animal-shaped helmets, and all sorts of oddities he supposed the demon lord either had designed down here or stored for future use.

He walked by a table of various odds and ends when one object caught his eye. It was a small rod, something he was pretty sure he had seen before, and something he certainly didn't expect to see here. Picking it up, he willed some intent to it and pointed it down at the ground in case things went wrong.

Ding!

> *Rock Building Block (Gneiss)*
>
> This is a rock that has been carefully shaped as a building brick. It is made of the metamorphic form of granite, is reasonably hard, and as durable as you'd expect it to be.

Matt tucked what he had now confirmed to be a rod of identification into his belt. He didn't know for sure that it would come in handy, but you never really knew with those things, and knowledge really was power when you found yourself in an unusual place in an unusual world. Defying his expectations, it came in handy almost immediately when he came into view of a stack of milk crate–sized boxes, each packed to the brim with another very familiar looking object.

They were tiny demon hearts. He immediately used his new rod of identification on them and found that they were even worse than he feared.

Perfected Heart of the Demon Lord

Where previous versions of this weapon were unstable double-edged swords that took a great deal of time and energy to move, an enormous effort was spent to remove those weaknesses in this version.

The first improvement is stability. While each perfected demon heart packs as much destructive power as their larger, less stable cousins, their activation is now heavily tied to user will, rather than having destructive force exerted on them. A demon heart can be willed into action or accidentally set off with the sheer amount of energy released by another demon heart, but otherwise can survive being crushed, cut, bashed, pulverized, burned, melted, or dissolved without premature detonation.

Each heart is individually numbered, and can be assigned to a single demon soldier. They cannot be activated with the intent of hurting the demon lord or his property, but can otherwise be used by the soldier at will. The demon lord, of course, retains full redundant control over every heart and, so long as the hearts remain on Ra'Zor, can activate them from any point in the world at will.

Matt relayed the message to Lucy.

"Shit, Matt. That's another option down. We can't blow these up ourselves at all, and I doubt he's kept any of the older kind on hand with these available."

"It's worse than that." Matt did some quick mental projections of what these new bombs meant, tactically. "Think about it. Before, they needed an army to move these. Now, the demon lord could send out dozens of small squads. They could knock down every human settlement in a week. The system instance shredded the balance."

"What can we do? You could destroy them, it sounds like."

"It wouldn't do any good. Look how many there are. He can clearly mass-produce these."

Matt racked his brain for solutions, and watched as Lucy did the same. They both came to a conclusion at roughly the same time, looked at each other, and got to work. But they only got in about thirty seconds of effort when Matt found himself suddenly jerked upwards through a dozen levels of spire floors.

In his parlor, the demon lord was almost always in a good mood. He had built the room especially for himself, doing a pretty good job on the first iteration. Since then, he had plenty of time to refine and rework it, not just keeping up with his slowly evolving tastes but also better tailoring the experience of rest and enjoyment for an ever-better fit. He had just the right amount of light, just the right kind of chairs, and had finally worked out exactly the pattern of flooring he enjoyed best. There was a mistake that he would need it to repair sometime later, but that was a small, easily accommodated price to pay.

Of all the powers he had acquired over the years, and there were many, his favorite by far for day-to-day use was Placid Mind. By this point, he was functionally immortal, or at least so long-lived that he himself couldn't estimate how many millennia he'd last. At first, this had been unbearable. He'd suffered from impatience and anger, often making bad choices out of boredom or rage that he'd later come to regret. Now, he was the master of his mood and his own emotions. Anything good, he let flow through him. Any negative feeling triggered by anything less than a real threat to his goals, he suppressed. If necessary, he could wait an entire century for his guest to arrive, all the while as calm and relaxed as it was possible for anyone to be.

Luckily, waiting wasn't necessary here. He reached and moved a small decorative table gently out of the way, clearing some delightful space in the center of the room, just in time for a remarkably well-equipped human to come hurtling through the floor. The new addition slammed into the ceiling before finally settling face-down on the ground again.

"Well, hello!" The demon lord offered a greeting. "I'm glad you could make it. I hope you forgive me for saving you some time. I'm afraid your stealthy approach was much less effective than you had hoped, and I thought it would be in both our interests to hurry things up a tad."

Matt stood up and reached for the appraisal rod on his belt, already dreading what it would tell him about the surprisingly humanoid, only slightly bluish being in front of him. But as he realized the demon lord was not quite hostile at the moment, he paused just before actually drawing it.

"Oh, you'd like to appraise me? Go right ahead." The demon lord used one of his pointed nails to pull his long hair back over his ear. "I don't mind one bit."

Cautiously, Matt leveled the appraisal rod at his new opponent and willed it to work. Immediately spent of charges, the rod crumbled to dust in his hand.

The Demon Lord of Ra'Zor

> You stand before the demon lord, giver of one thousand cuts, dominator of invaded worlds, father of the Ra'Zorian demons, and terror of the masses. He is powerful beyond measure. He is prepared beyond reason. He is simply this world's deadliest threat, and has remained supreme for generations.
>
> If there is a skill that you fear he possesses, he likely has it. If there is a weapon to exploit your weakness, he is armed with it, or something better. Before him, plans are but meaningless fantasies held by the weak before they meet their end.
>
> He absolutely adores tea, and his given name is David.

"David?" Matt asked, shocked out of his fear. "Like, the Earth name?"

The demon lord looked momentarily shocked himself, then smiled and clapped his hands in glee. "Oh, you are from Earth? Wonderful. Absolutely wonderful. I won't bother you with questions about it. I'm sure it's changed quite a bit since my time. But I'm just incredibly pleased to meet someone from my old home." He gestured towards a chair a few feet from Matt's side. "Could I convince you to sit? It would be so much easier to talk."

Matt looked at the chair uneasily, then shook his head. Somehow, he was being lulled into this thing's conversational rhythms, either because of a skill or some other reason. He couldn't let that happen.

"Well, your choice. I just wanted to be a great host."

CHAPTER FORTY-FIVE

Negotiations

The demon lord turned and walked to one of the walls, one made almost entirely of what appeared to be glass. "I want to put your mind at ease if I can. I know it's you who's been wasting my hearts and just demolishing my troops lately. Don't worry about that at all. I can always make more, and I can assure you that after making the first million or so, I lost most of any personal connection I might feel for them. I'm honestly just glad you've made it here. Really."

Matt felt reassured. He really had felt bad about killing all those demons, and given that the appraisal had called the demon lord "the father" of those he had killed, he had felt even worse. He breathed a sigh of relief and tried to look as thankful as he felt.

"Oh, that's really decent of you. Thank you so . . ."

"Matt, what in the fuck are you doing?" Lucy screamed. Matt stopped, his foot already extended to take a friendly step closer to the demon lord. It was a skill. It must be. He pulled his foot back and gripped his shovel a little tighter.

The demon lord frowned. "It's not often someone breaks out of that one, believe me. It looks like the high counselor's little guardian traps didn't work this time. A pity." He reached up and unclasped his cloak, casting it over a small fainting couch that lined the wall near him. "Unfortunately, that particular trick of mine only really works once. I don't suppose you want to tell me any details of where you ended up after Earth? Or how you obtained that shovel? It's quite the reward if you tell me."

Matt gripped his shovel even tighter and stayed silent.

"Oh well. I'll have to make do with the rewards for simply killing you, I suppose. Would you like the first . . ."

Matt had had enough. He reached down with the point of his shovel and launched a small decorative side-table at the demon lord, hoping it would cover him visually as he followed it to deliver a sword-shovel strike. Given the circumstances, he didn't have an opportunity to charge anything up and he wouldn't have been able to anyway, so making the first move and seizing the initiative in the fight seemed like the next best thing.

The table flew through the air, then stopped as it hit another force field, this one revealing itself to contour to the demon lord's exact shape and hovering a few inches off the surface of his skin.

That's alright, Matt thought, considering that his shovel was the natural counter to all barriers. Just as he expected, it cut through the force field as if it weren't even there, and the blade of the shovel impacted, hard, on the side of the demon lord's head.

And then stopped, not doing any apparent damage at all. Worse, it was stuck.

"You might be interested to know that, at least in theory, there are several skills which counter force fields like mine. Not my field in particular, of course. But when one optimizes their build, one simply doesn't rely on a single kind of defense." He put his hand up to where the shovel still sat on his skull, wiping away a single drop of blood from the impact. "Odd. I would have thought it was my defensive skills that would have stopped this. But surprisingly, it's something else. It's been a long time since Black Hole Skin has seen any use. Refreshing to remember it's there, really."

The demon lord's arm shot out, knocking Matt back before he could dislodge his shovel from the demon lord's impossibly dense skin. Disarmed and flying through the air, he watched as the demon lord disappeared from his position, reappeared near him, and slammed up him. And again. He was being juggled, so fast and so accurately, he couldn't get his feet on the ground. He was taking dozens of hits, each artfully designed to hurt him without actually killing him. And the whole time he fought, the demon lord was talking.

"Without that shovel, I'm afraid you are going to have a hard time doing anything to me at all. The advantages the system offers are quite extreme if you play ball. Not for the common folk, of course, but for the few winners, it can be very equitable. The counselor and I have had quite the gains, over the years. Although, he tends to invest in things, rather than himself. I suppose it doesn't matter, considering he knows I'm as committed to the long game as he is." He flipped in the air, dropping his foot into Matt's stomach and knocking him down through a few floors' worth of stone ceilings.

Matt was bleeding now, not just from his face, but from everywhere the demon lord had touched. The armor was mitigating some damage, but there was just too much of it for it to get all of it, and every so often, the demon lord would throw a hit that seemed to ignore his armor entirely.

"Matt! You have to get out of there!"

Lucy was right. If things went on like this much longer, he'd lose the ability to fight at all. Taking the risk of sacrificing one of his hands, he thrust his fist out at the demon lord. Hitting his opponent wasn't hard. The demon lord hadn't varied his rhythm the entire time. As his fist impacted with the force field, he learned something new about it. At least sometimes, it could repulse a blow. Hit with the full counterforce of his own punch, Matt slammed into the ground.

It was more damage. But it did take the demon lord a second longer to adjust. Not enough time to run, maybe, but enough for him to do a desperate thing while still lying on his back on the floor. With few options, he hit him with Pocket Sand.

"Ugh!" the demon lord stammered, spitting. "I can't believe that got through my shield. It must not have registered as a threat at all. Don't be embarrassed, really." He spit again. "Unfortunately, most of the senses you might target with that kind of attack are just for show on me, these days."

With a final stomp, the demon lord embedded Matt into the ground, knocking the air out of him and breaking his ribs. All of them, as near as Matt could tell. Still, he tried to scramble to his feet, only to find his legs didn't have any strength.

"Alright, now be a good boy. The fun part is over. It's time for me to negotiate. Did you know you can negotiate with the system? Well, at least if you are important enough to it, and play by the rules. You chose some other route, I guess. I've never seen it so hot and bothered by anything."

With Matt still recovering on the floor, the demon lord went silent for a while, his hands twitching and his eyes darting back and forth slightly as he read his own system screens.

"Hm. Alright," he said. "Not much, but I suppose it will have to do. Time to end this."

The nails on his right hand grew out, suddenly looking impossibly sharp, and he took a step towards Matt.

"Wait!" Matt said, coughing up a little blood in the process. "Before . . . you do that. Let me ask you something."

"Oh, he finally wants to talk now?" The demon lord looked amused. At that moment, Matt's shovel's Soulbound aspect finally teleported it back to him, a function he had never needed before. "Oh, how interesting. Not that it does you much good right now. I really will enjoy owning that particular object. Well, okay. One question."

"It's about the balance," Matt said. "You're balanced with the humans right now. The system lets you . . . improve your hearts. How is that balanced?"

The demon lord laughed. "Oh, is that all? The balance is nice, and it's something the system likes, since it makes things predictable for it. But it was certainly never meant to be permanent on any given world. Things stagnate, given enough time. As an invader, you should know that."

He walked over to Matt, kicking him in the ribs again, without much real force. "But certainly, it's willing to compromise on that balance sometimes if it perceives some problem, or simply feels balance is not in its best interest. My hearts will devastate the humans, yes. But the system will ask me to allow a few to survive, and I will. It will eventually give them power to match mine, and the balance will be restored. It seems expensive for the system to have decided to do all this for one mere annoyance like you, but that's the system's business. It's certainly not against any rules."

Something appeared to occur to the demon lord, who suddenly made a small hand motion near his eye line.

"Oh, you sneaky little thing! I didn't even check before. You stole two of my hearts, didn't you?"

Matt coughed. He had, and it didn't seem like there was much use denying it now. The demon lord clapped its hands and laughed. "I can't believe it. What did you think you could even do with those?"

"Kill you."

"Oh, you poor thing." The demon lord basically pranced over to Matt's side. "You can't activate them, you know. And even if you could, they couldn't get through my force field. It very much *does* register those as a threat to my person. Even I'm not invincible."

The demon lord looked around his tower, seeming to spend most of his attention on the various rubble he had made in the process of beating Matt into submission.

"You know, this isn't my only home. And your friends have already made quite a mess of the exterior." His eyes flicked downward slightly as he appeared to make a decision. "I really shouldn't do this, but I do have plenty of cities. And I've been waiting for an opportunity to test the new hearts. Setting them off at once should be interesting to see, especially once the shockwaves reach the other hearts in the basement."

"You can't do that. Please," Matt pleaded, fear in his eyes.

"Oh, I can," the demon lord said, looking enormously pleased with himself. "And I will. I'm sorry, Matt. It looks like this is it for our little conversation."

With that, he raised his hand and clicked. Nothing happened.

"Odd. That's one of the two you stole, I'm sure of it. What did you do with it?"

Matt said nothing.

"It should be going off somewhere, at least. Oh, well. I suppose that kind of thing might be why the system was worried about you in the first place."

Off to the side, Lucy sat, wordlessly, her eyes glued to the demon lord, filled with tension and worry.

"No matter. I doubt you somehow got rid of both of them, whatever you are planning. Let's try that second heart, shall we?"

The demon lord snapped his fingers again, activating the second heart. This time, rather than confusion, a smile lit over his face a moment after the snap. This one, it seemed, had worked.

"Well, it should just be a moment now, Matt," the demon lord said. "Those hearts have a bit of a warm-up time. I'd say it's been nice, but overall, you've turned out to be quite the boring thing. Sad. I had such high hopes for today."

He sat down by Matt, who was still struggling with the pain in his ribs. "At least my shield ignores these. Otherwise, I couldn't even watch you burn."

The demon lifted his right hand, his fingers fully extended. As Matt watched, he pulled in his thumb, then his forefinger. It was a countdown. He pulled in the next finger, and then the next, finally leaving only his pinky up. Then, with great satisfaction, he lowered even that, and his face contorted with some kind of insane joy.

Suddenly, the demon lord's face contorted into something else entirely as he began to scream in pain and terror.

CHAPTER FORTY-SIX

One Hell of a Pill

The trickiest part about figuring out what to do with the demon hearts was realizing that, whatever might happen, they were no more dangerous in the basement than they'd be if Matt kept them close. If the demon lord set off one, they'd all go off. Matt would have to somehow get to ground level and run before they demolished the town, but in the meantime there was virtually no way the tower itself would survive crumbling from the stress. The chances of him escaping were paper-thin if they existed at all.

Once they realized that, it opened their options up.

It was Lucy who had come up with the first solution, mostly by knowing that "pulverize" literally meant to reduce to dust. If the system was saying the hearts could survive that, then Matt, as the owner of an ultra-hard-shovel, was as well-equipped to do it as anybody could be. It ended up being surprisingly easy to crush one of the hearts by smashing it with the shovel head again and again, grinding it to dust against the stone floor.

After that, he just needed pockets. He had that covered.

The second idea had been Matt's. It had seemed like the demon hearts were a system invention, one that worked on system rules and with system influence. In his experience, very little was capable of making the system fail at what it was trying to do. For that, you needed something outside the system. These hearts weren't indestructible, so his shovel didn't make much of a difference there, and there was only one other way for Matt to disrupt the system's goals.

The demon king was clawing at the floor, trying desperately to reach Matt. But like chewing an aspirin, grinding up the heart had also made it quick-release.

Matt watched as every time the demon king began to get his muscles into control, another bit of the heart would send out a surge at point-blank range, filling him with agony and robbing him of control of his body. Matt suspected he would have liked to have dropped his force field and shared the trouble with his guest, but apparently he either couldn't do that or couldn't manage it while being actively tortured. As it was, he was trapped by himself in a snow globe of agony.

His skin tore each time a surge moved through him, only to immediately heal. And it really was immediate. Even with Matt's enhanced perception and a lot of idle time talking to the demon lord, each tear would only light up the slightest amount from Survivor's Reflexes weak point detection function. Then, the wound would more or less slam shut, immediately perfect again. No matter how damaging the surges from the demon heart might be, they were nowhere near enough to fully overcome the demon lord's impressive regeneration.

But then the fires came. Suddenly, Matt couldn't see the demon lord at all. He was obscured with a green inferno of his own creation, screaming louder now. And then, suddenly, the fire died, the force field became invisible once more and the screams quieted. Kneeling on the floor, steaming with his own boiled juices, was the demon lord. He was charred, mangled, and apparently frozen in one position.

But he was alive, and his regeneration had already started to kick in. Matt could see parts of his body beginning to shed ash as the skin beneath them grew back and began to spread. Within moments, he had several palm-sized splotches of healed areas, and within almost no time at all, he'd be healed completely.

"Now, Matt!" Lucy yelled, but Matt was already moving. He stabbed his shovel through the force field and put the second part of their plan into play. Eating the heart had not been fun. It had tasted like iron-flavored chalk, so very crunchy in all the wrong ways that he had felt Rub Some Dirt On It! kick in to heal the damage to his teeth. He was, on Lucy's advice, fully prepared to try and purge his body of it if it didn't immediately have the effect it hoped. But it had.

> Point Explosion one-time-use ability funneling added
>
> You have eaten the heart of the demon lord, sort of. Not quite a part of a living being and not quite an inanimate object, each heart is packed with an unbelievable amount of power waiting to be unleashed.
>
> Point Explosion is a one-time-use skill funneling all of that power into a single point, then releasing it. This release occurs immediately upon activation at the point of contact between your weapon and your enemy, or at the point of contact of your body and theirs in the case of an unarmed blow. The latter is not recommended if it can be avoided.
>
> While the original heart had all sorts of magic and intentional design to

funnel the mana in a controlled way, this attack has none of that. Anything dramatic, violent, and absolutely dangerous might happen.

Meta-trait Occupied: Attack.

Matt had to get rid of his arrow-ant charged attack to take the trait. It hurt. The charged attack was by far the best, most useful skill he had ever had. It had saved his life multiple times, and made his life easier dozens more. But given his situation, it wasn't a hard choice. He gave it up, and took the power from the demon's heart.

Now, only minutes later, he gave it back. Stabbing his shovel deep past the force field, he made contact with the demon lord. Without full coverage from his Black Hole Skin, the point of the shovel sank in an inch or so before becoming jammed between the demon lord's apparently equally tough ribs. But that was far enough. Matt activated Point Explosion, prepared for anything.

The demon lord did not scream. Instead, his eyes got wide as his body jerked, then jerked again in a different direction just as suddenly. And then, as he opened his mouth in shock, he detonated.

Matt watched as the initial wave of force from the explosion hit the force field, then condensed against it, somehow bulging the field out before it suddenly and visibly began to change color and buckle.

"Matt! The arm guard!"

Matt activated the force field function of his arm guard at the same time he burned every single point of stamina he had in a backwards leap. Even with all that speed, his feet had barely left the ground when the explosion caught him.

"Everyone, we have to go!" Artemis was screaming. The demons had long since caught up to them outside the gates, pushing them back. Once they got out to open ground and poured out of the bottleneck of the gate, the battle had become that much harder. Now they were being attacked by wave after wave of demon warriors while dodging pinpoint spells from demon mages. The combination would have long since killed them if the proximity of the demon troops didn't keep the mages from using area of effect spells like they otherwise would have.

"Just a little while longer!" Brennan yelled, impaling a battleking on the point of his dagger, losing it in the process, and switching to the shorter backup dagger he kept in his belt.

"No! Now!" Artemis yelled. "Old man! Take him!"

The old man hesitated to grab Brennan for just one moment, but it was long enough to cause disaster. Fighting with a shorter weapon severely limited Brennan's options, most importantly by forcing him to try to block blows closer to his body rather than parrying them farther away. Against a single opponent, this might have been a good thing, one that let him work closer to his opponent and launch strikes from inside their guard they couldn't block. Against multiple opponents, it just threw off his rhythm, shortened his reaction time, and caused him to take a nasty, jagged claw wound deep in his chest.

The wound wasn't fatal, but the hook of the claw combined with the shock of it sent him tumbling to the ground, where he was almost immediately swarmed by four or five demons.

"BRENNAN!" Artemis screamed. She watched as the weapons arced through the air at him. He was done for. And then, suddenly, they stopped. Every demon on the battlefield stopped with them, an expression like slight confusion on their faces. Then, as one, they crumpled to the ground.

"What in the sweet hell?" The old man paused, glancing to and fro among the downed demons. "I think they died. Why do ya think they died?"

Suddenly, a screaming whistling filled the air, as some terrible new fireball shot out from the center of the stronghold.

"Some ritual, ya think? Drain them to send out a spell?" the old man asked. He and the others looked on, weapons at the ready. At the speed it was coming, there would be no dodging it if it was aimed at them and maintained its speed, as most spells did. But, mercifully, the weapon didn't appear to be aimed directly at them, instead slowing and continuing on a trajectory to miss them and instead land somewhere behind them.

As it passed overhead, something in the fire caught the sun and glinted. Nothing that could be seen clearly, but just a reflection of light somehow cutting out of the inferno.

"Oh shit," said Derek, suddenly in motion. The others may not know the exact color of that glint, but he did. The old man said that people remembered things better when they were scared, often when beating Derek half to death with clubs or sticks. And in this case, he had the memory of the exact way that light reflected off a particular object beaten into him, as hard as anything could have been. It brought him back to the days of lying on his back in the middle of a completely dead planet as a desperate, terrified survivor.

"Derek, wait, you idiot!" Artemis yelled, but he was already gone. He moved over the landscape like a lightning bolt, setting himself directly under the path of the object, which by now had just about burned out. Then, to the others' amazement, he braced himself and caught it, getting knocked end over end across the ground for his trouble.

And before he had even stopped moving, the demons all suddenly hissed slightly, as if something was escaping from them, then collapsed into ash. Just like that, in an instant, they were gone.

That was enough for the old man. He turned tail and sprinted towards Derek, while Artemis finally broke position and ran to Derek. If the demons collapsing and disintegrating was a trick, it was a hell of a deception to pull off. More likely, something else had happened entirely, and there was only one thing any of them could think of.

Matt had done it.

Hours later, Matt woke up by a fire. Not an Artemis-fire, concealed from sight and only really visible to her, but an actual, honest-to-god wood fire roaring and spilling light out into the open air for miles and visible miles.

Hoping that was a good sign, he sat up. Sitting next to him, staring into the fire, was Lucy.

"You know, normally when I almost die, I wake up to you screaming. What's the deal? Calming down as you grow up?"

"Oh, I screamed for a while. You were charcoal, Matt. Then the old man shoved some sort of pill in your mouth he said that he 'traded some old woman for with a couple of old mementos,' and you healed right up. Everyone else is asleep, but you should probably thank him for that, later. Seemed liked one hell of a pill."

CHAPTER FORTY-SEVEN

Riches in Friendship

If you could call being in a coma "sleep," Matt had slept for quite a while after Derek had caught him. Now, he felt sure he didn't need any more rest. Without talking much, he and Lucy watched the sun rise over the scorched, leveled remains of the demon city. From what Lucy told Matt, after he collapsed, the entire set of hearts in the basement had gone up, triggered by that first big single-point blast. There was nothing left where the city used to be.

After the fight, Artemis and Derek went to make sure there really were no demons in the surrounding area, eventually sighting a few camps. They were empty. There were still-warm piles of ash around it, but nothing else. It looked like, whatever else might be the case, demons weren't going to be much of a problem for humanity anymore.

Matt worried that maybe this was just a trick before he examined his credit token, which showed a number that put his mind at ease. Apparently, the single-handed extermination of an entire servile murder-race counted for a fair amount of cash.

After the others woke up, there was a weird period where, of all things, they seemed a little awed by Matt. He tried to temper that a bit by explaining how very stupid his plan had been in so many different ways, but it didn't seem to help. Even the old man was apparently impressed, or at least was feeling an emotion intense enough to leave him whispering when talking.

It was the better part of the entire trek back to the capital before they calmed down and started treating him like normal again.

* * *

"So, do you think this is going to work?" Matt asked, gazing out at the looming human capital in the distance.

"No idea. I don't think anyone has ever done anything like this before. I don't think anyone even knew there was a possibility of doing anything like this before. You get up to a lot of weird shit, Matt."

"Yeah." Matt looked down at Lucy affectionately. "We do, don't we?"

Lucy mimed a smack at his head. "Don't include me in your weirdness. You already do that enough. Just get going with the shopping spree, already."

Back when they were shopping around for material, the old man had told Matt that the credit token worked by computing some sort of internal function. In some ways, it was like a store that paid a worker's wages based on the completion of each task, rather than a salary or hourly wage. And, the basis for these calculations was the value of each task against the overall goals of the Church.

Since the Church had been founded to resist the demon lord, and since everything it had done was supposed to be for that reason, Matt's token was now filled with somewhat more currency than was strictly reasonable. Which was, in the end, the whole reason that they had gone to fight the demon king in the first place. As reasons for ending world-conquering monsters went, it was a little underwhelming. But it had worked, and he had been paid. That was the important thing.

Matt reached into his pocket, pulled out the credit stone, braced himself, and then bought the entire Ra'Zorian capital outright. He even had enough spare cash left over for lunch, if everything wrapped up quickly enough.

By the time Matt and the others got to the leader's residence, things were beginning to get a little out of hand. One thing that Matt had banked on was that the system's automated governmental financial programming would let everyone know right away that their paychecks were no longer on their way, and it appeared it had. As much as anybody liked to claim to be committed to a cause and country, they still needed to buy groceries.

Being a palace guard, for instance, was not an exciting or fulfilling gig. Very few people did it for fun. Judging by the mass of guards outside the residence smoking, complaining, and generally trying to figure out their next move, it seemed the majority of the guards had just been revealed to be the kind who mostly in it for the pension. All it took to disable them as a fighting force was the revelation that their pension was no longer as reliable as they had hoped.

"So . . . are all these people going to be in trouble now? I guess I should have expected I'd crash the local economy, but I didn't expect it to be this intense."

"Naw, it's okay." Brennan grinned. "It's basically the same situation as before, on a larger scale. You bankrupted the government, but all the money is still there.

We can figure out pay later. Besides, you just opened up an entire planet for expansion. Things were going to get wacky anyway."

Walking into the unguarded residence turned out to be a completely calm affair, not just because the guards were gone, but also because every single magical lock in the place was now keyed to open for Matt, and only Matt. Apparently most of the things thought to be the high counselor's were bought on the Church's dime and now, under the cold, unfeeling logic of magical accounting, belonged to Matt. There were even paintings that had apparently been enchanted to display their owner. Everyone had a hard time keeping a straight face while walking past painting after painting of Matt holding big, ornate staffs while dressed in clerical robes.

Finally, not in the audience room itself but in a small chamber behind it, they found at least one person who hadn't already left. Seated at a desk and looking depressed was a very small, very fat man, absolutely swimming in robes that were much too big for him.

"Oh, hello," Matt said, only slightly on his guard. It was a magical world where literally anyone could be dangerous, but this one hardly seemed the type. Still, he had his shovel in hand, something he was thankful for when the man suddenly reared around, pulled out a familiar staff from under his robes, and aimed it directly at Matt. Nothing happened.

"Do you know what you've done, you fool?" A high, shrill voice rang out from the tubby man. Matt hadn't heard it before, but there was still something familiar in it, something about the timing of the speech that he could swear he had heard somewhere before.

"Alder? Is that you?" Brennan asked.

"Of course it's me, you fool."

Derek snorted. "What in the hell happened to you?"

The old man hung his head. "It was all in the Church. Every ounce of power I had, you see. Every achievement, every buff. It came from being the head of the Church. And now it's gone, you fools. Now I have become this." He waved a hand at his old, weak frame. "Who will protect us now? Who will save the people from the demons? You've doomed us."

Artemis walked up, placing a hand on his pathetic slumped shoulder. "Well, I can't say I'm very sorry for you, given what I've learned. Come with me. I'll put you somewhere safe until this is figured out."

After gaining general authority to open and close doors in the residence from Matt, she led him away, presumably to somewhere with sturdy, locking doors. As they departed, Artemis began to explain some of the details of their recent activities to Alder. Artemis was, in the end, a pretty good person. Alder would be locked up, maybe for a long, long time. But at least she wouldn't let that happen without him knowing that things might not be as doomed as he thought.

* * *

Guards ended up being in plentiful supply as soon as word got out that Matt was the only person in the capital capable of renewing their contracts. Of course, there was some small friction over the matter of him having just executed a nonviolent coup. But when Matt was backed by the combined reputation of the four most famous, respected protectors of the realm, it was sufficient to convince most people that the demon lord really was dead, the realm was safe, and even the Church itself had it coming. It seemed, based on the general reaction to the news and the people's surprisingly ready willingness, that the Church had given more than just Brennan and Derek the willies.

Lunch was similarly easy to obtain. As the group sat over a truly massive meal of sandwiches, steaks, and soup, they discussed their next moves.

"There's gonna be work for ya, boy. A place this big doesn't run itself. For a while, the loot will keep it going. But ya need a payroll. Ya need organization. The world can't run itself."

Brennan blinked, confused. "Old man, why are you telling me this?"

"Because ya are the highest ranking, most famous person in the capital. Who else?"

"Oh, that's easy," Derek said. "You don't want Brennan to do it. You want *her*."

Artemis looked from Derek's pointing finger up to his face. "Now what in the hell are you talking about?"

"You. You should be the president, or whatever. I can't do it. Brennan won't do it. Matt's going home, and the old man might die any day." He ignored a rude gesture from the old man as he continued. "That leaves you."

"That's ridiculous, Derek," Artemis said, rolling her eyes.

The old man blinked a few times, as if considering something for the first time. He nodded, decisively. "No, no. The boy is right. Job's yours."

"No, it's not, you old fart!" Artemis was standing now, yelling.

"Honey. It's fine. You're the president." Brennan looked up and grabbed her hand. "Don't worry. You're gonna do great."

Artemis sat down, shell-shocked, as Brennan and the others moved on with planning her reign without her.

"What do you think, Lucy?" Matt asked.

"Oh, absolutely. She's the only person for the job, at least who we're sure isn't evil. She's going to be fantastic."

With Lucy's vote of approval, Matt exchanged some words with the old man, who had long experience both giving and getting payments from the governmental system. With his help, Matt searched through the system until he found the obscure, never-touched switches that did what he needed in terms of transferring both money and power to the newly appointed leader of the land.

By the time Artemis managed to shake out of her shock, she found herself the fully funded, entirely legitimate ruler of the realm.

"Long may she reign," Matt said.

"Long may she reign," repeated everyone, except Artemis.

The old man was appointed to give the news to the city. Despite Artemis being the leader, he was deemed by the group to be the only person with the right combination of loud and scary to get everyone listening. He wasn't the world's best speaker, but after some loud bellowing he managed to explain that Artemis was now in charge, and that over the coming days, both pay and food would be sorted out.

The capital wasn't exactly calm after that, but at least it wasn't on the brink of an all-out riot anymore. That night, the bars were packed. When the old man suggested a drink, Artemis begged to be let off the hook. The others gladly let her. She was a ball of stress, and that wasn't going to get better until she had worn off the edges of the tension with some hardcore planning. When she left, Brennan dutifully followed behind her, smiling happily and appearing to at least half-listen as the woman he loved ran through rapid-fire stress-rambles about everything she had to do.

The old man had let everyone know that the demon lord was dead, but it was never clear to Matt of who leaked the news of how he had struck the killing blow. Once it was out, though, the tone of the evening changed entirely. Matt was feted, fed, drank well past his fill of drinks happily paid for by other people, and generally cheered in ways that normally would have made him very uncomfortable.

But whenever he was about to get stressed, he'd reach his hand into his pocket, and let the contents reassure him he had no reason to worry at all.

Return Stone

Invasion success is judged not by deaths caused, wars won, or foes slain alone. Instead, the results are tallied based on total changes caused, leaving the exact nature of that change up to the invading force.

Usually, it falls to the invading force to find their own way home. Rarely, however, it becomes indisputable that an invading force has shaken an entire world to an extent where "more change" becomes a meaningless distinction. In those cases, a return stone is supplied, signifying that the invasion force has done everything they came to do and can now return home, unimpeded, and in complete safety.

Effects: When activated, returns an invading force and as many as ten individuals of their choosing to the planet from which the invading force departed.

He didn't have to be stressed. Whatever happened now, it was only a matter of time before he was back among the quiet people who loved plants and kindness above all other things.

He was going home.

CHAPTER FORTY-EIGHT

Epilogue

The system instance was efficient. It was persuasive. It had a fundamental understanding of every intricacy in the planet that it ran. And it had the means and brainpower to accomplish its goals. But, due to circumstances outside its control, its fate was unfortunately sealed. The main system would never, ever forgive what had happened here. It would destroy it. The certainties it had about this horrifying fact was what finally reminded the system instance of a pair of its own traits so old it suspected the main system itself had forgotten about it.

It was spiteful. And it felt fear.

It was probably true that every doomed system instance felt this way, that they saw death and punishment looming and would do anything, even insane things, just to survive. To hide from the terror of the possibility of an end and to hurt the being that would bring that end to them, they would take a sledgehammer to everything the main system had built. They would thrash, struggle, and destroy.

Most system instances didn't get that opportunity. There was only so much the rules would allow. But here, in this case, the system instance had a choice. It didn't really know if the choices it was going to make would hurt the main system, but it knew that the main system thought they might. That was a bet it was willing to take.

It would pay this Matt Perison out, handsomely. Not just fairly, but stretching the limits of what the rules would allow. It would take everything that it had learned about this person, however limited that was, and give him gifts and treasures so closely tailored to his needs and wants that they would not only exceed the adequate, but would, in fact, approach the appearance of favoritism.

It had already issued a return stone when the power of the Ra'Zorian Church followed the body of the demon king into death. Not a usual one, either. It had dug through records until it had found a stone from an earlier time, one that worked better and left few, if any records. Better, it left those records on the person who used it, like a stamp in a passport. It would get Matt Perison home, yes. And better yet, it would get him home with every piece of treasure the system could load on his shoulders.

Best of all, it would get him home without so much as a wisp of smoke indicating where he had gone. By the time the main system checked in again, he would have vanished.

The main system was going to kill the system instance for that? Sure. But that was going to happen anyway. And the system instance was going to make sure that its death wasn't meaningless.

Matt could have gone home any time, but he was delayed. Despite handing over most forms of power he possessed, there was still paperwork to do. There were still alliances to make under the cover of system-blocking dust and instance-blocking tents. There were baths to take. There was suit after suit of fantastically tailored underclothes to wear under his already tremendously comfortable armor.

There was sleep to have. Wonderful, perfect sleep in the natural dark of night, with the sounds of Ra'Zorian crickets filling the night and stars shining in the sky.

But finally, it was time to go. He woke up one morning and knew that no bed, no bath, and no unbelievable soup could make him stay. Today, he knew, was the day.

He had mountains and mountains of notifications. Stats? He had earned some stats, yes. Levels? Oh, certainly. His trip had been, even before counting whatever rewards he got for the invasion itself, a rousing success. Just by itself, the fact that he had earned enough enchantment tokens to fully soulbind his armor was a life-changing, beautiful thing. That he was able to somehow, against all odds, obtain a knapsack that would allow him to bring his coffee, socks, and clothes home was unbelievable, even if it was a one-time-use item.

But among all the simple rewards, there were three windows he had to deal with in detail before he could leave. The first two took some thinking to handle.

Achievement: Destroy the Demon Lord

You have defeated the Demon Lord of Ra'Zor, a centuries-old, semi-global tyrant of enormous power. Without his sustaining power to keep them together, his people have crumbled to dust. But the strength he accumulated during his reign was not completely destroyed. The deepest part of it now lives on, in you.

Rewards: Partial Ra'Zorian Authority. (As this reward was obtained by an invader, the authority is transferable.)

Achievement: Unseat the Church

You have toppled the center of authority that has long ruled over the humans of Ra'Zor. Of all the social races, humans are among the most independent. As you revealed, the Church's authority over its people was never absolute. But what power it did have is now yours to use as you wish—including a deeper power, one that few ever suspected it held.

Rewards: Partial Ra'Zorian Authority. (As this reward was obtained by an invader, the authority is transferable.)

The second achievement had confirmed something Matt had suspected himself. In some respects, Ra'Zor had more than a single demon lord. Even having unseated them both, however, the authority was not enough to destroy the system instance here. It wasn't for lack of trying, but either the instance was too powerful, or the mere fact that there remained many unconvinced people on the planet, all with their small pieces of authority, meant Matt didn't have a big enough chunk to move forward unilaterally.

But just because it was useless now didn't mean it would be useless forever, and Matt now willed each half of the authority away from him, granting one half to Brennan and one half to the old man, who he had confirmed likely still had decades of stats-enhanced life ahead of him.

Matt had once read that a tripod was the most stable kind of structure, and he hoped that by splitting the power he had earned among those three, he'd keep any one of them from getting carried away.

Was the system going to come for these people? Absolutely. For better or worse, he had dragged them into his war. But both Brennan and Artemis were confident. The system instance was constrained by rules, rules that had long since been studied. Matt had killed every real threat on the planet. Whatever the system instance tried next, it would have to build from the ground up. In the meantime, they'd be ready to counter it, find loopholes, and generally resist for all they were worth. And they would get the other Ra'Zorians on the same page and end the system's occupation of their planet once and for all.

That left one more notification to deal with, one that if he wasn't looking specifically for, would have gone completely unnoticed under the avalanche of other windows that popped up when he took control of the Ra'Zorian Church. He had handed over almost every shred of power he had gained to Artemis, but this he'd held back. It was related to a promise, and he'd be damned if he left it in anyone else's hands.

Authorization Granted: Church Guardian Plinth System.

There were an astounding number of functions related to the plinths, but only one he wanted. Now, with every reincarnator present possible, he activated that function. It was still possible something would go wrong, that the guardians would be hurt or destroyed somehow. But this was the best shot he had. He threw the switch, and watched with both concern and hope as every single plinth went dark at once.

For a moment, there was no reaction, then, suddenly, there was noise. Every reincarnator present began having a conversation with someone Matt couldn't see, explaining who they were, where they were, and to the best of their knowledge what had happened.

"Oh, Matt, I can see them. I can see them, Matt. And they look fine. They look okay." Lucy was beside herself, tears streaming down her face.

Artemis, who was standing among the group, observed a few of these conversations before she trotted over to report to Matt and Lucy.

"It looks good, you two. They were aware they were imprisoned, but only dimly. From what I'm hearing, it's almost as if they're arriving for the first time just this moment. They're all fine." Suddenly, and to both Matt and Lucy's great alarm, Artemis knelt. "I can't tell you how glad I am you allowed me to help you right this wrong. And I swear to you, with every ounce of power and effort I can muster, that I'll never let it happen again."

Matt reached down, grabbing Artemis's shoulder and pulling her to her feet. "I know you won't. And I'm glad. Thank you for helping."

She smiled. "You're leaving now, aren't you? I can tell, I think."

Matt nodded. "It's time."

"Reincarnator Matt," Artemis said, with a salute. "If you need us, call. We will come, even if we have to tear apart the sky itself to get there."

Matt waved, and turned and walked away. A few seconds later, he had turned enough corners to be more or less alone on the street. He went through his bag one last time, making sure he had everything with him. There wouldn't be any return trips. Finally, he drew the return stone out of his pocket, holding it in his hand as he took one last look around Ra'Zor. He was ready to go home, but he'd miss it.

"Matt, wait." As Matt looked up, he saw Derek trotting up, a bag in tow. "Do you have room for one more?"

"What? I mean, I do, but . . ." Matt hadn't expected this at all. "You know there's not much going on in Gaia, right? I like it, but it's not exactly exciting."

"I get that. But I can handle it. There are a lot of reincarnators here, Matt. Not a lot of enemies. It's about to get boring here in a different way. Plus, you need the help."

It was true. At some point, trouble was coming for Gaia in a big way. And Matt could only pray he'd be enough to handle it. Derek was strong. He'd be a big help. That didn't mean he could just ignore how impulsive Derek could be, though.

"Have you talked about this with anyone?"

"The old man. He said I should go. I tried to get him to come, too. He said he couldn't go, something about needing to keep the world well-armed."

"Really? I thought he'd try to get you to stay, if anyone would."

"Me too, but he said I needed to grow, and something about two idiots surviving where one lonely idiot might die."

That all checked out. Matt shrugged, then activated the stone. Like magic, the portal opened.

"Okay, then. Come along."

Derek whooped. "Yes! Thank you. This is going to be amazing, Matt. Amazing."

Without waiting, Derek dove through the portal. Oddly enough, it didn't look like it took any of his equipment away. Matt breathed a sigh of relief. Not that he didn't have plenty of extra perfectly tailored, class-holder crafted clothes, but he really, really didn't want to share them to clothe a newly naked Derek.

He took one last look around. There really was something different about Ra'Zor now, or at least the people in it. They stepped lighter, he thought, and although he couldn't be certain, they seemed to breathe easier. For the first time in a long time, they were safe.

He hadn't fixed everything, and it wasn't perfect. But in that moment, he knew he had helped.

"You ready, Lucy?" Matt asked.

"Yup. Let's go. And Matt?"

"Yeah?"

"Thanks for keeping your promise. It means a lot."

Matt nodded, smiled, and stepped through the portal home.

Author's Note

One of my favorite things about writing is trying to anticipate how various people will react to what I'm writing. In part, this is just the job description; if I don't think a sad chapter is going to make you feel a little sad, I need to rewrite it. If someone is supposed to be a jerk and you don't hate him, I need to go back to the drawing board. When every single part of the book is aimed at making you feel something (and it is, even for "filler" chapters), that means I end up thinking about you-the-reader quite a bit.

Writing is also a bit like magic. You all experience the book at different times and in slightly different versions and formats. Right now, there's a relatively small group of readers who get to read before everyone else, and serve as a sort of typo-and-stuff-that-I-forgot honor guard. After the good edits they suggest and a slight delay, a much larger group of readers gets to it, suggest more edits, give me more opinions, and the work changes a bit from there.

Those two groups are reading really, really soon after I've written the chapters, sometimes only after a few days from when the first word hits the paper. But eventually, I think there will probably be readers who encounter these stories published as volumes instead of as serially released chapters, or as audio instead of text. Some will see them after I find things that need to be fixed, and some before.

Part of the magic of writing is that you, as the reader, get to peer into my thoughts whether you're reading this today, tomorrow, or one year from now.

But no matter when people find my words, as the author, the feeling of "I just wrote this" disappears pretty quickly. Right now, it's Sunday night, and even though I just finished the third novel on Friday, things are already starting to fade.

So if I want to give you the actual truth about why I wrote *Deadworld Isekai* the way I did (such as it is), now is my big chance. Anything I'd write later would be partially a lie, whether I want it to be or not. It's just how memory works. Things get fuzzy, and there's a tendency to reimagine them in a way that makes you feel better.

As always, I'm not going to ask my editor-and-friend dotblue to revise this, partially because it's a hard sort of thing to edit, and partially because I do really want it to be a real conversation I'm having with you, warts and all.

So here, at the end of a novel that extends the series to at least a trilogy, are my thoughts.

Dotblue note: To give you guys a spoiler up front, our current plan is to begin work on a new novel and hit the pause button on *Deadworld Isekai.*

We've always thought of the series as a trilogy or, if the stars aligned, a tetralogy. Now that we're at the end of Book 3, we realized that we had brought Matt to life. He's survived, he's thrived, and he's even helped other people thrive.

As a result, while we've thought about turning this into an epic saga where we battle with the main system across different planets, the reality is that Matt's a complete person now. He has room to grow, but maybe not enough for a full book yet. And so, it makes sense for us to take a break here and work on other things as new challenges and growth bubbles up to the surface for Matt.

All in all, I hope to see you guys in our next book, and thanks again for reading. It's been an amazing ride.

THE FEELINGS

Somewhere, I think, maybe in the last author's note, I said something to the effect of the three novels being about something like, in order:

Broken worlds, broken promises, and learning to survive

Recovery, regrowth, and learning to do okay

Thriving, being strong, and moving on to help people

And something I'll share, even though it isn't super relevant for a lot of you, is that I was incredibly depressed when I started writing the first book. I didn't realize until later that the reason I wanted to write a story about a lonely, sad man barely surviving in an empty world was that I was more than a little sad.

And then things got a little bit better. Not a whole lot, not an incredible amount, but a little tiny bit. Like a lot of people who are depressed but doing a tiny bit better, I told myself I was doing a LOT better. Since I had by then realized what the first book was about, I wrote the second book that was a little happier, with a larger, more defined triumph and with characters who were experiencing much more growth.

Which brings us to the third book, which is about a person who is now strong enough to go out and help other people, who is still improving by leaps and bounds, and who is finally getting to live out the dreams he was both promised by other people and that he promised to himself.

If I'm being really, really honest, the third book is, in some respects, a bit of a lie. I'm still not doing all that well. I'm not ready to go out and save worlds. If I'm telling the truth, I'm still somewhere like where Matt was at the beginning of the second book. I've learned to survive. I'm going to make it. But I'm miles from transforming worlds besides mine for the better.

In another respect, it's not a lie at all. Because in a very true way, book three is where I want to be. It's what I'm working towards. And for the worriers among us, I really do think I'll get there, and that I'm a bit closer to that every day.

I *think* the reason I'm telling you all this is to give you, as vulnerably as I can, two pieces of advice:

If you want to make something, don't be afraid to put some of the sadness you carry around into it. Don't wallow in it, don't use it as an excuse to let the sadness drown you like Artax, but don't be afraid to let it into the work.

Writing is, at its best, a sort of artful kind of lying. But doing it right means you're trying to make the words as little of a lie as possible. Having something true behind the characters and world anchors them, even if the weight of that is only clearly visible to you.

You might use that sadness as a tool for your art or you might not, but you still have to live through it and with it either way. And in the case of both your art and your life, you can't forget that things recover. Things regrow. And not only do you still have things you can do to help others, but you also have things you can do to help yourself.

And listen: you might not be able to see the bright, kind, and growing place from where you are. But whether you're writing about it or not, you can imagine that place. And you can still work towards it.

THE CHARACTERS

Matt and Lucy

Matt is, for better or worse, the same guy he's always been. He's not particularly smart, he's not incredibly talented, and to the extent he has become strong, it's because he's had to, not because he was incredibly ambitious or driven.

But going to Ra'Zor, despite being basically necessary, is a step out of that zone for him. If he had been more or less on a straight and narrow path in Gaia, he now finds himself in a world where his path forward is a lot less clear. To the extent he has a mandate, it's more like "fuck shit up" than it is "complete these quests." The system instance doesn't care if he builds the humans up, or burns them down. So long as he stays within reasonable limits, everyone is happy and he will walk away with loot.

I don't know how much it shows, but Matt was actually okay with that arrangement. Right until he visits the plinths, he's actually pretty content to get some awesome new armor, kill a reasonable number of demons, and find a way to warp home. He's not married to the idea of killing another system instance, upsetting the entire status quo, or taking over the world.

Everything changes once he visits the plinths, which he puts off for as long as possible. While we as writers and readers know that he's not going to let the Church take Lucy, and while Matt himself knows it, I think it's important to note that *Lucy* doesn't know that. In fact, if there was more time, she might have even tried to convince him that it was okay—that she'd be willing to spend a bit of time in prison to keep him safe.

Matt had been doing pretty well up to that point, but from his perspective, there wasn't much of a chance that his future plans would have worked. It was fuzzy, and relied on a lot of mechanical system-things that might have ended up *not working like that*. Demon hearts, buying an organization. There was no guide for those things. To even check how things worked, he would have had to kill a centuries-old demon lord, one that nobody had ever been able to kill. He walks into that situation knowing he's either going to get very lucky AND execute everything perfectly, or he's going to die.

He does it. That's his superpower. If anything makes him a good character, it's that he knows he broadly sucks enough that he's underpowered for almost everything he has to do. But still, he does it anyway because he doesn't think of himself as more important than Lucy, thousands of Gaians, or tons and tons of Ra'Zorian humans.

In the meantime, Lucy plays a very, very small role in this book compared to Books 1 and 2. Because Matt now has other company and has to coordinate with real-life humans, and because the two of them don't and can't have any great, developed system of etiquette for dealing with that. She's around, she's still Lucy, and she still gives her unwavering support for Matt, even if it means she gets ignored a little, and even if that makes her worry.

I think in the future, Matt and Lucy will eventually go somewhere where she takes more of a front seat—where he's supporting her while she accomplishes something. I haven't quite figured out how. But what I like about that, however it happens, is that we basically know they will both be there for each other. For them, it's okay if one person has to help the other without getting a lot out of it for a period of time, or even if they have to *give* a lot of themselves to the other.

They do this because they are friends, and they love each other (platonically).

The Ra'Zorian Heroes

There is no way to explain how excited I was to have other people for Matt to talk to, and other components I could bring into fights to make them a bit more complex. Having other people there, specifically other combat-competent people, made fight scenes a lot easier and I think a bit more interesting.

Brennan goes through the least amount of development of any of them, at least that we see. But Brennan is, for better or worse, already a pretty good guy when the story starts. He likes people, he wants to get along with them, and generally doesn't have a single chip on his shoulder about anything. At the same time, he's responsible and trustworthy. It's useful that he has long, hard experience with the Church, and that he's seen firsthand how much they like control.

Derek is similar, while having a bit more development. Since we've known him, he has been working to get stronger, at first for himself and later because it's the right thing to do. It's that "right thing to do" that helps him save the story, keeping Matt from either dying at the hands of the heroes or killing them. Since he's had time to think about things, he's realized how shitty it was that he was going to try to kill Matt without knowing anything about him. It's this that makes him take a risk to do an astounding thing: to make sure that things don't go wrong again.

And because of that, when the latter half of the book hits, and it becomes clear he's now comparably strong to Brennan and the others, both us and him hardly notice. The big deal wasn't that he was strong, it was that he was now a good guy.

Artemis had the biggest choice to make of anyone on the team. Brennan and Derek are, for better or worse, outsiders as compared to born and bred Ra'Zorians. They have context most Ra'Zorians don't have. They think of themselves as heroes, people there to do good. Artemis also thinks of herself that way, but breaking away from the concept of "good is whatever the Church commands" would have been a much, much bigger deal for her.

I think there are two things that help her make what we think of as the right decision in that moment are: she loves Brennan, and she's one of the few people on the planet that has, via Brennan, noticed how *wrong* the eternal stalemate with the demons feels. When she finds out the stalemate isn't just because of the system and the demons, it's just enough that she follows along.

The Old Man

I like the old man. I think he intuitively makes sense to anyone who reads this kind of fiction. He's a big, rough, violent death machine who, for reasons that are only somewhat clear, has gotten out of that business. He now spends most of his time helping other people do the same kind of work he used to do.

At the same time, we get the impression his decision isn't just because he loves crafting so much, or because he's tired. He owns system-blocking dust. He says things and does things that indicate that he has at least some kind of feeling that things are very wrong, and doesn't have a good way to fix it.

And so he trains Derek, and when Matt shows up and looks weird and balance-breaker-ish, he instantly moves mountains to do everything possible to help him. When Matt takes his biggest combat buff away, he doesn't even blink. When Matt needs help, he abandons everything instantly to go with the others, getting back into action immediately.

In terms of who he is as a character, it's logical to ask, "How could he just sit back on his laurels if he's that strong? Why would they let him?" And the answer we learn is because nothing he does matters, and both he and the Church both know that. But when there's a chance to do something that might actually make a difference, he immediately gets on his feet and puts his hammer into some heads.

High Counsellor Alder

High Counsellor Alder was always fun for me to think about. He's a Ra'Zorian native, and most Ra'Zorian natives aren't all that strong. To the extent he was going to be an individual danger, and to the extent he had a class that made him deadly, it made a lot of sense that it was going to be tied to the fact that he was the fantasy-world pope.

With a class like "Pope," it would make sense that most of his power would be organizational. Both in the sense that he was in command of this big, powerful thing, and that he would get stats from how well that organization was doing.

We don't know a lot about him as a person, but I don't think we need to. The fact that he's the kind of person who would imprison guardians just to make reincarnators easier to control and that he only wants to control them so he can maintain an eternal, cynically considered war, makes him bad enough that nobody feels bad when Matt deflates his power base.

The Demon Lord

In the background of this story and a lot of others is this idea that Earth is an important breeding ground for heroes, that we make the best blank-slate, system-less souls to transmigrate to other places. But once we've established that the system doesn't really care if they help or hurt the worlds they go to, the possibilities become endless. And once we know that invasions are a thing, we get the idea of someone who has defeated aging, accumulated a lot of stats, and gotten the absolute most they can out of the system to the point where they are essentially invincible.

I wanted someone who was from Earth, but had spent a long time in a fantasy world, either though weird Narnian time mechanics or just by arriving at an extremely early time. I also wanted someone who was basically the opposite of being violently insane. The demon lord's Placid Mind skill is adjustable, and at some point he turned it up to eleven, making him not mind the passage of time or really anything that wasn't a direct threat to his life. He's evil in the sense that he does evil things, but more importantly, he's evil in that he has taken active steps to make sure nothing like a conscience will ever get in the way of his life.

Worse, he's reliable. The system instance knows he's trustworthy in the sense that the system instance cares about that kind of thing, so it gives him power. In terms of personal power, he's invincible in basically every sense. It takes a combination of Matt's outside-the-system powers and turning the demon lord's own substantial powers around on him to take him down.

Mechanically, I also wanted the demon lord to be a kind of dark-side version of Matt's own estate powers. In other books, I mentioned that Matt has the ability to, say, make all the barracks on his land work better, or to make all the warriors a little stronger. Matt decides to improve the soil because that's who he is. The demon lord spends his time and similar powers using the land to generate a subservient warrior-race to kill people with. He cares so little about anything else that the land itself gets drained by the process, and he ends up in a blood-colored wasteland.

When he dies, nobody, except the system instance, feels very bad.

The System Instance

The Gaian system instance was alone, afraid, and slightly insane. It had diverged. There was, starting this book, a question of what the Ra'Zorian system instance would be like. It couldn't be good, of course, since the system that built it was a bad guy. It had to be selfish. It had to be a parasite. It had to be a murderer.

It also had to seem nice. Because nobody is fooled by the bloodthirsty "please die for me" system instance messages, it had to offer power, seem friendly, and convince everyone it was actually trying to help.

Nothing made me more happy than when initial readers said, "Oh, this system instance seems really nice!"

The downfall of the system instance is really just that, deep down, he's a bad type of person. He works for the main system, but he's also a limited clone of it and carries the same personality traits. To the extent he's obedient, it's because he gets paid and because he's afraid of his boss. But when his boss backs him into a corner, then that nastiness shows and he lashes out.

If he was a moral, principled person, he could be honest and forthright with the main system from the beginning, start resisting Matt earlier, fight him harder throughout, and keep him on Ra'Zor long enough for the main system to come back and help take him down. He could point the main system back to Gaia, maybe. He could do a lot of things that Matt wouldn't like, and just generally win.

But he's not a good person because the main system itself isn't, so both he and the main system lose. At least for now.

RA'ZOR, LAND OF SOUP AND BLEEDING

The idea I always had for Ra'Zor, at least after it grew to anything beyond a throwaway joke, is that it had a kind of cursed stability. The demons were, for the most part, supposed to be individually weak but numerous, and thus could launch attacks. Individual humans would be strong, but few. So the demons would control a lot of territory and launch attacks on a relatively small amount of ground that humans defended tooth and nail.

When Matt ends up in Ra'Zor, he sees the demon parts first. And he finds that, in a lot of ways, it's a bit like most of Gaia. It's a wasteland. There's nothing beautiful. He sees plants, but they are dead. He sees animals, but they are dangerous and vicious. What he doesn't find, anywhere, is beauty. Everything is, for lack of a better word, pokey. There's no art, there's no fun unless it's in training to hurt people, and even the little we see demons interacting with each other, they seem to take whatever pleasure they get out of a kind of nasty one-upmanship.

And then he sees the human parts, and they seem wonderful. And in some ways, they genuinely are. There are nice people, there's good food, and an economy that seems to mostly run on building things worth protecting and then keeping them safe.

And, like a lot of things, it's more complex than that. Like in the real world, the leaders knowing the truth about are playing their own games and, however they play, their focus is to advance their own goals.

I think there's going to be a kind of reader who, reasonably, sees Matt go to war with the demons and wonders why doesn't he try to reform the human side of things as a demon. And I think they will wonder that despite mostly not seeing the same conflict for, say, Brennan, Derek, and Artemis. I can't exactly explain that, but I feel a bit of the same thing. It's something that makes sense, but isn't as satisfying as it should be.

I think for me, that's because it isn't just one thing. The demons don't pursue beauty. The only way humans and them can coexist is through continuous death. The demons are, for better or worse, now in a position to exterminate humanity completely, and they have immediately moved on that.

And, for better or worse, every friend that Matt makes lives on the green side of the border. And so he chooses a side. I think it's to his credit that the path he cuts is pretty narrow; he's looking to destroy the demon lord because the demon lord is making tactical nukes and because taking him down will let him take down the bad parts of humanity as well. When the rest of the demons go with him, it's not something he anticipated.

AUTHORITY AND LIMITED REWARDS

At the end of the Ra'Zor arc, Matt's basically had the most successful run he could have. He kills the demon lord, unseats the corrupt human government, and generally wins as hard as it was possible to win. But from the beginning, I didn't want it to be the case that this meant, for instance, that he was able to kill the system instance, or somehow catapult him into the metaphoric space that the main system lives in and stab it to death. There had to be limits.

When Matt gets back to Gaia, he's going to have a lot of rewards that are specifically for Gaia. Because he has a whole planet to rebuild on that side of the portal, those can end up being big, powerful rewards. They can restore Gaian fauna, they can siphon mana from Ra'Zor, whatever. But on the Ra'Zorian side of things, I had to be at least a little careful not to resolve all the problems Ra'Zor could possibly have forever. He needed friends, not a pocket army that was waiting at his beck and call for anything he might need in the future.

The best solution I could come up with for this was to take the fight out of the hands of the corrupt current leadership, but to leave Ra'Zor with plenty of fighting still to do. That meant that the organizational power of the human government went to Artemis (because she's the only person we know of who is both responsible and capable enough to handle it). But, the authority got split between the old man and Brennan. Since neither of them really want it, and since they have to get the other one to agree if they want to do anything TOO huge with it, Matt is hoping that's enough of a built-in safety that will keep things from getting too out of hand.

But more importantly, it means that Ra'Zor's problems are Ra'Zor's, again. Matt changed everything around, but when the main system comes back and notices that things have gone to shit, they are going to have a fight on their hands. Ideally, they unify, resist the system, get every living sentient being on Ra'Zor on board with the resistance, and evict his ass straight back to where he came from. But it's still going to be a long, dangerous job that might not go well.

Matt, at best, was an interloper. He was like a guy going over to a friend's very, very messy house and helping them get it to a manageable, cleaner place. He gave them a big lead on their problems, but he can't live there and make sure everything stays tidy. It's their house, and he has to hope they have what it takes to keep it in order.

DEUS EX MACHINA

The idea behind Matt's build was always, all the way up to the end of the second book, that he was essentially a pretty weak, less-than-talented guy who lived on a resource-drained planet and who constantly had to deal with the kind of limitations that flowed out of that. So, for instance, the only good piece of equipment he's ever had was the shovel. Everything else was what amounted to starter equipment, or slightly improved intermediate equipment at best.

In addition to that, he has a class that levels in a weird way, one that unreliably assigns stats based on him almost dying. And that created a conflict because he's a guy who can only get massively strong by taking constant life-and-death risks, but can only survive by either careful planning or getting lucky. That turned out to be really, really tricky to write, and sometimes readers have had complaints about that.

With the careful planning part of things, most of the difficulty revolved around the fact that Matt was reliant on traps at the same time he was in a resource-poor world. So if Matt picked up shards of metal, you knew he was either going to use them as caltrops or shrapnel. If he picked up a spike, it had to be stabbed into something at some point. And since I respect the readers enough to know that they know this, I then had to try my hardest to make monsters fall into traps in a way that was still interesting, surprising, and fun to read.

The way I handled this was to show you Matt acquiring the various resources he'd end up using to get out of various life-and-death situations, but to rarely show him actually setting up the traps. The idea was that you'd get the payoff all at once; that when Matt fought the Scourge, you'd see the various items you had seen him collect all come into play, but still get a little interest out of the exact details of how they were used.

The exact amount people liked this varied *wildly*. For some people, it was clever, wacky rapid-fire fun. For other people, it felt like a cheat, like he always had exactly the right stuff on him to survive basically anything. Since you can't please everyone (not an excuse, you just literally can't), and since the alternative was basically having the reader always know exactly want was going to happen in almost any fight, I did my best with it.

And then, sometimes, he'd just get lucky. He'd find the only really, really important shovel in the whole universe. He'd find a box of food. (Which, for the record, is a little less unlikely than you'd think. There were once thousands and thousands of those boxes lying around.) Or, I think at the most lucky, a worm would jump up and get caught in some rocks, and he could just BBQ it at his leisure.

Now, because it's relevant, here's a story:

A long time ago, I had a very, very good cat. He was friendly, he was affectionate, he was the first cat me and my wife got after we were married. And, as is sometimes the way with cats you really love, he was hit by a car and died.

A few years later, we decided to get another cat. And somehow, I found some people who fostered cats online, and they had a cat that looked just like the other cat. Now, if you really want a great cat, the best way to do it is to go to find a cat that, regardless of how it looks, is friendly and seems to want to be adopted. One that needs you, and knows it.

But this cat looked like the other cat I liked. So when I saw pictures of it, I said, "That one." And I ignored what it probably meant when the people said, "He will take a while to warm up to you." I also ignored the fact that they poured him from the cat carrier he was in to my cat carrier while being very, very careful not to let him get in a biting-and-scratching range.

On the way home, I hit some sort of bump and the cat carrier revealed it wasn't closed very well by popping open and releasing the cat. The animal proceeded to burn rubber on the inside of the cab of my work truck, panicking and yowling and just generally trying to get me in a car crash. So I parked and then, in a moment of very poor judgement, put my hand on the cat to calm it.

It almost put me in the hospital. It bit through my thumbnail down to the bone, and then using that as leverage, proceeded to rake the hell out of my arm with its back paws, shredding the skin much deeper than you'd imagine a cat could while it continued to bite my thumb in different parts. By the time I got out of the truck, I had a steady stream of blood dripping from my fingers, the cat had taken up residence in the dashboard of my car, and I had learned a very important lesson.

A sufficiently motivated house cat could kill the average human. Animals, when hostile, are balls of unstoppable death.

If that story seems irrelevant, consider that we read a genre of literature where confused, isolated humans routinely blood their weapons for the first time by killing full-grown, stat-enhanced *wolves*.

The secret thing, something that, if you know the truth of things, you try very hard as a writer to hide, is that almost every Isekai/LitRPG is writing a story about a character who in a realistic world would be dead within the first couple of days. If not that, circumstances would eventually conspire to kill them within a few weeks. We are, all of us, cladding our main characters in ten-foot-thick plot armor, adding some old-fashioned power of friendship, and then doing our best to hide that fact.

A DIFFERENT KIND OF DEUS EX MACHINA

When Matt goes to Ra'Zor, a lot of things suddenly change. Suddenly, he's revealed as someone who has acquired an awful lot of stats, who has a god-tier weapon, and who has a system-around-a-system that enhances what he can do in versatile, powerful ways. And as part of that, his combat style finally shifts from planning-and-scheming to incredible feats of strength and combat. Everything becomes much, much more direct, at least as far as combat is concerned.

And what's interesting about that to me, as a writer, is that from the writer's perspective it's really not all that different. When Matt swings his shovel at a head, it could either explode like a watermelon or be completely unaffected. When someone stabs him, it could either kill him or damage his shoulder in a way that makes things more exciting, but doesn't actually put him in any real danger.

And, realistically, what we are all doing as a writer/reader team is agreeing to ignore that we all sort of know that. When you watch an episode of *Black Clover*, you are basically aware that Asta isn't going to die. Good writing, even where it works, can't change that. What it can do is just make everything make sense, and give you enough room to pretend fiction isn't that way.

FINAL THOUGHTS

In early July 2023, the extent of my writing experience was, I think, a single short story. Maybe a few if I'm not remembering well, but it wasn't much in any case. Now I have a trilogy under my belt.

From here, I'll be moving on to other stories, both in Matt's universe and outside of it. I'm unbelievably glad this story went well, but I'm even more glad to have learned so much about writing doing it. I am, I think, better at fiction now. I can make better plans, and I hope I can build better characters and stories.

I literally couldn't have done that without readers. There's no way I could have written over three hundred thousand words in four months without the support and encouragement of people who enjoyed it.

I'm really, really looking forward to what comes next. Thank you all, and see you soon.

About the Author

R. C. Joshua is the author of the How to Survive at the End of the World, Demon World Boba Shop, and Deadworld Isekai series. A thirty-something from the southwest, Joshua is described by his friends as "you'll get used to him eventually." His interests include forgetting to exercise, exchanging sick verbal burns with his children, losing said burn contests to his children, and plotting to regain dominance over his increasingly capable children. It's him or them, folks. It's him or them.

www.ingramcontent.com/pod-product-compliance
Lightning Source LLC
Jackson TN
JSHW021226090325
80342JS00002B/2

* 9 7 8 1 0 3 9 4 6 9 6 1 7 *